Raves for *The Alton Gift*:

"The late Marion Zimmer Bradley's influence can still be detected in her posthumous Darkover 'collaborations' with Ross. Though a slow start and arcane historical references might dissuade new readers, the teasing resolution will excite anticipation in those familiar with the memorable land of the Bloody Sun." —*Publishers Weekly*

"Sure to please Darkover fans." —*Booklist*

"Approved by the late Bradley to continue her Darkover novels, Ross remains faithful to Bradley's vision in this sequel to *Traitor's Sun,* creating a story filled with memorable characters, agonizing decisions, and powerfully subtle psychic forces." —*Library Journal*

And for Darkover:

"A rich and highly colored tale of politics and magic, courage and pressure . . . Top-flight adventure in every way!" —Lester Del Rey for *Analog*

"Literate and exciting." —*New York Times Book Review*

"I don't think any series novels have succeeded for me the way Marion Zimmer Bradley's Darkover novels did." —*Locus*

"Darkover is the essence, the quintessence, my most personal and best-loved work." —Marion Zimmer Bradley

THE ALTON GIFT

MARION ZIMMER BRADLEY

AND

DEBORAH J. ROSS

DAW BOOKS, INC.

DONALD A. WOLLHEIM, FOUNDER

375 Hudson Street, New York, NY 10014

ELIZABETH R. WOLLHEIM

SHEILA E. GILBERT

PUBLISHERS

http://www.dawbooks.com

First Printing, June 2008
1 2 3 4 5 6 7 8 9 10

DAW TRADEMARK REGISTERED
U.S. PAT. AND TM. OFF. AND FOREIGN COUNTRIES
—MARCA REGISTRADA
HECHO EN U.S.A.

PRINTED IN THE U.S.A.

DEDICATION

To all those faithful lovers of Darkover
who now rest in peace.

ACKNOWLEDGMENTS

Deepest gratitude to Ann Sharp of the Marion Zimmer Bradley Literary Works Trust; to Adrienne Martine-Barnes, for all her marvelous contributions over the years; to my trusted readers, Sue Wolven, Susan Franzblau, and Catherine Asaro; to Marsha Jones, nit-picker extraordinaire; and especially to my editor, Betsy Wollheim, for listening with an open mind to my wild ideas on how to chop the story up and put it together right.

INTRODUCTION

My own personal "voice" in the Darkover novels has always been the very first character I created for them: Lew Alton. Lew Alton was the hero of the very first pre-Darkover fantasy sketch I wrote as a young girl. It is very difficult to detach my own viewpoint from Lew's . . . I admit I have been curious from time to time to know how Lew, who is not, at least on the surface, a very attractive character, would appear from the outside. It is rather difficult for me to see him except from inside his own skin, and I have backed away, before this, from trying to see him through other eyes.

—Marion Zimmer Bradley

I think the only way to write about characters created by someone else is to fall in love with them yourself. Just as each loving relationship is unique, so is each creative vision. For everything that is good and true in these pages, I thank those whose vision formed a foundation for my own. The lapses and shortcomings are my doing.

—Deborah J. Ross

PROLOGUE

Four years after the death of Regis Hastur and the departure of the Terran Federation, in the Hellers Mountain Range . . .

The great red sun of Darkover rose above the mountain peaks, casting a sullen light through the bank of ice-crystal clouds. Although the worst of the winter storms had passed, the wind still carried an edge like a knife. A man in his middle years paused in his climb up the rock-tumbled slope and drew his threadbare cloak more tightly around his shoulders. A gust tore away his breath.

Turning his back to the wind, he looked down at the sheltered dale, with its cluster of stone cottages, livestock pens, barns for feed storage, stream, and fishpond. His people had farmed here, from time before memory, tending their flocks, fishing the streams and gathering nuts from the forest-lined slopes, trading furs and cheese in Nevarsin for those things they could not make themselves. Once, the community had supported a dozen families or more.

Now, Garin thought with inexpressible sadness, *there are only a handful of us.* A single curl of smoke rose from the cottages, the pens stood empty except for a pair of aged chervines, and the roof of the largest barn had fallen in on itself.

Garin lifted his gaze to the hillside, once thick with trees bearing nuts, amber-resins, and aromatic wood, now a tangle of blackened splinters. Some of the damage was old, from the fires a generation ago. Garin had been only a child, but it seemed as though the whole Hellers range had gone up in flames. The Hastur-lord, Regis, had sent food and seedlings to reforest the slopes. Lean years followed, but the trees had thrived and the goat herds increased. Garin had married a girl from Rockraven, near the Aldaran border, and settled happily to raising their children.

Then, three summers past, fires came again, as they always did. Only this time, no help had arrived, no fire-fighting chemicals, no crews sent by the Comyn. Garin and the other men defended their homes as best they could. They saved the village and the better part of the livestock, but they lost the forest.

The goats died, one by one, then the entire herd, and those who ate the meat sickened. Garin's brother, Tomas, wept over the graves of his two sons and said it must be a curse sent by the gods. Garin had replied, who would seek to punish little children in this way? Things would get better. They must.

He clung to that hope even as his own youngest daughter slipped away, and the others grew thin and weak. Last winter, they slaughtered half the chervines for food, but it was not enough. With the cold and damp came lung fever. The last of the grandparents died, and so did Garin's wife.

Now only ten of them remained, none either very young or very old. They had some apples and a little salted fish, nuts, and dried beans from last summer. There was nothing left to plant, for they had eaten most of their seed crop.

Better to go now, in the spring, while we still can. The thought tore at Garin's heart, that he might never again see the dale alive with flowers and laughter, sun sparkling on the water, kid-goats and children gamboling on the hillsides. He had come up here to take his farewells alone, to steel himself for the journey ahead.

We may die on the road, but we will surely die if we stay.

— ◆ —

In the cottage, where they had gathered for warmth and a last meal, Garin found a flurry of activity. Lina straightened up from tying a knitted scarf on one of the smaller children, a boy about six. She mothered them all, although only two of her own, a shy girl of ten and the adolescent boy out with the livestock, were still alive. Like the other two surviving women, she was a widow, and Garin's kinswoman. In short order, she had all the children dressed, each with a bundle and pack and walking stick.

Outside, Lina's son, Raymon, had laden the two chervines with tents and blankets, water skins, all their remaining food, and a small bundle of furs for trading. Garin shouldered his own pack, and they set off. Two of the children sniffled, and one of the women sobbed as the trail twisted through a cleft in the hills and the village was lost to sight.

As they traveled beyond the places they had known, the land grew wilder. They passed stretches of burned-out forest, earth etched with erosion gullies, mud slides and rock falls, and once a tangle of animal bones heaped together like deadwood. Some of the younger children woke screaming from nightmares for several days afterwards. Sometimes the trail was washed out or obscured by debris. Once they got lost trying to find it again and passed the night in tents under a splintered rock ledge, listening to the winds howl down from the peaks.

"Is it banshees?" Elena, the littlest girl, asked Garin.

"If it is, they're far away," he answered. "They live above the snow line, so we're safe down here." Yet, with so many strange, unseasonable happenings, who could say? He tucked the girl into Lina's arms and went to arrange for Raymon to keep alternate watch with him during the night. What they would do if a banshee did attack, he didn't know. They had no weapons against such a predator.

They made slow progress because of the children, but after four or five days the land seemed less barren. They came upon a travel shelter in a bit of scrub forest. Raymon set traps, and they breakfasted on rabbit-horn simmered with parched grain from the shelter's stores. Garin didn't begrudge their late start that morning, for full bellies eased fear as well as hunger.

Through the morning, they traveled through sparse, oddly stunted forest. Here and there, the whitened skeleton of a fully grown tree rose above the others. Garin wondered what blight had fallen upon the land, but he said nothing. He was lost in his thoughts when Lina, who was walking behind him, carrying little Elena, cried, "Look! There, up ahead—what is it?"

Garin shook himself alert. The trail curved beneath starkly bare, overhanging branches where leaves mounded against the boulder-strewn slope. Where Lina pointed, he made out a lumpy dark mass, sprawled half on the trail.

For an instant, he thought it might be a child dressed in stained fur. As he approached, he saw it was some kind of animal. He slowed his pace, cautious.

Lina came after him, leaving the children behind. "Is it a wounded *kyrri*?"

Garin frowned. He'd never laid eyes on one of the non-human creatures, but he'd always thought of them as smaller and covered with thick gray fur. "This is something else."

At the sound of Lina's voice, the creature stirred, its ribs shuddering. It gave a twittering cry, like a frightened bird. Lina flinched. Garin tried to push her behind him, but she followed close. Together, they took another step.

"It's all right, we mean you no harm." Garin tried to make his voice gentle and soothing. If the creature was wounded, it might lash out in terror.

They drew closer, and he saw ribs stark through pale skin covered with sparse, coarse hair. In a convulsive movement, the creature rolled toward them. Reddish eyes glinted up from a broad, chinless face. Tears streaked the creature's cheeks, and it squinted in the brightness of the day. It opened its mouth and gave another high, chittering cry. At the same time, it extended one arm, too long and thin to be human, toward them. At the sight of the elongated fingers, the unmistakable gesture of appeal, Garin's heart lurched.

"It's—I think it's a trailman," he breathed.

"What's it doing here, so far from its home?" Lina muttered. The trailmen kept closely to their own territory, the forests between the Kadarin River and the Hellers.

With a whimper, the creature let its arm fall gracelessly to the ground. Garin started toward it.

"Don't touch it!" Lina cried, seizing his arm. "It looks sick. It could give you the fever!"

"I don't think so." Garin's heart pounded in his ears, but he could not tear his gaze away from the poor creature. "There's been no trailmen's fever since the time of our fathers. Some *Terranan* magic brought an end to it. This one must be starving. See how thin it is? Its forests must have burned, like ours."

"What can we do for it? We have worries of our own. The children depend on us."

"*We* can live in other places," he said. "The plains, the Lowlands, Nevarsin, or, Aldones help us, even Thendara. But these beasts," he paused, corrected himself, "these *people* have nowhere to go. They cannot live without their trees. What if one of our own were dying alone in a faraway place? Surely, this one deserves our pity, if not our aid."

Lina glanced from Garin to the trailman. A mist passed over her eyes. She said in a choked voice, "I am ashamed of my selfish words. I thought only of our own sorrows. Would it accept food from us, do you think?"

Garin thought for a moment, then asked Raymon to bring him some dried apples and the smallest water skin. The boy came quickly with the food. Telling Lina to stay behind, Garin approached the trailman.

"See, I have brought you food and water." Garin crouched down beside the creature.

The trailman had stopped whimpering and seemed to be

breathing with difficulty. A film coated its red eyes. Its arm stretched toward Garin, palm upraised.

Garin did not think the creature could lift the water skin, even if it knew how to drink from it. He would have to cradle its head and hold the spout to its mouth.

He took a piece of apple, moistened it from the water skin, and placed it in the open hand. The skin felt dry, like old leaves. "Food. Eat, eat. Good."

The trailman did not respond except for the slow, hesitant ripple of its chest. Garin held the apple in front of the flat nose, hoping that the smell would rouse the creature. Nothing happened. His gut clenched. He had nursed enough of his own kinfolk through starvation to recognize the final stages.

The breaths slowed, the pauses lengthening. A fine quivering came and went in the little muscles around the mouth, then ceased. The trailman lay utterly still.

Garin refused to leave the body for wild beasts to scavenge. With the help of Raymon and Lina, he carried the trailman a little way off the trail. They laid it in a rocky depression and covered the body with what loose stones they could gather.

They went on in silence for a while.

The trail dipped downward, the hills opened out around them, and they reached the Nevarsin road. A short time later, a caravan came into sight, a dozen wagons pulled by shaggy-coated mules, and a small herd of sheep. The caravan halted when they saw Garin and his people. A man on a sturdy brown horse rode out to meet them. He carried a thick cudgel.

In a sudden sweat, Garin stepped away from the others. He held his hands away from his body so that the mounted man could see he was unarmed. "We are innocent travelers, not bandits!" he called out.

The rider nudged his horse forward. The animal responded placidly, clearly more accustomed to pulling a cart than engaging in battle.

"Who are you, and what are you doing on this road?" the man asked. "What do you want?"

Garin swallowed a prideful retort. They were outnumbered, and if it came to a fight, they had no chance with only himself and one half-grown boy. These looked like honest folk. If he bespoke them gently, they might let the family travel with them and share a little food ...

He told their story simply: the fires and floods, the hunger, that last terrible winter, and, finally, their decision to leave their home. ·

The rider nodded thoughtfully, lowering his cudgel. "I've heard that tale, or close enough to it, ten times over since I've been on the trail. Name's Dougal, by the way. M'wife and me, we farmed a smallhold up toward Stormcrag. The big fires missed us, but the last five years it's been one thing after another. Used to be, the lords'd mount fire-watch and send over Tower-made chemicals, and everyone'd turn out to help. Now it's every man for himself."

Garin nodded in sympathy. A look passed between them, the wordless understanding of country folk. Except for the unfamiliar accent, they might have been neighbors.

Dougal jerked his chin over one shoulder. "M'wife died in birthing, so I headed out. Met these people on the trail, decided we'd be safer together. All kinds of *reish* abroad these days that'd cut your throat for a morsel of bread."

Garin shuddered. "We'd be grateful if you'd let us travel with you."

"No need to ask." Dougal's weathered face crinkled in a wide grin. "Looks like some of your youngsters are fair done in. We'll let 'em ride in the wagons for a bit. Your woman there looks like she hasn't had a decent meal since last fall."

Garin turned back to the others and gestured them forward. "It's all right, they're friends. We'll be traveling with them for safety. Dougal, where are you headed?"

"Nevarsin village, m'wife's people. There's bound to be work in the city."

That sounded hopeful. If they could earn enough to buy seeds and a few goats, they might be able to return home.

Lina drew up to them, little Elena in her arms. She

looked up at Dougal and said, "We are grateful for your company."

Dougal blushed and ducked his head. Garin, watching them, thought that neither one would be lonely for long.

Together, they went on to Nevarsin, the City of Snows. Before they reached the outskirts, little Elena had begun to cough. When Garin touched her skin, she burned as if on fire. Lina, half out of her mind with worry, urged Dougal to hurry, for they could do little for her on the trail. At Nevarsin, there would be healers, warm food, blankets, safety.

The aged man posted at the city gates directed them to the Guildhall of the Society of Renunciates, who maintained a hospital for travelers. The Renunciates, hard-faced women with cropped hair and gold rings in their ears, wore men's clothing as if they had no shame or decency. Nonetheless, they took the little girl into their care. Men could not stay within their compound, they said, but Lina might remain, and they would have news of how the child fared on the morrow.

Garin passed the night in the rented stable, which was all he could afford. When he knocked at the Guildhouse the following morning, he was told that the little girl was no better. Not only that, but Lina, too, had fallen ill.

BOOK I

1

The year before . . .

On the day his grandmother died, Domenic Alton-Hastur spent the morning in the solarium of Edelweiss, reading aloud to her. Although bitter cold still clung to the shadows cast by the drifted snow, the little room with its thick mullioned windows stayed bright and warm. The house was unassuming, cozy compared to the great family estate at Armida, with old-fashioned, intimate rooms, lovingly worn furniture, and nooks that still resonated faintly with the laughter of children. Here Javanne had passed the happiest years of her life. When she became gravely ill, with little hope of recovery, her husband had taken her home to Edelweiss, surrendering the management of Armida to his oldest son.

Javanne Lanart-Hastur lay on a couch, propped up on pillows stitched in a pattern of ice-daisies and *kireseth* blossoms. Against the colorful embroidery, her skin looked chalky, her lips dry and cracked. Age and pain had withered her flesh, rendering the hand resting on the blanket as fragile as a songbird's foot.

Domenic sat in his usual place, a high-backed chair placed so that he could readily lift a goblet of water to her lips or stroke her hair if she became agitated. At twenty, he was tall and gracefully built, wiry rather than muscular, with a trace of the exquisite masculine beauty of the Hasturs in his eyes and mouth. His hair swept back from his forehead like an ebony cascade, unbound as he had always preferred to wear it. His eyes were gold-flecked gray, the irises ringed in black. A book lay open on his lap between his graceful, long-fingered hands. It was one of his mother's translations of fishermen's tales and song lyrics from Thetis, chosen because the softly musical rhythms calmed the old woman.

It wouldn't be long now, Domenic thought with a pang. He should tell *Dom* Gabriel.

How easy it would have been to miss this time together, Domenic thought. He had every reason to resent his grandmother. From the moment of Domenic's conception, the old woman had set herself up as the enemy of his father, Mikhail Lanart-Hastur. No member of the family had been immune to her vicious attacks. By the time the *leroni* at Arilinn had identified the cause of her increasing debility, the damage to her brain was irreversible.

Another outrage to lay at the feet of the World Wreckers, Domenic thought. Minute, deadly in their slow insidious action, the tumor-generating particles had lain hidden until it was too late. *What other weapons remain, waiting only to be triggered?*

At times, Domenic could sense a lingering taint in soil and rock. Since his *laran* had awakened during his adolescence, he had been able to sense the subtle changes in the planetary crust. The Gift, he understood from his teachers at Neskaya Tower, was related to the ability to detect precious metals below the surface, used in *laran* mining operations. Domenic's talent allowed him to reach deeper and farther. Sometimes it seemed that Darkover itself sang to him.

Domenic closed the book and brushed his fingertips over his grandmother's wrist. The featherlight touch brought a rush of *laran* impressions. Her life forces had sunk very low, guttering like a candle in its final hour. Barely a trickle of energy flowed through her channels. Focusing his mind through the starstone that hung on its sil-

ver chain, bare against his chest, Domenic embraced her
with a wave of love and felt the faint, poignantly grateful
response.

The impulse that had brought him here had been rebellion, escape from a life of courtly responsibility laid down
for him by his elders, rather than any fondness for his distant, critical grandmother. Why should he care, when she
had done everything she could to harm him?

And yet . . .

The first time he sat beside her and silently took her
hand in his, something had changed. She had gazed upon
him with pain-riddled eyes, and by some grace, some
wholly unanticipated insight, he had glimpsed the young
woman she had once been, tall and graceful, Gifted with
laran, pressured by her family and caste to marry a man
she barely knew and to bear him a host of children. He saw
her wasted talent, her withered dreams, the love she had
lavished upon her children, the tiny redemptive moments
of contentment. Then had come the slow, creeping doubts,
the fears gnawing upon her like leeches of the soul, the moments of shock as her own voice spewed venom upon
those she once loved. Finally, her own body had turned
traitor, and she fled here to Edelweiss, to the only place she
had known happiness.

That moment of compassion had touched a chord deep
within Domenic. All his resentment at the demands of his
rank, his longing to choose his own path, all these had
fallen away. He had seen himself in the mirror of Javanne's
sacrifice and found himself wanting.

A tap on the door drew Domenic from his reverie. He
set down the book and went quietly to the door. The Edelweiss *coridom* stood there, an anxious look upon his features. "Master Domenic, a rider in the uniform of the City
Guards has come from Thendara. He insists upon giving
his message only to you."

"I'll see him," Domenic replied. "Would you have one of
the maids sit with my grandmother and call me if there's
any change?"

Domenic went down to the ancient wooden gates. Even in the sheltered courtyard, bounded by stables and the stone walls of the house itself, the wind cut like a whetted knife. A Guardsman, his face reddened, stood holding the reins of a lathered horse. The animal pawed at the snow-laced ground.

"I was to give this to you and no other." The Guardsman held out a creased envelope.

Domenic thanked him. "Come in and warm yourself. I'll have the kitchen send you something hot to drink at once."

Having made sure both man and horse were properly attended to, Domenic took the letter into the little family chapel to read. It was an old room in the depths of the house, the four old god-forms painted crudely on the walls, lights burning before them even during the day.

Instantly, Domenic recognized his mother's angular script. She had learned to read and write Darkovan as an adult, and she had never mastered the smoothly looping calligraphy.

"Nico my dear," the letter began. Domenic smiled at her use of his childhood nickname.

"I hope this letter finds you well, although I understand there is small likelihood the same is true for Domna Javanne. *I cannot tell you how proud I am of your kindness in going to her. I hope with all my heart that you two have been able to achieve some measure of understanding on behalf of all of us. No one should end their life with such bitterness and unhealed wounds."*

How like his mother, to look for a reconciliation even though her own relationship with Mikhail's mother had never been close. Over the years, Marguerida had borne the brunt of Javanne's rages and had done her best to shield her husband from the old woman's vicious schemes.

"As much pride as your visit gives us, your father and I hope that your absence will not be long."

Domenic looked up from the letter. Even the gray light that filtered through the window seemed too bright. On the surface, he read his mother's gentle reminder that he was missed. She had already given him more freedom than he had any right to expect as the Heir to Hastur and, most likely, the next Regent of Darkover. Most of his last three years had been spent in study at the Tower of Neskaya, with occasional visits home or with his mother's Aldaran friends. He loved the way the mountains hummed through his mind, the sweet wild stillness of the glacial peaks, the lilting dance of the snowmelt streams.

"You must take all the time you need to sort out the priorities in your life," Marguerida had said the night before he left for Neskaya. "Please consider this, Nico. None of us are truly free to follow our own wishes. As ruling Comyn, we have great power to shape our world, but at the same time, our world shapes us. There is an old saying that we are as the gods have made us, but I believe the truth is that we constantly remake ourselves in striving to fulfill our destiny."

"Your father and I look forward to seeing you before the next Council season. I shall not rest easy until I have you once again home with us.

"Your loving mother,

"Marguerida."

Thoughtfully, Domenic refolded the letter. There was something more in the words than a mere wish to see him again or a hint that his presence was expected at Council season later in the year. Something troubled his mother.

Among Marguerida's psychic talents was the ability to sense the future, at least as it affected her and those she loved. She called it her Aldaran Gift. Had she received another such premonition? Did some vision of disaster lie behind the half-spoken plea?

———— ◆ ————

Javanne slipped away in her sleep that same day. The same messenger who delivered Marguerida's letter returned to Thendara with the news of her passing. It took the better part of a tenday to complete the preparations. A casket had to be built and a wagon procured to take her body to

Thendara, so that she might lie at the *rhu fead* beside her ancestors. An ordinary woman might rest in the family cemetery, but Javanne was Comynara, sister to the late Regis Hastur and mother of the current Regent. In addition, Domenic, as the Hastur heir, could not travel without a suitable escort. Supplies, pack animals, suitably warm clothing, and attendants all must be arranged.

Old *Dom* Gabriel was almost beside himself with grief. He had not loved Javanne when they wed, but a deep affection had grown between them over the years. A chill had settled in his lungs, and his coughing echoed through the house at night. He sat in the little parlor where once Javanne had nursed their children, staring into the fire.

The state of the old man's health worried Domenic. He seated himself on the footstool beside the broad patchstone hearth and took his grandfather's hands in his own.

For a long moment there was no response. Firelight reflected off the old man's fever-bright eyes. His shoulder bones jutted through the tartan shawl. The carpets and tapestries that had once warmed the room now seemed muted and threadbare.

"I know, I know," Gabriel muttered, "I should be attending to the leave-taking. But there is—Javanne used to—" A spasm of coughing cut off his words.

Domenic waited until the fit had passed. "You are ill . . ."

"I have been so before and will be again."

"Grandfather, I do not mean to be impertinent, but there is no one else to tell you the truth. You are not well, and travel in this weather will only make you worse. I would not have your death on my hands. What purpose would it serve to lay you in the earth at Grandmother's side?"

Except to bring an added measure of grief to your family.

Domenic thought his grandfather would brush away his arguments. Phlegm rumbled in Gabriel's lungs, and his head sank onto his chest. "She was my wife for all these long years, a good mother and a noble lady. How should I not show her proper respect?"

"You will honor her best by caring for yourself as she

would have," Domenic said gently. "In fact, my mother will say you have learned common sense at last."

"Yes, she would say that, wouldn't she? She always did speak her mind."

"When winter has passed and you have recovered, then you can come to Thendara. I will ride with you to the *rhu fead,* and you can bid Grandmother a proper farewell. She would not want you to risk your life in order to say those words a few months earlier."

"At which grave shall I stand? How will I know where she lies, when none bears any marking?"

Does it matter whether you say your prayers over Grandmother's remains, or those of Great-Uncle Regis? Or your own father, or Lorill Hastur, or any of the generations of Comyn who lie there? They are all at peace now.

A shudder passed through Gabriel's body, and he drew the shawl more tightly around his shoulders. "The day will come, all too soon, when I will make that journey."

"Not for some years, if you stay here now, in safety and comfort," Domenic said. "Let your people tend to you."

"I suppose an old man would slow you down. I do not ride as swiftly as I once did."

Wrapped in fur, Gabriel came down to bid farewell to Domenic on the day of his departure. Domenic's fine-boned gray mare, a gift from his mother out of her own Armida-bred favorite, pranced and pulled at the bit, eager to be gone. The gates stood open, the wagon and mounted attendants waiting. The breaths of the animals made white puffs in the chill air. Above, clouds scudded across a brightening sky.

"You're a good lad," Gabriel said, "and you'll make a fine Regent for the Domains in your time. Your father must be proud of you. Now get along, ride while you have good daylight. Give your mother my regards. Come back in summer, and we'll ride together."

2

The journey to Thendara passed uneventfully, except for the expected miseries of travel in early spring. Most days, rain lashed down, but there was little snow, and Domenic and his party were able to find an inn or travel shelter each night. The horses, accustomed to harsh weather, plodded on stoically, with lowered heads and tails clamped against their rumps. The wagon carrying Javanne's casket got bogged down in the mud several times, prolonging the journey.

Yet, through the damp and chill, Domenic heard a silver-bright melody. Men and beasts might shiver, but the land itself rejoiced in the fluid dance of seasonal renewal.

In the hills, they skirted blackened areas where forest fires had raged the previous year, abandoned orchards, stunted hedgerows, empty livestock pens, and farm houses whose roofs had fallen in. Here the wordless song of the land twisted, turning harsh, like the groaning of a living creature in pain.

As they came down into the Lowlands, they met travelers bent under heavy burdens, sometimes whole families with little children. Domenic asked the Guardsman why these people were on the road in such weather. The Guard shook his head and said they were most likely seeking work in Thendara.

The party clattered into the outer courtyard of Comyn

Castle late in the morning. The great stone walls provided a little shelter, but it had been raining steadily since sunrise, the wind gusting in slashes of sleet, and they were nearly soaked through. Mud spattered the animals up to their knees. The porter, who had been sheltering in an arched doorway that looked as if it dated from the days of Varzil the Good, called out a greeting.

A moment later Domenic's father, Mikhail Lanart-Hastur, emerged from the doorway, flinging on a thick cloak. In his late forties, Mikhail still had the same strong shoulders, the same body kept trim by regular sword practice, the same penetrating blue eyes. Silver hairs now frosted the pale gold, and lines of care bracketed his mouth. The skin around his eyes held shadows, like hidden bruises.

At Mikhail's shouted orders, grooms rushed about, unharnessing and attending to the horses, wagon, and baggage. His voice sounded hoarse against the rattle and clatter of wagon wheels and shod hooves on the paving stones.

Domenic kicked his feet free from the stirrups, slid to the ground, and handed the reins to a waiting groom. He turned, to be caught up in his father's hard embrace.

"Son, it's good to have you back with us again. Thank you for bringing her home."

Through the brief contact, Domenic sensed the depth of his father's grief. Whatever she had done in later life, this woman had borne him, nursed him, sung to him . . . loved him.

Memories, like motes of firelit poignancy, flashed from Mikhail's mind into Domenic's . . .

Mikhail lying snug beneath his blankets on his cot, with an infant's drowsy awareness of the rhythms of the house around him . . .

Edelweiss, Domenic thought, recognizing the indelible character of the place, *but long ago.*

Voices, edged with emotions beyond young Mikhail's understanding . . . his mother . . . a stranger . . .

"One thing more, sister," the man said. "I go where I may never return. You must give me one of your sons for my heir."

Javanne uttered a low, stricken cry. "Come then, Regis, and choose . . ."

Hands lifted Mikhail. A face bent over him . . .

"Once I take this oath," Regis said, "he is not yours but mine . . . and this claim may never be renounced by me while I live . . ."

Later, while Mikhail lay, restless and yearning, his ears caught the sound of weeping in the night.

From that moment, baby Mikhail ceased to be only the youngest of three sons of Gabriel and Javanne. He became a Hastur in his own right, the heir to Regis, the Domain, and the Regency of the Comyn. And so was Domenic, his oldest son.

Domenic looked into his father's eyes, his heart too full to speak. He understood why Mikhail had never lashed back at Javanne and why she had turned on him, of all her sons.

A shadow passed over Mikhail's features, still handsome but blurred, as if the spirit that burned so brightly within him were momentarily dimmed. Creases now marked the once-smooth brow and bracketed the generous mouth; the hollows of eye socket and cheekbone held intimations of age. Had the last three years, when Domenic had rarely been home for more than the briefest holiday visits, weighed so heavily upon his father?

Not just three years. Three years of being Regent in the wake of the departure of the Terran Federation.

"Go on, get yourself inside," Mikhail urged Domenic. "You're soaked through. When you're warm and dry, go greet your mother. I'll be a time making sure the casket is placed in proper state."

The Guardsmen went off to their own quarters. Domenic gave each of the Edelweiss servants a small purse of silver. Then he made his way through the labyrinth of halls and corridors to his own chamber in the family suite.

This part of the Castle had always seemed to him an accretion of centuries of architectural styles, all jumbled together. The stone stairs had been worn in the middle, polished by generations of feet. Here and there, a newer wall hanging or a panel of translucent blue stone brightened the passageway. At last, Domenic reached the familiar archway leading to the family quarters.

His father was right, he was wet through to his skin. The brief *laran* contact had drained him even further. Any moment now, he would start shivering. He did not want to face his mother without a bite to eat, a bath and shave, and a change of clothing. A drink might not be a bad idea, either. In this frame of mind, he hurried down the corridor, head down, slapping his sodden riding gloves against his thigh.

"Domenic!" Alanna Alar burst from an opened door and threw her arms around his neck. He smelled her faintly floral perfume, felt her silken cheek against his.

"Alanna! Don't hug me! I'm drenched and filthy from the trail. You'll ruin your gown!"

Alanna met Domenic's gaze with a disconcerting directness. He had seen her but little in the last three years. Somehow, in the time they'd been apart, she had changed from a pretty child into a beauty, with hair like spun copper and startling green eyes beneath dark, sweetly arched brows. He noticed a hint of shadow between the curves of her breasts at the neckline of her gown, her slender waist, her skin like velvet.

"Never mind about the dress!" she said, pouting a little. "Aren't you happy to see me? I've missed you so much!"

Something inside Domenic, some knot of tension, loosened. He and Alanna had been playfellows since they were young children, when she had come to live with his family. Her own mother had been too insecure and neurotic, not to mention utterly lacking in *laran,* to deal with a strong-willed, tempestuous daughter, so Marguerida had offered to foster the child. Domenic had taken the disconsolate girl under his wing, and he soon became closer to her than to his own siblings.

Domenic kissed Alanna's cheek. "I've missed you, too. I sent word—you must have heard—Grandmother Javanne died."

Alanna's cheerful expression faltered. Javanne and Gabriel were her grandparents as well as his, for her mother was Mikhail's younger sister.

"I ought to be sorry," she said, lowering her gaze but not sounding at all sad, "but I hardly knew Grandmother Javanne. She certainly made Auntie Marguerida's life miserable, and she wasn't very nice to you. I couldn't believe you went to stay with her when you didn't have to."

Domenic hesitated to remind her that Javanne's irritability and suspiciousness was not her own fault but an effect of her illness. It was too complicated to explain, and he didn't have the energy for a lengthy discussion. He remembered, too, how little grief Alanna had shown after the death of Regis Hastur, who had always been gentle and kind to her.

"It was the right thing to do," he said, "and we made our peace in the end."

Alanna slipped her hand into his. Her fingers felt smooth and soft. "Come on. We've only got a little while before Auntie Marguerida hears you're back."

As they walked toward his chamber, she told him about the latest street opera, a retelling of the adventures of Durraman's infamously recalcitrant donkey. Domenic remembered the times they had hidden in various places in the castle, the secret games they had shared, acting out tales of bandits or Dry Towners. Once, when they were about ten, she'd dressed in his jacket and breeches and announced she was going to cut her hair and run away with the Free Amazons.

Regretfully, he pulled his hand free. "Our reunion will have to wait. I must make myself presentable for my parents."

"So?" She turned back to him, eyebrows lifted like the slender wings of a rainbird in flight. For an instant, he felt as if he were drowning in the celadon light of her eyes.

"So," he said, trying not to blush, "no young woman of

good reputation should be alone with a man who is not her husband, especially in his own chamber. *Especially* if—in case you hadn't noticed—I am in sore need of a bath and a shave."

Rosy color seeped across Alanna's cheeks and throat. Her eyelids, fringed with amazingly long lashes, half lowered, and her blush intensified. Domenic thought she was the most beautiful creature he had ever seen.

"Please," he began, suddenly desperate to say something, "after I'm cleaned up, I must go to my mother. I'd very much appreciate your company."

"I will look for you afterward, but don't ask me to go in. Auntie Marguerida is expecting you, not me."

"Oh, Alanna, we are all family! You will not be intruding."

"It's not that . . ." Her eyes darkened, and she bit her lower lip. "I would not spoil your homecoming."

"Alanna—cousin—what is the matter?"

She gave a little, careless laugh. Domenic heard the forced quality, as if she were trying to put on a brave face for him. "She does not—we do not . . . she is always telling me . . . No, I will say no more. You are here, and everything will be better now, I promise."

With a smile that sent a curious sensation through Domenic's stomach, Alanna hurried away.

———— ✦ ————

Domenic emerged from his chamber clean and smooth-cheeked, wearing a suit of butter-soft suede dyed in Hastur blue and trimmed with silver braid, and made his way to the small office that his mother kept in her own suite of rooms. A lively fire warmed the hearth and scented the air with the familiar, comforting fragrance of balsam. An uneven tapestry, his sister Yllana's work, hung in a place of honor on the paneled walls, but otherwise the chamber with its cheerful carpet and lovingly tended furniture was exactly as he remembered it. Through the far door Domenic glimpsed his mother's specially built clavier.

Marguerida sat at her usual desk, piled with papers and opened books. Although she'd borne three children, now young adults, only a faint tracery of lines between her brows betrayed her years. Her hair was still a mass of silky flame-red curls, her eyes a curious golden color. She wore a gown of soft ivory wool, draped high on the neck for warmth, the skirts swinging from a gracefully dropped waist, and a matching embroidered glove on her left hand. The glove, hemmed with a tracery of satin-stitched flowers, was so much a part of her dress that Domenic could not imagine her without it. It insulated the psychoactive matrix embedded in her palm, the strange remainder of an Overworld battle before he was born. Domenic had seen it unveiled only once, at the Battle of Old North Road.

With a cry of delight, Marguerida came toward him. "Nico, my darling! Mik sent a servant to let me know you'd arrived. Here you are, home at last!"

Domenic returned his mother's embrace. "I'm sorry I was delayed. The weather was terrible, and it always takes longer to travel with a large party. Grandfather Gabriel sends his regards, but is too frail to make the journey this early in the season."

A strange expression passed over Marguerida's golden eyes. Domenic sensed the quick succession of her emotions—sadness tinged with relief at Javanne's passing, concern for her husband's grief, compassion for the old man who had been kind to her when she had returned to Darkover as a young woman and found herself caught up in the whirlwind politics of the Comyn.

"We will miss him," she said, "but it is better that he stay where he can be cared for. We have had enough deaths in the family."

She gestured to the divan that had been drawn up before the hearth. The two of them settled comfortably in the sphere of the fire's warmth.

"And *Domna* Javanne . . . ?" Marguerida asked. "You were able to say your farewells with an easy heart?"

"I believe she was at peace at last," Domenic said. "I read to her from one of your books, to ease her pain."

"Did you, indeed?" She looked pleased.

"She especially liked the song about the delfin prince and the pearl-diver's daughter."

"Javanne's passing marks the end of an era," Marguerida said thoughtfully. "Each year there are fewer left of that generation. My father, of course, and Old Gabriel."

"And Danilo Syrtis-Ardais," Domenic added.

"Yes, although he keeps so much to himself these days, I see very little of him. He took the death of Regis very hard. I'm afraid he may never get over the loss. And then Lady Linnea . . . since you were last at home, she left us for Arilinn Tower. She was trained as a Keeper when she was very young, you know, and gave it up to marry Regis. The work will give her a sense of purpose, and trained *leroni* are still so few that she will make a valuable contribution. But here we are, gossiping like a couple of old hens!"

As Domenic listened, he realized how much he had missed. Life had gone on without him, following its own rhythms. "It is good to be home again."

She took his hand, an unusual gesture of warmth among telepaths but characteristic of her. "I hope your stay will not be so brief this time . . ."

In his mind, Domenic finished her thought. *The time has come when you must take up your responsibilities. You are the Heir to Hastur and the Regency of all the Domains.*

"I have tried not to impose that obligation on you too soon," Marguerida said. "The people need strong leadership, and that takes not only talent but training. We must ensure a smooth succession."

"I know, I know. At my age, my father had had years of preparation. Great-Uncle Regis himself groomed him for the work. I appreciate the freedom you've given me . . ."

Where were the words to express the turmoil in his heart? How could he explain?

I don't want to be the most powerful man on Darkover.

I saw what it did to Great-Uncle Regis, what it is doing to Father!

Marguerida's eyes widened, and Domenic realized he had not kept his thoughts private. He braced himself for a lecture on responsibilities, but her expression softened.

"Regis used to say that if we did not like the lives we had been born to, we should have chosen our parents differently," she said. "Do you think he—or your father—or I, for that matter—*wanted* power? Oh, Nico, I would have given anything for a quiet, private life with Mikhail, with no greater fame than what I earned through my music. Goodness knows, I tried everything to avoid being named the Heir to Alton when I first came to Darkover. When I surrendered my right to Armida to old Gabriel, I thought I was at last free from Comyn politics. But my life didn't work out that way."

Neither will yours, she said silently. *Like me, you will always have the steadfast support of those who love you.*

Marguerida got up from her desk and stood beside Domenic's chair, resting her gloved hand on his shoulder. When he had left Thendara three years ago, thinking to make a new life for himself at Neskaya Tower, he had spared no thought for what it cost her to let him go. He had focused only on his own desires, his own needs.

In his memory, he saw Javanne as a young woman, setting aside her own hopes, fulfilling her duty to her caste, to her world. Releasing her own infant son to a harsh destiny. Her gaze, unflinching and direct, challenged him to do the same. She called upon him to set aside the toys—and the dreams—of his childhood.

"I am not my father, or Great-Uncle Regis," he said, his voice strangely thick. "But if I have no choice, then I must do my best."

Marguerida's fingers tightened on his shoulder. "I know you will, my dear, and I have every confidence in you."

As he forced a smile, Domenic imagined the walls of Comyn Castle closing in on him. One by one, the doors of his life swung closed, leaving only this narrow avenue.

How could he complain? He had already been given far
more freedom than any other young man in his position,
certainly more than his own father or Great-Uncle Regis.
Neither of them had had the luxury of studying in a Tower,
or swimming in the Sea of Dalereuth, or walking the marketplace in Carthon. Why should he want more?

If only Darkover did not sing to him in his dreams . . .

———— ✦ ————

Domenic did not see his father until later, in the cozy
room that served as the family parlor and informal dining
room. The sleeping chamber used by Marguerida and
Mikhail lay beyond it, and their children's bedrooms were
down a short hallway. The main hall, little used except for
formal occasions, lay in the opposite direction. The great
complex of Comyn Castle contained many such apartments, one area for each Domain. Most were used infre-
quently, only when the families came to Thendara for
gatherings of the Comyn Council. Domenic's family was
the exception, for Mikhail's duties as Regent required his
year-round presence.

These small, tidily appointed chambers were as familiar
to Domenic as any he had known. Through that door, his
mother had set up the office where she had received him
on his arrival; here she entertained friends and composed
music in moments snatched from her official duties. Farther down the hallway lay his father's study, part refuge,
part solarium, part library.

When Domenic entered the parlor, he found Yllana and
Rory bent over a low table, playing castles. Marguerida
sat nearby, picking out a melody on an old-fashioned *rryl*.
Yllana sprang up and accepted Domenic's embrace. She
was fifteen now, with tawny eyes and a girl's willowy grace.
From the fleeting touch of her *laran,* she had clearly inher-
ited their mother's quick wit and their father's cautious-
ness.

"So the exile has returned," Rory said, clapping Domenic's
shoulder. "For how long, this time?"

"I am not certain, for there is much to be settled."
Domenic felt Marguerida's eyes on him. He added, "I wish
the reason had been less unhappy."

In Domenic's absence, Rory had grown from an unruly
adolescent to a man, although echoes of the old wildness
still lingered in the roguish glint in his eyes. A curl at the
corner of his mouth reminded Domenic of his brother's
early penchant for mischief, the murals Rory had embla-
zoned on the parlor walls in chalk, the tarts stolen from the
kitchen. Rory now carried himself with an assurance and
restraint Domenic had never seen in him before. Clearly,
Rory's training in the Guards had given him much-needed
self-discipline as well as a sword fighter's muscular shoulders and supple strength.

Food arrived from the Castle kitchens. Marguerida had
ordered a light meal of late winter fare, Thendara-style,
buns stuffed with meat and onions, a bowl of dried apples
and another of toasted nuts, a beaker of watered cider, and
a pitcher of the ubiquitous *jaco.* Domenic found himself
surprisingly hungry.

While they were eating, Mikhail came in, trailing a gust
of air that smelled of leather and rain. "There you are,
Domenic! Come here, for a proper greeting!"

After embracing Domenic once more, Mikhail bent to
kiss Marguerida. Domenic felt the steady pulse of love between them. A ring sparkled on Mikhail's right hand, the
mysterious and extraordinary matrix given to him on a
desperate journey through time by the legendary Varzil the
Good.

Over the years, Mikhail had learned to harness the immensely powerful psychoactive gem for healing, as well as
less peaceful purposes. With his Tower training, Domenic
sensed how the ring crystal had become attuned to his father's personal matrix. One of the first things Domenic had
learned at Neskaya was never to let anyone else touch his
matrix. Only a trained Keeper could handle another's starstone without agonizing, even fatal, shock to the owner.
Since Mikhail was able to wear the ring unshielded, open

to casual touch, the stone of the ring must not have the same limitations.

The servants finished laying the meal on the table, and they sat down. One chair remained vacant, and a moment later, Alanna entered and slipped into it. She wore the same gown as before, but her hair had been tidied, plaited flame against the cream of her skin. Domenic noticed that she offered no excuse for her lateness. Instead, she kept her eyes on her plate.

"Alanna dear, will you not welcome Domenic back among us?" Marguerida said.

"She has already done so," Domenic said, accepting the bowl of amber-nuts Rory passed to him. "We ran into each other when I first came in."

Alanna's smile flashed like the sun after a storm. The air in the room brightened.

"Now we are all here together as a family," Mikhail said, "even if it is for a sorrowful occasion. Domenic, you did well in your kindness to my mother during her last days and in bringing her body back for burial. For all the unhappiness in her life, she was Comynara."

Domenic heard the heavy resonance in his father's voice, like the distant throbbing of a knell.

How would I feel if it were my mother lying in that casket, waiting to be laid in an unmarked grave? Domenic shuddered, unable to imagine a world without Marguerida.

"—do you?" Mikhail was asking.

Domenic had missed a beat of the conversation. He covered it quickly, excusing the lapse as fatigue from the journey.

"Of course," Marguerida said, giving him a tender smile.

The conversation shifted to Javanne's funeral. The ceremony itself required little preparation, for the ancient tradition was simple, but arrangements must be made for those relatives and dignitaries who were able to make the journey to Thendara at this season and on short notice. Lew Alton, Marguerida's father, had sent word that he would arrive from Armida, where he had retired at the invitation of the younger Gabriel, who would attend as well. The Elhalyn estates were close enough so that Dani Hastur, the son of Regis, and his wife and family could also be present.

"I wish some of the Aldaran folk could be here," Marguerida said. Katherine, the wife of Hermes Aldaran, was one of her closest women friends.

"Not even a weather worker could make the roads through the Hellers passable at this season," Rory commented.

"You're not afraid of a little snowstorm?" Yllana's eyes glinted with affectionate teasing.

Rory shrugged, refusing to be drawn in. "With a decent horse and proper gear, of course not. A caravan of wagons and pack animals is another matter."

"Our friends will be here soon enough," Mikhail said, "and then we will finish our discussion about Yllana returning with them to be fostered at Castle Aldaran."

"Would you like that, little sister?" Domenic asked. This was the first he had heard of the Aldarans fostering Yllana.

The girl lifted her chin, looking very much like her mother in a resolute mood. "I may have some of the Aldaran *laran,* and Mother says it would be better to learn how to use it from those who know it well."

Domenic nodded. In his grandfathers' time, Aldaran was still estranged from the other Domains. In isolation, they had learned new techniques to develop their distinctive psychic talents. A few of them now worked in Towers, but the rest of the Domains knew little of the Aldaran disciplines.

"It isn't fair!" Alanna's expression darkened. A frown twisted her beautiful mouth. "You made *me* go to Arilinn!"

"Child, that was for your own safety," Marguerida said. "We would never have sent you away if there were any other choice."

"But Yllana gets to live with *Domna* Katherine—"

"Yllana does not have your abilities as a telekinetic and a fire-starter, a dangerous combination," Mikhail said gently. He had always loved Alanna, even when she was at her most tempestuous.

"I hate Yllana!" Alanna shrieked. "I hate you all!"

Yllana flinched under Alanna's psychic blast. She clenched her dinner knife so hard, her knuckles went white. She looked as if she wanted to throw it at Alanna, but common sense and a naturally steady temperament restrained her.

"Alanna, you know you do not mean that." Marguerida struggled visibly to keep her own composure. "You are foster sisters, after all, and should not speak so to one another. We want what is best for each of you."

"It was not so bad at Arilinn, was it, little lady?" Mikhail asked. "Did they not teach you well?"

Alanna drew in her breath, clearly ready with a caustic retort. Suddenly, she grew very still. The hectic color drained from her cheeks. Her breathing slowed, and the fire in her green eyes dimmed.

"As you wished," she said in a flat, emotionless tone, "they taught me to control my *laran*. I do not light fires or hurl objects with my mind any longer."

"Now it is Yllana's turn to go away," Marguerida said, gently redirecting the conversation, "and we will miss her as much as we did you, Alanna."

"It is not my fault that life in a Tower did not agree with you." Yllana continued to regard Alanna with a mixture of caution and firmness. "I wish it had been otherwise, that you might have been happy there. Can you not wish me well?"

Alanna looked confused. "Of course, foster sister," she murmured in a subdued voice. "Why would I want anything else?"

The servants came in to clear away the remains of the meal. Rory excused himself to return to the Guards barracks and a previous engagement with one of his comrades. Yllana pleaded a headache, clearly to avoid becoming the target for any further outbursts.

Alanna rose also, but Marguerida gestured for her to stay.

"My dear, I will need your help with arranging a small dinner gathering tomorrow. Come to my office after breakfast and I'll give you a list of things to be done."

"As you wish, Auntie." Alanna dropped a curtsy before departing.

Domenic reflected that whatever his mother's intentions, there was no such thing as *a small gathering*. She knew too many people, and both she and Mikhail were outgoing, sociable personalities. Domenic suspected that in this aspect, he resembled his Great-Uncle Regis more than either of his parents. He, like Regis, was an essentially private person thrust into a public role. How had Regis done it?

He could not remember Regis without Danilo Syrtis, his sworn brother and paxman, at his side, or Lady Linnea, lending him her gracious strength.

Glancing at his parents, Domenic saw how they, too, formed a seamless whole. They were the right hand and the left, the darkness and the dawn. In that moment, he knew he could not face the future they had planned for him if he were alone. But he did not know where to find the other half of his soul.

3

Lewis-Kennard Alton stood at the window of the main hall in the Alton suite in Comyn Castle. Bitter storms had lashed the ancient stone walls for the past tenday, and the courtyard garden glistened. Even so, the worst of the winter had passed. Snow no longer lay thick on the ground, and buds swelled on the bare branches.

This room was one of the oldest in the Castle, the walls set with luminous stones from deep caves that charged with light all day and radiated a soft glow at night. Since Lew had last seen the place, someone, probably Marguerida, had covered the old stone seats with needle-pointed cushions in sea-wave patterns of blue and green.

Lew sighed. In his late sixties, one-handed, his face etched with scars, he felt as weary in spirit as the wet, gray world outside. He would just as soon have remained at Armida, the family estate, where he had useful work to do, advising the younger Gabriel, gentling young horses, riding the pasture boundaries, savoring the peace and nostalgia of his childhood home. Marguerida had specifically asked him to attend the funeral for Javanne Lanart-Hastur. He could not have stayed away.

This place is too full of ghosts.

Memory stirred, unbidden. Many years ago, Lew had ridden with Regis Hastur on the road to Thendara to attend Comyn Council. Regis had been only fifteen then, slender and earnest. His grandfather, Danvan Hastur, had been grooming him to take his place as Regent of the Comyn. Lew remembered the hunger in the younger man's eyes as he watched the Terran Federation ships roaring into the sky.

That was when the Federation still maintained its Headquarters at Thendara, while men of good will on both sides worked together—and women, too, for the Renunciates had been training as midwives with the Terran Medical corps and working as guides and translators since the days of Magdalen Lorne.

. . . Before the illegal, immensely powerful matrix known as Sharra drew them all into madness . . . Before he had loved and lost Marjorie Scott . . .

. . . Before interstellar civil war tore the Federation apart, before it closed its Base on Darkover, before the nightmarish Battle of Old North Road and its aftermath . . .

But all of that was over, best forgotten.

A chill crept along Lew's bones. With his one remaining hand, he clutched the front of his shirt, where his starstone lay wrapped in triple-insulated silk. He dared not look into its luminescent blue depths.

The past is too much with me.

"Father, you are here at last!" Marguerida entered, wearing a shawl of the Alton tartan over a gown of green like the cool shade beneath a pine forest.

He turned toward her, holding out his hand. She smiled, enveloping him with her special warmth, and stepped into his embrace.

How good it is to have you with us again, she spoke with her mind to his.

Lew broke the embrace, holding her at arm's distance to look into her eyes. Despite her outward poise, tension coiled through her muscles.

"What troubles you, my dear?"

"Come, sit down." Leading him into the smaller family parlor, she gestured to the cushioned seat beside the fireplace. The andirons were new, shaped like graceful, intertwined trees. The fire had burned down into a bed of glowing coals, radiating a gently seductive warmth. Marguerida offered her father a choice of *jaco* or hot mulled wine from the sideboard. He refused both, but she poured herself a cup of the bitter stimulant brew, stirred in a spoonful of fragrant sage honey to her taste, and sat facing him.

"I am so glad to have you here to talk to. Mikhail's tied up—a message arrived two days ago and he won't tell me about it—but he'll join us later."

Marguerida spoke lightly, but Lew sensed her distress at her husband's secrecy. Surely, any two married people as busy as Marguerida and Mikhail could not share every detail of their lives, but they had always been open with one another.

Mikhail has burdens enough, she added telepathically, *without my adding what may turn out to be baseless fears.*

This much was true. Even in Armida, where Altons farmed and raised their fine horses, and cares faded in the rhythmic passages of seasons, Lew sensed how difficult it had been for his son-in-law to assume the Regency of the Domains. Regis Hastur, who had held that position until his death three years ago, had cast a long shadow, one that might endure for generations.

Mikhail had all the makings of a brilliant Regent, trained for the work since childhood by Regis himself. Slowly, with his usual deliberate care, Mikhail was shaping Darkover without a Terran presence. Men by their nature resisted change, even when it was for the better. If some opposed Mikhail's leadership, just as many supported him. In the end, patience and time would win; Mikhail knew this, and Marguerida did, too.

There must be something else . . .

Yes, Marguerida answered, and Lew caught a flicker of fear from her mind.

"I'm probably just overly sensitive," she said, setting

down her *jaco* and rubbing her temples. "I've had one of my headaches on and off for a tenday now, not an ordinary one, but . . . I can't decide if it's my Aldaran precognition or just nerves."

Lew raised one eyebrow at the thought of Marguerida admitting to such a frailty.

Marguerida frowned. "I've never entirely trusted these premonitions. For one thing, they show only my own future or that of those very close to me. When Ariel Alar went into labor with Alanna, I *knew* Alanna would be all right because our lives would intertwine, but I had no idea what would happen to Ariel, how crazy she would become. Second, the foreseeings are far from certain. Third, and most importantly, I refuse to believe in predestination or hold with the superstition that our fates are sealed by the gods. Anyone's gods."

Lew could not restrain a smile. If ever a person were determined to create her own destiny, it was his headstrong daughter. From the day she returned to Darkover—no, from the moment of her birth—she had faced life on her own terms. Her early upbringing on the Federation world of Thetis had given her an independence and forthright approach to life unusual for a Darkovan woman. When her Alton relatives had pressured her to marry and assume her place in traditional Comyn society, she had forged her own way. She had married, but for love, not position; she had taken up her heritage and used her power to expand Darkovan literacy, to continue the music that was her passion. Now she stood at her husband's side, an equal partner in the defense of the world she had come to love.

Marguerida went on, "When Alanna was still in the womb, I had a vision of her—wild and rebellious, which she certainly has become, and also the cause of great troubles. In fact, I remember thinking she ought to be called Deirdre, for all the sorrow she would bring."

"Yet you took her into your own home and gave her the loving care her mother could not," Lew said.

"What else was there to do?" Marguerida replied with some heat. "If we are to avert disaster, we must guide her into a different path. I have tried my best to be patient and understanding, to make her feel accepted. Whether I have been successful remains to be seen. She did not take it well when I insisted she go to Arilinn Tower."

"The discipline of Arilinn is not easy," Lew said. "Was there no alternative?"

Marguerida shook her head. "Her *laran* had become too dangerous. Her tantrums were growing worse every day. Mikhail and I feared her mind might be too fragile to withstand the power of her talent. I could not save her, so I had no choice but to turn her over to those who could."

"In that case, you did right to send her there. If Arilinn could not help her, I doubt anyone could."

"Time and her season of training have indeed helped to steady her," Marguerida said. "I believe she is over the worst, although her temper is still uncertain. She came back to us with the same wilfulness, but she no longer started fires or threw pottery at the wall with her mind. In fact, she seemed to have effectively suppressed her *laran*. It did not distress her, so I assumed the Keepers knew what they were doing."

And your premonition about her?

She favored him with a wry smile. "You know me too well, Father. As you may have suspected, it has never entirely resolved, and now the sense of oncoming danger has returned. I don't know why. Alanna is much as she has always been. She is difficult, true, but her heart is good. She can be sweet and loving as well as contrary. I cannot see how she poses any greater threat now than she did before."

Lew sat back, rubbing his jaw with his one hand. "Are you sure your foreboding relates to Alanna?"

"What else?" She got up in a quick restless movement, tugging at the glove on her left hand, and began pacing. "The Domains are at peace, Francisco Ridenow is safely in exile, and the Terrans and that hideous Lyle Belfontaine are gone. After the Battle of Old North Road, they are not likely to return any time soon."

Memories, like a swarm of horrific ghosts, rose up in Lew's mind. The Terran ambush at Old North Road had been the last spiteful act of Acting Station Chief Lyle Belfontaine. The departing bureaucrat had almost destroyed Darkover's ruling Council as they rode to the funeral of Regis Hastur. What it might have meant for Darkover to lose so many Gifted minds at a single stroke was too terrible to contemplate. Combining their psychic powers, channeled through Mikhail's ring and Marguerida's shadow matrix, the two had defeated the attempt. And afterward . . .

Lew's gut clenched at the memory. After the battle, he and Marguerida had used their special talent, the Alton Gift of forced rapport, to selectively erase the memories of the Terran survivors, so that they remembered nothing extraordinary about the battle.

There was no other option, he told himself for the hundredth time. If the Federation ever found out what Darkovan *laran* could do, how it could be used as a weapon, any hope for his world remaining independent and free would swiftly come to an end. Afterward, Lew had gotten sickeningly drunk for the first time in years.

Marguerida was right. They had bought this current era of peace at a terrible price, but no enemies remained to threaten the Domains. The Terran Federation was gone, consumed by internecine war. Alanna offered no immediate threat. She had spirit, yes, and rebellion, but nothing worse.

And yet . . .

What if Marguerida perceived the approach of some other danger? Something perhaps masquerading as good? Had not great evil been done in the name of worthy causes? Was that not the story of the Ages of Chaos? Of Caer Donn and the flames of Sharra? Of the Battle of Old North Road?

Ghosts, he thought. *Nothing more.*

The conversation veered to inconsequential matters. Domenic and Yllana came in, chattering with the ease of affectionate siblings too long separated, something about Yllana's attempt to compose a new ballad about the spaceman, the *chieri,* and the Dry Towner's wife. Lew was surprised to see how both his grandchildren had grown. Domenic bowed politely, with a only a trace of the gangling awkwardness of a few years ago. Something in his reserve reminded Lew of Regis at that age. A hint of watchfulness around the eyes suggested that Domenic felt things deeply and that he had not yet found his place. Lew's heart went out to the boy, so clearly struggling to become a man, with all the uncertainties, conflicting emotions, and demands placed upon him.

As for Yllana, she would not look directly at Lew, clearly trying hard not to stare.

What did she see? Lew wondered. He knew what he looked like, a man aged beyond his years, a cripple with a face of scars, a mouth cut and twisted into a perpetual grimace, a man sick in his very soul . . .

"Ah, here is Mikhail," Marguerida said.

Mikhail entered, talking intently with his paxman, Donal Alar. Over the usual shirt and trousers, he wore a long, sleeveless robe, edged with white fur and bands of embroidery, vines weaving around a stylized representation of the Hastur fir tree. He looked up, his mouth curving into a smile. Yllana embraced her father with a child's unaffected warmth. Marguerida's edge of tension softened.

"*Dom* Lewis, you are very welcome," Mikhail said. "Perhaps Marja will be more easy about the upcoming session, with your keen eyes to spot any trouble. You are our elder statesman, and we value the perspective of your experience."

Lew made no effort to deflect the compliment, because it was true. His own father had schooled him in the intricacies of court politics, and his years as a Senator in the Terran Federation had given him ample opportunity to practice those skills. Absently, he rubbed the stump of his arm, where it had been cut away after the Sharra disaster in order to save his life.

Yllana excused herself and, with a parting kiss for both her parents, left the parlor. Donal bowed and followed her, closing the door behind him. Domenic remained, quietly watchful.

As Mikhail sank into one of the cushioned seats, Marguerida shot her husband a worried glance.

Mikhail leaned forward. "You may think I flatter you, Lew, but I cannot tell you how glad I am to have you here, especially at this time."

"Why now?" Lew asked.

"What has happened?" Marguerida said, almost at the same time.

Mikhail reached into an inner pocket of his robe and drew out a letter. "This came two days ago. I did not mention it before, because I have been considering how to answer it."

Mikhail handed the letter to his wife. The paper crackled as she spread it open. She read, her lips moving as she formed the words in Darkovan script. The blood drained from her face.

Is this the danger warned of by my Gift? ran through her mind, easily sensed by Lew.

"You cannot seriously—" Marguerida stammered aloud. "Mik, you *must not* agree to this!"

"Let Lew read the letter," Mikhail said. "Domenic already knows what it contains."

Lew took the paper and read slowly, trying to block out the distress radiating from his daughter's mind. The letter, addressed to Mikhail in his capacity as Regent, began with polite expressions of sympathy for the loss of his mother. The writer had an elegant command of the niceties of Comyn etiquette, at once respectful and intimate.

This could not, Lew thought, be what had upset Marguerida. He went on to the next section. The language was no less flowing, the desire for the reconciliation of old quarrels beautifully stated. It was, on the surface, a gracious request for permission for the sender to present himself at the upcoming Council meeting.

It was from Francisco Ridenow.

"I have already answered the letter." Mikhail spoke slowly, as if choosing each phrase with special care. "I have given him leave to attend."

In a tight voice, Marguerida said, "I wish you had not. That man is not to be trusted."

Lew felt a surge of compassion for his daughter. Losing Mikhail was the one thing in all the world that Marguerida truly feared.

"*Dom* Francisco is in an awkward situation, but we must give him a chance," Mikhail replied. "Very possibly, he is making an effort to establish a good reputation again."

"I'm afraid I don't have your enduring faith in human nature." Marguerida's eyes darkened, like weathered bronze. "I know we all change, and men can improve their ways, but I find it hard to forgive him. He was our friend once. We *trusted* him! And look at what he did!"

Francisco Ridenow had long claimed that the ring of Varzil Ridenow, called the Good, which now rested on Mikhail's finger, should have come to him as a family inheritance. Relentlessly ambitious, Francisco had seized the opening created by the Old North Road ambush, with all the attendant confusion, and attempted to assassinate Mikhail.

"You forget, dear heart, that he did not succeed," Mikhail said. "No lasting harm was done. We must give him the chance to make a new place among us, if that is what he truly intends. It will not help if we throw his past actions in his face, or turn everyone against him."

If all men were judged by their past, without any possibility of redeeming themselves, then we should all freeze in Zandru's coldest hell, Lew thought grimly. *And I, most of all.*

Why Mikhail had allowed Francisco to return to the family estate at Serrais after the assassination attempt, Lew could never understand. A generation ago, old Dyan

Ardais would have run Francisco through without a second thought. Maybe Mikhail thought there was still some good in Francisco, something worth redeeming, or perhaps he was simply less bloody-minded than other Comyn.

Mikhail did, however, remove Francisco as head of the Ridenow Domain, or rather, forced the Council to do so. Much of that, Lew suspected, was due to his very angry and determined daughter. Francisco's son had assumed control, a post for which his training as City Guards Captain prepared him well.

Was Mikhail wise in agreeing to Francisco's request? Rightly or not, traditions died hard. The Ridenow Domain was ancient and honorable, and Francisco was entitled to full Domain-right. For this reason, if no other, he would have supporters on the Council. If Mikhail denied such a request he would hand Francisco a powerful weapon of diplomacy. Lew knew the temper of the Council only too well. Javanne had forged a variety of alliances in her crusade against Mikhail, and his enemies would be only too happy to paint him as power-hungry and vengeful.

"I think you had no choice," Lew said slowly. "Despite all he has done, Francisco is still Comyn."

"Grandfather Lew is right," Domenic spoke up. "It would be difficult to justify a refusal."

"I see you are all ranged against me," Marguerida said with a wan smile. "I understand your reasons, even if I do not agree with them. Mik, if you have given your word, then I must make the best of it and stand by you. I do not think, however, that I will draw a single easy breath until that man is back on his own estates."

Relief passed over Mikhail's fair features. "It may all turn out for the best. We have friends on the Council— your father and the Elhalyn-Hasturs, and others who seek a peaceful, united Darkover. We will have time to prepare."

Mikhail took Marguerida's gloved hand in his, and for an instant, the jewel of his ring glowed with the light of their joined powers.

Watching them together, Lew thought that as long as these two people were together, nothing could dim their happiness. But if anything should happen to Mikhail, if Marguerida's premonition turned out to be right, what then?

What then?

4

That night, after the formal dinner following Javanne's funeral, Domenic went to Alanna's room. He was more than a little drunk, so he had an excuse to disregard his conscience and all his mother's rules of propriety.

The day had been the longest, most emotionally exhausting he could remember. The funeral cortege had departed early, in a drizzle of half-frozen rain, traveling the Old North Road from Thendara to Hali. Cisco Ridenow, as Captain of the City Guards, had taken charge of security arrangements with ruthless efficiency. Even so, memories of the ambush three years ago lingered in everyone's memory.

The younger Gabriel Lanart-Alton, as the deceased woman's eldest son, led the procession. His name, like his father's, had originally been Lanart-Hastur, but when he assumed control of the Alton Domain, he had taken that name as well. Mikhail and Marguerida followed him, along with Grandfather Lew, then Domenic himself and Rory, who had been released from his duties in the Guards to attend. Ylanna rode in a carriage further back, along with her aunt Ariel and Ariel's husband Piedro Alar. Miralys Elhalyn rode beside her husband, Dani Hastur, and his namesake, Danilo Syrtis-Ardais. Kennard-Dyan Ardais had not returned to Thendara for the funeral, nor had Mikhail's sister, the *leronis* Liriel. It was not as grand or large a party as the one that had accompanied the body of Regis Hastur, but it did honor to the woman who had been his sister.

They arrived at the field along the shores of Lake Hali. Pale green dusted the mounded earth. The drizzle cleared and clouds parted, revealing the swollen red sun. As Domenic took his appointed place, something roused his unusual *laran*. A silent keening rose and fell, reverberating through his skull. Perhaps it was a residue from the eerie cloud-lake of Hali, said to be the result of an ancient cataclysm, or perhaps it was only the accumulation of centuries of grief.

Domenic tried to shut out the waves of fear and suspicion that emanated from the assembly, masquerading as grief. Whatever the cause, his grandmother had been an ambitious, unpleasant old woman. At one time, she had formed an alliance with Francisco Ridenow to replace Mikhail as Regent and Head of the Hastur Domain. Half the mourners here had been forced to take sides. Perhaps, with Javanne's passing, the old quarrel might at last be laid to rest.

Family and friends had gathered in a circle as Javanne's casket was lowered into an unmarked grave. One by one, each person had shared a private remembrance of the departed. The two sons of the dead woman who had been able to attend came forward first. Following Gabriel, Mikhail spoke briefly of the mother who had nurtured him, with no mention of her later animosity. He concluded with the traditional formula, "Let that memory lighten grief."

When Domenic's turn came to speak, his throat had closed up. He wished there were some way to give voice to the sadness welling up from the layered mounds, from the ancient earth.

"The most important thing I know about my grandmother," he finally forced out the words, "is that she was loved."

He offered the words as a gift to her spirit. *Let her be remembered for this, and nothing less.*

Then he added, "Let that memory lighten grief," and in that moment, it did.

Emotionally drained, Domenic had returned with the others for the funeral dinner, laid out in the Grand Hall of the Castle, a vast echoing space better suited to a Midwinter Ball than to such a sad occasion. Rosettes and streamers of blue and silver, edged with black, intensified the gloom. It seemed half the Council attended the meal, all of them looking at him as if he were a high-bred horse they wished to purchase. Alanna had not been present, nor Yllana. Rory said he had City Guards duty that night, but Domenic suspected that his brother intended to spend the night drinking with his closest friend.

To make matters worse, Domenic could not shake the sensation of that mournful wail, like the cry of a banshee, now rippling through the stone foundations of the Castle. He had learned from experience that he could suppress the most unpleasant manifestations of his Gift with wine. At the time, getting drunk seemed the best way to deal with the social situation, as well.

The meal seemed to go on forever, through meat and fowl and cheese courses, sweet wine and pastries, and, when he feared he could hold no more, *shallan* and Thetan tea from his mother's dwindling private stores. The coffee she loved so much had been used up last Midwinter Festival. Only the prospect of seeing Alanna again sustained Domenic through the interminable hours.

Now back at the Alton quarters, Domenic paused outside her door, drew himself up to an approximation of steadiness, and raised one fist to knock. From inside came the muffled sound of weeping.

"Alanna?" He tapped gently and, when there was no response or pause in the sobs, lifted the latch and went in.

Shadows lay thickly across the room, the same one Alanna had used since she first came here as a child. A small fire flickered in the hearth, casting an uncertain light. The oval rug in front of the fireplace, normally a cheerful pattern of pink and red rosalys, looked as if it were covered with dark, irregular stains.

Alanna lay curled on her bed, facing the wall, fully dressed, clutching her favorite childhood toy, a stuffed rabbit-horn. Although he could not see her clearly, he felt her trembling.

"Alanna?"

"Domenic?" She sat up in a rustling of cloth and ran to him, tender and warm and exhilarating in his arms. When she pressed her cheek against his, he felt the wetness of her tears. He brushed them away with his fingertips.

"*Breda,* don't cry. What has happened?"

"Oh, Domenic, it's so awful here without you! No one cares anything about me! They all want me out of the way, or dead!"

Domenic put his arm around Alanna and led her back to the bed. He sat beside her and took her hands in his. "That cannot be true. It only appears that way because you're upset. I love you, and so does my mother and Aunt Liriel, and my father loves you, too. Remember how, when we were little, he used to say how bright you were, like his own little star come down to earth?"

Alanna gave a little hiccough, somehow endearing. "You—you love me?"

"Yes, of course . . ." Domenic's voice trailed off. His head was spinning again, only this time not from too much wine, but from Alanna's closeness.

She lifted her face to his. He felt the warmth of her breath on his cheeks, saw the tiny droplets on her lashes. Her eyes were pools of green-tinted shadow, deep and mysterious. Her lips parted, and he wondered what they would feel like against his, how she would taste, the smell of her neck if he buried his face in the graceful curves, the feel of her skin.

Just as he leaned toward her, Alanna shifted, wrapping her arms around his waist. Her face fit into the hollow of his shoulder. She sighed, and another thrill, part exhilaration, part rapture, rose up in him. An image sprang to his mind of them together and naked, how her body would look, what it would be like to run his hands over her breasts and thighs and the mysterious places between them—

Oh, gods . . .

A sensation like fire kindled in his groin and surged to his face. His heart beat like galloping hooves.

Domenic slammed his *laran* barriers shut. Like him, Alanna was psychically Gifted; they had each studied at a Tower, he for almost three years at Neskaya and she for one brief season at Arilinn. By every standard of proper behavior among telepaths, what he had just done—his lustful thoughts—amounted to assault.

How could he treat her like this? Domenic asked himself, horrified. How could he behave in such a barbaric way to this tender, lovely young woman, someone he had loved since they were children together?

Oh, Alanna! he thought, even though she could not hear him, *I would not for the world offend you, but I had no idea I felt this way, or what you could do to me . . .*

Alanna gave no sign she was aware of what had just transpired. Instead, she radiated almost childlike innocence. Yet there was passion, he sensed it deep within her, and *laran* too. Both her sexuality and her psychic talents seemed strangely muted.

Domenic shivered, suddenly sober. *She studied at Arilinn . . . once the most prestigious of all the Towers . . .*

Arilinn, where even now the *leroni* preserved the old ways of training Keepers. Because the same channels carried *laran* and sexual energy, Keepers once endured unimaginable training, remaining not only chaste but incapable of normal sexual response. It was all nonsense, of course. Cleindori Aillard, the Golden Bell of Arilinn, had proven that generations ago.

Surely, the workers at Arilinn would not have . . . no one today believed in such superstitions.

Gently, as if she were glass about to shatter, Domenic

took Alanna's face between his hands. In the dim light, her eyes shone. He could not read what lay in their depths—*fear, willingness, desire?* Or did his own wild hope put such answers there?

She did not resist as he bent his head and touched her mouth with his own. Her lips felt as soft as new-opened petals, yet firm and warm.

Domenic kissed her more deeply, moving his lips over hers. She tasted like honey, like flame . . .

She made a sound deep in her throat, or he thought she did. Had there been a flicker of answering desire in her kiss? Or had he imagined it, created it from his own yearning? He drew away, once more gazing into her eyes.

"Is this distasteful to you?" he asked, hoping that his voice did not tremble.

For a long moment, she was silent, and he wondered whether he had indeed offended her. His senses whirled, and he could scarcely hear his own voice over the pounding of his heart.

In response, she reached up and pulled him toward her. Her lips moved against his with an odd combination of hesitancy and eagerness. The touch of her fingers on his neck excited him more than he had believed possible.

The kiss seemed to go on forever. Domenic's blood sang in his ears, and waves of dizziness shook him. He could hardly believe this was happening to him. He wanted to touch her throat, her breasts, her thighs. Yet he was afraid to make the slightest move, for fear the movement would shatter what was building between them.

Alanna shifted, pressing her body against his. He tightened his arms around her. Wherever they touched, his skin seemed unbearably sensitive. A throbbing began from the deepest core of his pelvis, streaming upward along his *laran* channels through gut and lungs and heart. When Alanna opened her lips and ran the tip of her tongue over the inside of his mouth, the contact ignited a cascade of molten pleasure.

Domenic broke away, gasping.

"Is it—is it all right?" she asked, her voice a breathless whisper.

Gods, yes! When had he ever felt so intensely alive, soaring on each pulse beat?

He recollected himself enough to ask, "Do you want to go on?"

"I—I feel so strange, Domenic, as if my body belongs to someone else, and yet I am *remembering* something. Something strong and deep. Some almost-lost part of who I am. Do you recall how I once thought I was two people—"

"Hush, love. Don't think about that now."

Alanna took his hand and, wonder beyond wonders, placed it over her breast. She closed her eyes, curving his fingers around the soft flesh. Through gown and chemise, he felt a point, like a small nut, growing harder. She murmured—in pleasure, he thought—and each tiny sound reverberated through him.

Domenic slipped his free hand under Alanna's hair, aware that in the traditions of the Domains, the only man who might see—or caress—the nape of a woman's neck was her lover. Sweat dampened her skin. He cupped the back of her head and tilted her head up for another kiss. When her lips met his, parting eagerly, he gave himself over to the answering surge of exhilaration. Was he drunk on wine from the dinner or her closeness? He didn't care.

Somehow, his mouth slipped from hers. He covered her face with kisses, then the side of her neck and down the sweet slope of shoulder and the swell of her breast. The fragrance of her skin filled him, heady and compelling. He wanted to draw her in, to inhale her, to bury himself in her.

"Oh, Alanna . . . Oh, my sweet love . . ."

She shifted, her arms tightened around him. "Don't ever leave me," she whispered. "Don't ever let me go."

Some harmonic in her voice, a shade of childlike pleading, broke through his surging arousal.

What was he doing?

Domenic caught his breath and sat straighter, cradling her close. For a long moment, he could not speak as he wrestled himself under control. No matter how he felt, whatever impulses raged through him, he owed it to her— not to mention to all standards of proper, decent conduct—to treat her with all the respect due a Comynara.

"Whatever happens," he murmured, his voice trembling with effort, "I'll take care of you. We'll always be together."

Only when the words were spoken and could not be called back did Domenic realize that, as Heir to Hastur and the next Regent of the Comyn, he had no right to make such a promise. Not to Alanna, not to any woman of his own choosing. Moreover, they were blood kin, but what of that? Not so long ago cousins were permitted, even encouraged, to marry.

There were a hundred reasons why he must not think of Alanna as a lover. In that moment, with the weight of her head resting against him, his body trembling with fire and thirst and things he could not name but that only she could fulfill, he did not care.

5

As spring swung into early summer, the weather turned mild, with only a few thin clouds. Danilo Syrtis-Ardais began walking the streets of Thendara. In his late fifties, he still retained the slender, graceful form of a much younger man. His hair, worn longer than was fashionable, was still dark, but shadows haunted his eyes, and the creases around his mouth betokened his deep suffering. He had been handsome as a youth, pretty enough to attract unwanted attention, but time and grief had honed away that beauty, leaving his features stark but no less compelling.

The lung-fever the previous winter had left him debilitated, but now, with the coming of warmer days and burgeoning green, a new vigor rose in him. Wrapped in his fur-lined cloak, he paced the marketplaces, inhaling the awakening vitality of the city. Turning his face to the brightening sky, he sensed winter loosening its grip from his own heart.

When Regis died, he could not imagine how he could go on. Now, as that pain began to subside, he discovered new strength.

Once we have shared love with another human being, he is part of us forever. Danilo could not remember who had said those words, but with each passing day, he felt their truth. It would be years yet before the aching wound within him ceased to haunt his dreams, but that time would come.

Perhaps a man never recovered from such a loss; perhaps he should not. But life continued, and so would he.

Danilo paused at an open-air cookshop, where a woman, her face reddened from bending over a pot of hot water, scooped out steamed dumplings. The next food stall offered leaf-wrapped sausages, baked apples, and skewers of tiny golden onions. A half-grown boy in tattered clothing waited at the back of the shop, and Danilo watched as the woman filled his clay bowl with savory morsels.

He knew that secret meetings were being held within the Castle, schemes and shifts of power. As yet he had no place there. Here, in the marketplaces, the craft districts, the watering fountains and stable yards, along the poorer residential streets, he would find his true direction. He had already begun reestablishing the network of informants he had created during his years as paxman to Regis—innkeepers, stablemen, Travelers, a smith or two, people who might see and hear things hidden from the Comyn.

All was not peaceful on the street. Twice now Danilo had come upon groups of rough-garbed men lounging on the corners, who regarded him with frank suspicion. They muttered words like *"Comyn spy!"* followed by a curse, before they shuffled away.

He spotted Domenic at the edge of the market square, shadowed by two uniformed Castle Guards. A hooded cloak covered the boy's hair, but there was no mistaking his posture, both wary and excited, or those eyes of almost luminous gold-flecked gray. Something in Domenic's way of moving reminded Danilo of Regis as a young man, the way he held himself a little apart, diffident and intense.

Danilo had had little contact with Domenic over the last few years, but the boy seemed to have avoided the worst consequences of growing up with two charismatic parents; he was neither a bully nor a self-indulgent child. He'd had an independent spirit as an adolescent. Then he'd studied in a Tower for some three years. After such early freedom, it could not be easy to accept the presence of a protective escort.

Domenic smiled as Danilo approached and bade him good morning. The Guards bowed to him and retreated a step or two, remaining watchful.

"It's a fine day to be abroad," Danilo said.

"Yes!" Domenic agreed. "I thought winter would never end."

Some impulse led Danilo to say, "Shall we walk together and pretend for a moment that we are just two ordinary men?"

"If that were only possible!" Domenic rolled his eyes in the direction of the Guards.

"Some things never change." Danilo strolled toward the leather-workers' stalls, leaving the Guards to follow. "In his day, Regis longed to be accountable only to his own conscience and not the Comyn of all Seven Domains. He dreamed of one day traveling to the stars. Did he ever tell you that?"

Domenic shook his head, his expression astonished. "Great-Uncle Regis? No, he never said."

"Of course, as Heir to Hastur, Regis never had a chance to leave Darkover," Danilo went on. Anguish surged up in him, for his own loss, for his beloved's sacrifice. What choice had any of them had? "He often said that he did not choose his parentage wisely."

"Mother repeats that saying to me." Domenic grimaced. "Alas, I am guilty of the same lapse in judgment."

"You would exchange your mother and father for some other parents?" Remembering Danvan Hastur, that irascible old tyrant who had been grandfather to Regis, Danilo raised one eyebrow. "Whose?"

"Anyone's! No one's! I don't know!" Domenic picked up a tooled leather dagger sheath and, seeing the vendor come toward them, hastily replaced it on the table and kept walking. "Don't misunderstand me, I wouldn't trade them for the world. I love my parents very much, and they love me. They're wonderful people. It's just that . . . the things they have done, the choices they have made, are not mine."

I can't be them.

"I doubt they expect you to," Danilo said mildly, responding to Domenic's telepathic thought.

"In another tenday," Domenic rushed on, "the Council season will begin. Francisco Ridenow will arrive. He's even bringing his daughter! There's so much I have to learn yet. Yet here I am, walking the streets—"

"—getting to know the city that you will rule some day, the people, the rhythms and temper of the street—"

"—wasting an entire morning."

Danilo glanced at the younger man, wondering whether the time and effort of finding one's own path in life were ever wasted. Some things could not be rushed. This boy clearly needed someone besides his parents to talk to.

"Have you broken your fast?" Danilo asked.

Domenic shook his head in a way that indicated he had no interest in food. Danilo frowned, for loss of appetite was a sign of threshold sickness.

"Let us continue this conversation in my chamber," Danilo suggested, "but without your escort. You may be able to go without breakfast, but an old man like me cannot."

With a nod that might have been either shyness or gratitude, Domenic fell into step beside him. They slipped in through one of the Castle's side gates, where Domenic dismissed the Guards, and made their way up a back staircase.

Although he was no longer Warden, Danilo still retained a suite of rooms in the Ardais section of the Castle. The sitting room, with its wide, unadorned hearth, contained several chairs upholstered in worn wine-dark leather with matching footstools, a sideboard, and low serving table. The furniture had already been old when Dyan Ardais gave it to Danilo.

Once they had settled in Danilo's chambers, his servant brought in a pot of herbal tisane.

"I'm supposed to drink this revolting brew twice a day for my lungs," Danilo said. "Would you like some? I can as easily order *jaco* or spiced cider if you'd prefer." He took his usual seat by the fireside and gestured for Domenic to join him.

"*Jaco,* please."

"Smart choice." Danilo sipped the bitter tisane. Grimacing, he added a second spoonful of honey.

"You were the closest friend of Great-Uncle Regis," Domenic blurted out. "If he were still alive, I'd go to him, but he isn't. But if he were still Regent, not my father, everything would be different. As it is . . . I need to talk to someone."

Danilo felt a rush of compassion for the younger man, for too many times in his own early life, he had also *needed to talk to someone.*

The servant returned with a loaf of nut bread baked in the country style and still hot from the Castle ovens, a covered bowl of fresh curds and one of cherry jam, and a pottery carafe of unsweetened *jaco.* Danilo smeared a slice of bread with cheese and handed it to Domenic.

"First eat this, and then we'll discuss things."

Domenic's brows tensed, verging on a frown, but he took a tentative bite. Then, as if a floodgate of hunger had broken loose, he devoured the rest of the loaf, three cups of *jaco,* the cheese, and most of the jam. Color seeped back into his face. He let out a deep sigh.

"Thank you." Visibly gathering himself, Domenic said, "I wanted to ask you how I should go about choosing a paxman."

"Do you need one?"

The younger man sat back, looking surprised and a little scandalized. "I'm the heir presumptive to Hastur and the Regency. I can't perform my duties without a paxman!"

"On the contrary," Danilo said, "that is exactly the right thing for you to do. It would certainly be preferable to hire a secretary and let the City Guards continue to watch your back, rather than bind yourself to the wrong man."

"Bind *myself?*" Domenic frowned. "I thought it was the other way around."

Danilo leaned forward. The leather of the chair creaked

under his weight. "Why exactly do you need a paxman? What would he do for you that some hireling—or you yourself—could not do just as well?"

Domenic's eyes, gray flecked with gold, narrowed with understanding; the lad was sharp. "Are you saying it's not necessary? A relic from the time when every Comyn lord had good reason to fear a dagger in the back? What about you and Great-Uncle Regis? Didn't you protect and advise him?"

I did, Danilo thought, *all that and more, but none of it from duty.*

Aloud, Danilo murmured, "It was a gift Regis gave to me, not the other way around. We didn't choose to be lord and paxman. Fate and our hearts made us *bredin.*" He used the inflection that meant an even deeper intimacy than *sworn brothers.* "And the rest was a matter of tradition. You can't force that deep bond, any more than you can choose the form of your *laran.* If you want my advice, you will wait for the right person to appear—if he ever does—and not fret about it. There are plenty of others who can perform the necessary duties, and just as capably."

Domenic sagged in the chair. "It's all so complicated. I thought you could tell me what to look for in a paxman because you'd been one yourself. You know—the right skills, the right temperament. But that isn't what having a paxman—or being one—means. It's about love and loyalty and honor, isn't it?"

Danilo heard the hunger in the boy's voice, the passion and loneliness. Some chord deep within him responded. "We are not a society of impersonal laws, like the *Terranan.* It is those very things—love and loyalty and honor—that link the Domains together. When we go astray, these principles call us back to ourselves."

Domenic nodded. "I've been thinking I need a paxman to give me confidence."

"No one can give you that. You must find it inside yourself."

"I suppose. But my parents expect so much of me!"

"Do they expect any more of you than they do of themselves?"

"Well," Domenic said wryly, "my mother does accomplish more than any five normal people."

"That is not so bad," Danilo said. "Perhaps work is what she needs, a way she can use her knowledge and experience. *Domna* Marguerida is a highly competent woman—"

"Don't I know that!" Domenic burst out, and they both chuckled.

"What would you rather have her do?" Danilo asked. "Fret herself into hysterics, with nothing more useful to do than counting the holes in the linens? Or carry forth the vision she shares with Mikhail, helping to shape the future of Darkover?"

"Why does she have to shape *me* along with it? I never appreciated the custom of fostering out children until now. I always thought Uncle Piedro and Aunt Ariel were shirking their duty in sending Alanna to us. Now, I almost wish I'd gone to live with them in exchange! Why is it so much easier to talk to anyone but my own parents? I don't suppose *you* could adopt me?"

Danilo laughed. "I hardly think so. You're what, twenty? By all our traditions, you're no longer a child. A generation ago, you would have a wife and heir by now, and you'd be sitting in the Cortes or managing the family estate."

"These times are different," Domenic said. "There's so much I have to learn first, not the least of which is how to survive the political intrigue of the Council. I want to find my own way! I don't want to be like one of those string-puppets down at the marketplace."

"Neither did Regis." Danilo said quietly.

He remembered all too well that Regis had been under intense pressure to accept his responsibilities to Council and Domain. They both understood that he was expected to marry and father sons, to be everything his formidable grandfather demanded.

"Yet," Danilo said aloud, "in the end, Regis made up his own mind. He accepted his heritage and obligations freely, not because Lord Danvan expected it of him. You've probably heard stories of what Regis did then— leading the expedition to find a cure for trailmen's fever, using the Sword of Aldones to vanquish Sharra, standing up to the World Wreckers. None of these were Lord Danvan's ideas, and none of them had ever been done before. Regis made the position of Regent his own, with his own vision, his own talents. You will, too—"

Danilo broke off, his telepathic senses alert. There was another person nearby.

Domenic launched himself from his chair, crossed to the door in two strides, and jerked it open, revealing a beautiful and disconsolate young woman. Danilo recognized Marguerida's fosterling, though he had seen very little of her in the past years. She wore a mismatched orange skirt and lace-trimmed pink velvet jacket, as if she had thrown on the nearest garments to hand.

"Alanna!" Domenic cried.

With a cry, the girl threw herself into Domenic's arms. Danilo said, "I think you'd better bring her inside."

Within a short time, Alanna was seated in one of the leather armchairs, and a second breakfast, with an extra carafe of *jaco*, had been sent for. Domenic perched beside her on a footstool, chafing her hands between his. She looked pale except for twin spots of hectic color on her cheeks. Her hair curled in damp, unruly tendrils about her face. She had not yet stopped trembling.

"I know it was wrong to follow you," she said, between hiccoughs. "I couldn't help myself."

The girl's emotions, like an invisible turbulence, raked Danilo's nerves. Their gazes locked for a heartbeat as his mind touched hers. In that moment, Danilo saw her not as a gently reared *damisela* but as a creature of ice-pale fire. Strands of light, like colorless flames, flowed from her head and hands. She vibrated with their surging currents, wrapped in a confusion of light and motion—

With a sob, Alanna buried her face in her hands. "Whatever he's doing, *make it stop*!"

"*Dom* Danilo has done nothing to you, sweetheart—" Domenic said.

"He's in my mind, I tell you! He's putting things there!"

The girl swayed in her chair. Danilo caught her in his arms before she fell over. Her hands brushed his, her skin chill and damp. The physical contact intensified the telepathic rapport.

He stood in the middle of a whirlwind, not of ordinary air, but of light and energy. Images overlapped, like reflections from a ripple-touched pool.

. . . he saw himself, holding an unconscious girl in his arms; he saw Domenic do the same . . .

. . . he saw the room empty; he saw himself staring into a cold hearth, a husk of grief, holding a dagger to his chest . . .

. . . he saw Lew Alton burst into the room, the fires of Sharra burning behind his eyes . . .

With a soft cry, Alanna sagged in his arms, and the visions disappeared, leaving only a deep shaking in the marrow of his bones. With Domenic's help, he eased the girl back into the chair.

A tap on the door announced the arrival of more food. Alanna stirred at the entrance of the servants, and she devoured three fruit-laced spiral buns as if she hadn't eaten in a tenday.

"Zandru's Seven Frozen Hells, Alanna, what *was* that?" Domenic asked, his expression one of astonishment.

"You saw it, too?" Alanna whimpered.

"I think we both did, you were sending telepathic images so strongly," Domenic said.

Alanna looked as if she were about to burst into tears. "What is wrong with me? Am I going mad?"

"Hardly that," Danilo said, trying to interject a note of rational calm into the conversation, "although it can seem so if you don't understand what's happening to you. How long you have had these visions?"

Alanna sniffed and rubbed her nose with one delicate hand. "Visions? They seem more like streams in a river.

Each one takes me to a slightly different time or place. They started around the time of Grandmother Javanne's funeral."

She turned tear-wet eyes toward Domenic. "What is happening to me?"

The boy took her into his arms in a way no man but her promised husband should do. "It's all right, my darling."

"No," Alanna wailed, stomping one foot. "It's *not* all right! It's horrible and I want it to stop!"

"It's most certainly *laran*," Danilo said, although he had never heard of such a Gift. The Aldarans were said to possess precognition, but as far as he knew, Alanna had no Aldaran blood. Moreover, the girl was well past the age at which psychic talents usually manifested themselves.

"Auntie Liriel tested me when I turned twelve and said I had plenty of *laran* potential," Alanna said, frowning. "For a time, I could move small objects and start fires. Then Auntie Marguerida made me go to Arilinn. I hated it there, *hated* it! Nothing but rules and regulations and voices echoing in my head! After *Dom* Regis died, I refused to go back. If they'd made me, I would have run away rather than spend my life shut up in that stuffy old Tower, with everyone nagging me to control myself."

"I spent almost three years in a Tower, and it's not so bad," Domenic said.

Alanna shook her head, sending ripples through her tangled coppery curls. "I don't want to talk about it! All I want is to make this thing in my head stop!"

Leaping to her feet, Alanna snatched up the mug, still half-full of *jaco,* and drew back her arm to hurl it at the opposite wall.

Danilo caught her arm, deftly removed the mug from her grasp, and set it down again. "I think your energies would be far better served, *damisela,* by learning to master your visions. For one thing, it would be far easier on the crockery."

"If you're going to send me back to Arilinn, you can forget it!" Alanna snapped.

"That's precisely what I do advise," Danilo said firmly. "An untrained telepath is a danger to herself and everyone around her."

"I won't go!" Alanna shrieked. "I won't, won't, won't!" Her voice grew in loudness with each repetition. Her face turned red and tears wet her cheeks. Her delicate hands curled into fists.

Gently, Domenic took her in his arms and, surprisingly, she calmed almost immediately. He stroked her hair, murmuring, "It's all right, no one is going to force you."

"What are we going to do?" she asked, clinging to him.

"We'll have to find someone else to teach you," Domenic said.

"*You* could do it." Sniffing, she raised tear-bright eyes to his in an adoring expression.

"No, he *cannot*," Danilo said. A girl this willful, with *laran* this strong, needed a teacher who could not be intimidated or manipulated. He wished Lady Linnea were still in Thendara so that he might ask her advice. Perhaps in a less formal setting than a Tower, she might give Alanna the guidance the girl so desperately needed.

Alanna lifted her chin and smoothed her rumpled skirts. "Then I shall simply treat this as any other annoyance beneath the notice of a Comynara. It's like threshold sickness, after all, and that went away on its own."

"*Damisela*, you are proposing a very foolish thing," Danilo said sternly. "Your visions will not go away on their own. Only a Keeper trained in the old ways could safely suppress them, and I am not sure that is ever a good idea. It is likely they will get progressively worse unless you learn to control your Gift."

"You're only saying that because you hate me! You want to get rid of me!" she flung back at him.

Danilo glared at the distraught young woman, aware that he felt very little sympathy for her. As a City Guard and later as paxman and bodyguard to Regis, he had handled drunks and thieves, assassins and kidnappers. He was no stranger to physical violence. But young women in the throes of temper tantrums were another matter entirely. He wanted to grab the girl and shake some sense into her, but that would only intensify her resistance. As it was, she distrusted him so much at the moment that she might well refuse anything he suggested, no matter how sensible.

"Sweetheart, I agree with *Dom* Danilo," Domenic said, looking uncomfortable. "I don't think it's a good idea to ignore your visions. We both saw how they distress you. Surely, the *leroni* at Arilinn have the skills to help you."

"As long as *you* are near me, I shall be well." Alanna slipped her hand into Domenic's. Her voice softened and her eyes gleamed as she smiled up at him. Danilo sensed the spark of physical passion between them.

"Truly, I shall," she murmured. "Promise me you will forget all about my outburst."

As Domenic reassured her, Danilo wished the boy had not given in so easily. Alanna was an extraordinarily desirable young woman. Even though Danilo had never been attracted to women, not since he had given his heart to Regis, he understood the power of sexual attraction. From the way Domenic gazed at her, he was thoroughly enthralled.

It is not good for one person to have such influence over another. Danilo did not like to think what might happen if such a person, with so little self-control, felt rejected. He knew all too well from his own experience how easily passion, spurned, could turn into revenge.

"Does Marguerida know about your relationship?" Danilo asked. "Does Mikhail?"

Domenic shifted, clearly embarrassed. "No, we have taken care never to appear together before my parents, lest we give ourselves away telepathically. They must not find out until we are ready to tell them. Until then, will you keep our secret?"

"It is not mine to give away," Danilo shrugged.

Alanna had now regained her composure. Danilo sensed her Gift, like an interweaving of colorless light, quiescent but ready to flare up again. It was a pity she was so op-

posed to training at a Tower, for she desperately needed
the discipline.

A generation ago, Danilo thought, Alanna would have
been packed off to a husband and babies without a
thought. She was a respectable, marriageable young
woman, and there was no question about her *laran*. But a
man in Domenic's position needed more—a wife to stand
by his side, not sit at his feet.

As Linnea was to Regis. As Marguerida is to Mikhail.

Domenic loved Alanna, and in the warmth of that love,
she seemed to rise above her childish ill temper. Perhaps
over time she would also grow to become the woman
Domenic so clearly wanted her to be.

6

On the day of the opening session of the Comyn Council, Lew escorted Marguerida through the wide double doors that formed the main entrance to the Crystal Chamber. The Guardsmen on either side of the doors stood at strict attention. One of them looked vaguely familiar; perhaps Lew had known his father. Once, Lew would have stopped for a friendly word, a custom from his own time as a Guards officer. During his years off-planet, however, he'd become a stranger.

Sunlight streamed through the prisms set in the Chamber ceiling. Lew was struck, as he had been many times before, by the sensation of moving through the heart of a rainbow. The Chamber's eight sides included one wall in which were set the carved wooden doors through which Lew and Marguerida had come, and seven sections, one for each Domain. Railings separated each area with its benches and curtained-off enclosures. Banners in the colors of each Domain hung on the walls: Elhalyn, Hastur, Ardais, Aillard, Alton, and Ridenow. The double-eagle banner marked the Seventh Domain. Aldaran had been exiled from the Comyn, but now was reunited with the others.

In his mind, Lew remembered standing in this very Chamber so many years ago, waiting for the assembled Comyn to pass judgment on his fitness to be named his fa-

ther's heir. His nerves thrummed with the residue of all the
terrible things that had happened here, lives broken and
then given back, marriages decided, feuds declared and
ended.

*The past is too much with me. My father, Sharra . . . gods
help me, Marjorie dying! The Battle of Old North Road . . .
Will I ever be free of them?*

Lew forced his attention to the present. Dani Hastur was
already here, representing the Elhalyn clan of his wife.
He stood talking with some of the Aldaran folk, looking
friendly and relaxed, apparently enjoying himself. About
ten years younger than Marguerida, Dani was a pleasant-
looking man. He lacked the intense, charismatic beauty
that often characterized the Hastur men, but was calm and
easygoing in his manner. Unlike Regis, who had been
raised by an irascible grandfather, Dani looked out at the
world from the security of a loving family. Regis and Linnea had done their best to shield him from the tyranny of
his heritage, and if he had chosen a lesser place in the
world, he had carved out a niche of sunshine within his father's shadow.

Lew glanced around for the man who was Dani's namesake, his father's paxman and dearest friend. Danilo Syrtis
rarely attended such functions any more, yet there he was,
in earnest conversation with Kennard-Dyan Ardais, perhaps discussing which of Kennard-Dyan's many illegitimate offspring should be named Heir to the Ardais
Domain. Lew reflected that a *nedestro* heir would not necessarily be a bad thing, for the Comyn had grown too few,
too inbred in the last few generations.

A heavy, thronelike chair had been set up for Mikhail in
the Hastur section, with another beside it for Marguerida.
As always, Donal Alar stood at Mikhail's elbow. Mikhail
wore the Hastur colors, blue and silver, his jacket trimmed
with white fur, and today he looked regal enough to be
King. His hair, silver threaded through pale gold, shone
like a natural crown. When Regis had formally designated
Mikhail as his heir, Mikhail had legally become a Hastur,

entitled to sit under the fir-tree banner. Since becoming Regent, Mikhail had worn the Hastur colors of blue and silver at Council functions as an emblem of his authority.

Lew escorted his daughter to her seat and greeted his son-in-law. Shortly, more men and women arrived, arranging themselves under the banners of their respective Domains. Istvana Ridenow, who was the Keeper of Neskaya Tower as well as Marguerida's dear friend, took a seat in her family's section. Istvana was also kinswoman to Lew's second wife, Marguerida's much-mourned stepmother, Diotima Ridenow. The diminutive *leronis* had lost none of her aura of enormous authority with age. Her gray eyes were still clear and steady, although the passing years had bowed her narrow shoulders and added new lines around her mouth.

In these days, the entire assembly filled only a fraction of the available space. At the height of the Comyn powers, however, the Chamber must have been small for all who could claim Domain-right. Then, everyone present was Gifted with *laran*. By tradition, telepathic dampers were still placed about the Chamber at strategic intervals. Before the Council began its business, they would be set and adjusted so no trick of *laran* could be used to sway other men's minds. At one time, the Altons were so feared for their Gift of forced rapport that one of the supposedly random dampers was always placed directly above their enclosure. Although he understood the rationale, Lew did not look forward to feeling half-blind and half-deaf.

The official Ridenow contingent arrived to a flurry of interest, entering not by their private passage but through the main doors. Cisco Ridenow, as Acting Warden of his Domain, preceded his father. He looked fit, a strongly built man with the flaxen hair and distinctively shaped eyes of his family, wearing his uniform of City Guards Captain.

Francisco Ridenow strode into the chamber as if it belonged to him. He was a tall man, some years older than Mikhail, his dark red hair shot with gray, his once-handsome features marked with lines that suggested pain and disappointment rather than joy. He paused in the center of the room, his eyes taking in the assembly. A fire burned in him, igniting his every movement. He wore a close-fitting doublet and breeches in the Ridenow colors of green trimmed with gold, with none of the frills so popular that season. Only a faint hesitation, an almost imperceptible stiffness in one leg, remained from the wound he had taken during his unsuccessful attack upon Mikhail. From all appearances, the assault might never have taken place.

Francisco had always been charming and ambitious, good-looking as a young man. For a time, he paid court to Marguerida, but her heart had already been given to Mikhail, and his to her. To this day, Lew could not say how deeply Marguerida's rejection had embittered Francisco. Disappointed hopes, thwarted aspirations, jealousy, resentments, all had festered within him.

As Francisco approached, Marguerida laid one hand on her husband's arm. Francisco bowed to them, a fraction less deep than true courtesy required but not enough to constitute an outright insult, and then took his place behind his son. From the curtained back of the enclosure, a slender young woman with red-gold hair slipped onto one of the ladies' benches.

"He's up to something, I can tell." Marguerida bent close to her husband. "Be careful, *cario*."

"My love, all will be well," Mikhail said. "See, there is his daughter, sitting beside Cisco. Surely, he would not risk her safety by any rash action."

Lew made a few inconsequential comments, excused himself, and went to his own place under the Alton banner beside the empty chair designated for the senior Gabriel. A padded chair had been placed just inside the railing. Marguerida must have arranged it. How like her, to consider an old man's comfort. The younger Gabriel came in a few minutes later. Gabriel looked much the same as he always did, a sturdy man, swarthy instead of fair like his brother Mikhail. Clearly, the challenges of running a huge estate like Armida agreed with him, or perhaps it was a happy marriage to a widow with two half-grown sons. Gabriel had joked that in adopting her children, he was making up for lost time. The midwives had determined that their first child, a daughter, would arrive in the fall.

A page slipped in through the back of the Alton enclosure and offered cups of watered wine. Gabriel took one, but Lew waved his away. He had not touched alcohol since his tenday-long binge after the Battle of Old North Road, a desperate attempt to forget what he had done to protect Darkover.

The Council meeting opened with the traditional ceremonies. Mikhail, as Regent of the Domains and Warden of Hastur, presided with his usual easy grace. In the past, as Lew well knew, the roll call had been the occasion for a challenge, especially when the seat of a Domain was vacant. It was not unheard-of for another claimant to come forward. If Francisco were to challenge his son for Ridenow, now would be the time.

The roll proceeded, beginning with Elhalyn as the highest-ranking Domain. Dani Hastur stood in response, naming those members of his family who were also present, his wife, Miralys Elhalyn, and their son, Gareth. Hastur was next, with Mikhail himself answering and presenting Domenic. Domenic had already been confirmed as Heir, but he had not attended a Council meeting since. Heads turned as he stepped forward and bowed respectfully. A buzz swept through the ladies present, and Lew imagined their whispers. The boy was attractive enough, and with his rank and proven *laran,* he would be a splendid catch for one of their daughters.

Lew waited, watchful for any move on Francisco's part. The Ridenow lord sat quietly, following the proceedings with every appearance of courteous interest. When Mikhail called, "Ridenow," Cisco rose and bowed.

"*Vai domyn, Dom* Mikhail, I answer as Warden of Ridenow in place of my father, who is proscribed from serving as the Head of his Domain at this time. However, he is with us today, with your permission, and I ask that he be allowed to sit among us, according to the ancient traditions of Domain-right."

"*Dom* Cisco, your father is welcome in this Council," Mikhail said. "*Dom* Francisco, old quarrels have divided us for too long. Even as the Domain of Aldaran, so long banished from this chamber, now sits here as a valued and equal member, so do I hope you will once again find a place among us."

It was, Lew thought, a gracious speech, if foolhardy, giving Francisco an opening. When the Ridenow lord stepped forward, a murmur rippled through the assembly.

"I am sensible of the honor of your welcome to me, *Dom* Mikhail, both for yourself and in the name of the Comyn," Francisco said. "Since the days of our ancestors, we have met in this fashion, resolving our differences and working together for the benefit of all. It is said that even in the Ages of Chaos, before my kinsman Varzil the Good instituted the Compact, the great lords of the Comyn set aside their quarrels when they came together in Council. We can do no less, we who live in these times of peace."

Mikhail inclined his head graciously. "We welcome your part in it and a renewed fellowship in the future."

Francisco bowed again and sat down. Lew relaxed a fraction. Perhaps Mikhail had been right and Francisco was now prepared to make a new and honorable place for himself. His years of exile might well have granted him the time to reflect, for a better man to emerge.

During this exchange, Cisco had remained standing. "*Vai domyn,*" he said, "I have the additional honor of presenting to you my sister, who has now come of age. *Damisela* Sibelle Francesca Ridenow."

The girl with the red-gold hair came forward with her face demurely lowered as her brother began speaking. She halted just inside the railing and curtsied deeply. Lew had thought her pretty before, almost as striking as Alanna Alar. As she raised her face, the multihued pastel light bathed her for a single glowing moment before she retreated into shadow.

In the old days, as well as within Lew's own memory, feuds had been settled by marriage. He noticed the way more than one lord glanced from the Ridenow girl to Domenic.

A perfect solution to this lingering strife.

Whatever else he might be, Francisco was no fool.

The Council approved Mikhail's agenda for the season's business with only a few changes. The session ended at last, and the telepathic dampers were turned off. Lew felt a surge of relief at the return of his normal *laran*. A few Comyn rose, preparing to make their exits, but most turned amiably to their neighbors, discussing the social events to come or other everyday matters. Given the distances between Domains and the difficulty of travel in any but the best weather, most had not seen each other since last summer. Gossip and dancing, the latest fashions and amusements, a whirl of concerts and parties, a betrothal or two, perhaps even a breath of scandal, all these commanded as much interest as the official events.

When Lew told Marguerida of his plan to pay a courtesy visit to Francisco Ridenow, he did not expect her approval. He broached the subject to her and Mikhail that evening in the little family parlor of the Alton quarters. After dinner, Domenic had excused himself on business of his own, leaving the older adults to linger around the fireplace over their *shallan*.

"Father, you cannot be serious!" Marguerida set her cup forcefully on the table. The honey-pale liqueur splashed over the rim. She dabbed at the spot with her napkin, then got restlessly to her feet.

Dear child, please calm down, he said telepathically. *At least, stop pacing.*

I am calm. Marguerida sat down again. *It is* you *who are out of your mind.*

"Francisco has no reason to harm me—" Lew began.

"Except to get back at Mikhail. Or me."

"—And I have every reason to be courteous to him," Lew went on, ignoring her comment. "He was, after all, kin to Dio."

Mikhail looked thoughtful. "If we are to give him a chance to re-establish himself in Comyn society, then an overture must be made. With today's Council, we have taken the first step toward resolving this issue, but we cannot expect an instant reconciliation. If Lew is willing to undertake it, I think the effort might prove fruitful."

"I fail to see the point in such a visit, except to open old wounds or give that snake an opportunity to create new ones!" Marguerida insisted.

"I do not see any other honorable choice," Lew said. "To refuse to call on him, given the bonds of kinship by marriage, would be an insult."

Marguerida summoned a little smile. "I don't know what has gotten into me these days. Of course, you are right, Mik. Small, slow steps are essential to rebuilding trust and understanding. Father, do be careful."

Remember the warning of my Aldaran Gift . . .

———— ✦ ————

After a suitable interval, Lew sent a message to the Ridenow apartments within the Castle. An answer came back promptly, saying that Francisco would be honored to receive Lew at his earliest convenience.

Francisco himself greeted Lew at the door to the Ridenow suite. Lew sensed in him a mixture of pleasant surprise, friendliness, and anxiety. Like some of the Ridenows, Francisco did not possess *laran* but nonetheless had developed good natural barriers. He must have learned at a young age to live among telepaths without broadcasting his thoughts.

The Ridenow suite had not been used much since Cisco had taken up quarters near the Guards barracks. The efforts of the housekeeping staff under Marguerida's exacting supervision could not entirely dispel a trace of mustiness from the corners. Nevertheless, the chamber into which Francisco ushered Lew was well-lit by candles as well as natural daylight slanting through the thick glass windows, warm from the small fire, and pleasantly appointed. The cushions appeared new, even if the carpets looked as if they dated from the time of Damon Ridenow.

Bless Aldones for formal etiquette, Lew thought as they concluded opening pleasantries and took their seats. Francisco had known Diotima only slightly, being from a different branch of the family, but graciously welcomed Lew's visit on behalf of the entire Ridenow Domain.

If Francisco intended to put himself forward as the legitimate heir of Varzil the Good, he had studied the part well. Perhaps too well. Beneath the polished charm lay bitter-edged arrogance and a sense of indisputable privilege. Pride was not yet a criminal offense.

Not for the first time, Lew wondered what had happened to Dio's kinsmen. How convenient it had been for Francisco's ambition that so many had died.

Perhaps, Lew thought, he himself had grown too suspicious. After all, what Comyn had not been raised from birth with the knowledge of his place in the ruling aristocracy of Darkover?

Francisco's daughter entered, carrying a tray of wine and Carthon-style cakes in tiny diamond shapes, studded with crystalized honey. She wore a flowing gown of faintly iridescent fabric, and her red-gold hair hung in loose ripples to her waist. She served both men with an easy grace, scarcely disturbing their conversation, and then took a seat herself.

The talk moved smoothly through inconsequential matters, conditions on the road from the Ridenow estate, the weather, the upcoming ball. Sibelle's eyes brightened.

"It will be my daughter's first opportunity for the society of young people of her own age and station," Francisco said. "I fear that Serrais has nothing to compare with the delights and diversions of Thendara. We are rather a dull household."

"How shall you enjoy a formal ball, *damisela*?" Lew asked.

Sibelle lowered her gaze. "I believe I shall like it, *Dom* Lewis, even if I must confine myself to dancing with my own kinsmen."

"Are you fond of dancing, then?" Lew's heart lifted at the simple pleasure of discussing a dance with such a charming young woman.

When Sibelle smiled, a dimple appeared at one corner of her mouth. "Very much!"

"Then we must be sure to introduce you to the young men of the court," Lew said.

"Will *you* dance with me, *vai dom*?" She glanced at her father. "That is, if Papa says it would be proper."

"Indeed," Francisco said, "for he is your kinsman by marriage and a man of honor and good character, known to me."

"Oh, my dancing days are long since over," Lew said. "You would not want to drag your feet around the ballroom with an old man. You will not lack partners who are much more sprightly."

"But you are *Dom* Lewis-Kennard Alton!" Sibelle said. "You are the one who brought down the Sharra matrix at Caer Donn! They still sing ballads about it!"

Lew's euphoric mood evaporated. *Sharra again!* Would he never be free of it?

"Is something amiss, *Dom* Lewis?" Color drained from Sibelle's cheeks.

"It is no matter," Lew said, waving away her protests with his single hand. He heard his own voice, raw and strained from the permanent damage to his vocal cords, a poignant reminder that more than his face had been scarred at Caer Donn.

"You have done nothing wrong, daughter," Francisco said soothingly. "Take away the wine and leave us now. We have business to discuss."

"As you wish, Papa."

"She meant no harm," Lew said after they were alone

again. "How could she know that such things as Sharra are best forgotten?"

"Such things as Sharra . . ." Francisco repeated, his face darkening. "You are right, of course. What can any young person know of that horror?"

"We all pray there will never be a need for them to acquire such knowledge," Lew said fervently.

Francisco shook his head. "It is hard to believe that even in our time, after so long, we who have sworn to uphold the Compact should so easily forsake it. Varzil the Good, my ancestor, understood the temptations of necessity. When we are desperate, faced with an overwhelming adversary— the Terran Federation and its hideous technology, for example—how easy it is to justify the use of our *laran*."

"Are you referring to the circle that raised Sharra?" Lew shot back, stung. Francisco had touched a raw nerve, the core of truth. In the beginning, the circle at Caer Donn dreamed of using their *laran* powers to negotiate on an equal standing with the Federation. Only later, when they were already in its horrific grasp, did they realize that Sharra could never be used as anything except a weapon.

"In part." Francisco nodded, his eyes dark and unreadable. "And other things."

The Battle of Old North Road . . .

"*Dom* Lewis?" Francisco was leaning forward, and Lew realized that his own thoughts had wandered for an instant.

"Your pardon," Lew said. "You were saying?"

"I am glad you have had the chance to see Sibelle for yourself and will not hold such a small lapse against her."

"As I said, I do not consider that she has said anything in the least objectionable."

Francisco smiled. "Then you approve of her?"

"What reasonable person could not? She is a delightful young woman, a true asset to her family." He would not ask whether she had *laran,* as well. Too much misery had resulted over the centuries from valuing women only for the psychic Gifts they might pass on to their sons.

"Forgive my brashness in seizing this opportunity," Francisco said. "I would speak with you to the mutual advantage of our families and all the Comyn."

"I will listen," Lew said.

"As a man of the world, you know where the present state of affairs between Mikhail Lanart-Hastur and myself might lead. We have never come to outright warfare between Domains, but as long as the reason for a blood-feud persists, that potential remains."

Lew understood Francisco's veiled threat. Once, in the long-ago time of Allart Hastur, Hastur and Ridenow had been bitter enemies. That was before the Compact, and those very weapons to which Francisco had alluded—clingfire that burned a man down to his bones, bonewater dust that left the land itself sterile, lungrot, mind-warping spells and more—had been hurled at one another by the warring kingdoms. It had taken generations to resolve the conflict and bring the era of The Hundred Kingdoms to a close.

What was Francisco hinting? Was he searching for a means of reconciliation without loss of honor on either side? Had exile wrought such a change in heart?

"Please go on," Lew said. "If you have a proposal that would put this quarrel to rest, I am eager to hear it."

"Surely, you must have guessed that I brought Sibelle to Thendara for more than a round of parties and flirtations. I propose to approach Mikhail Lanart-Hastur with an alliance by the marriage of his son, Domenic, to my daughter."

So Lew's first thought on seeing Sibelle was correct. He almost wished it were not so, for the girl's sake. True, this was the way families had brought an end to hostilities since the beginning of memory. But not since Derik Elhalyn had attempted to force a political marriage between the Keeper Callina Aillard and Beltran Aldaran had anyone seriously considered it.

Look what resulted . . . Callina dead, leaving the Domain of Aillard without an Heir . . . Sharra threatening once more to rage out of control . . .

Flames in his mind, in his soul . . .

"Has Sibelle agreed?" Lew asked, wrenching his thoughts under control.

Would Domenic agree?

"As a dutiful daughter, she understands what is at stake. How many Comynara can render such service to their Domains? Considering the benefit to their families, the obligations of duty, and the suitability of the young people themselves, the marriage stands every chance of being happy. Domenic is reputed to be a fine young man, neither dissolute nor cruel. You see for yourself that Sibelle would make an exemplary wife. Of course," Francisco gave a shrug, as if to prove how reasonable he was, "if they find one another repugnant, we cannot force them. There is another son, I believe."

"Yes, Rory." Lew did not know his other grandson well, beyond the boy's wildly mischievous childhood pranks. Perhaps time and City Guards training had steadied him, as it had so many others.

"Sibelle will bring a rich dowry and new blood to Hastur. In time, Cisco will marry, and it is his children, not hers, who will inherit Serrais."

"You have given the matter careful thought."

Francisco gave a little, self-deprecating laugh. "I have had a great deal of time to consider such things. When we reach a certain age, our perspective changes. Things that seemed so urgent in our youth take on far less importance. We realize that we must put old struggles behind us and look to the future."

"Put old struggles behind us," Lew repeated silently. *If only it were that simple!*

"I see you understand me," Francisco said. "Will you convey my proposal? I believe it will receive a more open hearing than if I present it myself. Mikhail might well react to any gesture on my part with suspicion."

Francisco clearly wanted Lew to vouch for his sincerity as well. How could Lew refuse? Francisco had given him no reason to distrust his motives . . . no *overt* reason, that is.

Lew felt as if he had been holding two conversations with the Ridenow lord, one sincere and hopeful, the other veiled in disturbing references and hinted threats.

"As much as I hope for a return to amicable relations among all our houses," Lew said carefully, as he had learned to do during his years as Senator to the Terran Federation, "I cannot act as your agent, even indirectly. I am happy to communicate your willingness to enter into negotiations for a marriage alliance, but more than that, I cannot in good conscience undertake. I am sure you understand why."

"Forgive my eagerness." Francisco bowed his head a fraction, so that his expression was hidden. His voice, however, was warm and cordial. "I would not abuse your goodwill by placing you in such an awkward position."

"No offense was taken, and no pardon is necessary. It is a difficult business, but with time and goodwill on both your parts, all may be well," Lew replied, adding that even if the marriage did not come about, the effort would not be wasted.

With smiles and reassurances, Lew took his leave.

7

Marguerida gazed across the breakfast table at the man who had shared her life for these long years, enjoying one of the few peaceful moments together since word had come of Javanne's death. Sun drifting through the half-opened window glowed on Mikhail's hair, almost as bright as the day she had first seen him. Yet how much brighter was their love, both for the crises they had endured together and the thousand tiny everyday events that, like silken threads, bound their hearts into one.

He sensed her mood, as he always did, and creases formed a smile around his blue eyes. Without any need of spoken words, they shared a pulse of deep understanding, a moment only, for the day's business could not be long delayed.

A tap at the outside door broke the moment. Lew came in. His hair was combed, his clothing immaculate, but Marguerida instantly noticed the deep circles below his eyes, the scars etched into his face like erosion runnels.

Father, what is the matter?

Mikhail, always more deliberate, invited Lew to sit with them. Lew did so, although he refused *jaco* or herbal tisane.

"I have come to discuss my meeting yesterday with Francisco Ridenow," Lew said heavily.

"Yes, I wondered about that," Mikhail said, sitting forward in his chair. "Since you did not send word last night, I surmised the matter must not be urgent. Is it as we hoped, and does Francisco wish to re-establish himself among us?"

Lew's expression tightened minutely. Marguerida knew her father too well for him to disguise his unease, even though he had barricaded his thoughts.

"Whatever it is, let's hear it." Her words came out more forceful than she had intended. "It's always best to have it out straight."

"Very well," Lew nodded. "Omitting all the courtesies and indirect hints, Francisco proposes to end the animosity between you with a marriage between Domenic and his daughter, Sibelle."

Outrage flared in Marguerida. *What century does the man think we are living in, to barter our children for political gain?*

Years of living among the Comyn, however, had taught her to take a deep breath before she opened her mouth. What Francisco proposed was not unreasonable in Darkovan terms. Even today, many noble families arranged marriages for their sons and daughters, and, she had to admit, many of those marriages were as successful as those made for love alone.

Marguerida did not know what to think about this new development. Was it a good thing? A terrible mistake? Was it even possible? Being in light rapport with Mikhail, as she often was, she sensed his surprise quickly give rise to serious consideration.

He met her astonished glance. "*Preciosa,* set your fears at rest. Whatever happens, I will never pressure our son into a burdensome marriage."

Domenic—and Rory and Yllana as well—must be free to marry where their hearts lead them! she insisted.

"None of us are entirely free to do that," Mikhail replied gravely. "We Comyn cannot choose our lives the way ordinary people do. Even if we no longer command marriages in order to breed *laran* talents, there are other considerations. With power comes responsibility, and we cannot set aside our duty to please ourselves."

"You and I—" she began, her mind filled with memories of the opposition to their growing love. Javanne's antagonism had fueled most of the obstacles, but there had been other problems as well. As Heir to Alton, Marguerida had attracted more than one other suitor, including Francisco Ridenow. In a wild moment, she wondered if Francisco thought to ameliorate the pain of his own rejection by uniting their children.

Mikhail said, "In the midst of all we had to contend with, we were both Comyn, legitimate, *laran*-Gifted, with full Domain-right. Neither of us could have married a chervine herder or a scullery maid."

"No, I can imagine the scandal *that* would have caused," she said, laughing.

And neither can Domenic, he sent the gentle thought. *He is a true son of Hastur,* meaning the legendary ancestor of the Comyn.

Marguerida's temples throbbed, a sickening pulse so very different from a natural headache. *The Aldaran Gift again?* And did it warn of some danger to Domenic rather than Mikhail?

I will drive myself to distraction at this rate and be of no use to anyone!

Gathering herself, she turned to her father. "Is Francisco serious about this marriage? Do you think it wise? How does his daughter feel about it?"

"He says she understands her duty, so I would say, yes, she is willing. As to his own motives . . ." Lew's expression darkened. "I have spent half the night turning around the different possibilities in my mind and am no closer to any conclusions. He could have a dozen different schemes."

"Could it be a trap?" she asked. "A ruse to lure us into trusting him?"

"Anything a Comyn does could be a trap," Lew replied dryly. "We have had a thousand years to perfect the art."

"On the other hand, the offer could be exactly as presented," Mikhail said, "a sincere effort to establish closer ties, so that a generation from now, this quarrel and all its potential for blood feud will be forgotten. We must give him that chance."

"Or it could place Domenic within Francisco's reach," Marguerida muttered, and she saw in her father's eyes that he had considered the same thing.

"We will not allow Domenic to come to any harm, no matter what happens," Mikhail said.

"The Comyn Council is very likely to regard the offer as genuine," Lew said. "In fact, we must consider the possibility they may decide this match is in their best interest and force the marriage."

"They couldn't!" Marguerida cried. "They wouldn't!"

"I am afraid they could and might," Mikhail said. "Remember, even in our time, the Heir to a Domain cannot marry without their consent. We will not permit such a thing, not if Domenic is adverse to the match. But it is better that the issue not be raised in Council. Fighting it might cost us allies that we need for other, more important battles."

Marguerida wondered what could be more important than the happiness of her son, but she realized that was an impossibly romantic notion. On Darkover, duty to one's family, the responsibilities of rank, and the welfare of the greater Domain all took precedence.

"The marriage would not only reconcile Mikhail and Francisco but would ensure the future of Hastur and the Regency," Lew said. "The Council would argue, among other things, that Domenic is of an age to marry and produce sons to rule after him. They would be right. When Regis was his age, he had already fathered a number of *nedestro* children—"

"Are you suggesting that Domenic do the same?" Marguerida asked, appalled. Sometimes the loose morals of the Comyn were more than she could tolerate. It was one thing for someone like Kennard-Dyan to scatter his seed everywhere, with more illegitimate children than he could count, and quite another for her own, properly brought up son. She glared at Mikhail. "*You* did not behave that way!"

"I suspect Domenic is like me in this respect," he answered with a gentle smile. "Few telepaths are capable of intimacy with someone we do not love, someone we cannot touch mind to mind and share our deepest feelings with."

As we have, my dearest one, he added.

She melted inside, as she always did in the warmth of his tenderness.

"You are telling me that whether I like it or not, Domenic will be under pressure to marry," she said, gathering her wits once more, "if not from Francisco, then from the Council."

"Admit it, love, you would adore seeing him happily settled and producing grandchildren for you to spoil," Mikhail teased.

"Yes, but I did not expect it to come about in such a callous, calculating manner! Seriously, Mik, I cannot agree to any arrangement for Domenic without his consent. He may not care for Sibelle Ridenow. She is beautiful, to be sure, but can she make him happy?"

"I have met the young lady," Lew said. "I suspect she has led a sheltered life and is ready to fall in love with any man who fulfills her romantic notions."

"Hmmm." Marguerida frowned, not at all sure that was what Domenic needed in a wife. "We have not asked Nico's opinion of this scheme. He may consider the whole idea preposterous. For all I know, he may already be in love with someone else!"

"Is he?" Mikhail raised one eyebrow expressively.

"No, of course not! I only said that to make a point. Oh, he's fond of Alanna in the way of childhood playfellows, but he's never shown any serious interest in a young woman."

"We must put the matter before him and hear what he has to say," Lew put in. "He may surprise us in his understanding of what is at stake here."

Marguerida sat back in her chair. "I could live with that."

I think. "As long as you promise me, Mik, that if he says no, we will not pressure him."

"That goes without saying, but if it will reassure you, I promise," Mikhail said. "It will make for an awkward situation with Francisco, but we can deal with that."

"I do not think we should rush into an agreement even if Domenic falls head over heels with this girl," Marguerida said. "*She* may be innocent, but I still do not trust Francisco."

"We must use care," Lew said. "The situation, and Francisco's sense of honor, are volatile. An outright rejection will be taken as an affront. Francisco may be looking for an excuse to take offense."

Marguerida shook her head. For all the years she had lived on Darkover, the intricate, downright Byzantine convolutions of honor still left her baffled. Why couldn't these people just come out and say what they meant?

"That is certainly true," said Mikhail. "As Marja has pointed out, even if the young people take to one another, this marriage would be a complex diplomatic affair."

Marguerida bit her lip. Much as she disliked the idea of Domenic having anything to do with Francisco Ridenow, she could not refuse without creating a crisis where none existed. Difficult as it was, she must trust her husband and her father, who had far more experience in Comyn politics than she did, to act cautiously. After all, they too loved Domenic and would not place him at risk.

"Let us proceed, but slowly," Mikhail said. "Lew, if you are willing to deliver a reply on our behalf to Francisco, perhaps we can tread a middle path, without committing ourselves until we know more. Let him know how honored we are by his proposal and how deeply we appreciate the spirit in which it was made. Remind him of the complexity of arranging marriages in this day. Tell him that regardless of the outcome, we consider this as only the first of many steps together. Times change, Darkover changes, and we invite his participation in building the future together. Or something like that, in properly diplomatic phrasing."

"I will do what I can," Lew said with a weary smile. "It's strangely fitting that the skills I learned in the Terran Senate should be so useful now."

"Marja, will you discuss the matter with Domenic?" Mikhail asked. "I think he will take it better coming from you, and I cannot delay this morning's Council session any longer. You need not attend, as I know how boring you find trade negotiations."

"No, indeed!" she exclaimed with a little laugh. "I am happy for an excuse not to hear one more long-winded speech about nothing in particular. This would be an excellent time for a quiet word with Domenic."

Mikhail and Lew took their leave of Marguerida. She would have preferred to see her father rest, but she knew from the set of his jaw how useless it would be to suggest such a thing.

If I am not careful, I will let my own anxieties come out in mothering everyone around me!

After one of the servants had gone to ask Domenic to join her, Marguerida tried to quiet her thoughts. She found, to her surprise, that although she greatly disliked the notion of Francisco Ridenow as an in-law, she had more than a little of the matchmaker in herself. More than once, she had wondered where she was going to find a suitable wife for Domenic or, for that matter, for her wild, reckless Rory.

Why can't things be simple? Why can't Nico marry someone he loves and have some happiness, as I have had with Mikhail?

At the same time, Mikhail's question still stung. For all her fine words about giving Domenic a free choice, how would she feel if he chose someone she disapproved of?

Someone like Alanna?

Marguerida continued in her ruthless self-examination. Alanna was of good family, she certainly possessed *laran*, and was in many ways a suitable choice; yet the very idea stirred a feeling of desperate horror in Marguerida. From before Alanna's birth, Marguerida's Aldaran Gift had warned her of disaster. While Marguerida had done everything she could to temper that fate, she could never allow Domenic to be drawn into it.

Domenic deserves more from a wife than constant heartache.

There was no question in her mind that Alanna *would* bring sorrow. What if Domenic had set his heart on her, after all? Marguerida's head ached, threatening worse pain to come. Absently, she rubbed her temples.

Perhaps Francisco's offer was a hidden opportunity, a chance to direct Nico's attention away from Alanna. He had been too much in the girl's company, and Marguerida respected the power of hormonal attraction. If not Sibelle, then there might be any one of a number of suitable partners, young women with the spirit and intelligence to make him happy. One of them would surely please him. All it would take was a little encouragement and the right setting.

—— ✦ ——

Marguerida called Domenic into her office, where she could be sure they would not be overheard. She closed the doors, knowing that the servants had been well trained never to interrupt her work. Earlier, she had added a handful of balsam chips to the fire, so that the fragrance filled the cozy room. The flames reflected off the paneled walls and brightened the colors of her favorite rug.

She remembered sitting at this very desk, composing her first opera or studying Darkovan history while cradling a baby to her breast. Now that baby was grown, a man. Where had the years gone?

Domenic listened quietly as Marguerida explained Francisco's proposal. She could not read his reaction, for he kept his thoughts carefully shielded. Much as she tried to present the situation objectively, her own doubts kept creeping in. She could not see any good solution between playing into Francisco's schemes or leaving Domenic vulnerable to Alanna.

"I expected as much," he said when she had finished.

"You did?"

He grimaced. "You saw how the old biddies of both sexes on the Council looked at me on opening day. Even with the telepathic dampers on, I could hear them planning a Hastur wedding."

"Oh, Nico! How well I know the feeling that the entire Council has nothing better to do than plan out your entire life! Everyone expects the Heir to a Domain to marry early, and, like it or not, there are reasons for that. Someday Darkover may have a democratic government, but for now, the old feudal system is too deeply entrenched." She was babbling, she knew, but nervousness did that to her. Any moment now, she would make a bad joke.

"I'm sorry, Nico." She forced herself to slow down and take a deep breath. "I have been rattling on, haven't I? This isn't any easier for me than it is for you."

Domenic shrugged, feigning carelessness. "I can't expect to remain unmarried indefinitely. If anything happened to me, Rory would be the next in line, and—" he gave an impish grin "—if I weren't already dead, he'd come after me and do the job."

"I suppose he would," Marguerida replied with a chuckle. "I can't see him happily sitting through all those Council meetings."

"I also know," Domenic said in a more somber tone, "that the Council will have a say in who I marry. They still must give their consent, since I am the Heir to a Domain."

He sounded so bleak, Marguerida's heart ached for him. She wished she could wave a magic wand out of her childhood fairy tales and make all his troubles disappear.

She tried to sound encouraging. "Surely, the Council's approval is only a formality? After all, didn't your father and I marry for love? Didn't Miralys Elhalyn and Dani Hastur? Believe me, all the families involved had very strong opinions, and yet love prevailed in the end. Don't give up hope. I am sure the same will be true for you."

"To tell the truth, Mother, I don't know if I will ever find someone who suits me as well as you and Father do one another."

"I hope you will—I know you will! Meanwhile, won't you give Sibelle Ridenow a chance? If you don't like her, there are others," Marguerida hastened to add, not wanting to encourage him too much in that direction. "Francisco can hardly object if your affections are engaged elsewhere. Some very nice, eligible young ladies will be in town for the season. If you spend enough time with them, one may catch your fancy. I would be surprised if several of them did not fall in love with you."

Domenic looked away, his jaw set. Marguerida recognized that stubborn expression, for she had seen it enough times in her own mirror.

She sighed. "I do not want to see you unhappy or married to someone you cannot respect. It would have broken my heart if Mikhail and I had not found a way to be together. But your situation is different. You do not have to part with someone you already love. What I am *suggesting*," she put special weight upon the word, "is that you keep an open mind. Your father and I would dearly love to see you settled."

Domenic would not meet her eyes. She wished she could touch his mind with hers as she had so many times in the past, but his *laran* shields were closed tight. He was unhappy and hiding something, she could see that in his expression, in every taut line of his posture.

"You are quite right, Mother," Domenic said at last. "There are larger considerations at stake here than my own preferences. I will endeavor to fulfill my duty to the best of my ability."

Marguerida smiled as she rose, a signal the meeting was over. Once she was alone again, the smile faded. Tears rose to her eyes. Beyond words, she hoped to see him as happy in marriage as she had been, and she hoped that one day there would be no more secrets between them.

8

Domenic stood at the window of the second-story tavern room, watching the street below, seeing his own inner state reflected in its shifting turbulence: riders weaving their way between wagons and carts and pedestrians, liveried servants trotting along with sedan chairs, shawled women laden with baskets, nursemaids herding small children, men in ordinary working garb, street vendors hawking ribbons and hair trinkets, a couple of beggars on the corner, ragged street urchins darting in and out of the crowd, a City Guard or two standing watch.

Since Domenic had first spoken with Danilo Syrtis, the older man had become his informal mentor. The conversation had been so encouraging that Domenic had confided his jumble of conflicting emotions on the subject of his marriage. Danilo had listened gravely, sympathetically, perhaps remembering the time when Regis Hastur had been pressured to produce heirs. Eventually, Regis had married Linnea Storn. How the three of them—Regis, his wife, and his lifelong lover—had worked out the inevitable jealousies, Domenic could not imagine. What he did know was that his mother would not be happy about his relationship with Alanna, nor would Alanna accept his paying attention to Sibelle Ridenow or any other woman, and he had no idea how to broach the subject with either of them.

Even though he had no intention of going through with

an arranged political marriage, he resolved to make an effort to be courteous to *Dom* Francisco's daughter. Every instinct told him that Alanna would not like that at all. With her temper, there was no telling what she might do. In order to sweeten her mood, Domenic had brought Alanna with him to this morning's meeting.

Domenic had begun accompanying Danilo through the city and on several occasions had been introduced to some trader or minor lord, shopkeeper or traveling tinker. Often these meetings occurred in private, hired rooms like this, for men spoke more freely away from Comyn Castle. Danilo knew a surprising number of people in the city. Every time, Domenic had learned something new.

Domenic and Alanna had walked here with her hand tucked in his elbow, a public display of affection quite improper for an unmarried couple. Perhaps he unconsciously wanted to be caught and have their secret out in the open. He'd started dreaming of her, of the two of them in bed together. Such thoughts were dangerous. One of these times, they might become so tempting that he might not be able to stop himself.

As for Alanna, the outing was a special treat, for she had rarely been allowed to wander the city, even with an escort. She had pointed excitedly to goods displayed at the various shops and trading booths, bolts of spidersilk and *linex*, leather belts, boots of supple suede, and silver filigree jewelry. Even the scuffle outside the bakery, quickly broken up by City Guards, had aroused her curiosity rather than fear.

She had wrinkled her nose at the tavern room, with its low ceiling, unadorned walls, and table of scrubbed, unvarnished pine, the straight-backed chairs lacking even a single thin cushion between them, the steamy smells of boiled oat porridge and poor quality *jaco* emanating from the kitchen below. For Domenic, the place held a spartan appeal, clean and simple and, most of all, free from the ostentation of courtly venues.

Now Alanna moved to Domenic's side at the window. He slipped his hand around her waist.

"We have so little time alone," he said. "Let us not waste it."

Alanna snuggled into his embrace. Her lips met his, warm and pliant. Her body pressed against him. Domenic could not keep his hands off her. Through the layers of her tartan shawl and gown, he felt the softness of her breasts. His pulse danced in his ears.

Domenic bent to kiss her neck, following the smooth curve to the edge of her jacket collar. As he drew in a breath, the natural scent of her skin filled him. For the moment, nothing else mattered.

At a knock, the moment shattered. They sprang apart. The door swung open. Danilo Syrtis entered, wearing a hooded cloak that hid his features. At his heels came three other men. By the cut of their boots and fur-trimmed vests, Domenic guessed that two of them were small farmers from the Kilghard Hills; the straw-pale hair of the third suggested Dry Towns ancestry. The third man's clothing, although of good quality wool, warm and well made, revealed only that he was neither poor nor rich and said nothing in particular about his business.

Danilo threw back his hood. The morning chill had brought a flush of color to his cheeks, giving him the appearance of a much younger man. "*Dom* Domenic Lewis-Gabriel Alton-Hastur," he said formally, "allow me to present Zared and Ennis from your own Alton lands, and this is Cyrillon, who trades in furs and gold from Carthon."

"*Z'par servu, vai dom.*" The two Alton men bowed to Domenic and also to Alanna, although neither would look directly at her, as was proper. Domenic inquired how long they had been in Thendara and made small comments to put them at their ease.

The Alton men, who turned out to be kinsmen from the Mariposa Lake area, had come to Thendara hoping for an audience with Gabriel, as Head of the Alton Domain, during the Council season. However, commoners had no standing in Comyn Council, and their efforts to speak with

Gabriel—or anyone else in the Castle—had been soundly rebuffed.

Their great-uncle had died without any surviving heirs, for his sons had all perished in one way or another, some of the lung fever that had struck the area after the crop failures of the World Wreckers. One had fallen to bandit raids, and yet another had died in the period of upheaval following the Battle of Old North Road. This left the question of inheritance in doubt, and the caretaker steward who had been left in charge of Mariposa had been unable to resolve it. The various claimants had already come to blows.

Domenic listened to their story with a growing sense of unease. Traditionally, each major estate in the Alton Domain was ruled by a different branch of the family. Grandfather Gabriel lived at Edelweiss, unlikely ever to leave. The younger Gabriel had taken over the management of Armida. Rafael had married Gisela Aldaran and divided his time between her home in the far Hellers and Comyn Castle.

Mariposa had been left to the stewardship of others. Such men might manage the lands and livestock well enough, but they had no relationship of fealty with the people. They could not raise troops, pass judgment, or handle any of the thousand things a lord and his people owed one another.

There was nothing Domenic could say in defense of his own family. These men were Alton vassals and had every right to expect a responsive and responsible lord, one who knew them, their families and concerns. What could anyone in Thendara, no matter how well intentioned, know of their daily troubles?

In truth, the present Comyn were a small fraction of their numbers before the assassinations of the World Wreckers years. The death of Regis Hastur had weakened them further. Now it seemed that power was concentrated in the hands of a few, with too many estates going masterless. Some Domains were but a heartbeat away from a similar fate. Aillard rested in the hands of one aging woman, Marilla Lindir-Aillard. Kennard-Dyan Ardais had yet to marry or name an heir. Dani Hastur had abdicated his own position to rule Elhalyn for his wife.

We must take this issue up at the Council meeting, Domenic thought. *There are not enough of us to fulfill our responsibilities; that much is clear.*

Zared and Ennis shifted in their seats, clearly uncomfortable. Neither would look up. In a flash of insight, Domenic exchanged glances with Danilo. These were country men, by nature and upbringing conservative. He doubted either of them had set foot outside their own home lands before.

"If you will lay the matter before me," Domenic said, unexpectedly moved by the plight of these men, "I will render judgment to the best of my ability."

Zared dipped his head and said in archaic *casta,* "*Vai dom,* we place ourselves in your hands."

Domenic thought wildly that he was not worthy of such a gesture of loyalty, that he could never make a ruling by himself. Surely he must have someone to advise him, older and more experienced. Instinct kept him silent. To him alone these men had given their trust. He alone must fulfill the obligation.

What would Great-Uncle Regis have done? In a moment of insight, Domenic realized there was more to the issue than simple legality. Property rights were simple compared to the complicated lines of succession of the Comyn. There had been no intermarrying of lineages in this case, no previously unsuspected *nedestro* heirs, no contested parentage.

What was the *right* answer, the one that took the benefit of everyone involved into consideration? What would prevent injustice from festering into resentment and even outright feud? What would best promote harmony among these kinsmen, so that they would care for one another and the land?

Two of the claimants already had plots of their own, fertile enough to support their families; was it justice that they increase their wealth, leaving less for those who had nothing? After some thought, Domenic decided that the richest should make the division of the property into whatever portions he saw fit. The poorest man must then be allowed to select his share first, proceeding according in order, with the richest taking the last. However, he added, any claimant who wished a portion must add his own parcel to the land to be divided. As Domenic explained his idea, the two men nodded. They went away, clearly satisfied.

" 'Tis the word of an Alton lord," one commented as he left the room.

"Aye," said the other, "there will be no arguing with that. Greed will have its own reward, and no one's children will go hungry."

"That was well done," Danilo said, after the door closed behind the two Mariposa men. "Now, let us hear what Cyrillon has to say."

The third man, who had been listening attentively, said he needed no counsel, for his business prospered, but the lord there, he indicated Danilo, had said he ought to come and tell his tale.

He was, he said, of mixed Domains and Dry Towner blood, and spent his life in the rough border country between the two lands, supplying each with what it lacked from the other. At present, he carried furs, leather, and medicinal herbs from the Khilgard Hills to Carthon and returned with sulfur, salt, and gold filigree jewelry. Occasionally, he was able to purchase Ardcarran rubies as well.

"What's the news from Shainsa?" Domenic asked.

"Ah, much the same as always," Cyrillon replied. "The great chiefs snarl at each other like hounds over a bone. No one ever wins except to gain in *kihar*."

Cyrillon answered Domenic's questions about trade between the Dry Towns and the Domains, how the lords of Shainsa viewed the departure of the Terrans, and prospects for the continuation of an uneasy peace. It seemed to

Domenic that as long as the Dry Towns chieftains bickered among themselves, they could not coordinate an effective battlefront. Petty raids and forays into Domains territory would doubtless continue, as one hothead or another tried to prove his manhood.

"What about conditions on the road?" Domenic asked, thinking of the number of country folk he had noticed in the street. Two such men, ill-clothed and haggard, had been involved in the brawl outside the bakery this morning.

Cyrillon's fair brows drew together. "Aye, I have seen changes, and not for the better. Always, the less savory sort of vagabonds have more interest in wresting their living from yours and mine than doing any honest work."

"That's true enough," Domenic said, "or smiths would have no buyers for their swords."

Cyrillon shook his head in wordless agreement that such a time would never come. "This year I have seen many with all they own on their backs, but it's difficult to tell. Spring thaw often brings out wanderlust."

"They will not improve their lot in Thendara," Domenic said, thinking of how the City Guards had quelled the tussle. True, some work could be found in Thendara, menial tasks like loading wagons or mucking out stables, but Darkover was not like other Federation worlds, with a large urban industrialized base.

Danilo held out a small purse, which clinked softly as it fell into the trader's palm. "That's for your trouble, good *mestre*, and there will be more the next time you are in Thendara. Come and see us, even if there is no news. Perhaps we may have other uses for your abilities."

Beaming, the trader took his leave. Domenic waited until he no longer sensed Cyrillon's presence in the corridor before asking Danilo, "So you think I should cultivate men such as this?"

"I think the more sources of information you have, the more likely you are to hear the truth," Danilo said.

Alanna had been sitting quietly through the discussion,

her eyes shining. "That was splendid!" She clapped her hands in delight. "Auntie Marguerida never lets me stay when there's anything important going on."

"So you found the conversation interesting?" Danilo turned to her. "What did you think?"

"I think perhaps . . ." Unused to being taken seriously, Alanna answered slowly, her brow wrinkling in concentration. "Perhaps it might be better not to trust the trader's word entirely. A man like that thinks only of his own interests. If he passes some poor fellow on the road, his only concern is to protect his goods, not why the other has left his home or what other troubles he might have.

"Besides," she added, with a disdainful sniff and a toss of her head, "I did not like this Cyrillon at all. He looked at me as if he would like to carry me away to sell at the slave markets in Ardcarran."

Domenic laughed, but Danilo looked thoughtful. "Setting aside personal impressions," Danilo said, "we do not yet know the whole story. I too have noticed a rising unrest in the streets."

Domenic thought of the fight outside the bakery, the beggars on the corner, the way people on the street sometimes hurried away as he approached. He had been too long away from Thendara to know if this was unusual, and he had attributed his own sense of unease to his dislike of city life and crowds in general.

"This—this is new?" he asked. "Or worse than before?"

"I think so," Danilo replied. "Ever since the beginning of this Council season, something has been stirring up public sentiment against the Comyn, and the Regent in particular."

Something, Domenic repeated to himself, thinking now of his mother's premonitions. *Or someone.*

"The situation calls for a closer look," Danilo said. "Even legitimate grievances can be manipulated for a purpose. It wouldn't be the first time some malcontent or other has garnered support by blaming the Council. Yet the people have always looked to us when it has been necessary for one man to speak for many."

In Danilo's thoughts, Domenic caught the fleeting image of a young man, slight and intense, shimmering with unspoken power. But not the power of fist or sword. The power to inspire, to ignite the flames of idealism, of dedication. The power of the heart.

As quickly, the vision faded. Danilo had gone on, talking now about how the Federation had tried to impose its own form of government upon Darkover, with its own laws and economies.

"That's all over now," Alanna put in. "They're gone for good, aren't they?"

"That remains to be seen," Domenic said. Somewhere, out there in the stars, planets warred with one another. Perhaps they still did, or maybe they had bombed each other into ruin. He did not want to think what it would mean to Darkover if men like Lyle Belfontaine came swooping down from the skies, bent on taking whatever they needed, using Darkover for their own purposes.

"Nonetheless," Danilo said, picking up the conversation, "the *Terranan* upset the old ways, and we have not yet found new ones. Men like Zared and Ennis look to their lords to resolve their differences."

"It was lucky for them that you brought them here, where Domenic could tell them what to do." Alanna's mood turned petulant, as if the men had journeyed the long leagues to Thendara in order to annoy her. "Did they think they could march into the Crystal Chamber and lay their troubles at the feet of the Council?"

"Surely not the Council." Domenic wanted to laugh. What would that elegant assembly, in their brocades and jewels, think of the ragged men he had seen outside the bakery?

"We have always preferred to handle our affairs locally whenever possible," Danilo explained to Alanna. "In Syrtis, where I was born, our people looked to my father to resolve their differences."

"Who do they look to now, since you are here in Thendara?" Alanna looked genuinely curious.

"The farm is managed by a steward, and I visit when I can. It is the same everywhere. I wish I could do more, but the duties that have kept me in Thendara were more urgent, and I cannot be in two places at one time." Danilo exchanged a glance with Domenic. *There are too few of us.*

Some day, Domenic thought, he would have to divide himself between Regency and Domain. *And I do not yet have sons to take up those duties after me . . .*

Like it or not, his mother had touched upon an inescapable truth. He must marry. It must be someone acceptable not only to his parents but to the Council itself.

"What is the purpose of the Council, if not to rule over everyone?" Alanna asked.

"Over time, the Council's powers have narrowed in scope," Danilo explained. "Now it mostly resolves disputes between Domains and settles trade policy and inheritance rights. Once the Council was far more powerful, but even today someone like you or Domenic must still obtain the approval of the Council to marry."

Alanna cast a white-eyed glance at Domenic. "Could the Council forbid a marriage with someone they did not approve of? Or force you to marry someone else?"

Domenic reached out to reassure her. "Of course not. That is a bit of ancient history left over from the Ages of Chaos, when the Comyn used selective inbreeding to develop and strengthen their *laran* Gifts."

"I am sorry to say it, but the Council does still retain that right." Danilo's still-handsome face darkened, and he looked away. "Even Regis was not immune."

"Nobody today would suggest such a thing," Domenic repeated, sensing Alanna's rising hysteria. "Their approval is a matter of form only, of no consequence."

Color sprang to the girl's cheeks and her mouth quivered. "Domenic, do not tell me it is of no consequence! Tell me—" her voice broke, each syllable rising toward frenzy.

"What is the matter?" Domenic asked.

"I don't know which vision is true, what will come to pass!"

"Have you had another vision of the future?" Danilo demanded. "Of *this* future?"

Alanna gathered herself with an effort. "You were right, *Dom* Danilo, the visions did not go away. They're getting worse. Sometimes I have two or three at once, so mixed up I cannot tell what is real. I have seen *you*," she raised tear-bright eyes to Domenic, "standing beside a girl, dressed like a queen in Ridenow colors, and the *catenas* are locked upon your wrists while Auntie Marguerida and *Dom* Mikhail watch. Who is she, Domenic?"

Lord of Light! She has seen me marrying Sibelle Ridenow!

"Another time," Alanna rushed on before he could answer, "I saw you with a different woman. She looked familiar, but I can't think how I know her. You are laughing together. You are happy and I am not there! Am I dead, is that what's going to happen? I think I must be going mad!"

"There, there," Domenic said with an assurance he did not feel. "I will not forsake you. Have I not promised?"

"*Damisela*, it seems your *laran* is growing stronger," Danilo said, rubbing his jaw thoughtfully. "I suspect that you see not a single, inevitable future but a series of *possible* futures."

"That must surely be the case," said Domenic, trying to keep his voice light. "I cannot marry *both* ladies."

"No, of course not," Alanna said. Her fingers tightened around his, linking them in telepathic rapport. *Not when you are going to marry me.*

Domenic's heart gave a little jerk. Until this moment, the words had not been spoken, only assumed. He had behaved toward her as if they were betrothed. She had every right to expect the formal declaration to follow. Although they had not actually consummated their passion, they had touched and kissed in a way that not so long ago would have constituted an unbreakable commitment. She was no serving wench or dairy maid but a Comynara, not to be dallied with.

I must keep my promise to her. The word of a Hastur is as binding as any oath.

"What other visions have you had?" Danilo asked Alanna.

"Worse ones by far," she admitted. "This morning, as I was waking, I thought I looked out on a street—Threadneedle Street, where Auntie Marguerida used to take me when I was little. She had friends there, and they laughed together. Only this time, no one was laughing. In every house and outside, too, lying in the street, there were sick people. A woman ran through the street with a baby in her arms. She knocked on every door, and no one would let her in. I think the baby was dead."

Domenic had been listening to Alanna with his *laran* senses as well as his ears. Now, in a flash of inner sight, he glimpsed her as a pattern of energy. Around her body, lines of time streamed out like strands of light with figures moving back and forth upon them. Some were clear, others tangled, and yet more so turbulent that he could not make out any details.

"*Dom* Danilo," he asked, "what can it mean?"

Danilo shook his head, his dark eyes grave. "I do not know. May the Holy Bearer of Burdens grant it never comes to pass!"

"The vision need not be an omen of things to come." Domenic sought desperately for a happier explanation. "Perhaps Alanna has seen something from the past."

"I cannot tell," Alanna said. "Oh, Domenic, what am I to do? How can I bear it? Don't tell me to go back to a Tower! I want to lead my own life and not be shut up away from all the fun."

"I have thought much on this matter since we first discussed it," Danilo said to her, "and I agree. Clearly, you need additional training in mastering your *laran*. At the same time, it would do you no good to go to a Tower against your wishes. Not everyone is suited to that life. Regis did not study at a Tower, either. He felt called to live in the world, although for very different reasons. Once he made his peace with why he had suppressed his Gift, there was no need."

"Great-Uncle Regis—*suppressed* his Gift? How was that possible?" Domenic asked, stunned.

Danilo gave him an enigmatic look. "Many things can block the use of *laran* or warp its expression—trauma, conditioning, religious beliefs, even love. Sometimes, too, love is the key to unlocking it."

Domenic caught the older man's unspoken thought, *Could the same be true for Alanna?*

"What else, then?" Alanna cried, growing more agitated with each passing moment. "Do I simply let the visions come as they will and do nothing?"

Danilo raised one eyebrow. "That is one option."

Alanna looked deeply surprised, for clearly she had expected another argument about going to a Tower. Domenic opened his mouth to protest. Danilo's comment made no sense.

Danilo leaned toward Alanna without touching her. In a low, soothing voice, he said, "The only compelling reason to go to a Tower is to learn the inner discipline necessary to bear a Gift such as yours. It is a heavy burden indeed, as well as a talent so rare that no one else in present times has it. I do not think the *leroni* can teach you what to do with it, but they can instruct you in how to remain calm and focused. You can learn how to master your fears."

"You spent a season at Arilinn," Domenic said encouragingly. "Surely something you learned then—the basic meditation and focusing techniques—can help you now."

Emotion drained from Alanna's face. She seemed to freeze, except for the rapid rise and fall of her chest. When she spoke, an unearthly chill shivered through her voice. "I prefer not to think of those times. Ever. Again."

Domenic frowned. What could have happened to her at Arilinn? He hesitated, afraid to shatter her eerie detachment and provoke another outburst.

"I would rather die than go back to Arilinn!" Alanna shuddered and her eyes focused once again. "Therefore, I must do my best to—as you put it—master my fears. To not be so frightened."

Domenic found himself strangely moved by her words. He turned Danilo. "Is that safe?"

"I cannot say. I am no Keeper or anything like it," Danilo said. "Although it may be a terrible mistake, I do not know what else to suggest. People like Alanna should not have to choose between the cloistered life of a Tower and forsaking their Gifts. Who knows how many are out there, the descendants of Comyn liaisons over the centuries?"

Domenic remembered Illona Rider, the Traveler girl he had met during the adventures leading up to the Battle of Old North Road. Only a trick of fate had brought them together so that her Gift was discovered and nurtured. Only later was it learned that she was the *nedestra* daughter of Kennard-Dyan Ardais, although he had not yet legitimated her or any of his other illegitimate offspring. She and Domenic had studied together at Neskaya Tower, where he had remained, while she transferred after a season to Nevarsin. In his mind, Domenic saw her sweet features, the corona of flaming hair, generous mouth and pale, almost luminous eyes, heard her ready laughter. For all he knew, she might be under-Keeper by now.

What if he had never met Illona? What if she had spent her whole life in fear of her talent, with Darkover all the poorer? The Comyn were spread too thin, and they needed people like Illona now more than ever.

"How will we find them?" he asked Danilo. "What kind of training can we offer them? And what work will they do? What place will they find in society?"

"I don't know the answers to any of these questions," Danilo said, his dark eyes thoughtful. "But I think it is time we began the search."

9

On the night of the Midsummer Festival Ball, Domenic had rarely seen the Grand Hall of Comyn Castle so resplendent. Greenery bedecked with flowers and ribbons in a rainbow of colors hung everywhere. The floors and crystal chandeliers had been polished to mirror brightness, inundating the space with reflected light. Additional mirrors, many of them Terran imports, had been placed around the periphery at Marguerida's direction to heighten the effect of brilliance and rich color.

In the center of the long interior wall a small orchestra of viols, harps, wooden flutes, and several newer instruments played a lilting melody. Domenic recognized it as one of his mother's compositions. *Chamber music,* she called it. Later in the evening, between dances, a quartet of vocalists would perform songs from the opera she had completed last year.

Although the ball was traditionally a gathering of all the Comyn, Marguerida acted as resident hostess, supervising the decorations, arranging the music, checking guest lists, and ordering refreshments. Now she and Mikhail waited at the main entrance to extend their welcome to all the guests. Domenic took his place beside his parents.

Marguerida wore a glorious gown of elaborately layered, iridescent blue spidersilk trimmed with Temoran lace. At her side, Mikhail shone in an evening suit of bro-

cade in the same luminous shades, his doublet stitched with
silver thread, sleeves slashed to reveal a shirt of *linex* so
fine and white that it shimmered. The court-length cape
draped elegantly over one shoulder was trimmed in snow-
leopard fur and lined with the same spidersilk as Marguerida's gown.

What a sight we are! Domenic thought, reflecting ruefully
that neither of his parents seemed in the least uncomfortable with their finery. From their smiles and posture, they
enjoyed every moment of the richly textured pageantry of
the Festival. Their pleasure lay not only in their personal
ornamentation but in the sense of shared celebration. They
made themselves beautiful to honor their friends and kinfolk.

Domenic pulled his shoulders back and tried to breathe.
He could not think of his attire as anything but a costume,
for he had never before worn anything so complicated and
shiny. He had no idea of the cost of the velvet-soft suede
trimmed with outrageously expensive Ardcarran rubies. Instead of a serviceable blade, he carried a jewel-hilted dress
sword.

The room filled quickly with Comyn and Comynara in
holiday finery. Many of the women displayed their traditional gifts of flowers, either as small bouquets or incorpo-
rated artistically into their headdresses. Domenic had left a
basket of fruit outside Alanna's door, honey-sweet mountain peaches that reminded him of her skin. His offerings
to his mother and sister had been more modest, little
ribbon-tied nosegays of starflowers.

Katherine and Hermes Aldaran had already arrived, as
had Grandfather Lew. Marguerida embraced her friend
and the two women chatted in animated fashion for several minutes. Domenic looked around for Alanna, but she
had not yet arrived.

"A fine young man you've got here, *vai domna*," *Dom*
Marcos MacAnndra said, after Marguerida performed the
introduction. He held fertile lands toward the Temora sea-
coast, and, as far as Domenic knew, he had never before at-

tended a session of the Comyn Council. "You'll make us all proud, lad, of that I've no doubt."

Domenic stiffened as *Dom* Francisco approached with his daughter on his arm. The Ridenow lord stood out in the gaily colored assembly by his somber clothing. His sword looked functional rather than ornamental. In the green and gold of her Domain colors, Sibelle resembled a sunlit garden.

After the usual courtesies were exchanged, Mikhail said, "It is good to have you among us once more. Tonight, let us celebrate the joy of the season together."

"Few things would give me greater pleasure." Francisco paused, giving Marguerida a strange, unreadable look. "We were friends once."

"And may yet be again," she said, her voice carefully neutral.

"Lord Domenic, I do not believe you have been properly introduced to my daughter, Sibelle Francesca," Francisco said.

"*Para servite,*" Domenic replied politely. "*Vai dom, vai damisela.*"

Sibelle Ridenow curtsied and glanced at Domenic from under her lashes. She was, he admitted, extremely pretty, with strings of pearl and jade twined through her hair.

"Let the service be a blessing to the giver." Sibelle's voice was a sweet, clear soprano.

What have they told her? That if she snares me, she will rule Darkover as if she were a queen?

Quickly, Domenic stifled the thought. Sibelle Ridenow was a lovely, gently reared girl who had never given him offense. Indeed, on such a moment's acquaintance, he could not find any fault with her. He smiled, bowed again, and asked if she would honor him with a dance.

"Oh! Oh, yes, I would like that very much."

Obviously, no one had told Sibelle not to appear delighted. Her father, smiling, led her away as yet more Comyn came forward to greet Mikhail.

Domenic came instantly alert when Alanna entered, escorted by her brother, Donal. In her cream-colored satin crossed by a tartan in her family's colors, she looked poised and elegant. She caught Domenic's eye halfway across the room, but both of them were surrounded by clusters of people, and it would have been impossible to make his way to her. The air shimmered in Domenic's sight, or perhaps that was the heat rising in him. He ached with wanting to be with her.

Dani Hastur arrived somewhat later, accompanying his wife. Gareth was with them as well.

By this time, Domenic was no longer anchored to the reception line with his parents. Mikhail had taken Grandfather Lew aside, talking over cups of wine punch. Marguerida went off with her sister-in-law, Gisela, and Katherine, Hermes Aldaran's off-world wife, the three of them in animated conversation. Domenic spotted Rory in a corner, standing very close to another young Guard. They were so absorbed in one another that neither noticed Domenic's approach.

"Good Festival night," Domenic said. The two started, moving apart. "I'm sorry if I'm interrupting . . . will you not introduce me to your friend?" He inflected the word so that it could mean something more intimate.

Rory met Domenic's gaze, and a flicker of understanding passed between them. "Nico, this is Niall MacMoran. We've known each other since our first days as cadets."

Niall had a swordsman's muscled shoulders, narrow hips, and russet-brown eyes, hooded like a falcon's.

Domenic inclined his head. "I'm Rory's less disreputable brother."

"*Vai dom.*" Niall's eyes glinted as he bowed in return.

"This one thinks far more than he speaks," Domenic said to Rory, gently teasing. "Is he the reason you've reformed your wild ways?"

Rory slipped one arm around Niall's shoulders. "That depends on how you define *wild.*"

"And *ways,*" Niall added.

Domenic laughed outright. "Have you told Mother?"

"No, have you?" Rory said in riposte.

Domenic winced, then, seeing his brother's good-natured grin, shrugged in surrender. "I think she would be far more understanding in your case."

"That may be true," Rory said, shifting from playful to serious, "but we all need some part of our lives that is ours alone. There is a time to speak plainly and a time to keep silent. I am only the second son, not the Heir to Hastur and the Regency. Who I choose for my heart and bed affects no one but myself. The Domains will not fall into ruin if I decline to take a wife and produce numerous loud and smelly offspring. You, on the other hand ..." Letting his arm drop, he touched the back of Domenic's wrist. "You have no such freedom. I am sorry to say it, brother, but the world goes as it wills—"

"—and not as you or I would have it." Domenic completed the old proverb.

Leaving Rory and Niall, Domenic worked his way to where Gareth stood beside his mother, Miralys Elhalyn. The months since his return to Thendara had given him ample practice in the gestures and phrases of courtesy. As he circled the room, he acknowledged a number of minor lords and ladies, several clearly anxious to present their daughters to him. He avoided being drawn into conversation with any of them.

Four years had left Gareth tall and a little gangly, as if he were not yet accustomed to the new length of his legs. As far as Domenic knew, he had never served in the Guards cadets, and now, at eighteen, he was too old to begin. He bowed with impeccable politeness to Francisco Ridenow, who nodded in return before rendering Lady Miralys the full courtesy due her rank. The rudeness stopped short of outright insult; the Ridenow lord had just dismissed Gareth as if he were a child.

Gareth might have behaved badly four years ago, but he is an adult now, and the Heir to his Domain, Domenic thought with an intensity that surprised him.

"*Domna* Miralys, *Dom* Gareth, how good it is to see you

both again." Domenic put more than the required warmth into his words. He bowed, giving them each the courtesy of their greater rank.

Miralys returned his greeting with a graceful inclination of her head. "I have not had a chance to speak more than a word or two with your parents. How do they fare?"

"Very well, thank you." Domenic turned to Gareth. "It's good to see you again. Shall we try the sword dance tonight, as we used to do?"

Gareth's stiff expression melted into a genuine smile. "You'll still outshine me, I'm certain."

Danilo Syrtis emerged from the crowd, with Alanna resting her fingers lightly on his arm. Domenic struggled to keep from staring at her, a gross rudeness. He wanted to sweep her into his arms, devour her with kisses. Her very presence seared him. Every nerve quivered as if on fire when she tossed her head, sending her carefully arranged ringlets swinging.

As Danilo greeted the Elhalyns, his namesake joined them.

"Uncle!" Dani Hastur cried, receiving a kinsman's embrace. "I hoped you would come tonight."

"I never cared for formal occasions," Danilo said, "but it is good to see old friends again and for the young people to enjoy themselves."

The orchestra finished the last of Marguerida's compositions and played the introduction to one of the simpler reels. Couples formed lines down the center of the room, and the rest moved to the sides of the chamber.

"What a fine ball this is! And what splendid music!" Alanna glanced up at Gareth, pointedly expecting to be asked to dance. Looking delighted, he complied and led her out on to the floor.

Domenic watched them with a mixture of frustration and relief. Clearly, Alanna had seen him talking to Sibelle Ridenow and had decided to retaliate. For the space of a tune or two, Alanna would be happily occupied trying to make him jealous.

Domenic spotted his Aunt Liriel, graceful and imposing in a fall of emerald and silver crushed velvet. She caught his eye with a Tower worker's boldness and winked at him. He had always liked her and would have enjoyed a dance or two, as was perfectly appropriate with a kinswoman. Although large-boned and amply round, she was a graceful dancer, light on her feet, with an impeccable sense of rhythm. This evening, the pleasure would have to wait.

Remembering his promise, Domenic sought out Francisco's daughter. He could not ask a woman to whom he had not been introduced, but he had no doubt that within a short time, the attending fathers and brothers of all the *eligible young ladies* would remedy that.

Sibelle accepted his invitation with a shy smile. There was not much opportunity to talk, with the couples circling one another and exchanging places with their neighbors through the figures of the dance. As he escorted her back to her father, he found her just as pleasant as his first impression, well mannered, pliant, adoring. There was, in fact, no good reason why he should not agree to marry her . . . except his promise to Alanna. And the fact that he did not love her. He had no idea if, given time, he could. Alanna drew him like a lodestone, making it impossible for him to imagine himself taking any other woman to bed.

The evening went on, one dance after another, one lovely young partner after another. They were all from good families, with strong political connections, all educated but not overly intellectual. He felt his mother watching him from time to time and, in the background, Danilo moving about the room. Danilo did not dance, but he seemed to be involved in many conversations, especially with the Tower folk present.

As the older people finished their dancing, the music grew livelier. Simple reels and stately *promenadas* gave way to less restrained dances, a *secain,* a Terran waltz, and another dance, purported to be from Vainwal, that involved a great deal of swaying in close proximity to one's partner without any actual physical contact. Domenic's partner, a buxom, dark-haired girl introduced to him as *Dom* Lorrill Vallonde's niece, pretended to stumble so that he had no choice but to catch her in his arms. For an instant, she clung to him, pressing her body against his. He felt the roundness of her breasts, smelled her musky perfume and the hint of wine on her breath. Fluttering her eyelashes, she murmured that the dance had made her dizzy.

"Then you had best sit down, *damisela.*" Controlling his irritation, Domenic led her to a seat. "I would not risk you injuring yourself in a fall."

It was only going to get worse, he thought once he had performed the proper courtesies and disentangled himself, until a betrothal was announced, if not to Sibelle, then to some other young beauty. The matchmakers would not give up until, out of exhaustion or from some inadvertent indiscretion, he was trapped.

Even when the *catenas* was locked upon his wrist forever, he was not sure that some of these young ladies and their families might not keep trying. Not so long ago, many young women considered it an honor to bear a Comyn lord a son or daughter, even out of wedlock. He could probably father a dozen *nedestro* children upon eager *barraganas* to everyone's approval.

But I have no desire to lie with a woman I do not love.

"Why so glum? Are you not enjoying the dance?" In a swirl of creamy satin, Alanna skipped up to him. She'd clearly finished the entire dance, as well as several before it. The exercise brought a high, wild color to her cheeks. Tendrils of damp, coppery hair framed her face. "Or are you saving yourself for the famous sword dance? Will you astonish us all with your performance?"

Heat flared across Domenic's face. "Perhaps if I were halfway to being drunk, like some others, I might take more pleasure in the evening."

Alanna tossed her head. "Suit yourself, then, but do not expect anyone else to behave like a *cristoforo* tonight. Sweet Cassilda, it's hot! I'm nearly suffocated! Come on, let's get some fresh air before we turn grouchy and quarrel." Before he could object to the public indiscretion, she slipped her fingers through his and led him to the opened doors that looked out on the Castle courtyard.

On the veranda, couples strolled arm in arm, and he had no doubt that between the shadowed columns others were engaging in even greater intimacies. His mother would be outraged at his being seen in such surroundings with his cousin, and the thought gave him a pleasantly mutinous thrill.

The night air was cool and sweet. Inhaling, Domenic smelled rosalys and some spicy herb from the gardens. Three of the four moons hung like jewels in the velvet sweep of sky. Keeping hold of his hand, Alanna drew him across the courtyard. As soon as they reached the far side, he realized where she was headed—the tower where they had often played as children.

Domenic fully expected that once there, Alanna would make a scene about all the ladies he'd danced with. She might cry or scream at him, but her temper, although quickly roused, was as soon spent. It was not in her nature to hold a grudge. The stormy moment would pass, even as the evening did. In the privacy of the tower, they would be alone on Midsummer Festival night . . . His pulse leaped in his chest, and heat jolted through his groin.

Domenic took a lantern from the entrance alcove, kindled the flame, and held it aloft. Neither spoke as they climbed the old, familiar stone stairway. Breathing hard, Alanna lifted the latch of the door, strode across the room, and flung the shutters open. Below, the city blazed with light. Music and muted laughter floated on the night air. Festivities were well under way, dancing and merrymaking in the major streets and marketplaces.

Alanna braced herself on the window ledge and leaned out. Domenic stood behind her, waiting for her accusations. Instead, she seemed to grow still, inwardly focused. She pivoted toward him, her eyes glowing as if lit from within.

Unable to restrain himself any longer, he bent to kiss her. Her lips were soft, her breath sweet with the mingled smells of wine and flowers. A heady perfume arose from her skin. He felt dizzy, intoxicated, ravenous. Beneath his lips, hers parted, opening the slick warmth of her mouth to him.

With surprising intensity and hunger, Alanna kissed him back. She took his hand and placed it over her breast. Small whimpers, mingled pleasure and desire, rose in her throat. He felt her tremble even as he did.

The kiss went on, an eternity of rising, falling away, soaring. Domenic's heart hammered in his ears. Breath seared his lungs.

He fumbled with the complicated laces of her gown. She drew back, but only long enough to untie the little bows along the neckline. A slight twist, and her bare breast filled his hand.

He could feel her heart beating like mad, or maybe it was his own. Thought fell away, drowning in sensation. Her touch sent a surge of electric fire through the center of his body. Dimly, he realized that what they were doing could have only one conclusion.

Why not? This was Midsummer Festival, when all rules were forgotten. Were there not a dozen others doing the same throughout the garden, in the shadowed halls?

Were they not secretly betrothed? Did she not want it as much as he did?

Moaning, clawing at each other, they slid to the floor. His hands laced through her hair. The filigree clasp came away, releasing a cascade of silken waves.

She bit his neck. He felt the hard line of her teeth, the wetness of her tongue.

Oh gods, did she know what she was doing to him—what he was doing to her?

He lay partly on top of her, one of his legs between hers. She pushed his hip back and slipped her hand between them, stroking him. The touch excited him beyond anything he had ever experienced. He was almost painfully hard now.

Domenic gathered a handful of her skirts. The rumpled satin felt hot, alive. His fingers slid over her thighs. Gasping, he forced himself to slow down, to savor the smooth curves, but only for a moment. Alanna moaned again and shifted her body, opening her legs to his touch. Through the silk of her undergarment, her crotch felt hot and wet. He freed one hand to untie the lacing of his breeches.

With a sudden, hoarse cry, Alanna threw her head back. Her back arched in spasm. Her muscles locked, rigid.

Stunned, Domenic drew his hand back. Shock ripped through his body, as if she'd struck him. For a long, terrible moment, he feared she had stopped breathing. Then a bone-cracking shudder ripped through her body.

Domenic cradled Alanna's head and lowered her gently to the floor, then held her as her body twitched and flailed. The last of his arousal vanished into terror.

Convulsion! Threshold sickness?

Surely Alanna was too old for that, and she had studied at Arilinn . . . where the Keeper had suppressed her dangerous talent. What if her sexual feelings had been tied to her Gift?

Domenic's training at Neskaya Tower came back to him. He remembered one of his first teachers, an elderly monitor from Valeron, explaining that the same channels carried both sexual and psychic energy. Both awakened at puberty, sometimes resulting in the physical and emotional upheaval called threshold sickness. He'd had a mild case himself, but it could be deadly.

Lowering his *laran* shields, Domenic reached out to her. He sensed only a maelstrom of turbulent energy, radiating out from a core of madly swirling light. In that shifting chaos, figures formed and dissipated. Some of them seemed human, others misshapen like trailmen or tall as gods. Their images blew away like ghosts in a storm.

Alanna! Alanna, answer me!

She must be somewhere within that churning madness. No wonder she thought she was going insane.

Desperately, Domenic pushed against Alanna's mental

barriers. Deep within the chaos, he sensed a familiar presence. He called out again to her, silently, with all his mental strength. Was there a faint response?

Voices roared through his mind, but whether raised in joy or anger he could not tell. He heard rushing waters and then the crackle of flames, as if a whole range of forested mountains had been swept up into an inferno.

It was no good. He could not reach her through the power of her uncontrolled *laran*. He saw no way to create a link between their minds.

To create a link . . .

Alton blood as well as Hastur ran in Domenic's veins. He had *laran* and had been trained to use it. Moreover, he had the Alton Gift, although he had never used it before, had never had cause. The Gift of the Altons was forced rapport. His mother had the ability, although she rarely discussed it. So did his Grandfather Lew . . .

I must save her, even though I do not know how.

Domenic had heard of Terran explosives, utterly illegal under the Compact, but powerful. The image suggested a way to start. He abandoned his efforts to call out to Alanna. Instead, he focused all his strength on blasting through the wall of surging light. He imagined shock waves bursting through the tumult, fracturing the barrier between them.

Nothing seemed to happen. He sensed no change in the thrashing streams of light. Was his plan even possible?

Again, he thrust himself forward. The light parted for a moment. Exhilaration filled him—yes, it was working!

The shifting, chaotic brilliance of Alanna's vision closed in around Domenic, claiming him. Ordinary sensation fell away. The *laran* whirlwind buffeted him. He felt himself a tiny mote slammed this way and that.

Domenic lost all sense of direction; it took all his concentration to remember who he was, what he must do.

He was trapped.

How could he have been so foolhardy, so arrogant to think he could succeed—alone, without the safeguards of a monitor and Keeper? Now he had thrown away his own life as well as hers. Already the psychic storm ripped at his consciousness, shredding his boundaries.

Domenic saw himself collapsed over Alanna, cold and still in the tower room, his eyes vacant, his body a hollow shell. The image blew away, carrying pieces of his life force.

Somewhere in the unimaginable distance, a drum beat double time, lub-DUB, lub-DUB, and then faltered. The streaming brilliance faded to gray. He could almost make out the colorless sky of the Overworld, vast and arching into the far distance. The heartbeat fell away into silence. Strangely, he felt no fear.

Sensation crept over Domenic, as much remembered as real. In another instant he would feel the unyielding gray surface on which he stood. Something pulled at him—yes, there in the distance. People waited for him, called to him. He could not yet make out their faces. He knew only that very soon, he would belong with them. Nothing on earth, neither love nor duty nor honor, could hold him any longer.

10

Marguerida's heart gave a sudden lurch. She missed a beat of the *promenada* and stumbled. Only years of training in Darkovan dance kept her on her feet.

"Marguerida? Is something wrong?" asked her brother-in-law, Rafael Lanart, with whom she was dancing.

"I—I'm not sure." Blinking hard, Marguerida wavered on her feet. Pain lanced through her forehead, as if the simmering headache of the last few tendays had suddenly co-alésced into a spearpoint lodged in her skull.

"You look unwell." Rafael drew her away from the line of dancers. Music and movement swirled past, a lady in a coral-pink gown, Yllana dancing with one of the other young women, Rory laughing, tartans in a dozen patterns . . .

Her memory flew back to three years ago, when she had experienced a similar instant of disorientation. Then she had *known* something had happened to Regis Hastur, at the very moment he had suffered his fatal stroke.

Oh, no! Not again!

Her first thought was, as always, for Mikhail. She turned, searching for him across the seething mass of dancers. Rafael tried to restrain her. Pushing him away, she stumbled into the room. A few steps brought her to where she could glimpse her husband's golden head through a break in the dance formation. He was standing beside his pax-man and a group of minor nobles from the Venza Hills.

Mikhail!

Preciosa, *I am here,* he answered. *What is wrong?*

My Aldaran Gift is acting up again. I haven't felt it this strongly since Regis died.

Can you tell who is the focus?

Marguerida shook her head. The movement upset her balance. She barely felt Rafael's hands, guiding her to a cushioned chair along one wall. The music, a traditional tune that she knew by heart, dissolved into discordant notes.

The world fractured into shards of color and sound—Rafael, bending over her, his face grave with concern—her father, his face young, unscarred—Gareth dancing with Sibelle—Donal Alar—a girl she did not know, with dark hair and strangely familiar golden eyes—Regis—

But Regis died three years ago! And the girl . . .

Marguerida realized that she had glimpsed her own mother as a young woman. Somehow, she had come unstuck in time . . .

This is not happening to me! It is someone else . . . *but who?*

By sheer force of will, Marguerida wrenched her mind free. She had not survived a horrendous childhood in a Thendara orphanage and being overshadowed by the ancient Keeper Ashara, only to give in to someone else's nightmare now!

But who—?

"Where is Domenic?" She could not be sure if she whispered the words or shouted them.

Instantly, she felt Mikhail's response. *I do not see him.*

"Rafael, help me. I need to find my son."

"The last time I saw him, he was dancing with *Dom* Francisco's daughter."

Francisco, that snake! Fury shook her. *If he's done anything to harm Nico . . .*

Mikhail made his way across the room toward her. *Dearest, Francisco and his daughter are still here. Domenic is not with them.*

Danilo emerged from the crowd, his step as firm as a swordsman's. Concern shadowed his eyes. "*Domna* Marguerida, are you well?"

Marguerida gathered herself. The last thing she needed now was for the entire room to witness her distress, especially when she did not yet know the source.

Who—of course!

Mikhail reached her. "Mik!" she cried. "It's Alanna! I always knew she would bring disaster to someone close to me!"

"To Domenic?" Mikhail said. "Or to Alanna herself?"

"I don't know!" Marguerida struggled to control her rising panic, to think rationally. "Perhaps the same danger threatens them both."

"I will find them." Rafael strode toward the open doors, followed by Donal.

Marguerida's vision paled again. "Rafael will not find them . . ." Her voice sounded as if it came from far away, through a hollow tunnel. "They are not on the veranda, nor in the courtyard garden . . ."

Nico! she called with her mind.

To her surprise, she sensed a lingering imprint of where Domenic *had been.* His mind, the essence of who her son was, had already left the physical plane.

The headache dissolved into a wave of overwhelming fear. Domenic was the treasure she and Mikhail had brought back from their strange journey through time. He was the heir of their joined spirits as well as their flesh. Rory and Yllana were sweet children and she loved them, but she had only one firstborn.

With all the desperate love in her and all the power of her *laran,* Marguerida cried out, "*Come back! Come back to me!*"

To her astonishment, she felt her words make contact. It was as if she had thrown a lifeline to a man submerged beneath a storm-wracked sea and felt the slight tug as his fingers closed around the rope.

Nico! Where are you?

. . . not sure . . . came the muted response. The contact carried an odd reverberation, as if it passed through a dimensional barrier.

Heedless of the cost to herself. Marguerida poured more energy into the link between them. She might have only one chance to save her son before he drifted beyond any hope of rescue; she must not hold anything back. Colors flickered through her mind, fading to the gray of the Overworld. Yes, that would explain the subtle reverberation.

Mother of Oceans! How did he get there?

She had no time to speculate on the answer. From her own experience as well as her brief formal training in a Tower, she understood the dangers that the timeless, immaterial world held for the unprepared.

It did not matter *how* or *why* Domenic had strayed into the Overworld. She must get him back into the physical plane as soon as possible.

Hold on to me, she called. *I am going to pull you out.*

For a moment that could have been long or short, she could not tell, Domenic did not answer. When he did, his mental voice was stronger.

Not yet. I must find . . . His mental trace faded, but only because he had turned his attention elsewhere. *It's all right, Mother. You've showed me the way back. I know what to do from here.*

Before Marguerida could insist that Domenic return at once, his mind touched hers again. This time there was no dissonance resulting from the gap between normal reality and the Overworld. She felt his clear, immediate presence.

I'm all right. I'm back.

Between one heartbeat and the next, the world steadied. The pressure in Marguerida's temples vanished. Her vision snapped into clarity. Mikhail bent over her, chafing her hands between his. A few people had gathered about them with anxious expressions, Lew among them. Danilo dispersed them with quiet skill, undoubtedly learned from years of protecting Regis. Francisco watched from a distance, a brooding expression in his eyes.

Rafael returned, shaking his head. "I could not find either of them out there."

"Nico's all right—" Her knees threatened to buckle under her. She felt as feeble as if she had emerged from a tenday fever. Her eyes would not focus properly. She recognized the symptoms of *laran* exhaustion.

Mikhail caught her elbow. "Dearest, what is it?"

Oh, Mik! He was lost in the Overworld!

But you found him, love.

Yes, that's true enough. He is out of danger now.

"Let me get you some wine," Rafael said.

"No! No wine." The last thing she needed was alcohol. She was dizzy enough, sober.

"Water, then," Lew said firmly, "and something to eat. You are dangerously depleted and must rest."

It was useless to protest when her father used that tone of voice. Weakly, Marguerida nodded. She forced herself to sip the cup and nibble on the sugared nuts that Danilo handed her. At last, she managed to reassure Mikhail that she would not faint. After making sure Domenic was unhurt, she would return to their quarters and lie down.

She heard shouting through the open doors, from the direction of the outside streets. Donal came toward them, moving with the brisk efficiency that had served him well as Mikhail's paxman. His expression bore no traces of holiday merriment.

"*Dom* Mikhail, there is trouble at the Castle gates. You must come at once!"

——— ◆ ———

Sight returned to Domenic. He came to himself lying on his side, clasping an unconscious Alanna to him. His mother's mental linkage remained, still glowing, in the back of his mind. He doubted he could have found his way back without her.

Carefully, Domenic disentangled himself from Alanna without waking her and went to the window of the tower room. Weakness shivered through him, as if he had run all the way from Edelweiss to Thendara. It would pass in a moment, or so he hoped. Nauseated, gulping air, he braced himself on the window sill. The overlapping images of Alanna's vision and the Overworld faded to reveal the city below.

A crowd had gathered in one of the broader streets leading to Comyn Castle. These were not innocent holiday-makers, he felt sure. He was too drained to detect their emotions with his *laran,* but something in their massed purpose brought him alert. Torches bobbed, swarming toward the Castle gates. He heard raised voices, although he could not make out any words.

Alanna stirred and cried out, a muffled sob. "Nico, I feel so strange. What happened to me? Have I been ill?"

Domenic knelt at her side, afraid to touch her for fear of setting off another attack. "It's all right," he murmured. "Whatever it was, it can't hurt you now."

Alanna clambered unsteadily to her feet. She glanced down at her dress, her skirts in disarray, one breast exposed. "Oh! Oh, dear! Oh, turn around until I am decent!"

Domenic returned to the window to give her a measure of privacy. He heard the soft rustle of satin, and when he glanced back, she had covered herself, rearranged her rumpled dress, and was retying the little bows on the neckline of her gown.

The noise of the crowd outside had grown louder; the mob must have drawn closer. Should he give the alarm, summon the Guards? Did he dare to leave Alanna in this state? Could he reach someone with his *laran*? He was not sure he could summon the strength, and it might be dangerous to try so soon after his journey into the Overworld.

"Domenic, what it is? What's going on?"

"I must go down," Domenic said.

"No!" Quick as a snow-leopard, she seized his arm. Her grip was like steel. "Don't leave me!"

He did not want to hurt her by pulling away, and yet he could not remain up here. "Alanna, my place is down below. Are you able to walk? I do not want to leave you alone, but I have no choice."

Alanna's eyes cleared. "I don't know what I was thinking. Of course, it is our duty. We must both go. Just a moment." She finished the last bow, picked up the fallen clasp, and set her hair back into place with a few deft movements. By some female magic, her ringlets looked charming, rather than disorderly. He had no idea how she had done it.

He took the lantern, and together they hurried downstairs. The Castle gates stood open, as was traditional during Festival night. Torches mounted on either side, as well as a dozen or more in the hands of the mob, cast their light across the threshold. Guards took up positions between the crowd and the Castle.

Domenic pushed forward, trying to understand what was going on. Who were these people? What did they want?

"By my authority as Captain of the City Guards," Cisco shouted, "I order you to disperse! Go home, all of you, before someone gets hurt!"

"Not until we're been heard!" To Domenic's ears, the man sounded more than a little drunk. His comrades muttered agreement, although none of them moved forward. For the moment, there was an uneasy standoff.

"Where is the Regent?" yelled a man toward the back of the crowd.

"Aye, have him come down to us!" The crowd rumbled, a stormfront about to break.

"Zandru's frozen hells!" one of the Guardsmen cried, spying Alanna. "*Vai damisela,* this is no place for you. You must go back inside, where you will be safe!"

Alanna grabbed Domenic's arm and glanced at him with such mingled horror and despair that he wondered if she had seen this night in one of her visions.

"Stay close by me, then," he told her. Then, to the Guardsman, "I'll take care of her."

"If you have a complaint," Cisco shouted at the crowd, "bring it to the Cortes in the proper manner! This is Festival night."

Domenic had heard about flash fires, in which tinder-dry resin-trees and pitch pine, heavy with inflammable sap, would explode into flame at the tiniest spark. So now, the crowd hesitated, poised to ignite. To Domenic, half of them seemed too drunk on Festival wine to know what they were doing, but others were genuinely angry.

"We'll have our say when and where we please! Ain't taking no orders from . . ." The rest of the man's words were lost in a surging rumble.

The Guards raised their swords into ready position. Bare steel reflected the light of the torches.

I am the Heir to Hastur, Domenic thought. *I must do something.*

He could not think what action to take, except to jump between the mob and the Castle defenders, and what good could come of that? The ceremonial sword at his belt would be of little use in a real fight. Yet he could not let the encounter escalate, with no possible end but bloodshed.

Even as he reached for his useless sword, Domenic drew his hand away. What was he thinking? These men were not his enemies, they were his own people. For all he knew, Zared and Ennis were among them, men to whom he had an obligation of honor. Although his *laran* energies were severely depleted by his journey through the Overworld, he sensed their surging emotions; his original impression had been right—discontent and confusion, tinged by fear, blurred by drink and whipped to near frenzy by a few shouted slogans.

"Death to the Comyn!" a voice near the edge of the crowd boomed out. "Down with the tyrant Regent!"

"Wait here." Domenic nudged Alanna into the hands of the nearest Guard and stepped forward.

"What is going on?" Domenic gestured to the nearest man, thinking that if he could reason with one of them, he might calm the volatile mood. "You, there—why are you here, instead of at home, celebrating? Have you no wife or sweetheart, no sister or mother, to honor with fruit and flowers? No kinsmen to share song and dance?"

The man Domenic had spoken to hung his head. Domenic took another step forward. He lowered his voice, addressing this one man alone, his tones as soothing as if he were quieting a restive horse. The muttering died down as the others listened.

"My friend," Domenic went on, "whatever your sorrows, they cannot be solved here, on the street, and on Festival Night. This should be a time for fellowship and rejoicing, not brawling in the streets. Go back to your family, offer your devotion to your womenfolk as Hastur did to Cassilda."

"Who is this pup? This silver-tongued lapdog?" shouted a tall, rangy man with a soldier's bearing. Torchlight glinted off his pale hair. Domenic had not seen him clearly before, yet his had been one of the loudest voices, the one calling for death to the Comyn.

Domenic faced the heckler directly. "I am—"

"We'll not be put off!" the blond man interrupted. "We want the Regent himself!"

"Yes, have him come forth!" another man now took up the cry.

"Grab the boy!" someone else called. "Make the tyrant listen to us!"

"There is no need for force!" Holding his ground, heedless of the danger, Domenic raised his voice in an effort to make himself heard. "Listen to me. We are not enemies!"

Something gray and fist-sized shot out from their midst—a stone, Domenic thought, but things were happening too fast to be sure. Behind him, one of the Guardsmen let out a muffled cry and fell to his knees.

Fear shot through the air, mixed with the metallic reek of fresh blood and adrenaline. Two of the Guard's fellows, their swords already poised, lunged forward. Cisco Ridenow shouted out for them to halt.

"Enough!"

A single word, spoken with unshakeable confidence, shimmering with power, sliced through the escalating tension. As one, the mob hesitated.

Domenic turned, along with the others. His father stood there, silhouetted against the brightness of the Castle. Behind him came half a dozen Comyn lords in their glittering formal clothing. Domenic recognized Danilo Syrtis, Uncle Rafael, Francisco Ridenow. His mother pushed forward, leaning on Grandfather Lew's arm. Rory and his friend Niall rushed to stand beside their fellow Guardsmen.

"Down with the Regent!" the blond man shouted. In a flicker of torchlight, Domenic saw him draw back his arm to throw something.

The second rock struck Mikhail's head. He staggered under the impact. Marguerida and Lew caught him in their arms and lowered him to the ground. Domenic rushed back up the steps, thinking only that he belonged at his father's side.

Marguerida straightened up beside her fallen husband. She held out her left hand. Blood stained the fine embroidered cloth of the glove.

Domenic sensed her fierce protective rage through the waves of her exhaustion, for it had cost her greatly to reach him in the Overworld. Her face was hard and set, her golden eyes blazing, her chest heaving. There was no place on Darkover or beyond that she could not reach, nothing she would not do, to save the ones she loved. For Mikhail, the touchstone of her heart, she would blast her way through Zandru's Seven Frozen Hells.

Trembling visibly, Marguerida fumbled with the blood-stained glove. Underneath it lay the shadow matrix, the immensely powerful device she had used, along with Mikhail's ring, to defeat the Terran ambush at Old North Road.

MARJA, NO!

Domenic could not be sure if he had heard his grandfather's anguished cry or only felt it within his own mind.

Faintly, as if from a far distance, he heard a woman's inconsolable sobs, a voice hoarse with screaming. In the back of his mind, fire raged on the heights, a great form like a woman of flame stretched out her arms . . .

The next moment, Lew grasped Marguerida's free hand, immobilizing her.

No, Lew pleaded silently, *not again. Not against our own people.*

Mikhail clambered to his feet and stood on the steps. Blood, slick and dark in the torchlight, drenched one side of his forehead, but his gaze remained steady, his bearing proud.

The Castle defenders stood as if frozen, all except the injured Guard, who had gotten to his feet, clutching his shoulder.

Domenic braced himself for another tirade from the pale-haired man or one of the others who had been so belligerent, but no attack came. The crowd muttered among themselves, sounding more ashamed and confused than angry. He sensed they had not meant for the confrontation to escalate into violence, for blood to be shed.

"Good people!" Mikhail's voice rang out. "Let us not quarrel with one another in this holy Festival season. Whatever your concerns, surely they deserve our most serious and careful consideration." With the smallest motion of one hand, he indicated, *Not like this, with tempers hot and too much wine for clear thinking.* Animosity seeped from the crowd with each phrase.

One of the men, the one who had first demanded to be heard, held his ground. "How do we know the Council will listen to us and not turn us away, as they have before?"

Domenic recognized the man's mountain garb—worn boots, shaggy fur shirt-cloak, long hair braided with strips of dyed leather and eagle feathers. The man's skin was seamed and roughened by weather.

"What is your name?" Mikhail beckoned for the man to come closer. The crowd grew quiet, as if holding their breaths. At last, the man shuffled forward.

"Maury, *vai dom*. That's my cousin there, Raymon, and his wife's kinsman, Arnat. We came in from Kazarin Forst on the far side of the Venzas. We're desperate, *vai dom*. Our children are dying. But the Cortes judge said the matter was not for him, he had no power to help us, and no one else would even listen."

"Now someone will. Present yourselves at the Castle on the third day of the session of the Comyn Council, and whatever the matter is, we will hear you. *I* will hear you. I promise it. I, Mikhail Lanart-Hastur, Warden of Hastur and Regent of the Comyn, give you my solemn word. Will that satisfy you?"

"It is the Regent himself . . ."

"The Hastur-lord!"

"Hastur . . ." whispered through the crowd.

Domenic remembered the almost superstitious awe with which common people regarded Regis Hastur. It was not so long ago that the Comyn were believed to be half gods, descended from Hastur, Son of Aldones, who was Lord of Light. Most ordinary folk still considered *laran* to be akin to sorcery.

The man nodded. "The word of a Hastur is all my people have ever needed."

The word of a Hastur . . . an unbreakable oath.

Amazement passed over Maury's face. He inclined his head again and took a step backward. He spoke a few words to the crowd; the other men began to disperse. Domenic looked again for the pale-haired man, the one who had thrown the rocks and goaded the mob to violence, but he had vanished as surely as if the night had swallowed him up. Without his urging, the fight had gone out of the crowd.

Sobbing, Alanna rushed to Marguerida. Cisco took the injured man aside and sent him to the Guards infirmary.

"The rest of you, inside," Mikhail said. "Midsummer or not, lock the gates. See to it, Captain."

Cisco issued a string of orders, rescinding the leave granted to various officers for the Festival ball. Rory and his friend headed back to the barracks to arm and uniform themselves properly. The remaining Guardsmen held their position, for they would stay at increased alertness through the night while a search was made for the man who threw the rocks.

Grandfather Lew looked as if he were about to topple over, not from any physical injury but from psychic shock.

Danilo slipped one hand under the older man's elbow to steady him. "*Dom* Lewis, you must rest."

"Mik, come away," Marguerida said, as she tried to console Alanna. Her voice rang with fatigue. "You must let a healer attend to your head."

"There will be time for that later, as well," Mikhail answered gently. "I'm in no danger at the moment. Scalp wounds always look worse than they really are. First, I must see to the safekeeping of the Castle."

I can do my work better without worrying about you, should there be more trouble. Domenic sensed his father's unspoken thought. Marguerida clearly understood, for she hurried Alanna inside the Castle. The other Comyn lords put away their swords and followed them inside.

Mikhail gestured for Domenic to come close. "You did well out there, son."

Domenic grimaced and ducked his head. "Not well enough."

"Don't underestimate yourself. You dealt with a very difficult, dangerous situation as few men, even those your senior by many years, could have done. Many more would have been injured, perhaps even killed, if you had not calmed the crowd as you did. You showed true leadership, and I'm proud of you."

Domenic did not know what to say. He warmed inside at his father's praise, but was not sure he truly deserved it. He had done only what needed to be done, and, in the end, it was his father who had taken the lead.

Perhaps, he thought, *that is what leadership is about, the ability to inspire each person to do his part. Me, Father, Mother, Captain Cisco, even Grandfather Lew . . . none of us could have resolved the confrontation without the others.*

"There is something else you ought to know about," Domenic said, and he told his father about his meeting with the men from Mariposa, how they had come all the way to Thendara for the judgment, and how he had decided their case.

Mikhail nodded, thoughtful. "We've had a *coridom* at Mariposa. He's a competent estate manager, but he's limited in what else he can do. You handled the Mariposa situation well, son. I don't think even Regis himself could have done it better. I also agree with you, there is more going on tonight than rabble drunk on Festival wine.

"Meanwhile," Mikhail went on, "there is much to be done. Domenic, I want you to see to the inside of the Castle. Make sure everyone at the ball gets safely to their quarters. Those who live in the city must remain here tonight. Your mother will make all the arrangements." Mikhail's mouth softened. "You know that she will fret until I'm at her side again. Make sure she takes care of herself. You're probably the only other person besides me that she will listen to."

"I'll do my best, Father."

"That's all any of us can do."

———— ✦ ————

In the ballroom, very little was left of the festivities. The Castle staff were already clearing the tables of food and wine punch, and the musicians had put away their instruments. Domenic spoke with them, carrying out his father's instructions. Everyone looked less anxious as he explained what was being done to ensure their safety. Yllana, who had been ordered to remain inside, took the news of Mikhail's injury with calm practicality. Only the sudden paleness of her cheeks revealed her distress. She gave Domenic a quick hug and then hurried away to help Marguerida.

Francisco was still present, standing in the arched doorway leading toward the living quarters of the castle, talking earnestly with Sibelle. Her face was red and swollen. As

Domenic drew near, she broke down, sobbing, "I don't like this place, Papa! I want to go home!" She sounded so like a frightened child that Domenic wondered how old she really was.

Francisco said something to her, using a voice too low for Domenic to make out all the words, only isolated phrases. "You will behave with dignity, do you understand . . . not like a sniveling dairy girl!" Sibelle turned white and silent. Francisco went on, "You are Comynara, of an ancient and noble house . . . such a display brings dishonor to us all!"

Francisco spied Domenic and turned to him, quickly composing his features and delivering a formal bow. He inquired after Mikhail and the injured Guard. Domenic replied that his father was well enough to carry out his duties as Regent, protecting the Castle and everyone within its walls.

"I am shocked that such barbarity should mar this most important of all festivals," Francisco said. "It is unfortunate that better order could not be maintained in the city."

"Yes, very unfortunate," Domenic replied, stung by the implication that his father's incompetence had resulted in a breakdown in civil peace. If he had not seen Francisco at the ball earlier, he would suspect him of creating the disturbance.

Sibelle, her hand clutching her father's arm, gave a little whimper. Francisco glanced from her white face to Domenic. Noticing the calculating gleam in the older man's eyes, Domenic cursed silently. Francisco's next move would doubtless be to ask Domenic to escort his tearful, clinging, alluringly pretty daughter to her chamber.

This madness must end now!

After his aborted lovemaking with Alanna and its near-disastrous consequences, the very idea of wooing this distraught child sickened Domenic. Political considerations be damned, he could not, *would not* play such games.

Domenic remembered what Danilo had said about Regis, that he forged his own way through the demands and intense pressures of his family, the worst the Comyn Council could bring to bear on him. How he found a way to marry for love, to keep those he truly cherished close to him.

If Regis could do it, Domenic thought, then so could he!

"*Dom* Francisco," Domenic said, squaring his shoulders and fixing the older man with a level gaze, "your daughter is overwrought. You must take her home. Court is no place for such a tender flower."

Francisco responded with a condescending smile. "In the morning, the streets will be cleared and the rabble subdued. At least, I presume so. My daughter will be happier once order is properly restored. Won't you, 'Belle?"

"Yes, Papa."

Domenic's jaw muscles clenched. Sibelle glanced up at him beneath fluttering lashes, and he refused to smile in response.

"You misunderstand me." Domenic faced Francisco squarely. "I meant home to Serrais. I meant the schemes of the Council and all its members. Such an innocent should not be bartered in marriage like a side of meat—exactly how old are you, *chiya*?"

"Four—fourteen."

A year younger than Yllana! Domenic let her words hang in the air for a moment. Then he beckoned to one of the Castle servants, a round-cheeked, grandmotherly woman who was helping to clear away the remains of the buffet.

"The *damisela* is distraught, as you can see. Would you be so kind as to escort her back to her quarters in the Ridenow section?"

The woman dropped a curtsy and held out her arms to Sibelle. "You poor child, I know just the thing to settle your nerves. We'll get you snug in bed in no time."

Sniffling, Sibelle glanced up at her father. He murmured, "Go along, child. I'll be with you shortly."

Sibelle leaned on the older woman as they hurried from the hall. The last thing Domenic heard from them was the old servant asking, "Do you like hot honeyed milk?"

"You are making a quite unnecessary fuss," Francisco

said, once Sibelle and the servant had passed through the far doorway. "She is a woman and of an age to marry. I am certain of it."

Without the worry of shocking Sibelle, Domenic felt no need to mince words. "And I am certain that neither you, nor the Council, nor all the demons in Zandru's Forge, will induce me to marry for any other reason than my own desire, certainly not to a girl the same age as my baby sister!"

"The difference in years is of little consequence. A few seasons will remedy it."

Domenic felt the heat rising in his chest, unable to believe that Francisco was still pursuing his marriage scheme. Domenic drew himself taller and stepped toward the older man. Francisco held his ground, looking grim now, and subtly dangerous. Domenic was too irate to care.

"Can I make my position any plainer?" Domenic demanded. "I will not be your puppet and neither should Sibelle. She is your own daughter! Have you no care for her happiness?"

"I have every consideration for the welfare of the Ridenow Domain and of us all," Francisco retorted with equal fervor. "You have been cloistered away in a Tower for too long, or you yourself would see the necessity of this union. As for my daughter's happiness, that lies in doing her duty. She knows what honor demands of her. Do *you?* "

Francisco paused, his once-handsome features twisting in a way that sent alarms chilling along Domenic's spine. "Or are you saying you are not fit to marry? Are you mentally impaired, or dissolute and cruel, or perhaps you are simply unable to consummate a marriage?"

Domenic's temper flared, and he bit back the automatic rejoinder that he was none of these things. As quickly, he realized this was exactly what Francisco intended, to goad him into an outburst, to blurt out things that could not be unsaid, perhaps even to trap him into the choice between a duel of honor or a marriage.

"We are not living in the Ages of Chaos, when marriages were arranged by the Council for reasons of their own."

Domenic kept his tone even, although his nerves shrilled with outrage. "Sibelle deserves a husband who will cherish her, one she chooses with her own heart. I will never agree to less. I will select my own bride in my own time. If you think that renders me unfit, you are free to bring charges against me in Council! Explain to *them* how you schemed to get back into power by sacrificing a girl barely into womanhood!"

Stunned silence answered him. Before Francisco could say anything more, Domenic delivered a short, clipped bow and strode away. As he left the hall, Domenic wondered if he had done a very foolish thing, confronting Francisco like that. The man was capable of anything! It would be only one of a number of idiotic risks Domenic had taken that evening, from indulging himself with Alanna, to his reckless journey in the Overworld, to placing himself within reach of the mob at the gates, and now, taunting a man known for holding deadly grudges. Undoubtedly, the Ridenow lord would find some way to use the incident to his own advantage.

Aldones, I must be tired, to see plots everywhere!

Or was he at last learning to think like a Comyn?

11

Domenic found his mother and Alanna in the parlor beside a newly lit fire. Yllana had already eaten and gone off to supervise those tasks that could not wait. Several plates covered with crumbs and morsels left over from a hasty meal sat on the table. One platter of nuts, dried fruits, and various cookies was almost untouched.

Delicately, Marguerida licked the last of a honey-roll from her fingers. The sweet, rich pastry had restored a measure of vitality after her *laran* exertions. Already, she looked stronger and more alert.

The delicious aromas made Domenic's mouth water. Suddenly ravenous, he took a mouthful and let the concentrated sweetness flow over his tongue. His mind steadied as the food replenished his body.

Alanna, however, had gone quiet and blank-eyed. She took Domenic's hand, childlike, as he sat down beside her on the divan.

"I can't stay any longer," Marguerida said. "Nico, dear, see if you can get Alanna to eat." She left to find rooms for their city guests. When Mikhail finally returned, he would find a hot meal and a healer waiting for him.

"Alanna?" Domenic peered into her face, half afraid of what he might see.

"Yes, Domenic?" she said with alarming placidity.

"Are you all right? Can you try a few bites?"

A shudder passed through her. "I'm a little sick to my stomach."

"The healer will be here soon." Even as he spoke, Domenic knew that no ordinary healer could help her. This was more than physical shock or fright from the confrontation with the mob.

At Neskaya, he had learned what should be done. Food, rest, *kirian* . . . the care of a trained monitor. He could do the monitoring, since every Tower novice received the basic training. But would it be safe to touch her, even mind to mind? *Especially* mind to mind? No, it would be better for someone not emotionally involved to do the work.

Urgently, because he did not know how much private time they might have, Domenic bent close to Alanna. "I am sorry for my part in this . . . in what happened to you," he added, seeing her look of confusion. "Your vision."

"Oh," Awareness seeked back into her eyes. "Yes, I had another one, didn't I? It was rather unpleasant. I suppose I must have been frightened, but I don't feel that way now. I just feel . . . tired."

She stood up, holding on to the chair for support. "I will rest better in my own bed."

"Alanna, I promised Mother that I would make you eat. You know you need to replenish the energy drained by your *laran*."

"But I'm not hungry," Alanna whined.

"That's because your appetite has shut down, and it's not a good sign."

"I'm tired. I want to lie down."

Domenic felt a flicker of impatience. Hadn't she heard anything he'd said? In all probability, given the events of the evening, neither of them was entirely rational. He took a slice of iced spicebark cake, broke it, and held out one half to her.

"Here, taste this." He popped the other half into his own mouth. "It's good, just like the ones we used to steal from the kitchen."

With an aggrieved sign, Alanna accepted the sweet and nibbled a tiny bit. A moment later, she was avidly chewing, grabbing one cookie after another. A handful of nut candy followed, and then she paused.

"You were right," she admitted. "I *was* hungry. But I'm so tired, I feel as if I might faint at any moment . . . Please, Nico, let me go to my room. I'll take some dried apples and eat them later, I promise."

Unsure if he were doing the right thing, Domenic let her go. Alanna's lack of emotion worried him. She had always been so intense, so full of life. Now she seemed withdrawn, as if the events of the evening had happened to someone else. Did she remember what they had been doing before the vision seized her? Perhaps, like a Keeper of old, she had shut away that part of herself.

A few moments later, the Castle healer, a buxom, middle-aged woman named Charissa, arrived. The healer's gray-streaked auburn hair suggested that she had a small measure of *laran,* enough to enhance her sensitivity to her patients. She carried a basket of supplies: bandages, gauze pads, bottles of antiseptic and pain-numbing tinctures, silk-wrapped packets of costly needles and suturing materials.

"My father has not yet returned," Domenic said. "As you see, I am well, but Alanna seems dizzy and confused. She has gone to rest in her own room. Will you look in on her?"

"Yes, indeed, since she is the only one here who needs my care," Charissa said, clearly annoyed at having been summoned in the middle of the night, only to find that the people she was to attend had taken themselves elsewhere. "If *Dom* Mikhail returns, ask him to do me the courtesy of remaining in one place until I can examine him."

Charissa hurried off to Alanna's bedchamber and returned, frowning, a short time later. When Marguerida came in, Charissa took her aside and they spoke for a few moments in low, urgent voices. Marguerida sent a servant in search of Istvana Ridenow.

Relief surged through Domenic. Istvana was not only his mother's dear friend, but the Keeper of Neskaya Tower. She would know what to do for Alannna.

Istvana arrived at the same time as trays of hot food and

drink. Silver-haired and diminutive, Istvana carried herself with brisk authority. She stayed only a moment before going off to see to Alanna.

A moment later, Mikhail returned. Charissa made him sit down while she washed and bandaged his head.

"Scalp wounds often bleed freely, and this one will most likely leave a scar. I do wish you would allow me to suture it." Charissa frowned. "I cannot tell if there has been any deeper damage."

"Istavana must monitor him as soon as possible to be sure," Marguerida said.

"Love, don't fuss over me," said Mikhail.

"Fuss! Mik, that blow knocked you off your feet! You could have a hairline skull fracture, a brain hemorrhage, a concussion—"

Mikhail raised his hands. "If it will reassure you, then let Istvana examine my head. Thank you for your care, *Mestra* Charissa."

With a sympathetic smile, Charissa said, "I'll ask the *vai leronis* to come to you."

"As soon as possible," Marguerida said, adding, "if you would be so kind."

Later, Domenic lay in his own chamber, waiting for sleep. It was slow in coming. His thoughts jumped from one thing to another, going over the events of the evening. Who was the pale-haired man who had urged the crowd to violence? What if the rock had struck his father a little higher or lower? What if Charissa were wrong and Mikhail had suffered a serious injury?

Eventually, he convinced himself that his father would be all right. And at least, Marguerida had not asked what Domenic was doing in the Overworld.

As for Alanna . . . people survived threshold sickness, didn't they? Alanna could not be in better care than Istvana's. Domenic would make sure that nothing happened to trigger another crisis.

Now that the excitement was over, he considered the implications of Alanna's seizure. She might recover with time . . . but what would prevent another, possibly fatal episode the next time they tried to make love? Once they were married, how could that be avoided? They would be expected to produce children. Could he lie beside her, night after night, as chaste as a *cristoforo* monk? The sight and smell of her had been enough to drive him half-mad.

What kind of a marriage would they have, if he dared not touch her again? Yet, what choice did he have? He had made a promise, and could not forsake her now.

———— ✦ ————

Marguerida, having satisfied herself that the most pressing tasks had been attended to, allowed herself a moment of quiet in her office. With a sigh of relief, she eased herself into her favorite chair.

A faint, comforting fragrance of balsam still hung in the air. The fires had not been lit, but the air was warm enough. She needed no more light than the gentle glow from the candelabrum she had brought with her, and in any event, she could have found her way around the furniture in the dark, the room was so familiar.

She had been managing Comyn Castle for a number of years, gradually taking over the most onerous duties from Lady Linnea while Regis was still alive. The servants and stewards knew her expectations; even wearied as they were from the Midsummer ball preparations, they had aired out chambers for those Comyn who lived in the city, prepared hot meals for humans and cold ones for their horses, and the hundred other things that Marguerida did not need to specify. Everyone who had been hurt was being treated, everyone else had been informed and reassured, no one was hungry or without a bed to sleep in, and the Castle was secure for the night.

Closing her eyes, she rubbed her temples and tried to decide if this particular headache was simple stress, an aftermath of *laran* exhaustion, or yet another nudge form her

Aldaran Gift. The night's events certainly qualified as a crisis, but she felt certain that the worst was not yet over.

The constant state of apprehension was wearing her down, making it harder to think things through. She needed a good night's sleep. More precisely, she needed a good night's sleep in the arms of her husband. Just thinking of him, his breath warm on her hair, his love sustaining her, sent a wave of relaxation through her body. She thought of reaching out to him with her thoughts, of speaking with him mind to mind, as they so often did, but he was hurt and weary and still had work to do this night. They would be together soon enough.

Meanwhile . . . there were too many things from this night that she did not understand. To be sure, she had been caught off-guard by the mob. She was familiar with various complaints from farmers and herdsmen; there was always some difficultly: drought or mud slides, the ever-present danger of fires, diseases of livestock, or trading conditions. What could have stirred them up so? *To violence?*

In her mind, Marguerida relived that heart-stopping moment as the rock sailed through the air, the sickening sound as it struck Mikhail, the way her entire body shook with the impact, as if she herself had been hit. And when she looked down at her hand and saw his blood—

He could have been killed!

With a sob, Marguerida buried her face in her hands. She had not realized how tightly she had been holding her emotions in check.

I've got to get hold of myself! There's too much still to be done. The children need me—Mik needs me. I can't break down like this!

Mikhail had *not* been killed, she reminded herself, nor had the injured Guardsman. She and her husband would face the next day together, and the day after that, as they had always done. They had come through the Battle of Old North Road, Francisco's attempted assassination, Ashara's menace, and the death of Regis, not to mention Javanne's schemes . . .

Just as Marguerida was beginning to feel more herself, she heard a tap at the door.

"Father!" She ran to the door, opened it, and let him in. As he took the proffered seat, she noticed how weary he looked, and how grim.

"Has something else happened? Should you not be in your own bed, resting?" she asked anxiously.

"Yes, I ought. But there is a matter of more importance we must discuss first."

He sounded so like the distant, critical parent of her childhood that Marguerida held her tongue with an effort.

Suddenly, the moment after the rock had struck Mikhail flashed before her eyes.

"Marja, no!" Lew's mental voice reverberated again through her mind. She had been half out of her wits with desperation at the time, yet his words had held her immobile for a crucial moment.

"Not against our own people!"

Remembering, her gaze flew to the glove on her left hand. She had not had a spare moment to change clothing, and the bloodstains on the palm and fingers were dry. When Lew had cried out, there on the Castle steps, she had been struggling to remove the glove, to bare the shadow matrix embedded in her skin, to use it . . .

. . . as she had used it at the Battle of Old North Road?

Marguerida gulped. Was that truly what she had intended? To blast those men—*our own people*—as she had Belfontaine's soldiers? It was impossible, for the fireball that brought an end to that battle had required the combined power of her shadow matrix and Mikhail's ring. But the sight of Mikhail's blood had driven out all rational thought. She had acted out of pure instinct. If Lew had not stopped her . . .

"I don't know what got into me," she stammered. "I'm not a violent person. I've always tried to use my Gifts," and here, her eyes flickered once more to her gloved hand, "only for good."

Lew nodded, and for an instant his eyes took on a

strange, faraway look. Marguerida remembered the stories about how he had willingly joined the Sharra circle, hopeful to use the great matrix to trade for Terran technology and Darkovan independence. Worthy goals, indeed, but in the end, impossible. Sharra might have been created originally for another use, but by the time it came to Caer Donn, its only possible function was as a weapon. The great matrix would warp any other purpose, and it was too powerful to control, as Lew had found to his sorrow.

The shadow matrix had been imprinted on Marguerida's palm during a wild battle in the Overworld with the disembodied spirit of Ashara, the ancient *leronis* who had overshadowed her as a child. Ashara had prolonged her own existence by taking over the minds of others. As Marguerida and Mikhail had struggled to free her from that malign influence, Marguerida had broken off part of Ashara's psychic Tower, and the result had been the living crystal in her own flesh. What if—the horrifying thought came to Marguerida now—what if the shadow matrix were tainted with Ashara's venomous spirit, the way the Sharra matrix was tainted?

No, it could not be possible! Ashara was destroyed, gone! The stress of the night's events, the terror of losing Mikhail, that moment of panic, had put the notion into her mind. It was a baseless fear, nothing more!

"Your heart is good," her father said, giving no sign he had sensed her thoughts, "but you may not fully appreciate the power of what you are dealing with. This—" he pointed to her gloved hand, "is no toy. And neither is *laran,* most particularly the Alton Gift."

"I most certainly do not need to be reminded of that!" With an effort, Marguerida controlled her irritation. Her father was not her enemy, and he was always harder on himself than on her. He deserved patience and understanding, not a fit of temper.

"I did not come here to lecture you." Lew's usually hoarse voice was low and gravelly. "I see I've made a bad beginning of it."

"We're both tired," she said with a rush of sympathy. "That does make it harder. What did you want to talk about? And must it be tonight?"

"Always the practical one, my Marja. There are two things on my mind, neither of which can be instantly resolved, but I do not want them to be forgotten in the business of the season. The first is the proper use of *laran*."

"The Alton Gift, you mean?" She raised one eyebrow.

"You did not use your *laran* to restrain the crowd at the gates tonight, but you have worked long and hard to master your temper."

Just barely, Marguerida reflected, carefully keeping her doubts to herself.

"There is no point in hashing over tonight's events. However, I am reminded that Yllana and Domenic both possess the Altoh Gift, as does—what was her name, the Traveler girl?"

"Illona Rider. She is still at Nevarsin Tower, and likely to become under-Keeper there. Surely, her teachers would not have let her progress so far if she showed any instability."

Lew nodded. "Nico's Tower training should also serve him well."

"Yllana has an exceptionally steady temperament, like her father," Marguerida added with a smile. "Tonight, she was a wonder of efficiency under pressure. I don't know what I would have done without her. I have no reservations about any of them."

"Doubtless you are right. All three are fine young people. You know them better than I do. Nevertheless ..." Lew paused. "Perhaps I am too old-fashioned about Comyn responsibility, but I would feel easier if I made sure for myself that Nico and Yllana understand the responsibility incurred by having the Alton Gift."

"I have no objections to your teaching them whatever you think they need to know." Marguerida shifted, a little uneasy. There was something more, still unspoken, some shadow behind her father's words. She remembered how shaken he had looked after the mob dispersed.

In typical fashion, she faced the problem directly, laying one hand gently on his single arm. "Father, what else distresses you? What brought up this concern for *laran* ethics?"

He shook his head, his eyes shadowed, and for a long moment did not answer. "Ghosts," he said at last, half-whispering. "The past is too much with me in this place. I do not know why my mind keeps bringing up old memories. I wish I had stayed at Armida, but I am not sure I could find peace there, either." He sighed and shook his shoulders, as if trying to shed whatever bothered him.

"You cannot leave us now, not in the middle of this crisis!" Her words came out sharper than she intended.

"I have no intention of going anywhere. Not yet, anyway. You do not need to convince me I am needed here. It's just . . . I have been reminded of too many things I wished to forget. I am not so foolish as to think that I can simply run away from them. Not even in my dreams."

"Shall I ask Charissa to attend you? Or Istvana?" Marguerida asked, genuinely concerned for his health. "Something to help you sleep, perhaps?"

He got to his feet. "Ah, my Marja. Some things cannot be solved with a sympathetic conversation and an herbal tincture. I have lived with these memories for many years, and no doubt I will continue to endure them."

With those words, he bent to kiss her cheek, and then left her. Marguerida remained in her chair, watching the candle flames, now still and steady. It seemed that everywhere she turned, the people she loved harbored painful secrets. Nico, and now her father.

By the time Marguerida gathered the family for breakfast the next day, it was well past noon. Sunlight drifted, bright and clear, through the half-opened windows of the family parlor.

Mikhail came in last. The night before, Istvana had examined him with her *laran*. Below the darkening bruise, she found no damage to his skull or bleeding in his brain, but the blow had left him with a mild concussion. Despite her instructions to remain quiet, he had been up since dawn, after only a few hours' sleep.

Marguerida sensed her husband's struggle to concentrate through the nausea and fatigue. It was all she could do not to pin him down and force him to take proper care of himself.

Leave him alone, Marguerida scolded herself. *He will not heal any faster for your fretting.*

At least, the city was quiet this morning. The City Guards patrolled the streets and stood watch beside the locked gates. There had been no new reports of disorder in the streets. She worried a little about Rory, on patrol duty, even though there was nothing she could do to protect him.

The meal began poorly. Everyone seemed preoccupied or irritable. Domenic picked at his food, his expression shuttered, his mental shields firmly in place. Yllana had dark circles under her eyes and kept fidgeting until Marguerida excused her to practice her music.

Istvana glided into the room, wearing an ordinary summer gown of very fine, pale yellow wool embroidered around the high neck and cuffs with the Ridenow colors. She went to Marguerida and embraced her.

"How are you, Marja my dear?" Istvana asked in her no-nonsense tone. "Mikhail, you are not resting enough, that much is clear."

Good for you! Marguerida thought. *Maybe he'll listen to sense when it comes from someone else.*

"When there are fewer urgent matters that require my attention, I will rest more," he said with deceptive mildness.

Marguerida sighed. Sometimes, her beloved could be infuriatingly stubborn.

"Sit down, Isty," she said, gesturing to the empty place. "We are well, considering what a night it was. How is Alanna this morning? Has she recovered from her fright?"

Istvana took a seat and began piling food on to her plate.

"I told you last night, Marguerida, the girl does not suffer from fright any more than *you* do. What is wrong with her is not that simple."

Domenic looked up sharply. Marguerida noticed that he had been shoving his breakfast around his plate without eating more than a mouthful or two.

"Alanna is something of a mystery," Istvana said, between bites. "I understand she studied for a time at Arilinn."

"She did," Marguerida said.

"That explains it, then." Istvana nodded.

"I don't understand," Mikhail said, frowning His blue eyes reflected his deep concern. "She stayed only one season. After that, she refused to go back. As she seemed so much improved, we did not force her." His fair brows tightened, pulling on the swollen bruise on his forehead, and he winced. "Should we have?"

"Marja told me that Alanna demonstrated emerging talents of fire-starting and telekinesis—a very dangerous combination with her poor self-control," Istvana commented. "The circle at Arilinn must have felt impelled to deal with the situation immediately, for Alanna's own safety as well as that of those around her."

Istvana's expression darkened. Because of their friendship, Marguerida almost forgot that Istvana had all the authority and ruthless power of a Keeper.

"I know I can trust you not to repeat this," Istvana said, "but since Jeff Kerwin retired, I don't know what Arilinn Tower has been up to. Aldones knows, we have few enough with the strength and talent to do the work. Sometimes, though, I wonder if they could not have found someone besides Loren MacAndrews to succeed Jeff as Keeper. I have no right to criticize another Keeper, and I certainly am not the guardian of her conscience. However, in my opinion, she is leading the Tower backward."

Mikhail's head came up and Marguerida caught his shiver of alarm. "What do you mean, *backward*?"

"Just that. Arilinn has long been known as the most con-

servative of the Towers. The Archives there must date back
to the Ages of Chaos, they're so old."

"But of incalculable historical worth, are they not?" As a
scholar, Marguerida appreciated the value of such a library.

"Indeed," Istvana agreed, and speared a piece of meat.
"But not merely as obsolete records. They represent a
treasure trove of forgotten techniques, just waiting to be
rediscovered."

"Including things better left alone?" Mikhail said, nodding as he followed Istvana's train of thought.

Marguerida bit her lip, remembering her brief, unhappy
time at Arilinn. She had been older than the rest of the students, and, having been raised offworld and possessing the
Alton Gift, had become an object of thinly veiled hostility.
Loren, one of the oldest students at that time, had been
openly relieved when Marguerida left.

"I remember that Loren was fascinated with tradition,
not that I ever knew her well." Marguerida wondered if
Loren's resentment had not been rooted in jealousy. "She
wasn't exactly friendly, but she seemed competent." *And
ambitious.*

"Oh, she is that." Istvana gestured with her fork. "I didn't
mean to imply otherwise. Arilinn Keepers have always
been highly qualified, and Loren is no exception. I meant
that she might have tried one of the old methods on Alanna
as an emergency measure, assuming that Alanna would remain for some time at Arilinn, so there would be plenty of
time to reintegrate her talents as she attained greater self-
discipline."

"Old methods?" Marguerida asked. "I'm not sure I understand what you mean."

"Someone at Arilinn—and I can only assume it was the
Keeper—implanted certain involuntary safeguards within
Alanna's mind. In effect, Loren cordoned off the more
dangerous parts of Alanna's *laran* in order to protect her
sanity."

"You mean, they destroyed her *laran*?" Mikhail gasped.
Marguerida sensed his instinctive recoil. *Laran* had been

revered by the Comyn since time immemorial; only a short time ago, no Comyn could marry or inherit without demonstrating that he possessed it.

Istvana quickly reassured Mikhail that Alanna's talent was not burned out, only quiescent.

Like a cancer in remission, Marguerida thought. A twinge pulsed through her temples, an echo of her earlier headaches.

"Fire-starting and telekinesis were not Alanna's only talents," Istvana went on. "She also had—*has*—a form of unreliable precognition. No, Marja, it's not at all like your Aldaran Gift. In fact, faced with multiple possible futures, it is a wonder the child's mind did not break down entirely. Fortunately, this seems to be a recent development, and I wonder if it was not in response to the earlier suppression."

"Like weeds popping out in new parts of the garden, once you've weeded them in one place?" Marguerida frowned. "So, if this ability is cordoned off, who knows what Alanna will come up with next?"

"She isn't doing it deliberately!" Domenic burst out.

Istvana gave him another intent look. "No, I am sure none of this is voluntary on her part. And Loren did what she thought best. We cannot question the decision of a Keeper."

Istvana went on to explain that last night, something had disrupted Alanna's safeguards, resulting in a resurgence of threshold symptoms. Out of the corner of her eye, Marguerida noticed Domenic shift uneasily in his chair, but she could sense nothing of his thoughts.

"Is she—" Domenic stammered, "is she still in danger?"

Istvana shook her head. "Alanna's mind is stable for the time being. I was able to reinforce the Arilinn safeguards. I dared not meddle with what Loren did, not until I understood all the implications, so I thought it better to leave her precognition alone. She may find it troublesome, but is should pose no direct danger to her or anyone around her."

Mikhail looked unhappy. "Should we sent her back to

Arilinn? She would not have gone willingly before, but perhaps now . . ."

He blames himself, Marguerida thought, her heart aching for him, *for not having insisted she return after that first season. Oh, Mik! We had no way of knowing what would happen, and Alanna was so set against it. Who knows what she might have done if we had not relented—run away, set the castle stables on fire as she threatened to do, caused even more mischief?*

"A person with Alanna's powerful *laran* and volatile temperament would definitely fare better in the disciplined environment of a Tower," Istvana said with a sigh. "Not Arilinn again, but perhaps with Laurina MacBard at Dalereuth. The decision, however, must be hers, and she would have to submit to the training willingly and wholeheartedly. Her consent cannot be forced. Given her previous resistance, coercing her would do more damage than good. She should be safe enough, for the time being, if she is not subjected to another destabilizing incident."

Domenic's expression of concern intensified. It was sweet of him, Marguerida thought distractedly, to be so concerned about his childhood friend.

At least, I will not have to send her away, back to the mother who cannot love her. That would ruin her for certain. Perhaps with this incident, whatever trouble Alanna might have caused had been averted. Alanna appeared biddable enough for the moment.

"What should we do, then?" Mikhail asked. "How do we avoid triggering another incident?"

"Alanna's *laran* is unusually complex," Istvana said. "You know that the same energon channels carry *laran* and sexual energy."

Mikhail nodded. "That is why threshold sickness often arises in puberty, when both become active."

Domenic blushed and looked away. Istvana politely ignored him.

"At one time," Istvana explained for Marguerida's benefit, "it was thought that no one working in a matrix circle could be sexually active. Either there would be no energy left for sex—the man would become impotent and the woman, unresponsive—or else, the channels would overload with potentially fatal results."

"What superstitious nonsense!" Marguerida exclaimed. "Using our *laran* never prevented Mik and I from—er . . ." She broke off as Domenic's face reddened even further. Poor boy, he wasn't used to his parents discussing such intimate matters.

Istvana nodded. "Of course, we know that now. But for centuries, Keepers were required to remain virgins, and nowhere as stringently as at Arilinn. You see, Keepers carry far higher energon levels than do other Tower workers, and for their own sake, as well as the safety of everyone in their circles, their lower channels must remain clear."

Domenic shifted uneasily in his chair. "Surely, that does not apply to Alanna."

Istvana looked sharply at him. "In Alanna's case, her earliest-manifesting talents and her sexuality arose at about the same time. I suspect, from what I found in her mind, that Loren used the old techniques to shut down *both*."

"Oh!" Marguerida exclaimed, lifting one hand to her mouth. "How terrible! And yet . . . that does make sense. When she came back from Arilinn, she struck me as childlike and curiously free from the usual teenage hormones. I was actually grateful we didn't have that to deal with, as well as her temper."

Marguerida bit back her next words. Loren might have acted in what she thought was Alanna's best interests, but that could not justify what amounted to psychic neutering. Before she could put her thoughts into words, Mikhail spoke again.

"These safeguards are temporary, aren't they? Alanna will be able to live as a normal woman, to . . . ah, to marry and have a family?"

Shaking her head, Istvana gave her empty plate a little

shove. "It would be better to delay, until we can sort things out properly. Eventually, it might be possible to remove the safeguards. Once she has matured in her self-control, that is. Or the sexual inhibition itself might be released, perhaps through the careful administration of *kireseth*. The Forbidden Tower circle rediscovered some of the old Years-End rituals."

Istvana paused, her eyes thoughtful. "You say that Arilinn will be sending a representative to the Council season. I hope it is Loren, so that we can discuss what she did. For the time being, let us leave well enough alone. Unless . . . the girl is not betrothed, is she?"

"No, thank all the gods!" Marguerida breathed in relief.

"If you say that Alanna is in no danger," Mikhail said, "I do not see what else we can do."

"Where is *Dom* Lewis?" Istvana, having satisfied herself, changed the subject. "I hoped to see him this morning."

"As I do," Mikhail said, in between sips of unsweetened *jaco*. "I want to ask his advice about how to handle those men from last night."

"You mean, how to get you out of the pickle you made for yourself," Marguerida said, gently teasing him. "I believe Father took breakfast in his own room. Isn't that so, Darna?" She glanced over her shoulder at one of the serving maids.

"Yes, *vai domna*. Cecilia took a tray to him a little while ago." The girl began clearing away the breakfast dishes. Istvana excused herself to check on Alanna again and to attend to her own duties.

"I suppose last night was exhausting for an old man," Mikhail said when he, Domenic, and Marguerida were alone again.

"He's not that old—" Marguerida stopped herself. Lew was not yet seventy, barely out of middle age by Terran standards. The years had worn hard on her father; one look at his poor scarred face, or the way he rubbed the stump of his arm when he thought no one was watching, reminded her of how much he still suffered.

What will I do when he's gone?

Why am I indulging in such morbid thoughts? Father will be with us for a long time yet.

"I would not disturb Lew's rest," Mikhail said, "but I must prepare to receive those men in Council the day after tomorrow. I would prefer not to go into such a meeting without knowing as much as I can about their situation. I'm going to have enough difficulty convincing the Council to accept such a breach of protocol as it is. I'd rather not make a fool of myself by my own ignorance."

"You could ask Danilo Syrtis," Domenic said. All three heads turned toward him.

"That's an interesting suggestion," Mikhail said. "Danilo was once part of the inner workings of the Council, through his association with Regis, his Wardenship of Ardais, and later, his service to us. He has withdrawn so much these last few years and then was so ill last winter, I was surprised to see him at the opening session."

Hesitantly, as if revealing a confidence, Domenic said that Danilo had arranged a number of meetings for him in Thendara with various sorts of people. "Traders, craftsmen, a few minor lords. I've learned far more about the city and the surrounding lands than I could behind these walls. *Dom* Danilo spends a great deal of time outside the Castle, I believe. He may have heard of these men."

So that must be the secret Domenic was hiding. Marguerida didn't know whether to be proud of her son or furious at him for taking unnecessary risks. Thendara, like any big city, included districts where a young man was not safe wandering alone. Possessions that Domenic took for granted, such as a finely woven cloak or a belt with a metal buckle, might well tempt a thief. Even a man trained in self-defense could be overcome by sufficient numbers or caught by surprise.

She tried to remember what it was like to be twenty and how she would have felt if her parents had forbidden her to stray beyond an armed fortress or worse yet, had someone trailing her everywhere, reporting back to them. She would have been so angry, she would have gone out and done the most outrageous thing she could think of.

I was a University student, nobody of importance. Nico is the heir to the Regency and most powerful Domain of Darkover. He has no right to risk himself.

"I agree it is unwise to take foolish chances," Mikhail went on. "But, if Domenic is to rule in his own time, he must know the city and its people. He must learn to gauge those risks for himself, to rely on his own judgment, nor out protection, no matter how loving or well meant. I do not think he could have a better guide than Danilo Syrtis."

Who, Marguerida reminded herself, *kept Regis safe for many years, against World Wreckers, assassins, and many other dangers.*

She sighed inwardly. When Domenic was born, she had wanted him to be self-sufficient, confident in his abilities, and capable of making his own decisions. Now, she reflected ruefully, it was too late to change her mind.

12

Domenic spent the next day and a half in frustration. Alanna slept most of the time. He knew this was a good sign, that her body and mind needed rest, but the thought did not make waiting any easier. When, finally, she woke, she refused to discuss the events leading up to the riot. Clearly happy to see him, she chatted excitedly about their secret engagement. What Istvana had said was indeed true, he decided. Alanna had returned emotionally to the condition the Arilinn workers had created in her, spirited and capricious, but sexually oblivious. She might have been made *emmasca*, she was so unresponsive. The passion they had shared had disappeared as if it never existed. When he kissed her, she turned her head, so that his lips pressed against her cheek.

The Castle bustled with more than the usual Council season activity, and Domenic's family seemed to be in the center of it all. Marguerida, with Yllana's help, managed the added housekeeping until all the unexpected guests could return safely to their own homes, as well as all the usual arrangements necessary for Council season. Danilo met several times with Mikhail, coming and going with his usual quiet discretion. Domenic did not have a chance to speak more than a few words with him, for his father had delegated a surprising amount of boring but essential Council work to him. Nor did Domenic see much of his grandfather. Lew appeared for one or two family meals, saying little and eating less. Only a stern look from Mikhail restrained Marguerida from fussing over him.

The riot at the Castle gates granted Domenic an unexpected reprieve. Francisco Ridenow did not send his daughter home, but he seemed to have given up the idea of a marriage alliance, at least for the time being.

Yllana mentioned in passing that she had seen the Ridenow girl playing at hoops and streamers with Katherine Aldaran's daughter, Terése, who was the same age. Yllana spoke of their game so wistfully that Marguerida suggested she take a break from her household duties to join them. Yllana happily went off to do so, looking more like a carefree *damisela* than a young woman struggling with new responsibilities. Domenic hoped the friendship would be good for all of them. At least, he doubted even Francisco could exploit it for a political betrothal. In addition, Terése had spent the first decade of her life on Terra, among diplomats, and was unusually sophisticated for her age.

As for the Council meetings, once the initial furor had subsided into attempts to place blame for the incident, business resumed as usual. Discussions degenerated into each side jockeying for advantage, regardless of the merits of the case. Domenic found himself looking forward to the audience with the Kazarin Forst men. At least, something real might happen then.

———— ◆ ————

The mob at the Castle gates might have been drunk, egged on by a few vocal malcontents, but they had legitimate grievances.

Danilo sat in the Crystal Chamber and listened to the men of Kazarin Forst tell their tale. As he had reported to Mikhail, they had been in the city since the passes opened up in the spring. What they said was also true, that they had tried for a Cortes hearing and were turned away. The information was not difficult to gather. The men had told their story throughout the poorer areas of the city, generating sympathy and outrage. Unfortunately, theirs was not an isolated case.

On the day of their hearing, the two brothers stood together, dressed in their mountain garb. Their fur shirts looked even shabbier in the opulent glitter of the Chamber. They were proud folk, and nothing less than the gravest extremity would have driven them here to beg for help.

They told a story as old as Darkover itself—forest fires, followed inevitably by mud slides and erosion, then drought. The natural cycle of fire and flood was an essential part of Darkover's ecology. In settled areas, everyone from Comyn to the poorest farmers banded together to control the worst blazes, for the forests provided food for man and beast as well as fuel and shelter for wildlife and, hence, furs and meat. Even in modern times the importance of fighting fires was so great that the penalty for breaking fire-truce was exile or death.

In Danilo's memory, another scene played out with other men. It was early in the World Wreckers time, before anyone knew that the destruction of forest and soil and the assassinations aimed at decimating the Comyn were part of a deliberate and far-reaching plot to reduce Darkover to such desperate straits that they would accept rescue from the Federation at any cost.

Regis had sat under the blue and silver fir tree banner of the Hasturs, listening to a grizzled old man with a profile like a sharp-toothed crag.

"I swore thirty years ago that I'd starve before I crawled down to the Lowlands to ask the Comyn for anything," the old man had said.

In the end, Darkover had had no choice but to negotiate with the Terran Federation. Regis had been adamant about not placing themselves in debt to the *Terranan*. He insisted on full restitution from the World Wreckers and poured out his personal fortune to import food and also medicines, for people weakened by toil and hunger were especially vulnerable to disease.

Even the most heavily damaged areas recovered as the World Wreckers brought in special equipment to speed the restoration of soil and forest. Yet the natural cycle of fire and flood continued, and therein lay the current problem. Even though Darkover remained independent, able to purchase what it needed, it never acquired advanced technology. The planet was too poor in minerals to support industrialization. The population was too thinly distributed, and it was not suited by either temperament or training to factory regimentation. There would always be things too expensive or difficult for Darkover to make for itself and other things Darkover could offer in exchange.

Now the Federation was gone, having withdrawn to fight its interstellar civil war. Where could people like these Kazarin Forst men turn except to the Comyn who had always guided them?

Danilo blinked, and it was no longer Regis who sat across the room, but Mikhail. Mikhail had made good use of the foreknowledge of the complaints and he had an answer ready for them. His plan was innovative but sound. The strange illnesses besetting beasts and crops might indeed represent some new threat or might be only a recurrence of older ailments. A trained matrix technician and one of the Renunciate healers who had been working alongside the Terrans as part of the Bridge Society exchange would accompany them to determine what kind of assistance would be most efficacious.

Humbled but clearly moved by Mikhail's thoughtful response, the Kazarin Forst brothers withdrew. The Council concluded the rest of its business for the day and adjourned.

As the Council members rose to leave, some lingered briefly to discuss the session. Mikhail's brothers, Rafael and Gabriel, gathered with Marguerida and Gisela Aldaran, Rafael's wife.

Since they were a small group, the most convenient place to meet was the antechamber between the main Hastur enclosure and the private entrance. Members of the

Domain once used the place to speak undisturbed before making a formal appearance in Council. The antechamber had not been used much since the time of Danvan Hastur; the wood paneling was dark with age but richly grained, carved in designs of interlocking fir branches and leaping stags. The benches that lined the walls had been newly refurbished, however, and covered with long flat cushions. The air smelled of wood polish and herbs.

As Danilo joined them, Marguerida was saying to her husband, "That was well done, love."

"Aye, but a hundred more such men stood outside our gates the other night." Gabriel had not yet taken his seat. He shifted from one foot to the other, slapping his fist against his open palm for emphasis. "For each one who dares to come forward, there are as many others, fomenting discontent and rebellion." He scowled at Marguerida, who had opened her mouth to reply. "Don't look at me that way, sister-in-law. I speak only what we all know."

"I saw them in the streets as I rode out this morning," Rafael commented.

"Gabriel, please sit down," Marguerida said, holding out her hand. "There's room here on the bench, and you'll make us all nervous, pacing about like that." With a grunt of resignation, Gabriel complied.

"Danilo," Mikhail said, smoothly changing the subject, "you have my deepest thanks. I doubt the hearing would have gone as smoothly without your information."

From his own place in the corner, Danilo inclined his head and said he was happy to be of service, but the credit was due entirely to Mikhail's skillful handling of the situation.

"Modestly spoken," Mikhail replied graciously. "I nonetheless value your wise counsel."

"You shall always have it."

"Mikhail, you cannot seriously propose to give an audience to every malcontent in Thendara," Gabriel said, returning to the previous topic. He had always been the most tradition-minded and conservative of the three brothers.

"You know as well as I do that the Council barely tolerated today's hearing. If you press them or abuse their patience, you will lose their support on issues of real importance."

"And *this* isn't important?" Marguerida put in.

"What else are we to do?" Domenic asked. "We cannot turn these people away. As Comyn, we have a responsibility to them."

"There speaks the idealism of youth," Rafael said, but not at all maliciously.

"Rest assured," Mikhail said, "I will not underestimate the seriousness of the problem. That's why I want to know how you see it and what suggestions you have for how to proceed."

Marguerida ran her fingers over the embroidered cushion cover and looked thoughtful. "As Gabriel says, the men at our gates are just the tip of the iceberg. The old ways are breaking down. We need to put something new in their place or run the risk of going the way of the dinosaurs."

"The *what*?" Gabriel said. "What are dinosaurs?"

"I forgot there were none on Darkover. Just think of them as slow-witted, wingless dragons, lumbering blithely on their way to extinction, like some Council members," Marguerida said with a chuckle, then sobered. "What we need right now is a better way to use our existing resources."

"You clearly have something in mind," Mikhail said, grinning at his wife, "some scheme that will no doubt send the traditionalists on the Council into apoplexy."

"Don't tease me, Mik. I don't *mean* to upset them. I just don't cope well with people who think nothing should be ever done for the first time."

Mikhail laughed outright, but Gabriel looked unhappy. Gisela, who had been sitting beside her husband, listening, said gently, "You must admit that Marguerida's ideas—like setting up a publishing company with Thendara House— have been of great benefit."

"*I'm* not the one she must convince," Gabriel muttered. He leaned back against the paneled wall, then scowled at the sharper edges of the carvings.

"Like illiteracy, this problem won't go away on its own," Marguerida said. "If these people don't get help locally, they will come here and expect *us* to do something."

"My point exactly," Gabriel said. "If we attempt to hear every case brought before us, the Council will be swamped with every trivial dispute in the Seven Domains. It would be better to handle these things as we have always done, each Comyn governing his own lands."

"If that were possible, if there were enough of us, would those men on the street be here?" Domenic asked. "Isn't this proof that the old ways are no longer enough?"

"I say we should send those people back where they belong, using the force of the City Guards if necessary," Gabriel said. "Times of unrest have come and gone before. If we are steadfast in our determination, matters will resolve themselves."

"That may have been true once." Domenic refused to back down. "But we've never faced a situation like this, not since the *Terranan* first landed on Darkover. I believe we have not yet seen the fullest impact of their departure."

"Or replaced the benefits they brought," Rafael added.

"Domenic's right," Marguerida said. "When the Federation left Darkover, they created a vacuum—of power, of resources, of people. In time, we will adjust. A new balance will emerge. The question is, how do we make that transition as smooth as possible?"

Danilo seized the opening. "I believe there are far more people with *laran* than are presently represented in the Comyn. Some of them may be *nedestro* offspring, like that Traveler girl, Illona Rider. Others may be from collateral families or possess only minor talent, not enough for Tower training, but—"

"I don't understand your point," Gabriel interrupted. "Are you proposing throwing open Council membership to every by-blow or commoner with a touch of *laran*? The result would be chaos!"

Danilo paused. He had not been thinking of the Council itself but of the other ways Comyn served Darkover with

the talents of their minds. At the same time, *Why not?* The
Federation Senate included representatives from every
level of society.

"In the meanwhile," Mikhail said in a quiet voice that
drew everyone's attention, "we must do what we can to
minimize the suffering of the people in our care."

"My thought, exactly." Marguerida nodded, her golden
eyes shining the way they did when she got a new idea.
"We need a way of sorting out the more serious issues and
dealing with ordinary things on a lesser level, the way the
Cortes does, or referring them to the appropriate authority. We could set up a screening center—not here in the
Castle, but somewhere more accessible."

"The City Administrative Office would make an excellent location," Mikhail suggested. "That would have the
advantage of being available all year round, not just in
Council season."

"It's true, there's room in the building," Rafael said,
catching their enthusiasm. "But who would do this screening? We're stretched too thin as it is."

"Since it's my bright idea," Marguerida said, "I'll be the
first to volunteer. I'll get Domenic and Rory, when he's off
duty, to help. It will be good training for both of you," she
added to Domenic. "Who knows? The idea may be catching, and then we can enlist young people from other families, too."

Danilo said to Marguerida, "I will take my turn, if I can
be of use."

"As will I," Gabriel said, more out of duty than real interest.

"And I, as much as I am able," Rafael added. Since he
lived at Aldaran much of the year, this was not likely to be
much. Fondly, Gisela laid a hand on her husband's arm.

"By your leave," Danilo went on, "I will discuss the proposal with *Dom* Cisco. We could use a cadet or two, those
with legible writing, to keep records for us. That might
make a useful rotation of duty."

"Which is a nice way to say, for those who've overdone

it on the practice yard or who need a little concentration to sharpen their minds," Mikhail said.

"So you see," Marguerida concluded delightedly, "it is to everyone's benefit!"

As the meeting broke up, Domenic glanced in Danilo's direction, but there was no possibility of a private word. Danilo could not help thinking that although Marguerida's suggestion would undoubtedly relieve some of their current difficulties, it was a temporary measure only. He doubted that Darkover's rural population would adapt well to such centralized authority or to the disruptions in home and farm caused by the necessary travel. Despite all the years of Federation presence, Darkover had few roads, no mechanized transportation, and no means of communication except mounted messengers and telepathic relays.

There are too few of us ...

Then he must find more.

———— ✦ ————

The next morning, Danilo left the Castle early. Although he had a meeting to attend, one he had taken a great deal of trouble to arrange, he paused at an open-air stall selling hot drinks and fried meat pastries. A knot of workmen stood waiting for the next batch to emerge from the oil pots, steaming and fragrant with spices. Danilo bought a mug of *jaco* and took it to a sheltered corner to sip. The sounds of men's laughter, the clatter of cooking implements, horses and carts, the street vendors crying out their wares, washed over him. Nearby, another cookshop sold fried fish and mushrooms on skewers; shawled women stood in clusters, baskets under their arms, gossiping while their children played between the stalls.

As he passed into the market area, he noticed a group of idlers listening to a speaker who was clearly worked up about something. Above the heads of the listeners, Danilo caught a glimpse of the speaker's lanky frame, his emphatic gestures, and pale hair partly hidden beneath a cap. Danilo moved closer for a better look, but as soon as the speaker noticed his interest, he cut short his oration and vanished into the morning traffic.

Danilo made his way through a district of parks, past high, wide houses whose walls shimmered with panels of pale translucent stone. At one of them, the servant at the door showed him to a workroom hung with insulating draperies, a matrix laboratory.

Matrix mechanics, trained at the lowest levels, had been licensed in the city since the time of the Forbidden Tower, but there had never been very many of them at any one time. The earliest licensed mechanics had been *leroni* who, for one reason or another, by their own choice or involuntarily, did not remain within a Tower. That austere life did not suit every temperament. Nowadays, they might have acquired their training without ever having studied in a Tower. They accepted mostly small domestic projects like creating matrix-keyed locks. The Terrans had hired them for other things as well; the shabbiness of the laboratory suggested that those commissions had not been replaced with other work.

In the laboratory, a man and four women, one of them old enough to be a grandmother, sat in armless wooden chairs in a rough circle. They were quietly dressed, and all except the white-haired woman had reddish tints in their hair. The man could not have been more than twenty-five or so, with restless eyes and angular, homely features. Danilo bowed and, after suitable greetings, took the single empty seat.

"You lend us grace, *vai dom,*" said the tall, poised woman, Varinna, who owned the house. "To what do we owe the honor of this visit? Has there been some complaint against us?"

The matrix mechanics existed in a gray zone, neither Comyn nor commoner, mistrusted by both, tolerated only because they provided services too trivial for Tower *leroni.* They had no powerful friends and were always vulnerable to charges of illegal activities.

"No, no," Danilo said quickly. Until now, his contact with

these people had been oblique, discreet. "I do not come in any official capacity, at least not at the present time. Rather, my aim is to explore the possibility of working together to the mutual benefit of yourselves and latent, untrained telepaths throughout Darkover."

The young man, who had been introduced as Darius-Mikhail Zabal, turned to Danilo with a frankly curious gaze.

"Do not toy with us, *Dom* Danilo Syrtis," said the white-haired woman, regarding him with an expression of unmasked suspicion. She touched the cane leaning against her chair as if she would like to beat him with it. "We know who you are. You serve the Hasturs, now as before. Are you not, even now, spying on us for the Regent?"

"Spying, no." He paused, unsure how much to tell them. Yet, trust must be earned.

"Once, *laran* Gifts may have been restricted to the Comyn, but over the centuries they have been diluted." Danilo did not need to point out that all of them had some talent, or they could not manipulate the small crystals they were permitted by law or operate monitor screens like the one in the corner of this very laboratory.

"You have had the benefit of training," Danilo went on. "You can use your *laran* to earn a respectable living. For each of you, might there not be others less fortunate—dozens, perhaps hundreds more—unknown, untaught, tormented by powers they can neither understand nor control?"

One of the women shrugged. "I am sorry for them, of course. It is a shame they have not the opportunity to use their *laran*."

"It is a *disgrace*!" Danilo exclaimed. "Not only do those people suffer, but all of Darkover is the poorer for it."

"I too have wondered if those with such gifts could be found, taught, and given useful work," Darius-Mikhail said quietly, "but as one man with slender resources, I can do little to help them."

"Together, we could," Danilo went on. "With the backing of the Council, we could train matrix healers, set up relays for everyone to use, not just Towers—"

—a planet-wide communication system, far better than anything the Terrans could offer—

"—track weather patterns—"

"For what purpose? We are not Tower folk. We cannot control storm and flood, like the Aldarans," the old woman pointed out.

"Perhaps not," Darius-Mikhail said, "but with forewarning, dwellings could be safeguarded and livestock saved. Losses would be minimized and help brought more speedily."

Danilo said, "We can stabilize hillside erosion and make firefighting chemicals available to everyone who needs them."

"The affairs of the *vai* Comynari are nothing to us, nor ours to them," Varinna said stiffly.

A long, uncomfortable pause followed. Danilo had hoped to excite their interest and their hope for a better future, not just for themselves but for all of Darkover. He had known they might be reticent, that his overtures might be met with mistrust.

Still, Danilo thought as he bade them good day, it was a beginning. The matrix mechanics agreed to meet with him again. They were wary, but he sensed that underneath the thinly veiled animosity, he had piqued their curiosity.

Darius-Mikhail accompanied Danilo into the street. "I hope you are not too discouraged by your reception. The others mean well, but they all have good reason to go carefully. Some ordinary folk still regard us as sorcerers or worse, and the Towers have never been friendly."

"I did not think it would be easy," Danilo said.

"Even so, I believe you," Darius-Mikhail said. "And if—when, you have a place for me, I will gladly join you." He glanced back at the house. "You understand that I must earn my bread in the meantime."

And that means maintaining a good relationship with those who refer work to me.

"Zabal is an old, honorable family name," Danilo said. "I know I have heard it, but I cannot remember where. I am sorry, but should I know you? Could you be a distant kinsman?"

Darius-Mikhail's expression turned guarded. "Whatever dealings my family had with the Comyn were a long time ago. I do not ask for preference or privilege, only honest work."

Danilo nodded, understanding all too well the difficulty of being poor and friendless in a large city, too proud to accept overt charity. "Then honest work you shall have, when there is any to be done."

Darius-Mikhail inclined his head in an impeccably respectful bow and then went on his way. Was it a trace of precognition, Danilo wondered, or only his liking for the younger man that made him certain they would meet again?

13

Flames . . . flames burning in his mind . . . a woman, chained, her molten hair blown on a firestorm wind, hovering . . . rising . . .

"No! Merciful Avarra, no!"

Pain . . . agony flaring in his hand . . .

"No!" The cry, torn from his own throat, wrenched Danilo awake. His vision blurred with overlapping images—his familiar chamber, night-darkened . . . a woman, burning eternally, spanning the heavens, leaning down, reaching for him—*Sharra!*

No, it could not be! The immensely powerful, illegal matrix that had been used for such destruction a generation ago had been destroyed. Regis had taken up the legendary Sword of Aldones and shattered the hold of Sharra upon Darkover.

Gradually, the image of Sharra faded. Danilo's pulse slowed and grew steadier. The panic-fueled tension in his muscles eased, replaced by shivering. The embers of his small night fire had fallen into a pile of ashes. Half unconsciously, his fingers moved in the safeguarding sign of *cristoforo* prayers, one he had not used since childhood.

A dream, it must have been a dream. But not his own, of that he was certain. Although he and Regis had been taken prisoner while Sharra raged over the Hellers, he himself had never been forced into the circle of *laran*-Gifted workers who were trying to control it. Lew had intervened, almost at the cost of his life—

Lew.

Cold receded, replaced by rocky certainty. It had been *Lew's* dream. Lew had been freed from Sharra when Regis destroyed the matrix that housed the Form of Fire ... but perhaps that infernal image still persisted in Lew's memory.

Without hesitation, Danilo pulled on his indoor clothes, a *linex* shirt worn to flannel softness, long lambswool vest and pants, and low boots. He tried to contact the other man's mind with his *laran* but without success. Lighting a candle, he headed toward the Alton quarters.

Around him, Comyn Castle lay still as bedrock. Every sensible soul was still abed at this hour. As Danilo approached the Alton quarters, he felt a vibration of psychic energy, a twist of pain—

"Come to me, burn forever ..."

And silent weeping, *"No! No!"*

Danilo broke into a run. His *laran* guided him unerringly. A door loomed ahead, a shadow in the wavering light of his candle. He jerked the latch up. It slid easily under his touch. He shoved the door open and rushed through the outer chamber. Beyond lay a series of smaller rooms, and from one of them he heard—*sensed*—the silent, anguished moan.

This was one of the older portions of the Castle. The walls were bare, dense, dark gray granite set with slender panels of pale blue stone that glimmered faintly, giving the room the look of a jewel-studded cavern. Not a cavern, Danilo thought, a tomb, a place suspended in time. The furnishings, a huge four-poster bed, dressers and chairs, were old, too, from before Lord Kennard's day.

Danilo rushed to the bedside and set the candle on the nightstand beside it. An odor of honey and sleepweed rose from the half-empty goblet.

"Lew! Lew, wake up!"

Grasping the older man's shoulders, Danilo turned him

on his back. Never before had he seen such an expression—horror, desperation—on a human face.

"Lew! It's me, Danilo!"

What would he do if Lew did not respond, if he had gone so deep within his private nightmare as to be beyond human reach? Danilo had heard stories of how, to save a man's life or his sanity, a *leronis* might take his starstone into her hands. No, that was one thing he would not do. Kadarin had taken Lew's starstone and then drugged him, to break his will and force him into the Sharra circle. The shock had almost killed Lew. Perhaps it had also driven him mad, and no wonder.

Poor tormented soul, Danilo thought. Gently, he lowered Lew back on his pillow and smoothed the limp, sweat-damp hair. His fingertips brushed the knotted scars over cheek and lip, the deeply incised lines. *How you have suffered.*

Danilo took Lew's one hand and cradled it between his own. The Holy St. Christopher knew, there were burdens enough in the world. Over the years, nourished by love and useful work, he had made his peace with his own sorrows, all but one, the single gaping wound, the death of Regis. Even in that, he admitted, he had discovered a kind of solace. If he had lost, he had also loved and been loved.

The flaming image spreading across the heavens . . . A woman's form, laughing as the fire consumed her . . . A mind, pressing on his, the terrible crushing force . . . his own mind giving way . . .

Peace . . . Danilo prayed. *Bearer of Burdens, let this man's sorrow be lifted from him. Let there be an end to his pain, a healing, a cleansing . . .*

How long Danilo sat there, filled with that poignant mixture of grief and tranquility, he could not tell. At last, he felt a stirring, a movement between his hands. With a heart-rending cry, Lew jerked his hand free.

"No! Stay away!"

"It's all right, Lew. I won't harm you. It's me, Danilo."

"It *is* you. I thought—I must have been dreaming." Lew

covered his face with his hand. "Dark Avarra, it's still there! *She's* still there, in my mind! I'll never be free, never!"

Danilo made no attempt to touch the older man again. "The Sharra matrix was destroyed. She can never harm you again."

How can you be sure? She was real, I tell you, just as monstrous as when she drew us into the madness at Caer Donn ...

Danilo flinched under the power of Lew's unspoken thought. Hesitantly, he asked if he might see Lew's starstone.

Lew, like many of his generation, wore his matrix on a cord about his neck, shrouded in insulating silk. He slipped it over his head, unwrapped it, and held it out. Danilo bent for a closer look, careful to avoid any physical contact with the stone. Shadows shifted in the glinting blue light.

Danilo sensed the residue of Lew's *laran*, etched there by decades of use. Here lay a record of Lew's strength and courage, but also of self-doubt, bitter regret, and, running through them all like a river of poison, guilt. Guilt for what he had done, guilt for the death of his first wife, who had perished in order to give them all a chance of escape.

No taint of Sharra remained in the starstone, although the memories might well persist in Lew's mind.

"I saw no trace of Sharra in your matrix," Danilo said, indicating Lew's starstone. "We must look deeper."

Danilo was no Tower-trained *laranzu*. He knew his limits all too well, and he was not entirely sure he had been right in his treatment of young Alanna. But Lew desperately needed help and, in this moment, was open to him. Such a moment might not come again.

Danilo did not know how much goodwill, compassion, and his own experience supporting Regis through threshold sickness could do in this case. But he had to try. He himself had once been the victim of *laran* invasion of his mind, even as Lew had.

Hesitantly, Danilo asked, "Will you allow me to examine your mind as well?"

Eyes dark with anguish met his. "Are you sure you want to do that? Do you know what you will find?"

"I know something of the abuses of *laran*," Danilo forced himself to say. "I too thought I would go mad, that there was no way out, no one who would accept my word or take my part. I was wrong, as we both know. Regis believed in me. He believed in you, as well. For the sake of what we have each endured, will you not trust me?"

For a long moment Lew's mind was silent. Perhaps he had suffered too much. "You have never been false to me, Danilo Syrtis," he said in a harsh whisper. "I do not believe there is any hope for me, but if you are determined, you may try."

Lew lay back, and Danilo shifted his position. Instead of looking directly at Lew, Danilo closed his eyes. Breathing deep into his belly to calm his own thoughts, he allowed himself to slowly descend. Bits of color and sound swept past him. He caught fragments of music and speech, faces—a girl-child with haunted golden eyes, a room with odd geometric furniture, a single moon rising above a placid sea, soaring glaciated peaks washed crimson in dusk, a beautiful young woman with flame-red hair, eyes of gold-flecked amber and an expression of heart-melting tenderness—*Marjorie!* An ancient city—*Caer Donn!*

No, Danilo thought, *that way lies madness.* Without knowing how, he guided the other man's thoughts. *Let the past rest. There is nothing you can do to change what happened. Let it go . . .*

Like a flash flood, soul-deep revulsion spread across Lew's mind, directed not at the Sharra circle but at himself.

You do not understand! Lew raged at Danilo.

Danilo could not imagine what Lew had done that he should look upon himself with such disgust. The catastrophe of Sharra, the deaths, the madness, the ruin of a beautiful and ancient city—these all lay in the past, and none of them had been Lew's fault. Lew had acted honorably, had tried his best to prevent the disaster, and had himself been a victim. Perhaps, in the manner of victims, he blamed himself for not doing more, but Danilo did not believe that was the sole cause of the older man's self-loathing. There was something else, some memory buried even more deeply, that now ate away at Lew's soul like a hideous cancer.

No wonder Lew had gone through bouts of drunkenness, years when he did not show his face in Thendara.

Shivering, nauseated, Danilo found himself back in his own body. A faint light touched the eastern-facing window. Beside him, Lew had turned his face away.

That unhealed hurt, that festering wound spread its poison into Lew's mind. Eventually, it would kill him, either from overwhelming despair or by driving him back to drunken forgetfulness.

"Lew," Danilo said gently, "listen to me. Whatever it is you have done, whatever has been done to you, it is devouring you from within. I know a little about living with nightmares. I don't—" he broke off, searching for words. "I don't think this is the kind of thing we can survive alone."

After a long moment, Lew stirred. "What do you suggest I do about it?" His tone indicated he had little hope, that this was a useless exercise.

"I don't know why these memories have resurfaced now," Danilo said, changing the subject slightly. "The Keepers tell us such things can lie dormant, only to awaken when some person or event triggers them. It's as if, in some corner of your mind, that terrible time is still going on."

Lew's face went stony. "I don't need you to tell me that. I've lived with those memories for a long time."

"If there is a way to make peace with the past . . ." Danilo captured Lew's gaze with his own. "Isn't that why you drank so much? To forget?"

Lew's head jerked back, like a startled horse.

"I know only one place where a man can find true peace,

not just the oblivion of the bottle," Danilo went on. "Where even the heaviest burden can be eased."

"I studied at Arilinn long ago," Lew said, "but I do not think the discipline I learned there can help me now."

"I did not mean a Tower. I meant the monastery at Nevarsin, St.-Valentine-of-the-Snows. No, Lew, I do not say that because I was raised in the *cristoforo* faith. I studied there, yes, but so did Regis, and he was not. I say it because I have seen men whose minds and lives were shattered find hope again. Even if they could never return to the outer world, they discovered a measure of contentment. The past cannot be changed. We both know that. But what we do with it, that is up to us."

"I as much as promised Marguerida I would stay—"

"At the cost of your own sanity? Lew, if there is any chance that the good brothers at St. Valentine's can help you, isn't that more important? How can you be of service to Marguerida or anyone else if you continue like this? How much of your own life, your own needs, have you set aside for others? And has it been from love, or guilt?"

"I should ask you the same thing," Lew replied, "you whose whole life was devoted to Regis Hastur."

It was a valid point, Danilo admitted with a pang. In a voice suddenly thickened, he said, "I never asked for anything except to serve the one I loved. I have done so with a clear mind and an easy heart. Can you say the same?"

"No, and that is the difference." Lew went to the window. His shoulders rose and fell in a deep sigh. "I would not convert."

"No one would ask it of you. The Holy Bearer of Burdens opens his arms to all in need."

"It is strange," Lew said, still gazing out over the courtyard, "but in this moment, I feel a hint of that peace you spoke of. Perhaps it is just knowing there is someone who understands. For the first time in more years than I can count, I wonder if there might be a way out of this darkness. I do not know how much time will be granted to me, but I would wish . . . Danilo, you always had the clearest writing of any of us. Will you write a letter of introduction for me to the—how is he called, the head of the monks?"

"Father Master Conn." Danilo bowed his head. "I would be honored."

14

Several days later, Lew was even more certain that Danilo's suggestion of going to St. Valentine's was worth trying. Danilo was also right that the nightmares had another, deeper root than old memories of Sharra. He could not go on as he had, that much was certain.

With some trepidation, Lew went to tell Marguerida of his decision. He found her breakfasting with Domenic and Yllana in the family apartment. Sun streamed through the half-opened windows, glowing on the wood paneling, and filling the air with warmth. A bowl of rosalys adorned the center of the table, surrounded by a half-empty basket of spiral buns, a bowl that once contained hard-boiled eggs, now filled with broken shells, and a platter of sliced peaches.

Although the conversation drew to an abrupt halt at Lew's entrance, he caught his grandson's quickly masked look of misery, the subtle hunching of his shoulders, the exasperated tautness around Marguerida's eyes.

"Good morning, Grandpapa." Yllana had shed her initial hesitation and looked directly at him.

"My apologies for the intrusion," Lew said.

Marguerida's expression softened. "It's a pleasure to see you, Father. You aren't interrupting anything. I think we've beaten that particular horse into the ground. Come, sit down with us. Will you take a cup of *jaco*? Something to eat?"

Lew took the seat she indicated, at her right side, but declined any refreshment.

"Since Domenic and Yllana are both here, perhaps we can have our discussion." It was fitting that Marguerida be present, as well. The talk would give him time to find the right way to tell her he would be leaving.

"You mean the matter we spoke of the night of the Festival ball?" Marguerida asked.

Lew nodded, and then turned to his grandchildren. "You both have the Alton Gift, and it would be irresponsible not to caution you about the seriousness of its use."

"Oh, Grandpapa, Mother has lectured us about that since we were babies!" Yllana said, rolling her eyes.

"Yllana, you will speak respectfully to your grandfather," Marguerida said.

"It's all right, Marja," Lew said, giving Yllana a smile. "I'm the one who has been neglectful, and you, clearly, have not."

"Of course, I talked to them!" Marguerida shifted in her chair, her golden eyes clouding momentarily. She had had no warning, and when her Gifts awakened in full on her return to Darkover, she had been frightened and confused. "I had no idea what I was capable of, if I was caught off guard, or frightened . . . or angry. After what happened to me, I was not about to let my own children grow up unprepared."

"My father drilled it into me even before we knew I had the Gift." Lew glanced at Domenic and Yllana. *"The unbridled anger of an Alton can kill."*

"Any *laran* can be dangerous if misused," Domenic pointed out. "That's one of the first principles I learned at Neskaya. 'We swear never to enter the mind of another, save to help or heal, and then only with consent.' "

"But ordinary *laran* allows contact only with other telepaths," Lew said. "With the Alton Gift, you can force rapport with anyone, Gifted or not. You can control not only their thoughts, but their actions, their emotions." He hesitated to use frank language with his young granddaughter, but ignorance would be far worse. She was Alton and therefore capable of great harm through ignorance or carelessness. "Unasked for, uninvited, such a contact amounts to psychic rape."

Yllana flinched, then regained control of herself. Her previous saucy mood evaporated, replaced with seriousness. Her expression reminded Lew of Mikhail; she was, after all, Mikhail's daughter, with much of his steadiness of temperament.

Marguerida reached out to brush her daughter's wrist in a telepath's light touch. "You need not fear losing control and abusing someone in that manner, *chiya*. I have every confidence in your good judgment. And in yours, too, Nico."

Lew sat back, sensing the deep bond between his daughter and her children. Her faith in them clearly helped them to think of themselves as responsible, to become the best they could be. He did not know how she had managed such a connection with her children while adapting to Darkover, supporting her husband, and continuing her own work.

He gazed at Domenic, with his intent, carefully guarded expression, and bright, steady Yllana. They had not been taught as he had, and that was not necessarily a bad thing. No one had thundered warnings at them or forced them to submit to a potentially fatal ordeal in order to prove their place in the Comyn. Their minds were unscarred, their outlooks open and earnest. Perhaps they would not make his mistakes.

"I hate being afraid of what might happen if I lose my temper," Yllana said, wrinkling her brow. "I've never understood why such a talent was developed in the first place. It's of no use in everyday life, like telepathy."

"It's said to be a very ancient Gift, from the breeding programs of the Ages of Chaos," Lew explained. "When I was a boy, it was even rarer than it is now. In fact, only my father and myself were known to have it." He omitted mentioning his dead brother, Marius, seeing no point in dragging up that tragedy. "Then, it was believed that only an Alton by blood could possess the Gift, but the old Comyn lineages have been so intermixed, this is no longer the case."

"Yes, Illona Rider has the Alton Gift, too," Marguerida said, nodding. "I was relieved when she agreed to study at a Tower, so there would be no question of her responsible use of her *laran*."

"Since she is *nedestra* and has the Gift," Domenic added thoughtfully, "it is likely that others outside of the Comyn, perhaps even those who do not know their lineage, might have this or other Gifts." He glanced at his mother, and Lew felt the leap of tension between them.

"That would be horrible, wouldn't it?" Yllana said, "for someone who didn't even know they had the Alton Gift to use it. They could kill or cripple someone without even meaning to! Oh, this should not be called a Gift, but a Curse!"

"No, you must never think of yourself as cursed!" Marguerida cried, her voice resonating on the edge of alarm. "*Laran* is a tool like any other, and it can be used for great good. We must take care to never use it for petty or selfish purposes."

"That is a worthy ideal," Lew mused, "but one that too many fall short of."

Domenic's head shot up. "Do you mean Alanna?"

"No, why would I think of her?" Lew said, surprised. "I spoke only of myself."

"Father, surely you have nothing to reproach yourself with!" Marguerida laid one hand on his good arm, so that Lew felt an outpouring of concern. "You are the least self-ish and most self-critical man I know. Darkover owes you a tremendous debt."

Perhaps, Lew thought, *but at a cost I can no longer bear.* For a long moment, no one spoke. Then Lew roused himself to pick up the thread of conversation. "I, too, wondered about the original purpose of the Alton Gift. Surely, it was meant to be used with the greatest care and deliberation and only in desperate circumstances."

"A weapon when all else had failed?" Marguerida said. Images of the Battle of Old North Road and its aftermath flickered across her mind.

"A final defense for the Comyn," Lew added, although the words brought little comfort.

The conversation went on only a little while longer. Domenic answered questions about his training at Neskaya, reassuring Lew that he had been properly taught. Yllana was to return with Katherine and Hermes Aldaran at the end of the season.

"We will miss her terribly," Marguerida said, "but I believe she will benefit from exposure to other techniques ... as well as getting away from home, with all its irritations."

Yllana rolled her eyes again, but Domenic's face tightened in a scowl, quickly suppressed.

"That reminds me," Yllana said, brightening. "I've been meaning to ask you, Mother. Terése and Belle—Sibelle Ridenow, that is—and I have come up with the most wonderful plan! Wouldn't it be lovely if Belle could come with us to Castle Aldaran? We could take our lessons together and keep each other company."

"Lessons? Has she *laran*?" Lew asked.

"Oh, yes! She has the Ridenow Gift of empathy, at least Terése and I think so. One time, when I fell and scraped my elbow, Belle cried as if she were the one who was hurt. You should see how gentle and kind she is with the horses, as if she knows what they are feeling."

After an instant of awkward silence, Marguerida said, "Surely the matter should be taken up with Sibelle's father."

"Lady Katherine said she must discuss it with you first. She'll say yes if you agree. Please do! It will be so good to have friends there."

Marguerida looked to Domenic. "What do you think of this scheme? How would you feel about Sibelle going away?"

Lew caught the faint lightening of Domenic's expression. "It might be the best thing for her, to be away from home, fostered by someone like Lady Katherine, who has lived offworld and does not bow down to her kinsmen as if she had no will and no intelligence of her own."

"Of course not!" Yllana giggled. "What do you think we girls are, spineless rabbit-horns?"

"Certainly *not* traditional Darkovan women!" Marguerida had started to take another sip of *jaco* and sputtered.

"I'm not being flippant," Domenic continued. "Sibelle only agreed to her father's proposal because she thought she had no choice. She mustn't be punished for trying to please her father. I'm not going to marry her, as I made abundantly clear to *Dom* Francisco after the ball."

"Marry her?" Yllana's mood went from amused to aghast. "But she's younger than I am, and I'm not nearly grown-up enough."

"You are more mature than many young ladies your age," her mother said, "but I have always thought it barbaric to consider women good for nothing more than producing sons and heirs."

"Or for the alliances and advantages their marriages bring to their families," Domenic said forcefully.

"I think Domenic has the right of it," Lew commented. "I knew the *damisela* was young, but I had not realized—I had not thought Francisco capable of pressuring a child into marriage."

Marguerida gave him a sharp, dark look. She, at least, had had no qualms about suspecting the Ridenow lord's malice.

"It won't be the first mistake I've made," Lew said, as much to himself as to the others, "or, I fear, the last."

"Father, you are not responsible for that horrible man's

misdeeds," Marguerida insisted. "Nico, I must say I am relieved that you know your own mind in this matter."

"Oh, I do. And expressed it rather forcefully."

"Did you, now?" Marguerida was clearly pleased. "Well, then, I shall do my part and enlist Katherine's help in salvaging poor Sibelle's future."

Yllana clapped her hands in delight. "We are all going away at the end of the season, then. May I go and tell Terése now?"

"You may go, but you must find some way to keep quiet until things are sorted out with *Dom* Francisco," Marguerida replied. "It would not do for him to get wind of the plan before Katherine has secured his permission."

"Please forgive me," Domenic said, rising as his sister left the room, "but I also have business to attend to. Mother, Grandfather." He delivered a short bow to each of them and left.

Without the two young people, the room seemed empty, the gentle sunlight too still. Sighing, Marguerida turned to Lew, "I don't know what's gotten into Nico lately. He just won't listen."

"He seems reasonable enough to me," Lew commented.

"That's because he was on his best behavior, but if you had been here earlier, you might think very differently."

Lew had rarely heard Marguerida so distressed by the behavior of her children. Trying to be supportive, he said, "As I remember, you were the same at his age. For several years neither Diotima nor I could make you see sense."

A hint of a storm flickered across Marguerida's features, for during most of her childhood Lew had been a cold, distant parent, and she had retaliated by becoming rebellious and headstrong. Since her return to Darkover, however, they had become closer than either of them had dreamed possible.

"The lad will come into his own, in good time," Lew said. "He handled himself well the other night at the Castle gates, and he's learning more all the time."

Marguerida picked up her cup of *jaco* and stared at its

congealed surface. "It was one thing when he wanted to wander through Thendara. Now he's got it into his head to make a tour of all the Towers, trying to enlist the Keepers in a search for latent telepaths. Where he got the idea, I don't know, maybe from Danilo's stories of Regis."

"His wanderlust developed at an early age, as I recall."

"I suppose you mean that it is too late to change his basic temperament," Marguerida said. "Or mine."

"I am not saying that Domenic should go alone and unarmed wherever he pleases in the Seven Domains," Lew said. "Instead of forbidding him the freedom he so obviously craves, why not encourage him to do it safely? Give him the advice you yourself would have heeded when you were his age."

"At his age, I had already left home for University! I was an adult, I—" Marguerida halted in midsentence. One corner of her mouth quirked upward. "I have been behaving like a cross between the High Inquisitor and a smothering mother, haven't I? It has been a long time since I was young and unruly. I've almost forgotten what it was like."

"You've done a splendid job with Domenic," Lew said. "There comes a time when every young eagle must test his wings. He will not disappoint you. Just as you have never disappointed me."

With a little cry, she got up and wrapped him in her arms. They had long since resolved the pain of her early years, but even so, he felt how deeply touched she was to hear the words spoken aloud.

Lew's heart sank, but there was no way to avoid what must come next. As gently as he could, he told her that he had decided to go to the Nevarsin monastery for an indefinite period of time.

"I had hoped to persuade you to remain here at the end of Council season, rather than returning to Armida," Marguerida protested. "Francisco may have given up on the idea of marrying his daughter to Nico, but what if he should try something else?"

"Then you and Mikhail will deal with him, seeking advice from those you trust." Lew raised his hand. "I am not irreplaceable, or the only man on Darkover with a little diplomatic experience."

Marguerida shifted tactics. "Isn't it dangerous for a man your age to travel in the mountains? You haven't developed some new religious calling, have you?"

"I don't think so," he said. "As for the dangers of the trail, I have traveled throughout Darkover all my life, and I will have competent Renunciate trail guides. I am sorry to leave you at a time you have every right to expect my help, but some things cannot be endlessly deferred."

"What things?"

Carefully, he said, "We have seen dark times, you and I. Some of those shadows still cling to me. In the quiet and isolation of St. Valentine's, I may find some measure of peace."

I do not know how many more years will be granted to me. I would not leave this life with fears unfaced, guilt unresolved, questions unanswered. If I do not go now, when will I have another chance?

Marguerida's golden eyes widened slightly, and Lew realized she had sensed his thought. She answered with an outpouring of love and concern.

What will I do without you? she spoke to his mind.

"Why, what you have always done, my dear. Face the future with courage and determination. Remember that you are not alone. Surround yourself with people of wisdom and insight, most particularly those who see things differently than you do."

"But none so tactful in their criticisms as you are." Marguerida smiled, a flash of radiance like the sun emerging from behind storm clouds. As he rose, she slipped a hand through the crook of his elbow and walked with him to the door. "You will take care, won't you? And come back for the next Council season?"

"I . . . I cannot say how long I will be gone."

"Well, then, until you have settled matters with yourself?"

Lew leaned over to plant a kiss on her forehead. "You will never cease to be in my heart, my Marja."

"As you will be in mine."

Marguerida was especially happy for an excuse to take time from her duties as chatelaine of Comyn Castle for a visit with her friend, Katherine Aldaran. The two women had first met a few years ago, when Katherine's husband, Hermes, returned to Darkover just before the Federation withdrawal. Like Marguerida, Katherine had not grown up on Darkover; they were both educated women, and they had each rebelled and finally reached an uneasy compromise with the oppressed, confined lives most Darkovan women were expected to lead. Moreover, Katherine was also an artist, a painter who understood Marguerida's passion for music. With her temper and beauty, lustrous, waist-length black hair and milk-pale skin, Katherine would have attracted attention anywhere. At Aldaran, where she lived most of the year, she encountered fewer restrictions than she would have in the Lowlands. The Aldarans were long known as rebels and noncomformists.

With obvious pleasure, Katherine welcomed Marguerida's visit. Katherine and her family still occupied the old Storn apartments in the Castle, adjacent to the Aldaran suites. The sitting room, redecorated only a generation ago for Lauretta Lanart-Storn, had been painted in shades of pale spring green, and the tapestry dominating one wall depicted a party of ladies working together on a needlework project. The scene made Marguerida think of the Darkovan equivalent of a quilting bee. It might have been a portrayal of an everyday event or a subtle reminder of the traditional place of women, but Katherine had commented that women had always worked behind the scenes, managing political power through just such associations.

The two friends settled into armchairs, drawn together for comfortable conversation. To one side, a small table of carved ash-pale wood bore a beautifully glazed teapot and cups and a bouquet of tiny yellow starflowers in a glass vase. The delicate lemony smell of the flowers blended with the slightly pungent aroma of the drink. Katherine poured out cups of steaming herbal tisane and offered one to Marguerida.

"I take it," Marguerida said as she accepted the cup with a pang of resignation, "that you don't have any coffee left, either."

Katherine shook her head. "Nor real tea, I'm afraid. Sometimes I think I'd kill for a cup."

Marguerida put her feet up on the little footstool, leaned her head against the back of the chair, and sighed. A comfortable silence settled over the two as they sipped their tea, each pretending it was something else, but only for a moment. Neither woman was the sort to sit still for long.

"I take it that Yllana has told you of this scheme the girls came up with, to abscond with Sibelle Ridenow," Katherine said.

"Yes, she did," Marguerida nodded, setting down her half-full cup. "There's no question that fosterage with you, away from her father, would benefit the girl, but what about you and your family? That is, assuming *Dom* Francisco would agree in the first place."

Katherine cradled her cup in her hands and blew across the steaming surface, her fair brow wrinkled in thought. "I have met Sibelle once or twice in passing, seeing her as no more than my daughter's friend. There is no problem in including her; she seems a sweet, biddable child, and Castle Aldaran has more than enough room. But . . ."

"The question is," Marguerida finished her friend's unspoken thought, "did our daughters come up with this idea because they truly enjoy Sibelle's company, or were they encouraged to do so? Is this some new ploy of Francisco's?" Katherine was one of the few people outside of the family who knew about the marriage alliance proposal and its outcome.

"I have been considering that possibility," Katherine

said, "and I cannot see what advantage Francisco might derive from our fostering his daughter. Aside from getting her out from underfoot, that is, which he could do as well by sending her back to Serrais."

"Could he be hoping for an alliance with Aldaran, like the one he proposed to us?"

"If he is, he will simply have to wait until Sibelle is old enough to make up her own mind," Katherine replied tartly.

Marguerida laughed. "Whenever young people are thrown together at a certain age, they will fall in love with each other. Or think they are in love, when they are really in the grip of rampaging hormones."

"Yet we managed to survive those years, and find satisfying marriages based on something deeper," Katherine said, smiling. Her marriage to Hermes, despite its own share of difficulties, continued to be a source of joy and fulfillment. "I don't doubt that will happen to Sibelle in her own time. It will be my job to make sure she has a solid enough sense of her own worth to insist on being treated with respect by everyone involved. Including her father."

"It won't be an easy task," Marguerida mused. "Sibelle has years of early conditioning to overcome."

"Yllana will help," Katherine said. "I would be less optimistic without her. You and Mikhail have brought her up to think of herself as a strong, competent person. She and Terése will be the best possible examples for Sibelle."

Before Marguerida could reply, she heard a timid tap on the door. At Katherine's invitation, Sibelle Ridenow entered, followed a step behind by a servant in green and gold livery. Sibelle's red-gold hair had been braided in a simple style suitable for a young girl, and she wore a child's smock of fine wool embroidered fancifully with flowers and rainbirds over long, full skirts.

"Your escort can wait outside," Katherine said, motioning for the servant to close the door behind him. "Come here and sit down, *chiya*. Do you know why I asked you here?"

Sibelle glanced after the departing servant and then pulled up a third chair as she was bidden. She glanced at Marguerida with a look of such unease that Marguerida wanted to wrap the poor, terrified child in her arms. Had Francisco been badgering her again, as Nico had described on the night of the Festival ball? What sort of instructions had he given the girl? The very thought aroused Marguerida's maternal instinct and cemented her determination to extract Sibelle from his clutches.

Between them, Marguerida and Katherine soon put the girl at her ease. Sibelle spoke with delight about her new friendships. Although she did not say so aloud, for doubtless she knew it was improper to criticize her family home, she had been desperately lonely. She had not been allowed to play with those her father considered below her, and there had been few visitors of her own age and sex. Often, books and animals had been her only companions.

As Sibelle talked, Marguerida sensed the young girl's *laran,* still unformed and untrained, but present. As Yllana said, Sibelle seemed to have the empathic sensitivity of the Ridenows. It was a shame, Marguerida thought, that Francisco was so entirely lacking in the ability to experience the emotions of others, or he would never have acted in such a callous, manipulative fashion. Nor did she wonder why Sibelle was so unhappy at home, shut up in the huge manor house.

Marguerida emerged from her reflections just as Katherine was asking Sibelle if there might be any objection to her staying at Castle Aldaran. To her astonishment, Sibelle burst into tears.

Before Marguerida could react, Katherine, who was closer, put her arm around Sibelle. "Whatever is the matter, child?"

"He doesn't want me! I failed him, and now he hates me!"

"No, I'm sure he does not." While speaking soothingly, Katherine exchanged a knowing glance with Marguerida.

"There is a certain time, you know," Marguerida said in

a confidential tone, speaking of things only women could understand, "when fathers simply don't know how to cope with their daughters."

"Yes," Katherine picked up the idea, "you know what men are like, helpless in the face of a little emotion."

"He . . . he does get angry if I cry," Sibelle sniffed. Clearly, she had never considered that she might not be in the wrong.

"And if you should happen to have a thought of your own, he would be seized by the demon cats of Ardryn," Katherine said.

Marguerida wondered if this were carrying the notion too far, for certainly the girl had never heard of Ardryn, but "demon cats" sounded a bit strong. "This is exactly why we Comyn have so often fostered one another's teenaged children. It saves a great deal of wear and tear on everyone concerned. You know my own foster daughter, Alanna?"

Perhaps it was dangerous to use Alanna as an example, but Marguerida could truthfully say that she had given Alanna a far better home than her own mother ever could.

"I promise you," Katherine was saying, "that if you come to live with us, Hermes will not get angry at a few tears."

At the mention of Hermes, who had succeeded Lew as the Federation Senator from Darkover and knew how to handle difficult negotiations, Marguerida felt hopeful. Katherine's forthright manner might be too abrasive for Francisco, proud as he was, and quick to take offense, and obviously of the opinion that women were subject to command of their male kinfolk.

"Kate," she said, as a considerably happier Sibelle left them, "I think we should bring your husband in on this scheme, and have him talk to Francisco. I'm sure Francisco would be more amenable to the proposal if it came from a man as respected as Herm."

"Why, Marja, I think you are right. When I'm with you,

it's easy to forget how recalcitrant and sexist these Comyn can be. For Sibelle's sake, it would be better to avoid provoking her father. Herm is just the person to do it, too."

Neither woman was surprised when, a couple of days later, Terése and Yllana ran to their respective mothers with the news that Sibelle was to join them at Castle Aldaran.

15

As Council season drew to an end, Lew made his final plans to leave Thendara. The guides he had hired from the Thendara Renunciate Guild House completed their arrangements. He felt a surge of restlessness, as if he had stayed indoors too long, a yearning to be gone from the confines of castle and city, to feel the wind in his hair and a horse between his knees, to look again on the untamed heights.

The leave-taking was as difficult as he had feared. Beneath her hopeful words and cheerful demeanor, Marguerida fought back tears. Mikhail looked grim, and Domenic, who had been persuaded by his mother to delay his own travels to the various Towers until the following year, radiated resentment and misery. Alanna was nowhere in sight, and Yllana had already departed on the long journey to Aldaran.

The journey passed uneventfully. Still some leagues from Nevarsin, Lew caught a glimpse of the ancient city, clear and pale in the morning light. The gray walls of the monastery jutted like ancient bones through the eternal glacial ice. The trail wound downward into the valley, which they reached in time for the midday meal and rest. The Renunciate guides kept Lew warm and well fed; they pressed hot tea on him, reminding him of the need for extra liquids in the altitude. Then they mounted up again, proceeding along the broad, well-traveled road that led to the City of Snows.

They arrived at the gates of Nevarsin just as dusk fell. Rain blurred the sky, heralding the swift fall of night. Within, they rode single file along cobbled streets, up narrow winding lanes and finally the steep, snow-covered paths that led to St. Valentine's.

Lew and his party paused before the inner gates, where the statue of St. Christopher, the Bearer of Burdens, bowed beneath the weight of the world beside the smaller image of St. Valentine. Lew shivered, despite the layers of fur and thick wool.

The older of the two Renunciate guides pulled on the knotted rope hanging beside the lantern on the gates, and Lew heard the slow, deep tolling of a bell. A few minutes later, a short, dignified man in a brown robe came out to greet them.

"I am Brother Tomas, and I bid you welcome to St. Valentine's." The monk shifted his cowl to reveal a bald head, a face crinkled by lines, and merry blue eyes. "I also greet you, my sisters, but I regret I cannot permit you to enter here, not even the guesthouse."

"We respect your rule, for we have a similar one in our own Guild Houses," the older Renunciate said. "We have no need of your hospitality this night; our sisters in the city wait to welcome us. *Dom* Lewis, we have completed our contract with you. We leave you in the care of this good monk."

Passing through the gates behind Brother Tomas, Lew found comfortable stables for his horse and the pack animal carrying his personal belongings. Robed, cowled figures hurried silently across the courtyard. Some of them looked too young to be monks, and Lew supposed they were students. Danilo had attended the school here, as had Regis.

The monk did not inquire about Lew's business but led him to the guesthouse, a square stone building set a little distance from the main monastery. A fire warmed the common room, and a simple meal had already been laid out on a trestle table. Two men in sheepskin vests and leggings were about to sit down. At Lew's arrival, they set aside their meal and helped him carry his packs from the stables to the small room that was to be his. The stew and crusty, nut-laced bread were still warm when they all returned. They stood, looking awkward and hesitant, while Lew helped himself to a portion.

"Please sit, eat," Lew urged them. "You have already delayed your dinner in order to assist an old man."

They glanced at one another, and Lew was reminded poignantly how much in awe these Hellers mountain folk held the Comyn. With some convincing, they agreed to join him.

Afterward, Lew settled himself on the narrow cot in his room with a sense of profound relief. He did not trouble to light the stack of wood in the fireplace. His chamber lay just a wall's thickness from the common room, and he was warm enough beneath the soft wool blanket.

Although his bones throbbed with weariness, Lew lay awake for some time before sleep overtook him. A faint radiance, the light of a single moon, drifted through the thick, wrinkled glass of the window. Rarely had he been surrounded by silence so profound. Thendara, like any major city, was never truly still. Comyn Castle always held some distant hum of activity. Here, in the isolation of the monastery, no dogs searched the garbage for scraps, no men staggered home from a tavern, no midwives sat with their laboring charges. The immense brooding quiet of the mountain permeated the air.

In that silence, the beating of his heart grew slower and softer, until it seemed he could hear other things between the rhythmic pulses. Voices long since muted reverberated faintly through the bedrock.

Bits of memory, images of fleeting brightness, swept through him. From the marrow of his bones came a cell-deep vibration, the echoes of a scream. His own, he thought, yet so distorted, torn from his throat so long ago,

leaving his voice permanently hoarse. His own voice, and
the reeling agony in his mind as his *laran* barriers gave way
under that relentless, crushing pressure. His mind bending,
collapsing, until he was a thing of dust and ashes, nothing
more—another's voice ringing through him, another's will
guiding his actions.

Even now, at the deepest level of his bones, some part of
himself writhed in anguish, pleaded, fought . . .

It is over, he told himself. *I survived, I am myself again.
No taint of Sharra remains in my starstone.* Why then could
he not shake these memories?

Why then did this other voice, this echo upon echoes,
still cry out in his mind? He heard it as from a distance, as
if he were outside, heard the inarticulate howl, the shame,
the violation—

No!

And now another voice came to him, his own, repeating
with hideous, inexorable force, *You will forget what you
have seen . . . forget the fireball, the sorcerous lightning . . .
that is not what happened here today . . . the battle was ordinary, nothing more . . .*

In his memory, he pressed on, thrusting past the wisps of
defense, seizing control, planting his command deep and
sure. *Forget . . .*

What had been done to him in Caer Donn had been
done unwillingly, for they had all been caught up in the
madness that was Sharra. What he had done to the Terran
soldiers after the Battle of Old North Road, *that* had been
deliberate, a fully conscious choice. Their minds had lain
open to his, defenseless. Once or twice he had felt a spark
of awareness as he drew upon the Alton Gift.

It did not matter why he had done it, how noble his motives, or even that the future of Darkover depended upon
it. Knowingly, he had used his *laran* to enter the minds of
those men; he had twisted their will and warped their
memories.

He had assaulted another person in the same way that
he himself had once been violated.

Wave after wave of self-loathing swept through him. His body shuddered. Sickness filled his mouth. If he could have fumbled his way to the knife in his pack, he would have taken his own life.

No, he thought as a renewed spasm of nausea shook him. He did not deserve such an end to pain. A quick death and the peace of the grave, these were for worthy men, not himself.

Somewhere a voice moaned in wordless anguish, a voice he should recognize. Somewhere lungs struggled for breath, an aged heart faltered but kept on, the stump of an arm burned with long-forgotten fire, an old man hugged his trembling arm to his bony chest.

Eventually, exhausted muscles loosened and the shivering eased. The dense stillness of the mountain, the glimmering light of the far-off moons seeped into the chamber. He breathed it in. Almost, he could hear a voice whispering.

Rest now, lay your burden down. You are in a house of peace . . .

In the end, he slept, and no dreams came.

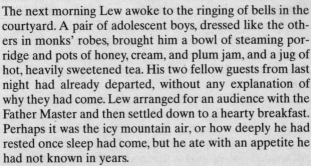

The next morning Lew awoke to the ringing of bells in the courtyard. A pair of adolescent boys, dressed like the others in monks' robes, brought him a bowl of steaming porridge and pots of honey, cream, and plum jam, and a jug of hot, heavily sweetened tea. His two fellow guests from last night had already departed, without any explanation of why they had come. Lew arranged for an audience with the Father Master and then settled down to a hearty breakfast. Perhaps it was the icy mountain air, or how deeply he had rested once sleep had come, but he ate with an appetite he had not known in years.

The novices returned with the message that Father Conn would see him after morning prayers, and he was welcome to join them in chapel beforehand.

A light snow had fallen across the courtyard. Lew drew

his cloak about him and made his way across to the monastery building. The chapel was in the oldest part of the structure, hundreds of years old, and Lew had once heard that it was a matter of pride that every stone had been cut and placed by human hands. No *laran* had been used in its construction.

Within the chapel a single light glowed in the shrine to the Holy Bearer of Burdens, gently suffusing the entire chamber. Daylight sifted through the ancient windows, pieced together from shards of brilliantly colored glass. As Lew took a place on a bench toward the back, his eyes adjusted to the light. He had known music all his life, whether ballads sung to guitar or *ryll*, trail songs, or Marguerida's formal compositions, but rarely had he heard such soaring, almost ecstatic melodies.

Men's voices, a blend of rumbling bass, sweet tenor, and the pure high sopranos of the boys, rose and fell in chant. The words were so old as to be barely recognizable.

"One Power created
Heaven and earth,
Mountains and valleys,
Darkness and light . . ."

Listening, Lew felt a strange sense of coming adrift in time. He could have been any age from seven to seventy, and it could have been now or a hundred, five hundred years ago. These stones, these voices, these ageless words, remained the same. The snow on the mountain, the stone floor beneath his feet, the slow flickering of the vigil light . . .

He saw his own sorrows as fleeting, no more than ripples in the vast firmament of time. In another decade or perhaps two, he would be forever at peace, his pain and struggles forgotten as if they had never existed, and his joys too. This, *this* would remain, and for the moment, he was part of it.

The last sustained chord died into silence. Lew held his breath. Then someone coughed, feet shuffled, and a loose wooden railing creaked. The younger boys whispered among themselves as they filed out.

The monks moved with noiseless grace, even the older ones. Lew sat and watched them leave, catching glimpses of their faces. Young and old, well-formed or homely, each reflected the same inner serenity. Hunger stirred within him, the desire to relive that moment of transcendent grace.

Toward the last came a tall, angular man whose clothing was no different from any of the other monks but who held himself a little apart. He paused beside Lew.

"I am Father Conn. Will you accompany me to my office, where we may speak privately?"

The monk's voice was deep and melodious, as if the hymn still sang through him. Lew followed him along a short passageway, lined with panels of age-darkened wood, and through a door. The room beyond was graciously proportioned and pleasant, with pale walls and leaded-glass windows overlooking the courtyard. Bookcases held rows of leather-bound volumes, some of them very old, and more books sat on the battered wooden desk. The only ornament was a carved wall-hanging of a man carrying a laughing babe on his shoulders, the Bearer of the World's Burdens with the Holy Child.

Lew seated himself on one of the plain chairs, unsure of how to begin. He did not want to use his Comyn rank to gain admission to the community, and yet he could not think how to tell his story without revealing his identity—or his crime.

"You have come here in search, Lewis-Kennard Alton," Father Conn said. The daylight turned his gray eyes luminous, almost silver. "As many have before you. Rest assured, nothing you say will leave these four walls. I am no judge, but a fellow pilgrim like yourself, a servant only. How may I ease your burden?"

Lew shook his head, thinking that he was a fool to have come so far when there was no help, no possible forgiveness. He could not go home again, knowing what he had done. The burden, as Father Conn referred to it, was past all human bearing.

How could he tell Marguerida, who had done the same,

adding her Gift to his? Would that not amount to accusing her of the same atrocity? Or Danilo, who had suffered from psychic torment at the hands of old Dyan Ardais? Or any of the Tower folk, whose first and most basic oath was: *Never to enter another mind, save to help or heal, and then only with consent?*

No, his crime was beyond forgiveness, the vilest imaginable act to another telepath. Their response would surely be to cast him out and condemn him utterly.

Yet in the Father Master's unflinching gaze, Lew found a glimmer of hope. Slowly, with many stammering missteps, he began his tale. Often he paused, overcome with shame. Father Conn did not press him but sat with that same expression of careful, compassionate listening. The words tumbled out, framing the images in Lew's mind. With each syllable, he felt an infinitesimal lightening of the sickness in his soul.

"I do not know how to live with what I have done," Lew concluded. "I only know that I cannot go on as I have before."

"No, that much is clear," Father Conn said. "What new beginning would you make of your life?"

"A friend suggested I might find peace here. I suppose he meant the relief of confession. But that changes nothing!" Lew cried with a sudden rush of passion. "I cannot go back into the past and undo the damage to those men's minds. Even if I found a way off-planet and tracked each one down, how can there be forgiveness for me? What could I do that would ever make such a thing right?"

For a long moment Father Conn sat, watching him quietly, until Lew grew uneasy, wondering what the monk must think of him. "This monastery owes its beginning to a question very like yours," Father Conn said. "How is unendurable guilt to be endured? How is unbearable shame, or pain that sends men to the brink of madness, to be borne? How is life to be lived when all hope is gone?"

A shudder passed through Lew's body. The old monk had spoken his deepest fears, his most elemental questions. Lew felt the very depths of his soul had been exposed, yet there was not the slightest tinge of censure or recrimination in those words.

Lew's gaze went to the opposite wall, where the saint bent beneath the weight of the world and all its sorrows. The carved wood had been worn to shadows, the unseeing eyes filled with such gentle sadness, such compassion, that Lew had to look away.

Raised to worship the four gods of the Comyn, Lew had never given serious thought to any other faith. The *cristoforos* were said to pray for the strength to carry their burdens. Could it be that they were answered? That he himself might find some ease, some power greater than his own flawed efforts?

"Will you not bide with us a time," Father Conn asked gently, "and see if you can discover that answer for yourself?"

If only it were possible! "What should I do here?"

"Sing," Father Conn said. To Lew's astonished response, he added, "Pray, but only if you feel moved to do so. It isn't required. Work. Listen. Walk. Sleep. Let the solitude and peace of this place grow in you, little by little."

"I—I would like that."

A smile curved the corners of the old monk's mouth. "Then let us begin."

BOOK II

— ✦ —
16
— ✦ —

Earlier that same year, winter reluctantly eased its grip on the village of Rock Glen. Nestled in a vale along the road between Nevarsin and the wild Kilghard Hills, the little community prepared for spring, when the routes to the Lowlands would open. Men repaired harnesses, tended pack chervines in their sheds, and sorted the season's harvest of furs. Children ran shrieking through their homes, no longer content with the quiet indoor pursuits of ballad singing and storytelling, until their frantic mothers shooed them outdoors.

One day, as blue shadows crept across the mounds of layered, compacted snow, the man who called himself Jeram returned from checking his traps. Two of the older boys accompanied him, carrying a brace of mountain rabbit-horns. A healthy flush covered their exposed cheeks, and their eyes were bright from the exercise. Jeram led, placing each foot in the prints they had made on the outward journey.

The edges of the snow had softened in the warmth of the afternoon. Although the meltwater would freeze again that night, it was a good sign. The animals from the traps were thin, their stores of fat almost exhausted. Soon the smaller beasts would begin to starve or sicken. At least the wolves had not yet been driven to attack the village livestock. Before then, Jeram thought, the first green

shoots would push through the snow to nourish the prey
animals.

Having drawn ahead of the village boys, Jeram paused,
exhaling plumes of vapor. The little rise on which he stood
looked down upon the village. Smoke rose from chimneys,
and paths crisscrossed the open space from houses to storage barns to livestock sheds. Everything looked snug and
neat.

It was, he thought, a good life. Fur-trapping in the winter,
farming ice-melons, hardy rye and red wheat, then root
vegetables and cabbages during the summer, caravans in
spring and fall, and through the seasons, the songs and stories, the lore and gossip, the births and deaths and the thousand details of living. He had never dreamed of such a
place, where excitement meant Sarita's baby had at last
taken her first step or Collim's half-blind chervine doe had
given birth to twins.

The brightness of the day stung his eyes. He blinked and
cleared his throat. The boys caught up with him, laughing
over a joke they had told a dozen times during the dark
winter months. Something about a spaceman, a Dry
Towner and a *leronis*, undoubtedly bawdy from the way
they turned even redder as they caught his glance.

"Enough dawdling," he told them. "Let's get those rabbit-
horns back, or they'll stew up tough as leather." In all probability, they would be dry and stringy no matter how long
they simmered.

Jeram turned, glancing down at the snow before his feet.
Without warning, the world slipped sideways. In his sight,
the footprints elongated as if they were gel-plas. The snow,
gray and crusted, rippled, shifting into a living, breathing
thing. Colors merged and twisted.

Again he felt that terrible pressure against his mind, saw
that face he did not recognize. Eyes glowed, burning
through his insubstantial flesh.

"Who are you?" Jeram gasped. "What do you want with
me?"

The ground reeled and dipped beneath his feet. For an instant, he seemed to leave his body, hovering in space. He tried to yell for help, but he had no voice. Gray rimmed his vision, condensing into blackness . . .

"Jeram! Jeram, say something, please! Are you hurt? What is the matter?" Liam, the older of the two, was shaking Jeram's shoulders. The boy's brow furrowed with concern.

With a jerk, Jeram came back to himself. He lay on his back in the snow with no memory of having fallen. Gingerly, he wiggled his toes, checking for sensation and motor control. After determining that he could move all four extremities and there was no pain along his spine, he sat up.

"It's all right," he told the boys. "I'm—all right," and he prayed that he did not lie.

The younger boy, more shy than his brother, stared at Jeram. Both looked uncomfortable.

"What is it, lads?"

"You—you shouted something in another tongue. It didn't sound like anything we've ever heard."

Jeram clambered to his feet and ran a suddenly trembling hand over his rough-bearded cheeks. This was a moment he'd dreaded, one of them anyway, when he let down his guard, forgot all the d-corticator sleep learning tapes, and blurted out something in Terran Standard.

"I don't remember what I said." He tried to keep his tone casual. "I must have used one of the more bizarre dialects I've picked up over the years. I told you, didn't I, that I traveled a lot when I was young? That's why I've got this awful accent."

Jeram chuckled, as if it were a joke. Then, to demonstrate that all was well, he took the rabbit-horn carcasses and headed down the final slope.

"It would be better if you didn't say anything about this, especially not to Morna," he said after a while. "You know how women are. She'll only fret."

The boys were old enough to remember the fuss when Morna, widowed young, had taken in a half-frozen stranger and later married him in the freemate custom of the mountains. They shrugged, clearly content to leave their elders to their eccentric ways.

———— ✦ ————

It snowed again that night, flurries that found their way through every chink in the cottage walls. Jeram fell asleep in Morna's arms, the two of them warmed by furs from animals that he himself had trapped. He awoke later to silence and the pounding of his heart. The bed-chamber, one of three rooms, for Morna's family had been comfortably well-off, felt unnaturally still. Moving carefully so as not to awaken her, he slipped out of bed and went to the window. Through the slitted shutters, he made out two of the four moons, awash in their pastel, multihued light. He wondered if he would ever get used to more than one moon swinging across a tapestry of un-familiar stars . . .

I chose this world, I chose this life. I am Darkovan now, and everything else is past and buried.

The man who had once been Jeremiah Reed had come to Darkover battered and weary in spirit, darkly cynical. He had seen men and beasts and mountains valuable only as strategic tools.

What was he doing here, he had once grumbled, on this Closed Class-D world where natives settled their differ-ences by hacking each other to bloody bits with swords? The Terran Station Chief wanted a heavily armed force, in-cluding tech specialists like Jeram, for some unfathomable reason.

When Jeram was deployed in a routine action on Old North Road, it had begun like any other policing mission. The local bigwigs were making trouble, they'd been told.

Take them out, read the orders. *Get rid of the whole med-dlesome, elitist Council with a single strike.*

The team had worked together with their Aldaran con-federates, scoping the territory and laying out their am-bush. Everything had gone according to plan, that much Jeram remembered. The locals were greatly outgunned, fighting only with primitive edged weapons. They should have been no threat at all.

But then . . .

Then he had woken up in the blood-drenched mud, with his head pounding and a sickness like nothing he had ever known shivering through his nerves. His mind kept telling him that the enemy had been greater in numbers and more skillful than anyone anticipated. Something had happened to him, something that made his stomach twist and acid rise in his throat every time he tried to think about it.

The others in the team had gone back to the Thendara spaceport to wait for the last Federation ship home. Part of him longed to *get off this goddawful frozen twilit planet,* the same part that told him that the defeat had been a miscalculation, nothing more. Instead, for reasons he did not entirely understand, he had slipped out of the city. He would never find the answers if he left.

It was a stupid risk. If the native rulers, the Comyn, found out he had taken part in the ambush, they would probably execute him on sight.

Luck was with him, for no one stopped him or asked his business. No one demanded his identity. His d-corticator training allowed him to pass well enough, explaining away his accent as a distant dialect. With his fair skin and rust-dark hair, he blended in with the native population.

Days passed, weeks—no, they called them *tendays* here. He found work of one kind or another, striking up casual friendships on the road. As the bruises of the battle faded and the slash on his left shoulder healed, he felt a veil lift from his eyes. For the first time, he saw the world around him.

Darkover was cold, yes, but so were the Rocky Mountains, where he'd spent much of his childhood. The great Red Sun cast glorious shades of color upon color. The air smelled clean with wild herbs, pitch pine, and resin-trees.

The Hellers, that vast and towering mountain range, called to him. Something in their sheer heights and the crystalline beauty of the glaciers tugged at his soul. Perhaps these peaks reminded him of happier boyhood times, or perhaps it was something in their uncompromising starkness that stripped away the artifice of his former life. Here at last was a place where he could put the past behind him and start anew.

It had been a simple thing to change his name to something more Darkovan, to find a village beyond the traveled paths, where he could settle without too many questions. No one knew he was here. The Federation would never come after him with charges of desertion. His neighbors suspected nothing of his role in the Battle of Old North Road. His new life would have been perfect if it were not for his bad dreams.

Dreams were one thing, but this episode, with its lingering disorientation and loss of consciousness, was something else. If there was something seriously wrong with him, it might prove fatal. There were no antiepileptic drugs on the planet, let alone this far into the wilderness, or any effective treatments for a brain tumor or meningitis.

If I die, I die, he thought as he slipped back into bed. After what he had been through, the thought had no power to frighten him. Dying was easy; men had died all around him on Old North Road. Living, that was the hard part.

———— ✦ ————

"Jeram! Oh gods, Jeram! Answer me!"

He felt cold air on his face, hands on his shoulders, the creak of a mattress on its supporting leather straps beneath him. The world moved sickeningly. His vision thinned at irregular intervals, dissolving . . . dissolving him with it . . .

He heard the voice again, a woman's voice, a voice he should know, but the words no longer made any sense. Sounds washed over him, resonated through his bones. The world swung ponderously, pendulum-like, up and down, in and out. It took him with it, further and higher with each enormous swing, out into nowhere with each swooping breath. Stars streaked past him, atoms, vibrations like the very rhythm of the universe . . .

"... threshold sickness, I'd stake my life on it ..." said another voice, a woman's voice, but one he did not know.

"How can he possibly?" That was Morna: warm arms in the night, gray eyes alight with sadness and passion. "A good man to be sure, but a drifter out of nowhere?"

"I don't know, maybe some lord's unacknowledged—" The strange woman spoke again, with the kind of brisk authority that Jeram associated with nurses and kindergarten teachers. She said a few words in *casta* that he did not understand. "—families all through these mountains have *laran,* or so I've heard."

But I'm not one of you ... Jeram's breath came in gasps with the effort of containing his secret, holding back the fateful words.

He drifted in the far spaces between the stars, frozen like comet dust, stretching thinner and thinner on the interstellar cosmic wind ...

The next moment, he shrank to microscopic size, tissues and cells, the intricate colorless patterning of mitochondria, the flash and sparkle of biochemical reactions, the drifting crystal-like particles of disease. Almost, he could reach out and touch them, change a receptor site in the protein coat of a virus, turn a virulent prion into an inert, harmless particle. They clung to his body like pollen, like grains of star-stuff.

— ◆ —

"He's worse, isn't he?" Morna again. Sweet, loving Morna.

"We must take him to the Tower at Nevarsin," said the second woman, an undercurrent of fear in her voice. "If the *leroni* there cannot help him, then no one can."

A cup pressed against his lips. He had not realized how dry and chapped they were. "Drink," said a voice, and he did.

Fire washed through his body. He burned with it. Vision shredded into flame.

"More."

He swallowed again and again at the insistence of the voice, until he dissolved into darkness and felt no more.

— ◆ —

Jeram came to himself sitting on a pony—Morna's pony, the flea-speckled gray—on a broad, well-traveled road a short distance from the steep gray walls of Nevarsin. He must have been fading in and out of consciousness for some time, for he remembered snatches of trail and trees, the smell of horse dung, the creak of oiled saddle leather, the wind tugging at his beard.

So it was real, not more hallucinations.

"Are you feeling better now?" He recognized the woman's voice but not her face. She reined in her own mount, a sturdy mountain pony, a bay with black points and such heavy feathering the length of its legs that it looked like a miniature draft horse. A chervine on a leading line carried supplies, perhaps trade goods as well.

"I—I think so." Jeram's mount moved off, following the other animal. "I'm afraid I can't remember how I got here, or who you are, for that matter."

The other woman swiveled in the saddle, and he got a good look at her face, pleasant mouth, wind-roughened cheeks, ginger hair hacked off like a boy's. Something in her eyes reminded him of Morna, a cousin perhaps. She introduced herself as Nerita n'ha Caillean, without any family name.

"I remember being sick. You came to tend me." Jeram tried to sort through the chaos of impressions, some of which were clearly hallucinations. Although he did not feel delusional, he knew of half a dozen agents, biological and chemical, that might produce what he had just lived through. So far as he knew, none of them had ever been imported to Darkover.

"You've been through a bout of threshold sickness, pretty bad, too," Nerita said, nudging her horse forward. "I've never heard of someone as old as you getting it. It's usually adolescents, and Comyn at that. Were you ever tested for *laran*?"

Hell, I don't even know what it means!

"The folk at the Tower will sort it out," she said, "or else Morna will take it out of my hide. Here we are."

They had reached a little village nestled in a little depression. Rising in his stirrups, Jeram made out the outlines of the city itself, as gray as the mountainside. Above it, sheets of glacial ice shimmered in the sun. The village was nothing special, houses of wood and stone, pens and sheds for livestock, an inn with its stables, a cookshop or two doing business with travelers to the city. He had a vague recollection of having passed through the village before, stopping for a tankard of steaming, spice-laced cider on a frosty morning before going on to the city, where Morna bargained for salt and sewing needles. He had watched silently as the men of the village sold their furs and ice-melons, buttons carved from chervine antlers and blankets woven from their soft fur.

The familiar wariness settled on him. *Stay quiet, unnoticed, do nothing to attract questions.*

He swayed in the saddle, his stomach unsettled. Perhaps this weakness was due to his recent illness or to simple lack of food. He could not remember having eaten.

Never before had he felt so exposed. The smallest gesture—the movement of his hand to the blaster no longer at his hip, an inadvertent expletive in a language no Darkovan spoke—would betray him. Something else now flowed through his every thought, colored his vision and his breath.

What was this laran *Nerita had spoken of, which now had sunk its claws into the deepest recesses of his mind?*

17

Through his wavering vision, Jeram spotted a towerlike structure at the far end of the village, neither fortress nor lookout. Yet, he sensed, it was not undefended. An invisible barrier walled it away from the rest of the world.

"What—what is that place?" he asked.

"The end of our journey—Nevarsin Tower," answered his Renunciate guide. "Mayhap you'll not have heard of it, for the folk there do little to draw attention to themselves. They will lend their magic in time of need, for healing beyond what we can give. Otherwise, they are as reclusive and close-mouthed as the *cristoforo* monks."

A man in warm, ordinary clothing, his face grave and lined with care, his hair carrot-red streaked with gray, met them at the base of the Tower. After hearing Jeram's story, he took him inside.

As soon as the heavy wooden door closed behind them, a flood of impressions assaulted Jeram's senses—colors, swirling and melting into one another, music from a dozen different directions, fire flaring and then subsiding into the narrow flame of a candle . . .

He put out one hand to steady himself and almost fell. The walls around him, stone partly covered with carved wooden panels, dissolved into sparkling powder.

"You are unwell, but we will care for you," the man said with a kindness that surprised Jeram. "Do not fear, we are not sorcerers, as they call us in the city, nor are we devils or men cursed by the gods. Everything we do here lies within the power of the trained human mind. Come now, lean upon me. I will take you to a place where you can rest, and then our *leronis* will see to you."

Leronis . . . That was some kind of seeress, a fortune-teller or herbalist perhaps. Whatever was wrong with him, this *threshold sickness,* the last thing he needed was the ministrations of a native witch-doctor.

Something tugged at Jeram's memory, some detail from the sleep tapes or his field briefings. Something, perhaps, he had heard during his brief time stationed in Aldaran.

Something about extrasensory powers, women and men, cloistered and trained in unimaginable ways to use these talents. Was that what was wrong with him, Jeram wondered, some psychic malady? He had no detectable psi; he'd been tested as part of his Federation placement evaluations. Everyone knew that such talents, assuming they were genuine and not an elaborate hoax, were worthless . . .

Jeram could not think straight. The world was thinning again, twisting and melding. Somehow, his body managed to keep going, propelled by the gentle pressure on his shoulder.

They passed through a narrow hall, a common room, and up a winding staircase. Here and there, softly glowing globes had been set in brackets on the walls. They looked like solar lights, but that was impossible, Jeram thought dazedly. Darkover was a low-tech world, wasn't it?

Jeram leaned heavily on the railing and kept going. Moving helped the disorientation. After what could have been only a few minutes but seemed much longer, they came to a landing.

Jeram's guide lifted a latch and swung open a door to what was surely a bedroom, one wall curved with the outer shape of the Tower, windows of surprisingly good glass, a bed and chest, and a cabinet with bowl and ewer of beautifully glazed blue pottery. He stumbled to the bed, which seemed to reach out to receive him. As he closed his eyes, the twisting in his stomach enveloped him.

Some time later, he became aware of thirst and the presence of another human being in the room. A woman in a long red robe, her features partly shadowed by a gauzy scarf of the same color, sat on a stool beside his head, leaning over him. She could have been any age from twenty to forty, with smooth, milk-pale skin, peculiar colorless eyes, and copper-bright hair.

She smiled encouragement. "The worst of the threshold sickness has passed. I don't understand why you were not better prepared. Surely, someone must have warned you of the danger when your *laran* awoke."

Jeram sat up, half expecting the world to slip and grow thin, but it remained normal. His body felt sound enough, without injury or undue fatigue. Despite his thirst, he felt unusually well, his vision clear and steady.

How much could he say? The less, the better.

"I didn't know I had it."

She looked at him with a strange intensity. At the back of his mind, he felt a whisper touch, as if she had gotten *inside* his skull.

Memory came roaring up, of terrible crushing pressure in his head, of himself disintegrating under its weight, of fighting back with every last morsel of will and desperation—

—*the face with the burning eyes*—

The next instant, the butterfly touch vanished. The woman sat back, staring at him with an expression he could not read. "I most humbly beg your pardon for the intrusion," she said. "I am Keeper here, and you have been under my care. You were near death when the Renunciate brought you to us. I entered your mind only to save your life."

"You . . ." *saved my life*, Jeram thought, and knew in the pit of his belly that she had.

He struggled for the right words. "I don't understand any of this. What you say *feels* right. I know it's true, and I also know . . ." *that entering the mind of another against his or her will is a kind of rape.*

How exactly did he know that?

"Among telepaths, it is indeed a grave offense. When we speak one mind to another, however, there can be no pretense, no dissembling. If I may—" she reached out one hand. Her fingers were graceful and slender, and, Jeram noticed with a little shock, there were six of them.

Although every nerve shrieked in denial, he forced himself to hold still. "Go ahead. You saved my life. Do whatever you have to."

He closed his eyes, expecting another assault. What came instead was a cool, featherlight touch on his temple. A sensation like silk slipped across his mind, and he caught the distant arpeggio of an Old Terran Welsh harp. He had not heard such an instrument except in recordings since he was a child. The melody, half remembered, half heard, stung his eyes.

She's in my mind, he thought, and this time there was no reflexive panic.

I am Silvana, Keeper of Nevarsin Tower. From girlhood, I have been trained to match resonances with another mind in such a way as to do no harm.

Only Jeram's long years of training kept him from jumping to his feet—he had *heard* her thoughts.

"Open your eyes, man who calls himself Jeremiah Reed." Silvana's voice carried neither censure nor surprise. She sat on her stool, watching him with careful eyes. For a long moment, neither spoke.

Jeram's heart pounded in his ears. She had read his mind—she must know who he was.

"We of the Towers do not judge a man by his origin or pedigree, as if he were a race horse," Silvana said, "only by the quality of his character. I have seen enough of yours to believe you are a good man. While you are here, you are under my protection. Let no more be said." Silvana nodded, clearly accustomed to unquestioned obedience.

"A different matter concerns me," she went on. "Clearly, you were not prepared for the awakening of your *laran*. Here at Nevarsin Tower, we can teach you to control those powers, lest they in turn control you."

He caught, like a whisper from another room, the Keeper's thought, *An untrained telepath is a danger to himself and everyone around him.*

"I don't suppose there's any way of getting rid of it?"

"Why would you wish such a thing?" Silvana frowned, and he wondered how he had offended her. "*Laran* is a rare and precious Gift. So few of us have it, and even fewer yet have the strength to put it to use."

For all he cared, she could keep it. "My threshold sickness—will it come back?"

"I cannot say. In most cases, once the crisis has passed, the symptoms subside. However, you may be vulnerable to a relapse simply because you are older." At his quizzical glance, she explained, "The channels that convey *laran* also carry sexual energy. Frequently, both become active at the same time."

"During puberty?"

"Exactly. I've heard of cases in which, for one reason or another, *laran* was shut down or deliberately suppressed. In the old times, Keepers were expected to remain virgins, but nowadays, we know this is cruel and unnecessary. In any event, that cannot be true in your case. You are no *emmasca,* but a functioning, sexually active male."

Silvana said this with such unemotional, almost clinical detachment, she might have been discussing a biochemical reaction. Jeram was accustomed to the earthy candor of the village folk, but he had not expected it from this beautiful, elegant lady. He felt heat rise to his face.

"Your talent seems to have lain dormant, never awakened," Silvana went on without a pause, oblivious to his reaction, "until something happened to overwhelm your natural defenses."

"Like an—a psychic assault upon my mind?" Jeram blurted out before he could consider the full meaning of his words.

"Yes, forced rapport—if that is what you mean—could break through even strong natural barriers." She leaned forward, brushing her fingertips over the back of his wrist. Once again, Jeram felt the silken touch on his mind.

What happened to you? whispered like a scented breeze.

"I—I don't know."

Nausea rose up in him, and for a terrifying moment, objects at the edges of his vision elongated, plastic melting under heat.

What's wrong with me? Why can't I remember? Why does this happen to me every time I try?

"I believe that you have answered your own question." Silvana's voice was low and mild, trained to conceal rather than express deep emotion. "Something—or someone—has tampered with your memories and, in the process, broken through to your deeply buried talent."

"Tampered with my memories?" Jeram repeated, stunned.

His first response was to insist that wasn't possible. During his psi testing, he had been told he was highly resistant to hypnosis. Darkovan pharmacology simply wasn't sophisticated enough to produce drugs that would affect only memory, and only such a small part, a few hours at most. Even if such things existed here, how had it been administered?

And yet . . .

The Battle of Old North Road—the missing hours—the sense of twisting *wrongness* whenever he tried to think of it—

Quickly, he shut away the thought. The last thing he wanted was to reveal his role in the attempted assassination of the Comyn Council.

A light tap sounded, and the door swung open. A much younger woman, another stunning redhead, entered. She wore a simple belted robe of gray-green and carried herself with the same dignified reserve as the Keeper.

"This is Illona," Silvana said, "my under-Keeper."

Illona carried a small wooden tray with a vial filled with

clear liquid, another glass tube marked for measuring, and a cup. She handed the tray to Silvana.

Silvana measured out a portion of liquid from the vial into the cup and offered it to Jeram. "Here, this will help to settle your symptoms. It is honey-water with *kirian*, one of the safer distillations. We keep a supply for youngsters with threshold sickness, and other uses."

Jeram took the cup and sniffed. The liquid had a vaguely citrus aroma. He hesitated, remembering the warnings about native botanicals. The Darkovans might be descended from Terran colonists, but that didn't mean it was safe to eat or drink everything they did. "What does it do?"

"It lowers the telepathic threshold," Silvana said.

"No, thank you. I'll get through this without any drugs." Jeram set the cup aside. He'd had enough of other people inside his head.

Illona exchanged a quick glance with Silvana, then turned back to Jeram. "I am a trained monitor. Will you permit me to examine you?"

Despite Silvana's earlier words of reassurance, Jeram did not want her or anyone else rummaging telepathically around in his memories. "I'm very grateful for all the help you've given me, but this isn't necessary. I'll be fine now." He pulled the bedcovers aside and swung his legs over the edge of the bed.

As soon as Jeram's feet touched the floor, dizziness swept through him. His body seemed to divide in two . . . eight . . . twenty overlapping images. Thought splintered. The world slipped sideways.

Strong, slender hands lowered him back to the bed. The rim of a cup pressed against his mouth. "Please, let us help you. Drink."

Jeram swallowed. The sweet, aromatic liquid warmed his gullet as it went down.

Breath rushed through his lungs. Blood ebbed and surged behind his eyes to the rippling doubled-beat of his heart. Delicate lines of glowing white light, like skeletons of lightning, shot across his vision.

He opened his eyes and the images faded, replaced by a soft blur of shape and color. His pupils must be dilated. He tried again to sit up, but his arms and legs had gone limp.

Illona bent over him, smiling. She was very young, twenty at most. There was a small dimple at one corner of her mouth.

"It's all right," she said. "The worst effects will wear off in a few minutes. One of us will stay with you the whole time. I can imagine how strange this must seem."

She knows! Panic lapped at him.

"I wasn't brought up in the Towers, either," Illona went on, unconcerned. "I lived with the Travelers, performing from place to place. It took me a long time to get used to having *laran*. Just imagine being born deaf and suddenly being able to hear."

Listening to Illona's calm, assured voice, Jeram felt his panic seep away. If he were ever to get through this *threshold sickness*, he reasoned, he needed help.

Despite his misgivings, Jeram found himself trusting Illona. He felt a *presence*, as real and indescribable as the knowledge he was not alone in a lightless room. He felt no pain, no fear, only Illona's curiosity and a lingering touch of gaiety.

"Don't worry," she said, "I'm not reading your mind. I'm just listening to your body, nothing more."

He closed his eyes, aware of the voices of the two women. Gradually, the sensation of disorientation lifted. His body felt whole and strong, as stable as bedrock.

Illona turned back to him, and this time her eyes were somber. "Jeram, there is no question your memories have been altered. They are still there, but a compulsion spell prevents you from gaining awareness of them."

"I don't believe in spells and magic," Jeram muttered.

"It's not magic," Silvana said with a trace of impatience, "but matrix science, a system of knowledge and skills we of the Towers have cultivated for millennia."

Chill rippled up his spine. "You mean that all of you can take over another man's mind? What did you call it, *forced rapport*?"

Silvana said, "There are very few now alive with this particular Gift. As it happens, one of them is currently in Nevarsin, *Dom* Lewis Alton."

Alton? That was the name of one of the Darkovan ruling families.

"Oh!" Illona said, delighted. "I didn't know he was here."

"I do not believe he wished it generally known," Silvana said. "He came here quietly, last fall, to enter retreat at the monastery."

A strange expression crossed Illona's face. "Lord Alton surely knows more about forced rapport than any man living. His expertise would be invaluable now. But should we intrude upon him, when he has not made his presence known to us?"

"I do not know if he will break his seclusion," Silvana said, "but I would not make that choice for him. It will do no harm to ask."

The two *leroni* stayed with Jeram until the last effects of the *kirian* had passed, then left him to sleep. As he lay on the bed, his muscles trembled with fatigue, as if he had just run a dozen miles in full battle gear.

He wondered if this Lord Alton had been one of the funeral cortege he had helped to ambush. These natives were primitive by Federation standards, and such people took matters of honor and revenge very seriously.

There was nothing for it but to go along. Jeram was too weak to leave the Tower on his own, and he did not fully understand the nature of his affliction. He could not go back to hiding, to living in disguise. This thing within his mind had roused and must be dealt with. Like a folk-tale genie, it could not be put back into its bottle.

If what Silvana and Illona had told him was true—and he had every reason to believe them—he needed Lord Alton's help.

Hope and fear and survival instinct roiled together in him. His body exhausted, he drifted through formless dreams punctuated by shadowy figures, faces with burning eyes . . . a woman of flame . . . a city of corpses . . .

Afar, a voice cried out, and he knew it for his own.

18

Lew Alton sat at his accustomed place in the back of the chapel of St.-Valentine-of-the-Snows. The monks had departed after the morning hymns, but Lew remained, savoring the silence. It had become his habit to spend time in quiet contemplation following the chanting of the morning office. Around him, the ancient stone walls still held the final sustained chords.

The voices of the monks, from the reedy tenor of the youngest novice to the rusty quavering of the oldest, never failed to evoke Lew's wonder, that so many disparate tones could come together in a single soaring harmony. Individually, they were far from beautiful, yet from the indrawn breath before the first syllable to the last sustained note, they formed a transcendent wholeness.

Early in his sojourn here, Father Master had set him to reading the words of the holy saint.

"The truest words are not spoken by the mouth, but by the heart; the deepest silence is not heard by the ears, but by the spirit. Speak then with your heart, and listen with your soul."

This early in the day, shadows wreathed the chapel. A single lamp burned in the shrine. The monks came and went, threading their way between the rows of benches with their eyes closed, relying on their other senses. Lew supposed he was too old to learn their unerring inner sense of direction, but Father Conn had encouraged him to try, beginning with sitting here, eyes closed.

Breathe in . . .

Breathe out . . .

Bits of thought and memory drifted through Lew's mind, a line of fire sweeping through forested mountains, walking with Marjorie Scott on a frosty morning through Caer Donn, the aching void where his right hand had been . . .

Breathe in . . .

Breathe out . . .

At last, tranquility crept over him. He felt the air whispering through his lungs, the faint pulsation of his heart, the repose of his arms and legs. Even the mild stiffness in his neck, he accepted without complaint. On some days, stillness never arrived, and he would pass an hour or more, wrestling with his thoughts until he gave up or the bells summoned him to some other activity.

Gradually, Lew's awareness returned to the chapel around him, the pressure of the worn wooden bench, and the chilled flesh of his one hand. He had not learned the technique of warming his body from within. The monks, it was said, could sleep on the glacier ice in perfect comfort, wearing no more than their sandals and robes.

Moving slowly, Lew made his way along the darkened aisle. Once he would have bounded up the stairs to Father Conn's office, but his knees had endured too many winters. Now it was part of his discipline to be gentle with his limitations. Warm food was provided for him, as well as extra blankets and time to get where he needed to go. Slowly he climbed, letting his muscles and joints work within their capacity.

Father Conn looked up from his desk as Lew entered. Morning sun poured through the leaded glass windows, filling the room with gentle golden light. A beautifully calligraphed prayer book, its illuminated initials spots of bright color, lay open on the desk beside a pile of papers covered with notations.

Pausing just inside the doorway, Lew bowed. The saluta-
tion was not required, as Lew had not taken vows, nor was
he likely to. He bowed out of genuine respect. From its alcove, the carved statue of the Bearer of Burdens seemed to
smile in welcome.

Lew settled himself in his usual place, the cushioned
chair set aside for guests. Monks and novices used a back-
less bench. After exchanging greetings, Lew said, "I've
been thinking about what you said."

"Indeed? What in particular struck you as worthy of
thought?"

"You said that I knew a great deal about living with guilt
and that I'd gotten comfortable with it. I don't understand.
How else should I feel, after everything I've done?"

Father Conn folded his hands together. Ink stained the
skin of the right forefinger, and a scar ran down the back
of one hand like imprinted lightning. "I have never noticed
any correspondence between how a man thinks he *should*
feel and how he actually *does* feel."

This was, Lew thought, typical of Father Conn's comments, so different from what he expected from a man who
lived bounded by rules, from the first oath of a novice to
the final Creed of Chastity. In all the tendays since his arrival at St. Valentine's, the old man had never once lectured
him. Instead, he had offered Lew encouragement, instruc-
tion in meditation, and commonsense observations.

"I have told you the part I played in the destruction of
Caer Donn," Lew said, "not to mention everything that
happened during my exile on Vainwal and Thetis. Are
you saying I ought *not* to accept responsibility for those
things?"

"Are guilt and responsibility the same thing?"

Add to the list, *infuriating rhetorical questions.*

"No," Lew said, trying not to feel irritated, "they are not
the same. Responsibility is a fact—I made choices, I did
things for reasons that seemed good at the time, yet the results will haunt me all my life. Guilt is what I *feel* when I
think of them."

"Exactly how does your guilt change what you have done? You say you regret your actions. You offer up your own pain in the form of guilt, as if it were holy penance. I ask you again, how does tormenting yourself help those you have wronged?"

It cannot. Neither I nor any man can change the past. I must live with it forever.

A long moment of silence passed. Gently, Father Conn leaned forward and said, "The holy St. Valentine was no stranger to guilt, either. He believed it was a prison of his own making, that as long as he remained wedded to remorse, he could never move beyond it to true healing."

"I do not deserve healing."

"Perhaps. But the world does. The people you harmed do. Take your guilt, my son, and turn it into right action. Repair what you have broken."

"How?" The question burst from the very depths of Lew's soul. "How can I undo what I have done? Where in this world or the next is there any forgiveness for me?"

Father Conn sat back, once again regarding Lew with quiet compassion. "That I cannot tell you. Each man must discover the path to atonement for himself. I know you are not of our faith, yet the Holy Bearer of Burdens answers prayers regardless of the beliefs of those who offer them. You could do far worse than to ask for guidance."

With those words, Father Conn rose, signaling an end to the audience. Lew bowed again, a brief, distracted movement, and headed back toward his chamber in the guesthouse. Had he been given such an answer when he first arrived, he would have stormed away from Nevarsin without another thought. The insufferable arrogance of the old man, to suggest that he, Lewis-Kennard Alton of the Comyn, descendent of Hastur, son of Aldones, Lord of Light, would pray to an obscure penitential saint! But in the tendays and months of daily meditation, of song and discussion and gradual delving into his own heart, Lew had come to an abiding respect for this place and its people. If Father Conn thought prayer would help, then he would try.

Even as Lew crossed the courtyard, drawing his cloak
about his shoulders, words formed in his mind.

*I don't know who You are, or if You even exist, but if You
do, have pity on me. Show me what I must do.*

Upon entering the guesthouse, Lew found a young man, a
stranger, sitting there. From the lad's ginger hair, aura of
trained psychic power, and Tower-style clothing, he must
be a *laranzu*. The young man introduced himself as Anndra MacDiarmid, matrix mechanic of Nevarsin Tower.

"*Dom* Lewis Alton, I am sent by my Keeper to request
your assistance. She believes your particular experience
may shed some light on a problem that has newly presented itself." Anndra had clearly rehearsed the speech.

Particular experience? Lew stiffened. Could there be
some lingering trouble from the Sharra disaster, after all
this time? Perhaps some poor soul had escaped the flaming ruin of Caer Donn, eventually making his way here.

"If there is any help I can offer," he said, "I will gladly do
so."

Lew's horse, a black Armida-bred gelding he had trained
himself, with perfect manners and a mouth like silk, was
kept in the monastery stables. As Lew could not easily
manage, one-handed, Anndra went about saddling the
horse. Within a short time the two of them set out toward
the village and the Tower beyond it.

As Lew entered the gates of Nevarsin Tower, he sensed
the ordered discipline of a working circle, the cool sure
touch of its Keeper, the intricate patterns of matrix lattices.
He remembered his short time at Arilinn, among the happiest in his life.

Anndra escorted Lew upstairs, where the Keeper
awaited him. Although Lew had no memory of having met
Silvana before, there was something tantalizingly familiar
about her. Perhaps it was some family resemblance to
someone he knew, for the Comyn were so inbred that he
would not be surprised to learn they were all cousins to

one degree or another. She could well be a *nedestra* daughter of one of the great lords, or she could be from an obscure collateral branch.

After they had exchanged the courtesies usual among matrix workers, Silvana said, "A man has come to us for healing, and there is no one here at Nevarsin Tower with practical knowledge of the use of *laran* to overpower another man's will or experience in how a mind so shattered may be mended."

Lew flinched. Was he never to be free of that terrible time of enslavement to Sharra?

He had prayed for guidance, not knowing what form it might take. Could this plea for help be the answer, a chance to wrest some good out of all the evil that had come before?

Silvana opened a door and stood aside to let Lew enter, carefully drawing back to avoid any inadvertent physical contact. Morning sun touched the unadorned stone walls, revealing an infirmary with two beds, a couple of stools, folding tables and storage cabinets along the walls. The air held the faint, unmistakable residue of *laran* power. A man lay in the far bed, and a young woman looked up from where she sat beside it. With a start, Lew recognized her as Domenic's friend, Illona Rider. She and Domenic had begun their studies at Neskaya Tower together. Lew had forgotten that she had transferred to Nevarsin after the first year.

Illona rose and stood back so that Lew might approach. Lew's first thought was that the patient had none of the characteristic features of the Comyn, and yet he clearly possessed *laran*. The man's eyes, a shade of brown unusual on Darkover, widened as he met Lew's gaze.

"It's him!" the man shouted in Terran Standard. The words reverberated through Lew's skull. *"It's him!"*

Screaming inarticulately, the man scrambled to his feet. Illona grabbed his nearest arm. Quick as a mountain cat, he twisted free. The movement sent her sprawling.

The man, wearing only an ordinary shirt and loose pants,

stood with his legs braced in a fighting stance. There was nothing Lew could do—he could not run, he certainly could not mount any kind of defense. By instinct, he reached for his only weapon, the Alton Gift, and in that instant knew he could never use it again, not even to save his own life.

This is the answer I prayed for, this choice, he thought, and drew himself up to face the attack.

"This is a Tower, not a tavern! Cease this brawling immediately!" Silvana took a step into the room. The air shimmered with the power of her *laran.* Lew's vision went white. Warmth suffused him, a rising sense of well-being.

Enough. Lew was not sure whether Silvana had spoken aloud or only in his mind. He heard Illona's quick indrawn breath, the rustle of a gown and a soft step on the carpeted floor, and then a moan from the other man as he crumpled to the floor.

Vision returned. Illona and Silvana were lifting the nearly unconscious patient back on to the bed. Lew himself was still braced against the wall beside the door. *Laran* flooded the air, the twisted patterns of an unstable talent. He recognized the distinctive tang, like overheated metal.

With a hoarse cry, the man arched upward, arms and legs flailing.

"Merciful Avarra!" Illona cried. "Threshold convulsions!"

"He's gone back into crisis," said Silvana.

The two women pulled up stools beside the bed and quickly established psychic rapport with the sick man. Lew hesitated; it had been decades since he had worked in a circle at Arilinn. He could, however, act as a monitor, making sure that neither woman suffered any physical harm or distraction while they worked.

Lew slipped his starstone free of its wrappings, closed his eyes, and focused his *laran.* To his inner sight the man on the bed glowed like a furnace, his body a tangle of furious reds and browns, jagged yellow streaks, the throbbing crimson of critically overloaded *laran* channels.

The two *leroni* linked their minds, encircling the man with cool blue-white radiance. Lew was a little surprised by the strength of Illona's *laran*, clear and supple as liquid diamond.

As he went deeper into rapport with Silvana, searching out the patterns of her body as well as of her mind, Lew felt as if he were seeing double. He recognized the resonant vibration from her starstone but also the brilliance of her *laran*. She was not only using her starstone as any trained *leronis* would do, she *herself* concentrated and focused the mental energy. Only one lineage in all Darkover had ever possessed that ability.

She was Hastur, the living matrix, graced with the full Gift of her Domain.

Lew was so surprised that he almost dropped out of the linkage. Until Regis had used the Hastur Gift in the struggle against Sharra, it was thought to be extinct. Regis was gone, and with him this rare and precious talent. His only son, Dani Hastur, certainly did not have it.

This Keeper, hiding here in an obscure Tower, disguising her heritage, might very well be the lost daughter of Regis Hastur. With her strength of *laran* and unmistakable natural ability as a Keeper, she must be Linnea's child as well. Lew had heard of such a daughter, born soon after the World Wreckers withdrew. She had been called by another name, he could not remember what. He had been offworld during the years following the World Wreckers. Since there had been no trace of her when he returned from exile, he assumed that she had perished. He had never had the heart to ask Regis about her.

Why had she remained hidden all these years, using another name? And who was he, with his own dark secrets, to judge a Keeper's motives?

During the few moments Lew was distracted, Silvana drew upon Illona's mental energies, weaving them together with her own to buffer the worst of the unstable *laran*. Lew caught the image of wrapping the man in a soft, thick blanket. Volcanic, the man's psychic power battered against the restraints. Silvana's aura turned incandescent in response.

Acting on instinct alone, Lew plunged into rapport with the *leroni*. His powers were not what they had once been, but he was still Alton and Comyn, trained at Arilinn. With a Keeper's sure touch, Silvana reached for him, blending his mind into the unity, attuning their linked energies.

Through the lens of the Keeper's mind, Lew's mental vision deepened. He no longer saw the stranger as a pattern of *laran* channels and nodes but as a maelstrom, images and emotions as vivid as if he himself had experienced them . . .

. . . Lew felt the rough-woven cloth of the man's Darkovan disguise, the ice-edged breeze and dappled shade of the trees overhead, the occasional call of a rain-bird. Adrenaline sharpened his vision. He was seeing and feeling everything this stranger had. Behind him, one of the heavy flyers took off from the encampment where the other techs had set up their equipment . . .

. . . Along the Old North Road, the funeral train came into view, riders and wagons hung with draperies, black trimmed with blue and silver. They moved with cumbersome grace. Beside him, one of the younger men shifted, *Come on, closer* . . .

. . . Through the stranger's memories, Lew understood the battle plan. At the right distance, at the right moment, they would attack. Their cudgels would bring down the horses, their arrows take out the Guardsmen, and their knives do the rest. If all went according to plan, no one would ever know the ambush was not by a dissident group of natives . . .

. . . The first unit burst from the trees, running hard, swinging their sticks. The Guardsmen, expert riders, drew together, slashing back with swords and spears. The horses pranced, churning dust. At the rear of the train, men spilled from the carriages, swords drawn . . .

. . . "Go!" His team leader barked out the command. He surged forward with the rest of his unit, racing toward the knot of riders. The man beside him had already drawn his blaster . . .

Lord of Light defend us! Silvana's anguished cry interrupted the flow of images. *A Compact-forbidden weapon!*

Trapped in the stranger's nightmare memory, Lew caught flashes of blaster fire, a rearing horse, confusion and explosions, and the reek of death . . .

. . . They must have been better prepared than we anticipated. The thought etched itself in his brain. And yet . . . how could swords and horsemanship stand against *blasters*? . . .

. . . He lay in a pool of half-frozen, stinking red mud, and heard the moans of the man next to him . . .

. . . A face . . . a man's face, framed with hair that was red and silver, a mouth twisted by an ugly scar, bending over him . . . and a woman's, much younger but hard with purpose, with the same red hair and a tiger's golden eyes . . .

Rupturing the mental linkage, Lew reeled away in horror. Shock ripped through the circle as its unity fractured. His heart convulsed within his chest. Crushing pressure shot through his physical body as well.

The face . . . he cried out silently, *it was mine,* mine! *May all the gods forgive me!*

Lew's pulse beat fast and brittle, a desperate patter. His lungs ached for breath. His hands clutched his chest.

"*Dom* Lewis, what is the matter?" Silvana rushed to his side. He felt her touch on his forehead and another over his breastbone. Relief, cool and silver-white, swept through him. The pain lifted. Air flowed into his lungs.

"Illona, help me get him to the bed," Silvana said. "Then you must monitor him."

The two women lifted Lew to the bed, silently coordinating their strength to handle his weight. Illona focused her healing psychic energy with the quiet competence of one who would soon advance to Keeper, answerable to no man but only to her own conscience. Lew hardly noticed when Silvana left the room.

Illona continued to monitor Lew until she was certain

the episode of angina had passed. In a short time Lew felt
well enough to get up. The pain in his chest seemed to have
completely resolved.

Lew sat up, tested the steadiness of his legs, and walked
over to the bed where the Terran stranger lay, sleeping off
the exhaustion of his convulsions. From sharing the man's
memories of the Battle of Old North Road, Lew knew his
name, Jeram. Jeram's skin was roughened by weather and
recent illness, but he had strong bones, eyes bracketed by
lines of vigilance, a complex, mobile mouth.

Silvana came back just as Lew was preparing to return
to the monastery. As before, she treated him with the professional detachment of her rank. Nothing in her bearing
suggested that she was aware of his discovery of her identity. Why she disguised her lineage was, after all, her private
affair.

"Thank you for your assistance, *Dom* Lewis," Silvana
said. "Illona tells me that you have made a good recovery.
Do not overexert yourself, for these episodes of transient
chest pain can indicate a more serious heart ailment, one
that is beyond our skill to remedy."

"Vai leronis," Lew said, using the honorific address, "I
also thank you. May I—I would like to impose on your
hospitality and request an audience with Jeram."

"Why?"

"Domna, you know that I used the Alton Gift to suppress this man's memories. I do not deny it. For that deed,
I must answer to the gods themselves. But the gods are not
here. Jeram is, and there are amends to be made."

And forgiveness asked and granted, she added mentally,
for both your sakes.

Silvana tilted her head to one side, considering. "This is
my Tower, and whatever happens here is my responsibility.
If both of you agree to such a meeting, then I will permit it.
But until the two of you reach a reconciliation, I must insist
upon being present. Is that acceptable to you?"

Lew bowed his head. A sense of unexpected gratitude,
mingled with terror, filled him. After all, he had prayed for

guidance. He had not expected the answer to come in this particular form. Perhaps that was just as well, he thought as he met her gaze and nodded his agreement. Trapped by his own guilt, he would never have imagined such a meeting.

"Yes, I accept."

19

Lew arrived early at Silvana's sitting room, a pleasant chamber decorated with a distinctly feminine touch. A small fire cast ribbons of light over a mantle carved with ladies dancing with Midsummer garlands. The furnishings, low table, chairs and sideboard of silver-gray wood, made Lew feel as if he had entered an enchanted forest. Any moment now, a *chieri* might step forward.

Lew took the seat that Silvana indicated, one of a pair of chairs that had clearly been brought in for this meeting, sturdier than the rest, more suitable for a man's frame. Leaving the place facing it empty, Silvana took her own seat.

A knock sounded on the outer door. Lew tensed and gripped the wooden armrest. Silvana raised her voice in greeting, the latch lifted, and Jeram entered.

He was no longer the pale, convulsion-ridden man Lew had first seen, but shadows still haunted his russet-brown eyes, his jaw and compressed lips. He moved like a sword fighter except for the slight hunching of one shoulder and the bend in the elbow as if reaching for a weapon holstered at his belt. Refusing to meet Lew's gaze, he lowered himself into the second chair.

He does not want to be here, facing me. This meeting is as difficult for him as it is for me.

"I don't remember everything that happened the other

day," Jeram began without preamble. He spoke *casta*
surprisingly well, his off-world accent tempered by a
mountain-style lilt. "I was pretty disoriented. It's not every
day you meet the boogeyman from your nightmares. Until
that moment, I had no idea you were real."

"I am flesh and blood, even as you are," Lew said.

Jeram kept his gaze on his hands. "Silvana says you did
something that stirred up this *laran* thing in my mind. She
says you can help me."

Even without telepathic contact, Lew heard the desperate courage behind the other man's words.

*We are brothers in this, having endured the imposition of
another's will upon our own.*

He would make no excuses. He forced himself to meet
Jeram's tortured gaze, to open his mouth, to form the
words.

"My name is Lewis-Kennard Alton. I am, as you may
surmise, a telepath, and I possess the Gift of my family, that
of forced rapport. I used this Gift upon you and the other
Terran survivors of the Battle of Old North Road to
tamper with your memories."

How did he find out my part in the ambush? Jeram had
not the skill to barricade his thoughts. He scowled at Silvana.

"She told me nothing," Lew hastened to say. "When we
first met, you went into threshold crisis. Do you remember?"

Now Jeram looked directly at Lew. "You walked into the
room and all hell broke loose—" Jeram lifted one hand to
his forehead—"here."

"You recognized me," Lew said. "Then I used my *laran*
to help Silvana and Illona pull you through the crisis. In
the process, I—I'm not sure how to explain this so you
can understand—I shared your memories of the Old
North Road ambush. I saw the battle through your eyes."

"So now you know who I am." Jeram's eyes went bleak.

"And *you* know who *I* am and what I have done."

"I know there is a hole in my memory, but I don't know

why." The muscles of Jeram's jaw stood out in stark relief as he bit off each word. "What, exactly, am I not supposed to remember?"

Lew closed his eyes. "That question would be better answered if I removed the block to your memories. Then you would understand for yourself."

"You think I'm crazy enough to let you into my head again?" Jeram shot back.

"No, I can understand why not," Lew said, gesturing with his one good hand. "I will tell you, then. The fighting ended when my daughter and son-in-law, who is Regent of the Comyn, used their *laran*—their mental powers—to overwhelm your military forces."

Jeram looked incredulous. "This—this *laran* mind stuff stood up to blasters?"

You were not at Caer Donn. You did not see the real reason the Compact was made law—not to control your Terran technology but for the far more terrible weapons we can produce with our own minds. Weapons capable of bringing down a starship, turning a city into flaming ruins, opening a gate between dimensions, or perhaps even worse.

The moment stretched on. Silvana sat immobile, her expression inhumanly calm, unreadable except for the faintest whitening of her already pale skin. Even the fire seemed to pause, expectant.

Slowly, Jeram's eyes widened in understanding. Lew could not tell if the Terran had glimpsed the image of fire raining from the sky or whether the moment of silence answered his question. Jeram's unguarded thought shimmered in the air: *If what Lord Alton says is true, the Feds would stop at nothing to get their hands on a weapon like that, one that could be carried in a man's head! Undetectable, unstoppable . . .*

"We could not allow any of you return with that knowledge," Lew said. "The Comyn had expended a great deal of effort in persuading the Terran Federation that our matrix sciences—that is, the use of *laran*—was not worth investigating."

Jeram's expression darkened. "I understand why."

"You do?"

"I . . ." Jeram hesitated, his gaze wavering, his face momentarily taut. "I know something about the nastier side of warfare."

"As long as we had nothing you wanted, especially nothing with a military application, we hoped to remain safely overlooked," Lew continued, caught up in the need to tell the whole story. "With the Senate in disorder and the Federation on the brink of civil war, we were determined to keep Darkover neutral. As it happened, we were right. The Federation withdrew, and we stayed out of your war."

"So you did it to protect Darkover, without considering the cost." Jeram looked thoughtful rather than angry.

Lew said, "I do not mean that I was justified, only that the cause seemed good at the time. I cannot excuse what I did to you. I wish I had the power to undo it, but as I have not, I can only ask your forgiveness. Under the honor code of the Comyn, the one wronged may demand restitution of the offender. What would you have of me? What can I do to make amends to you?"

You're asking me? Jeram's startled thought rang in the air.

"Before you answer, Jeram, consider this." Silvana spoke quietly, yet with absolute command. "When you went into crisis for the second time, you very nearly died. Lew gave freely of his *laran* strength, heedless of any risk to himself."

"How could I have done anything else?" Lew wanted no credit, no thanks.

"You really . . ." Jeram's brows drew together, and a look of uncertainty passed over his face. "You really *believe* it, don't you? That you did a terrible thing?"

Heat rose to Lew's cheeks. The scars on forehead and upper lip, where Kadarin's rings had slashed him, burned. Somehow, he stopped himself from burying his face in his one good hand.

"I have done you injury," Lew said. "How else can I say

it? I do not know how to repair the harm. That is why it is for you to say."

No one moved. Tension thickened the air. One of the small logs in the fireplace broke apart with a hush and a fall of ashes. Silvana turned her gaze from Lew to Jeram, her gray eyes almost luminous with intensity.

As the moment lengthened, Lew's heart sank. Surely, if Jeram were willing to accept his confession, if there were any possibility of amends or forgiveness, Jeram would have responded by now.

Father Conn was wrong. There is no hope. Not for me.

Even as the words passed through Lew's mind, they shed much of their former power. He had done everything he could to clear his conscience. He could not demand forgiveness from Jeram or anyone else. Neither had he any right to judge. His only power was to let the matter rest.

In that moment, Lew felt a glimmering of compassion for the tormented man he had been. Perhaps the forgiveness he needed most must come from himself.

"All this is beside the point." Abruptly, Jeram got to his feet. "What's a few minutes of memory, anyway? You've found out who I am. Just arrest me and get it over with."

"Arrest you?" Silvana said.

"Turn me in," Jeram explained. "Report me to your law enforcement, to this Comyn Council of yours."

Lew stared, caught off-guard by Jeram's outburst. He had interpreted the Terran's silence as a rebuff. He had not considered the possibility that Jeram might have guilty secrets of his own.

Silvana drew herself up, slender and strong as tempered steel. "As Keeper of Nevarsin Tower, I am answerable to no man, certainly not a pack of Lowland *Hali'iym*. The Council has not yet grown so mighty that it can issue commands within the walls of my Tower. Nor will it, while I still draw breath."

Jeram was an off-worlder, Lew reminded himself, and could not appreciate the magnitude of his offense in questioning the decisions of a Keeper.

"I don't understand." Jeram turned to Lew. "You people have the strangest mixed-up priorities! All you can talk about is how you wiped out a few minutes of my memory! What about what *I* did—attempted murder?"

Murder? Jeram was a soldier following the commands of his superiors. The men responsible for the ambush were dead or gone, recalled in ignominious haste. In any comparable Darkovan skirmish, the defeated troops would have been allowed to return home in honor.

"I cannot speak for the Council, any more than you can for the entire Federation," Lew said. "I speak only for myself and what lies between us."

"*Dom* Lewis is not the keeper of your conscience in this matter," Silvana pointed out, "and neither am I. If you have unresolved business with the Council, you must bring it before them. Lew has asked for my help in addressing his own concerns with you. Will you hear him and allow him to discharge his burden of guilt? Or will you turn away, clinging to your bitterness?"

"I'm not . . ." *bitter.*

"Then *what are you,* Jeremiah Reed?" Silvana's words, resonant with all the authority of a Keeper, shivered through the air.

Brown eyes widened. "I don't know anymore."

"If you would find out," Silvana suggested, "you might begin by finding out what was done to you. I realize this requires an act of trust in permitting Lew to enter your mind again."

"Then what? I'll still have this *laran* business going on," Jeram said.

The resentment in the other man's voice startled Lew. *Laran.* The foundation on which the Comyn, and hence the Seven Domains, stood. *And this* Terranan *would throw his away?*

"I cannot remove your *laran,*" Silvana told Jeram, "not without risking permanent damage to your brain. You will have to make your peace with your talent and learn to master it."

"I was trained at a Tower," Lew told Jeram, "and I would be grateful for the chance to pass that knowledge on to you. It was my action that woke your talent, and it is therefore my responsibility to teach you how to use it wisely."

"I don't seem to have any choice." Jeram sounded reluctant but resigned. "It's said there's nothing so terrible as a devil in the dark. All right, then. Let's get this one into the sunlight."

——— ✦ ———

Throughout the autumn, Jeram studied with Illona and the other teachers in the Tower. As he mastered his *laran*, he seemed to resent it less. He slowly integrated into the Tower community, although his strongest friendship was with Lew.

By steps, Lew guided Jeram through the restraints that had been set on his memories of Old North Road. The process was slow, both to protect Jeram's fragile mental balance and to give him time to master his new abilities. Silvana attended their early sessions, gradually shifting from participant to observer.

They sat together on many long nights, when their discussions ranged as widely as the far Hellers. Often they talked as they strolled along the streets of Nevarsin. Winter was fast approaching, and even on sunny days, ice edged the wind and brought a ruddy hue to the faces of both men. All too soon, snowstorms would keep everyone indoors except for the most needful tasks. Lew and Jeram took advantage of every opportunity to stretch their legs in the open air, to explore the old cobbled streets and narrow winding lanes shadowed by ancient gray stone houses, to stop at a tavern or forge or bootmaker's shop.

"I don't understand why you fight with swords when you're capable of so much more," Jeram said on one such occasion, when they had spent an hour examining a display of beautifully forged knives and daggers.

"*Laran* weapons, you mean?" Lew asked.

"Yes, exactly!"

"We went down that road during the Ages of Chaos and very nearly destroyed ourselves," Lew said with a trace of grimness. "Only the Compact saved us, that and the fact that when you are linked telepathically, you feel your enemy's pain as your own."

"You fought back at Old North Road," Jeram pointed out. "I don't see any saints among you."

"We Darkovans are no better than any other people. We love and hate and bleed and try to live the best lives we can. But it is one thing to lash out from desperation or when taken by surprise, and quite another to deliberately obliterate a helpless enemy."

They left the shop and came out onto a wider street. The sky, which had been clear when they left the Tower, had clouded over. A shadow closed over the city. The air smelled of snow and lightning.

"I have heard this Compact mentioned before," Jeram said after a long pause, "but I don't understand. I thought it was just a superstition about modern technology."

"It is a pact of honor, kept throughout the Domains for the last thousand years." Lew drew his cloak more tightly around his shoulders. "It forbids the use of any weapons that do not place the user at equal risk. He who wields a sword must come within reach of his enemy's blade."

"But a distance weapon . . ." Jeram broke off, nodding. His skin turned ashen. "So there are no innocent victims on Darkover?"

"Of course there are. We are not perfect. We make mistakes, and some of us choose to do things we know are wrong."

Jeram nodded, and said no more on the subject.

———— ✦ ————

Late one afternoon, as the first storm of the season lowered over the Nevarsin peaks, Lew and Jeram sat together beside the fire in Jeram's chamber, Lew in the single armless chair, Jeram on a stool borrowed from the infirmary. The room was simple and spare, for Jeram had added nothing to adorn the stone walls or cushion the floor. Jeram's saddlebags sat in one corner, his cloak hung on a peg beside the door, and a few personal items, a comb made from chervine horn and a razor, had been laid out beside the basin on the single table. Otherwise, the room might well have been unoccupied.

The last of the memory suppression had been lifted, and now Jeram could recall everything that happened to him during the Battle of Old North Road and afterward.

Jeram stared into the flickering embers, silent. Lew knew better than to intrude on Jeram's thoughts. It was hard to wait, half in fear, half in relief at having finished what he set out to do.

In Lew's mind, Father Conn stood at his shoulder. *"Sit. Breathe. Wait."*

At last, Jeram stirred. "You took a big risk in telling me all this. I don't think I would have been so brave."

It was not courage. I had no choice.

Jeram looked down at his folded hands. "You could have walked away. Stayed home, said nothing."

"I would still have to live with myself. Perhaps if I had been some other man, if I had not been part of Sharra, my own actions would not have tormented me to this degree."

"And the woman with the golden eyes?"

"My daughter, Marguerida."

"I'd like to meet her some day," Jeram said. "Not to point any fingers, mind you, as if I had the right to do that! Just to see her for myself and put the last of this affair to rest. If she can stop blasters with her mind, she must be really something."

A thought crept across Lew's mind, staining the moment of brightness. If he had done wrong in using the Alton Gift after the Battle of Old North Road, was Marguerida not guilty as well?

"Let it go," a voice whispered in his mind. *"You are not the keeper of her conscience."*

Jeram's head lifted. Russet eyes met Lew's. Lew could not tell how much of his own thoughts Jeram had followed.

"I do not think you are evil, either of you," Jeram said. "Even knowing . . . everything."

Lew heard the faint catch in the other man's voice, the momentary hesitation.

Jeram is hiding something, too.

"You know that I took part in the ambush," Jeram said. "And that afterward, I deserted. I stayed here on Darkover and hid my Terran identity. What you do not know, what nobody on this planet knows . . . Blast, this is harder than I thought!"

Jeram got up, scraping the legs of the stool over the stone floor, and raked his hair back from his face. Flames shone on the beads of sweat on his forehead. Lew sensed his shame, his fear of discovery, but also his desperate need to tell *someone* . . .

Lew's first thought was that he was not worthy to hear Jeram's confession. What right had he to pass judgment?

If you could admit what you did, Jeram said telepathically, *maybe I can do the same . . .*

Have you betrayed your oath, too?

"It's a long story," Jeram said.

"We have time."

Jeram paced a few steps, as far as he could in the cell-like dimensions of his room. He paused, took a deep breath, and burned back to Lew. His mouth twisted in indecision. Then, from one moment to the next, his eyes cleared, his expression altered to determination. He still radiated anxiety. Smoothly, not taking his eyes off Lew, he lowered himself to his seat.

"When I enlisted, there wasn't much chance of outright war, just peacekeeping and exploration. That's what I wanted to do, climb mountains on alien worlds. So I joined M and E—that's Mapping and Exploration."

"Yes, I know." Through the light rapport that had sprung up between them, Lew sensed the other man's enthusiasm.

"One thing led to another. There was a small Xeno-pathology Unit on Ramos V, focused on protecting our troops against native diseases. Since I'd taken courses in med tech, I interned there before going into the field."

Jeram had been part of First Contact and Colonization teams on five planets. His words tumbled out, describing the intensive d-corticator training, the arduous wilderness conditions, the training to screen for infectious microbes and design immunization protocols.

"Then . . ." Jeram paused, his face clouding, "the Expansionists took control of the Lower House. There was that nasty business on Ephebe. But you wouldn't have heard about that, here on Darkover."

"Actually, I remember it well," Lew said. "For many years, I represented Darkover in the Senate, so I am no stranger to Federation politics. I've lived on Terra, and Thetis and Vainwal as well. Does that surprise you?"

Jeram gave a wry smile. "Nothing about you can surprise me."

"As for Ephebe," Lew said, "the sanitized public version was that Transplanetary Corporation claimed ownership of the planet, and when the locals sabotaged the spaceport, the Federation sent in troops to restore order. At the time, I suspected the story was a cover for a military takeover. In the light of subsequent events, and President Nagy's grab for power, I am certain of it."

"I was recalled during the Castor Sector war games." Nodding, Jeram went on. "Policy changed, and so did orders. They didn't want protection against naturally occurring infectious agents, not any more. They were developing new biological weapons of their own. They wanted to vaccinate their troops in order to deploy them safely, which is where I came in."

Lew shuddered. *To deliberately create a plague and to turn it loose on an unsuspecting, unprepared population . . .*

"They put it to us that we'd still be protecting our troops." Barely suppressed outrage simmered beneath Jeram's words. "The work wasn't so different from what we'd already been doing. It didn't take a genius to figure out their real intentions."

"What did you do?"

"What could I do? I had a friend—we served together on Ramos V—who resigned his commission and met with an *unfortunate accident* the next week. I knew they'd never let me go, even with the nondisclosure oath. So I went along, I did the work I'd been trained for . . . and more."

"You . . ." Lew paused, swallowing the bile that rose to the back of his throat. "You *created* a plague?"

Jeram stared into the fire, his eyes dark and bleak. "I designed systems to identify and isolate pathogenic microbes, or to take a harmless organism and mutate it into a virulent form. No, I never turned one of those nasty little bugs loose, but it was only a matter of time before someone else used my work to do just that." *And I would be just as responsible.*

"But you don't know that." Lew bit off his words. He was trying to justify Jeram's past because of their friendship. Was he really helping Jeram by excusing his actions? Would he himself have found any resolution to his guilt if he had not faced his own choices honestly?

"When I got reassigned here," Jeram went on, "I suspected a typical bureaucratic foul-up."

"Why would a disease-weapon specialist be needed on Darkover?" A terrible inkling shivered up Lew's spine. What *had* the Federation been planning in those last days?

"You tell me," Jeram said, his eyes glinting red in the light of the flames. "This planet has no technology to speak of, a hideous climate, no significant metal resources, and a sparse, largely agrarian population. Why would the Acting Station Chief request a bioweapons development specialist?"

"Belfontaine!" Lew spat the word out like a curse. "The *bre'suin* would have used any means to bring Darkover to its knees. But he never had a chance, did he? The Federation pulled out too soon, forcing his hand. That's why he ordered such an ill-planned ambush!"

"Out of desperation," Jeram nodded. "You actually did me a favor, covering my tracks in the ambush. Sooner or later, some Federation bureaucrat would have stumbled across my records and wondered what I was doing on this forgotten snowball. Now I'm listed as dead or missing in action. I have a chance to start over."

He drew in his breath. "I've spent my professional career in violation of all your rules of ethics, your Compact. If what I've done makes me a monster in your eyes, let's have it out now."

This time, Jeram met Lew's gaze fully. Slowly, awkwardly, Jeram lowered his mental shields. Lew reached out, as gently as he could . . . and for a glowing instant touched Jeram's mind.

Everything in life can be manipulated or misused, Lew said silently. *Your knowledge, my Gift . . . The Federation would have used them both for its own purposes.*

Understanding flowed between them, giving way to compassion. Compassion for the hurt man who now sat before him. Compassion for his own reflected anguish. Lew felt the ripple of response from Jeram, the sting of tears, the upwelling sob of relief.

You are no monster, any more than I am, Lew thought, and knew for the first time that it was true.

20

Midwinter came to Nevarsin, with celebrations and observances that were modest by Lowland standards, at least so Jeram understood from Lew and the others. Many of the people of the village and the city itself followed *cristoforo* ways, and did not worship Hastur and Cassilda.

The Tower folk, as usual, kept to themselves, with a Festival dinner and singing. Everyone participated, even the usually aloof Silvana. Accompanying herself on a lap harp, she soon had everyone laughing with a long ballad about a wandering monk and the contents of his many pockets. Jeram was no ethnomusicologist, but he could have sworn the melody was Terran and very old.

Sitting in his corner, fortified with a tankard of hot spiced wine and tapping time to the music with one foot, Jeram felt more relaxed than he could remember. If having *laran* meant acceptance into such a community, it was indeed a gift.

With the passing of winter, the great Red Sun swung higher in the sky. The days took on a lingering, honey-sweet quality. Wildflowers covered the slopes of the Hellers. Snow still fell almost every evening, but the days were mild.

Jeram took advantage of the fine weather to go home. Morna fell into his arms, tearful with relief. Of course he must return to the Tower, she agreed, if it was needful for his recovery. Such a change the folk there had wrought in him! she'd exclaimed. He looked almost his old self again.

Not my old self, Jeram had thought. *Never that self again.*

As he parted from her, she gazed into his face for a long moment, as if memorizing his features. She had never promised anything beyond the sharing of a meal, a hearth, and a bed, which in these mountains was all that was necessary for a freemate marriage. Either might dissolve the bond at any time.

Jeram's threshold sickness passed, even as Silvana promised it would, and the suppressed memories no longer haunted his dreams. Instead, as he gained in mastery of his *laran,* the events of his life took on a new pattern. He might have stumbled into this world by a combination of luck and instinct, but he was at Nevarsin Tower for a reason, beyond his own personal concerns; perhaps he was on Darkover for a greater purpose, also.

Although the realization came slowly, working with Lew Alton was as restorative for the older man as it was for Jeram himself. Standing at the open window of his chamber in the Tower, gazing southward down the sloping hills toward the Lowlands, Jeram thought, *If there is hope for Lew, if there is healing and peace, then there may be hope even for me.*

A breeze tugged at his hair, now grown out to shoulder length. He could return to Rock Glen and Morna's warm arms, to trapping furs in the winter, farming hardy rye and red wheat, root vegetables and cabbages during the summer. It was a good life, a rich life. A simple life. But not his, yet. For all the peace of the Tower, a kernel of restlessness still wound through his guts, a piece of the puzzle that did not yet fit.

Jeram? Illona's mental voice brushed his mind.

With deliberation, Jeram shaped his answer. He would never be very good at projective telepathy, for he had learned it too late in life. Only someone like Illona, with her powerful Gift, could pick up his thoughts without difficulty.

I am here.

Will you join us in the common room? We have a visitor! Excitement lilted through her thoughts, as if she were singing.

Jeram smiled to himself. If he were ten years younger, he would have been half in love with her. She was a lovely girl, as talented as they came, and anything that gave her such pleasure was to be welcomed.

He took a breath, concentrating on his words. *On my way.*

Jeram paused in the doorway of his chamber, one hand on the latch, to look back at his chamber. How anonymous it seemed, how few the traces of the personality of its inhabitant. In his years in the Federation forces, he'd accumulated few worldly goods. His assets were his skill and knowledge. Then, as a deserter, he dared not keep anything that would give him away. Now . . . Until he knew where he was headed, it was best not to tie himself down.

Was he doomed to be a drifter? Or, as Lew suggested, a man who had not yet found his purpose?

Jeram proceeded down the stone stairs to the common room. Half the Tower workers had gathered there, with Silvana noticeably absent. A table had been laid with festive foods, spiral buns redolent with spices, bread studded with toasted nuts and dried berries, bowls of tiny mountain peaches and sweetened cream, pitchers glossy with condensation.

A young man stood in their midst. He could not have been more than twenty, slender and black-haired, yet he held himself with unquestioned command. His clothes, although travel-stained, were beautifully cut, jacket and pants of embroidered, velvet-smooth suede. Fur lined the short cape thrown back over one shoulder.

Lew sat in the most comfortable of the chairs, his scarred features lightened by joy. The newcomer, who had been talking in animated fashion with Illona, bent to say something to the old man and rest a hand upon his shoulder. Jeram had lived among telepaths long enough to recognize the intrusiveness of such a touch. Yet Lew only smiled and patted the boy's hand.

Illona gestured for Jeram to join them. "Domenic, may I
present Jeram, your grandfather's student? I am glad you
had the opportunity to meet him, for I fear he will leave us
soon, having exhausted what we can teach him. Jeram, this
is *Dom* Domenic Alton-Hastur."

A Comyn lordling and Lew's grandson! That explained
the boy's aristocratic bearing, as well as his affectionate fa-
miliarity with the old man.

Jeram felt safe enough, for neither Illona nor anyone
else here would give him away as a Terran deserter. Silvana
had spoken truly when she said the Towers did not judge a
man by his past.

"Vai dom," Jeram said, bowing awkwardly.

"Titles are unnecessary in a Tower," Domenic answered
in a gracious tone, "but I thank you for your courtesy."

He regarded Jeram with a steady gaze, his expression
composed but open. Jeram had never seen eyes like
that—gold-flecked gray haloed in black. In the instant it
took Jeram to remember how to secure his own psychic
barriers, their minds touched. Domenic's *laran* was utterly unlike any at Nevarsin Tower, complex and resonant, like a windstorm sweeping down from the Hellers,
like the vast, echoing ocean depths, like the molten heat
of a volcano.

"We are all friends here," Illona said, her eyes sparkling.
"Domenic and I met as children and studied together at
Neskaya Tower. It has been three years since we've seen
one another. Come, let's sit down, and Domenic can earn
his bread by telling us the latest gossip from Thendara."

"I'm afraid my news is some months out of date,"
Domenic said as he took a seat beside her on the padded
bench. "I've been on the road since the passes opened at
the end of winter."

"And what excuse did you concoct to run away this
time?" Illona teased. "Don't tell me you've been seized by
a desire to join the Travelers! I assure you, that life, for all
its romantic reputation, is far from enviable. So much so,

you never know when some well-meaning busybody will carry you away to a Tower for your own good!"

"Yes, and look where it has got you," Domenic replied, clearly refusing to take offense. The banter had taken some of the stiffness out of him.

"You could consider my adventure a last fling before I settle down to my duties as Regent-in-training," Domenic said with a sigh. "I hoped they'd put it off another year, but who knows? Before I'm tied to Thendara, I wanted to see more of the Domains, especially the Towers." He had, apparently, visited most of them, and this was to be his last stop before returning home for the annual meeting of the ruling Council.

"Glad as I am to see you, Nico, do you have other business here?" Lew asked. "Nevarsin Tower is hardly a place one comes for pleasure."

"The Comyn are still too few and spread too thinly," Domenic said, his tone now earnest. "The Towers, with their knowledge and insight, must play a greater role in Darkovan affairs. Actually, the idea came from Danilo Syrtis, but Father took it up, and Mother let me indulge my wanderlust to persuade as many Keepers as I can to join us this Council season."

"Giving the Towers a voice on the Council is a dangerous road to tread." Sammel, the senior matrix technician, had been listening to the conversation and now spoke up. "Even the most disciplined among us are vulnerable to corruption by power. Would you have us return to the Ages of Chaos, with the tyranny of *laran*? I assure you, the reasons the Towers withdrew from worldly affairs have not changed."

Jeram, listening, could not help but agree. If a pair of *laran*-Gifted Comyn could defeat an elite Federation force and then erase the very memory of that battle from their minds, what could a whole Tower of trained telepaths do?

Domenic shook his head. "I do not mean a return to the days before the Compact, but moving forward to the days to come. To begin with, we propose a Council of Keepers, advisory at first perhaps, a forum for discussing our mutual concerns."

"Such as?" Illona asked.

"Finding and training telepaths like yourself."

"Ah!" she said, and clapped her hands.

"It is true," one of the women said, "that we are isolated here at Nevarsin. We speak but rarely over the relays with the other Towers and never with the Comyn lords. Yet we heal those who come to us—" her gaze flickered to Jeram—"so why should we not also apply our minds and talents to other problems?"

"That would be for Silvana to decide," Sammel intoned gravely. There the discussion ended, for the Keeper was not among them.

The conversation spun away in other directions, news of births and deaths, weddings, horse races, and petty scandals. Jeram paid scant attention, as he had little interest in the doings of Thendaran high society. After a time the gathering dispersed, and those workers who would form the evening's circle went to rest.

Illona went off to see to quarters for Domenic within the Tower and for his entourage in the village. The young lord, it seemed, was to visit for a tenday or more.

Domenic paused to speak again to Lew. "I am glad to see you in good health, Grandfather. I hope you will be able to return with me for the Council season. We have too few counselors with your experience and insight."

For a moment, the old man looked pained. Jeram sensed how much Lew missed his daughter, Domenic's mother, and the lad himself as well.

"When I first came to Nevarsin, I had no thought of ever leaving again, except perhaps for the last journey to the *rhu fead*," Lew said. "Now . . ." His gaze flickered to Jeram and a faint smile softened his scarred mouth. "If Darkover still has need of me, I will be happy to serve."

— ✦ —

As he had often done before, Jeram accompanied Lew along the path back to the monastery. Lew walked slowly, for the past winter had brought new stiffness to his joints. Jeram wished Lew had ridden his horse, but Lew insisted on walking when time and weather permitted, saying that the day would come all too soon when he would have no choice.

On this day, Jeram did not leave Lew at the monastery gates. He escorted Lew into the chamber once reserved for guests but now given over to Lew's use. Lew lit a fire in the hearth and set the kettle to heat water for spring-mint tea.

"You are disturbed, my young friend," Lew said, as they settled beside the fireplace to sip the pungent, refreshing drink.

"I can't hide anything from you, can I?"

Lew smiled so gently that the scars on his face merged with the creases. "When one lives in a Tower, where men and women speak directly to one another's minds, there is little room for pretense. I will return to Thendara with a lighter heart and a burden lifted. For all the work you have done here, however, something remains, some kernel of grief within your soul."

Jeram looked away. *I could have hated this man all the days of my life. I could have become a shell of bitterness around a festering wound. I could have never learned the truth.*

"Lew, you and I have come a long way over these long winter months. There's so much I understand now—about you and why you did what you did. About myself and what really happened at Old North Road. About Darkover and what's really important. You don't owe me anything; I hope you know that."

"I have done what I can," Lew murmured. "Yet, I cannot be truly easy, knowing some inner turmoil drives you still."

Jeram got up and paced to the door. *I'm tired of running, tired of hiding.*

Be at peace, my friend, and may we each find the answers we seek.

Jeram could not be sure which of them had spoken that silent prayer. This, then, was the gift and the wonder of *laran*, this timeless space without dissembling or misinterpretation. This simple truth between them.

Tired of running, tired of hiding.

Jeram had spoken more truly than he knew. He had seen the courage it took Lew to confess, to humble himself, to ask forgiveness. The peace it had brought to Lew shone like a radiance through his every gesture. Jeram hungered for that same release.

There was nothing he could do about his participation in the Federation's bioweapons program. If people had died as a result of his work, he could not bring them back to life. He must find a way to live with that possibility.

One thing, however, he could do, and that was follow Lew's example: He could go to those he had harmed or tried to harm—to the Council in Thendara, to admit his part in the ambush. He did not think they would execute him; Lew's reaction and his own limited knowledge of Darkovan ethics suggested that enemy combatants, once defeated and disarmed, were treated with honor. They might punish him in some way—a jail term, public service, however this culture defined restitution. When that was over, he, like Lew, would have done everything he could. He would be as free as his conscience would allow him to be.

Then he could return to Morna's village, or go wherever the road took him, without having to glance over his shoulder. The time of hiding would truly be over.

———— ◆ ————

The next morning Jeram said his farewells to Silvana. During his time at Nevarsin, they had never become really friendly. That was not possible with any Keeper, he had learned. Illona, with her easy warmth and infectious good humor, was an exception. Holding the centripolar position in a circle required almost inhuman control, and many Keepers could not endure the discipline for more than a handful of years. Silvana had lasted longer than most, and this emotional isolation was the price. She regarded him with her steady, penetrating gaze, as if she could see clear through him to truths he himself had yet to discover.

"We have done all we can for you," she said. "Your life is not here among us. The world calls you. Go with our blessing."

He bowed, took his leave of her, and headed down the road to Thendara.

21

Dawn swept across the Nevarsin peaks. In the light of the great Bloody Sun, the glacial ice glowed like pink-hued pearl. On the lower slopes, the chill of the night lifted, along with the evaporating dew.

Domenic had left the Tower before breakfast, while the workers who had operated the relays or labored in the circle during the night gathered for a meal and a little relaxation before sleeping through the day. Since his arrival, he had been tied up in one formal meeting after another, with the city fathers, the Father Master of the monastery, everyone but the one person he had come to see. Silvana had still not found the time to speak with him. She was not ill, simply absent. No explanation had been offered, and everyone had been apologetic but firm. Here they kept to the old ways; the Keeper's will was law, not to be questioned. He had passed from expectation to disappointment and finally to exasperation, and if he did not remove himself, he ran a serious risk of a fit of ill-temper.

The idiosyncracies of the Keeper of Nevarsin Tower played only a small part in Domenic's current mood. His sojourn was coming to an end; this was to be his last stop before returning to Thendara. He had no reason for delay, and his parents would expect him to arrive in time for the opening of the Council season. His mission had been largely successful. Istvana Ridenow had been delighted to see him and promised to attend the next Council meeting. The Keepers of Dalereuth and Corandolis had received his invitation with polite interest.

The village outside the Nevarsin city gates bustled with activity. Its narrow cobbled streets filled with local men and women, bundled against the morning chill, carrying baskets or work tools, travelers on tough mountain ponies, traders readying their stalls, and drovers with strings of laden chervines. Peddlers hawked their wares on every corner, adding to the clamor.

Domenic stopped at a food stall to buy a mug of hot cider and a pastry filled with spiced meat and onions. Half a dozen pedestrians paused to stare at him while he ate. As he finished his meal, his original plan, spending the morning with his grandfather, seemed less appealing. What he needed, he decided, was to get as far away from people as possible.

A trail at the far end of the village led Domenic to the rocky slopes. As he climbed, the exercise warmed his muscles. His face tingled in the brisk mountain air. The tension in his back and shoulders eased. He found himself humming beneath his breath.

At the back of his mind, he sensed a low rumbling, too slow and deep for ordinary human hearing. Through it wove a descant, wild and sweet, like sunlight sparkling on flowing water. Domenic gave himself over to the shifting harmony, slow as a glacier and quick as a mountain stream. As the moment of resonant joy faded, he wished there were words to capture it.

Domenic paused at the edge of a long sloping meadow. Wildflowers grew here in profusion. He had not realized there could be so many shapes and colors, sprays of brilliant red and purple, heavy-headed bells of waxy white, daisies shimmering with gold and orange, starflowers and sky-on-the-ground. As he crossed the field, he saw that many had already gone to seed. The blooming season was all too short at this altitude.

At the far end of the field, rocks jutted from the hill-

side in slantwise layers, their edges softened by seasons
of wind and rain. He headed for them, thinking to rest in
the sun.

Catching a hint of *laran* ahead, Domenic recognized Illona's mental signature. He quickened his pace. The last
days had given him little opportunity for private time with
his friend.

Illona?

Domenic! Gladness danced through her mental call.

He saw her now, wrapped in a cloak of tawny chervine
wool almost the same color as the rock. She pushed back
the hood, revealing copper-bright hair, and waved to him.
She had been sitting so still, he might not have noticed her
otherwise.

Domenic reached the place where Illona stood. A high
color glowed on her cheeks. On impulse, without thought,
he held out his arms. For an instant, they were children
again, thrown together under desperate circumstances. She
was the uneducated Traveler girl, living by her wits and the
talent she did not yet know she possessed, and he was the
rebellious son of a Comyn lord, terrified and exhilarated
by the Terran plot he had just discovered.

In a heartbeat, time shifted, and he held a vibrant young
woman in his arms. Several curls had come free of her butterfly clasp. They brushed his neck like tendrils of silk,
smelling of honey and wildflowers. Her arms held him with
wiry strength, her body supple against his.

He released her. She was no peasant girl but a *nedestra*
Comynara and under-Keeper, never to be assaulted by a
man's casual touch.

Jade-green eyes widened as she caught his momentary
distress. "Come now, Nico," she said, using his childhood
nickname, "you offered me no insult. I have not become
such a stuffy old pudding as to insist on formalities with my
dearest friend."

"We were friends once," he stammered, "but that was a
long time ago—"

"Oh, has it been? What, all of three years?" She gathered the folds of her cloak around her. "Enough banter! Let's walk."

Domenic followed, keeping pace with her easy, swinging stride. Clearly, the years of Tower study had not affected her vitality.

"You're out early," he said, trying to make conversation.

She smiled over her shoulder at him with a hint of her old mischievousness. "I like to be about when the sun's shining. It was so dark through the winter, I thought we would all turn as pale as maggots."

"That is natural, I suppose, when one is snowed in for much of the winter."

"Indeed! The main gates were completely covered for tendays at a time, but we were prepared. When the Tower was built, the upper windows were designed for such times."

From Illona's mind, Domenic caught the picture of herself and one or two younger companions clambering down a drift of snow, strapping on snowshoes of laced rawhide, and making their way into the village. Their laughter rang in the frozen air. Under the visual image ran a sweet wild singing in the blood, of reveling in being outdoors . . .

Deep within Domenic, a renewed longing arose—to escape the walls of Thendara, the rooms filled with intrigue and responsibility, the faces peering at him, gauging what use he could be to them . . .

Domenic?

He poured out his yearnings into Illona's steadfast care. How, from his earliest boyhood memories, he had hated the city, the demands of court and Council. The joy he had felt when they first met, when he had been able to travel wherever he wished. The crushing weight of guilt and duty, as with every passing day the Castle became a prison and his life narrowed, all the color and life seeping away. His regret at leaving Neskaya, the brief respite for those few seasons. The lifeline Danilo had offered, a time to climb mountains and walk the shores of lake and ocean, an escape too soon ended.

Oh, Domenic! Of course you feel that way! How could you not, being who you are? Illona's response swept through him like balm over scoured wounds.

They had come to a halt, facing one another. Domenic had not intended to be so open with her; until that moment, he had not realized the depth of his longing, woven into the very fabric of his breath.

Illona stood before him, compassion shining in her eyes. She was not conventionally pretty, not like Alanna, but her entire being shimmered with something that stirred him far more deeply. She made no move to brush aside the torrent of his feelings, to lecture him or to shame him into duty. She simply listened, and in that silence, infinite possibilities opened before him.

Domenic had grown up surrounded by rank and privilege, adored by his parents; if he had been hungry or cold or alone, it had been by his own choice. Illona, watching him with those calm, knowing eyes, had led a far different life, one of struggle and uncertainty. Yet she had made a place for herself by her own talent and efforts. Someday she would be a Keeper, beholden to no lord. She had not taken this path out of duty or desperation, but had shaped her own life.

He wished with all his heart that he might have a place in it.

"Nico?" Illona's voice, low with concern, broke into his thoughts. "Is something wrong?"

Lord of Light, what was I thinking? Am I not pledged to Alanna?

"I'm cold, that's all," he stammered.

"We've stood too long in one place for such a morning. Are you ready to go back? No?" Illona took his hand, her fingers warm and strong around his, and brought it under her cloak.

As they went on, wind tore at Domenic's hair and stung his eyes. His heart beat faster with exertion but also with excitement. For a long while, neither of them said anything. Illona, too, was breathing hard, but she showed no sign of fatigue.

No, he thought, *not her.*

When they stopped to catch their breath, he felt awkward. The morning had turned as pure as a flawless crystal, and even a casual misstep might shatter it.

Domenic turned, looking down the way they had come. He had not realized how far they had climbed. Images flooded his mind, of riding back to Thendara with Illona at his side, laughing, talking, hours and days together . . .

He wanted her with him, more than he had ever wanted anything in his life.

"Tell me," Illona said, "about this Keepers Council of yours. If Nevarsin participates, I will most probably be its delegate."

"Why, isn't Silvana coming? Where has she been, anyway?" he said, using his irritation to cover his feelings. "Why is she avoiding me?"

Illona shrugged. "She is a Keeper, answerable only to herself, certainly not to a Lowland Comyn lord. Whatever her reasons, they are her own."

"You're not curious? You don't care?"

"I certainly wouldn't disturb her solitude just because it makes *you* uncomfortable," she replied with spirit. "Some of us have better things to do than pry into other people's personal affairs."

Domenic had forgotten how direct and plainspoken Illona could be. "I'm sorry, I was rude just then," he said, trying to sound humorous. "I can't help it, it's my upbringing, to think I have a right to know everything about everybody."

Her eyes twinkled. "Oh yes, I agree completely, it was very rude! What shall we set for your punishment? Bread and water for a tenday? Latrine duty? I know—reciting verses from 'Honorio at the Bridge'."

Domenic groaned, remembering how the novice mistress at Neskaya had made them memorize from the epic poem.

" 'A mighty oath swore he,' " Domenic chanted in a sing-song voice,

" 'An oath of blood he swore,
That the great house of Aldaran
Would suffer wrong no more.' "
Illona giggled and chimed in, gesturing dramatically,
" 'And bade his messengers ride forth,
East—and west—and south—and north!' "
She threw her arms wide and spun around in a wild
dance, missing the correct directions entirely. Domenic
could not remember when he had laughed so hard or so
freely. He wiped tears from his eyes. Illona too was flushed,
radiant.

"I'd all but forgotten that idiotic poem," Domenic said
as they recovered sufficiently to continue walking. Around
them, the sun had risen well overhead. A heady sweetness
rose from the earth. Even the ice on the facing hillside had
yielded to the warmth of the day.

"I don't suppose they could have us memorize anything
interesting," Illona said. "The point was to teach us to concentrate, even on something tedious. Gods, it *was* ridicu-
lous, wasn't it?"

"With training like that, it's no wonder we take everything so seriously."

"There is a time for that, certainly," she said. They
walked on for a while in companionable silence, lightly in
rapport.

"You asked about the Keepers Council," Domenic said.
"The idea came from Danilo Syrtis. He's been like a mentor to me. He sees things . . . Darkover's changing, Illona,
even more than Great-Uncle Regis dying and the Federation leaving. Things have been set in motion, like fracture
lines in a sheet of ice."

"What things?" she asked.

"The old ways were dying even before the World Wreckers
came, the Comyn too inbred and isolated, the people hungry
for off-world ideas and goods. For a time, Great-Uncle Regis
held the world in balance, old against new. Now that balance
is gone, and we're being ruled by an increasingly small number of hidebound aristocrats. People out there—" he jabbed a

finger back toward the Lowlands—"look to the old ways, in vain."

He faced her, knowing that she could read his face as well as his emotions. "We live off their tithes and their loyalty, but we have little to give them in return. Something new must come into being. Someone must answer them."

Me.

"The Lowlands must have changed indeed, for you to say such things," Illona said thoughtfully. "Here at Nevarsin, in city and Tower, life goes on much as it has in the past. Indeed, I would not be surprised if Varzil the Good, returning to us, noticed no difference."

"At Dalereuth, you would see it," Domenic said. "Or any of the small towns in the Kilghards now held by bandits. We passed a dozen caravans of refugees headed for Thendara or Corresanti, displaced by drought. They turn to the Comyn for aid, as their folk have done since the beginning of time. Only now, there is no answer for them. What can we do, penned up in Thendara, with no one to send?"

"You believe the Keepers, acting together, can help?" Illona's brows drew together and she pursed her lips. "What exactly do you think we can do?"

"I don't know." Domenic sighed. "We must try *something*. We cannot just continue as before, and it seems to me that the more minds focus on a problem, the greater chance of one of them coming up with a solution. Danilo said that was what Great-Uncle Regis was trying to do, first with Project Telepath and then with the Telepath Council. We cannot go back to those times, but we can take the best of their ideas and move forward. We're hoping that someone from each of the working Towers will attend Council season this year."

"We don't need to be physically present to talk to one another," Illona reminded him. "True, the relays don't work as well over greater distances, but we are not completely cut off."

"From each other, of course not," he said, "but to the rest

of Darkover, the Towers are indeed remote and mysterious. Most people have no idea what you do."

"Are you saying we've become irrelevant?"

For a long moment, Domenic did not answer. He felt a whisper touch on the back of one wrist. Illona's presence filled his mind.

"I—I'm not sure. Perhaps we have, all of us."

You will never be irrelevant to me.

In her luminous green eyes he saw himself, now wracked by dreams and doubts, now sure and steady, stepping into a future of mingled fear and hope. He took her hand in his, and the rapport between them intensified.

No longer seeing through his physical eyes alone, Domenic floated in an ocean of radiant light. Illona's mind enclosed him at the same time as he held her. Her strength astonished him, the trained supple power of a Keeper's *laran.*

Domenic felt a tinge of envy, because although he had enjoyed his studies at Neskaya, he had known he would never make his home there. The Tower had been a place to train his psychic talents and to achieve a measure of self-discipline, as well as a reprieve from his duties in Thendara. Had he been anyone else, he could have found a place in a circle, perhaps as a high-ranking matrix technician. But for a Comyn heir, destined to rule, such a life was unthinkable. Moreover, there was no place in the Tower—or anywhere else he knew—for his ability to listen to the heart of the world. He had no idea how it might be useful. Most people, he thought dispiritedly, could not even conceive what it was like. He himself had no words for the deep, textured sense of presence. *Song* did not even come close to its immensity or power.

In answer, Illona sent a ripple of music through their joined consciousness. At once, Domenic heard the throaty mellow tones of a reed flute, the arpeggio of a *ryll,* and more, viols and cymbals, drums and trumpets. He understood what she was telling him, that each instrument sang in its own fashion, that none was flawed, only different.

That each was necessary to the soaring harmony of the whole.

You have not yet found your true place, she spoke to him, mind to mind, *but when you do, the whole world will sing!*

Illona! Preciosa!

In that unintended moment, she was indeed precious to him, a mirror of his dreams and yet entirely herself.

The music in his mind built, chord upon rising chord, waves of delight like laughter, like breath. Each surge carried them higher, linked them more deeply. Beneath their feet, he imagined the mountains humming with joy.

—— ◆ ——

Cold brought Domenic back to his physical senses. He had no idea how much time had passed as they stood on the windswept hillside. Never in all his days, not even his time at Neskaya, had he ever entered into such a deep, engulfing unity with another human being. He had not even known it was possible.

Illona stirred. Domenic put his arms around her. Her cloak had fallen open. She drew its folds around them both. Leaning into him, she lifted her face. In a movement as natural as breathing, their lips met. He felt the kiss in the pit of his belly—lust, certainly, but also something deeper. A forging, a uniting. Never had he felt such balance, each of them giving and receiving in equal share. Their hearts kissed, not just their lips.

They broke apart like dancers who knew their steps perfectly. The space between them warmed with the closeness of their bodies. He could think of nothing to say, no words that would not fracture the perfect moment. There was no need to say anything. As one, they clasped hands and turned back toward Nevarsin.

They were still in rapport but able to converse about ordinary things when they neared the Tower. Several riding animals, mules and hardy mountain ponies, stood saddled in the front yard. Tower servants bustled in and out the front gates. Sammel and Fiona, the youngest member of the circle, stood talking in agitated tones with a *cristoforo* monk.

Fiona looked up, seeing them. "Illona! Praise to Evanda, you've returned. Sammel could not reach you with his starstone and we feared something had happened."

A delicate flush brushed Illona's cheeks. "My attention was diverted for a time."

"I am to blame for that," Domenic said. "I went walking on the hills, and Illona guided me back. What is the trouble?"

The monk, a small, wiry man of middle years, answered. "We of St. Valentine's tend the sick in honor of the Holy Bearer of Burdens. Of late, a number of poor folk have come to us, driven from their homes by fire or hunger. The women and children we send to our sisters of the Renunciates, for no female may enter the holy confines." Here, his glance went uneasily to Illona.

"Pray continue, good brother," she said serenely.

"Usually, all these poor men need is good care—a warm bed, nourishing food, and a little rest. Their bodies return to health, and they go on their way. But two days ago one of our patients became very ill. Despite our best efforts, he grows worse. He burns as if on fire."

"What is wrong with him?" Illona asked. "I assume your infirmarian is familiar with the various fevers and their treatments."

The monk gestured impatiently. "This case is beyond even Brother Kyril's skill. Father Conn has bidden me ask for help, and quickly, too, before the poor soul is beyond any remedy."

"Sammel is the only man with monitor's training," Fiona pointed out. "If the case that serious, it will take more than one of us."

"I will go, too," Domenic said. "I trained for several years at Neskaya."

"Then we will have enough for a healing circle," Illona said. "That is, good brother, if it is permissible for this female monitor and myself to enter?"

Some of the antagonism left the monk's weathered features. "Father Conn has made provision, for this one time." He gestured for them to mount up and follow him.

Domenic brought his own horse from the Tower stables, saddled her himself, and they set off for the city.

So this is where Grandfather has hidden himself away, Domenic thought as they passed through the heavy wooden gates of St.-Valentine's-of-the-Snows.

Illona, who had entered first as ranking *leronis,* glanced back at him.

Hardly hiding, Domenic. It was he who urged Father Conn to summon our aid. This will not be the first time that monastery and Tower have worked together.

Yes, that felt right. In Domenic's imagination, a redrobed Keeper joined hands on one side with a monk in a cowled robe, and on the other with a richly dressed Comyn lord.

A worthy vision, indeed! came Illona's unspoken agreement, *and one I pray we will live to fulfill. Perhaps this is what your destiny will be, to weave us all together, even as a Keeper draws the minds of her circle into harmony.*

She hurried after the monk. In his sandals, he moved silently across the cobblestoned yard and into the main building.

Glancing up at the gray stone walls, Domenic saw that they had been shaped and placed entirely by human hands. Wind and weather had softened the gouges left by the chisels but could not erase the lingering dissonance, the invisible fracture lines left by metal slicing through stone. He wanted to stroke the walls, as he might the neck of a restive horse, to coax the discord into wholeness.

Inside the building, darkness enveloped them, but Domenic's eyes quickly adjusted to the dimmer light. They climbed a short flight and went down a colonnade along one side of the building.

"This is the infirmary," the monk said, swinging open a

door. Inside, four or five cots formed a neat row, each with a pillow and blanket. A monk lay sleeping on one, cowl pulled over his face, hands folded over his chest. The blanket was still folded neatly at his feet.

At the far end of the room, a monk bent over another patient, sponging his head and chest. Lew sat beside the bed, cradling his starstone in his single hand. He smiled as Domenic and the others entered, walking quietly to avoid disturbing the sleeping monk.

"Grandfather!" Domenic exclaimed. What was the old man thinking, to expose himself to a serious disease?

"Where else should I be, if not where I am needed?" Lew said without the least sign of concern.

Their guide excused himself to go in search of stools for everyone. The infirmarian straightened up, carefully avoiding looking directly at either of the women. Domenic got a better view of the patient under the layers of blankets. The man appeared to be of middle years, deeply weathered. Fever flushed his skin, which hung on his bones. He broke into weak, wheezing coughing.

Seeing the reluctance of the infirmarian to deal directly with females, Domenic spoke up. "Who is he? How long has he been like this?"

The monk looked relieved as he answered, "His name is Garin, and as far as I can interpret his answers, he is a farmer who brought his family here to Nevarsin in search of work. Two have already died, a woman," he used an inflection to cast doubt on whether she was really his wife, "and a girl-child. They were taken ill shortly after their arrival in the city and perished after a few days of illness, or so the Sisters who cared for them said. As to how long this man has been ill, I cannot say. I have tended him for two—no, three—days, but I believe his symptoms began some time before that. As you can see, he is sturdy and must have been an active, useful person. Such a loss of flesh does not occur overnight. A strong man can sometimes go about his work for some time after the onset of an illness."

"A pity," Fiona said tartly, "if he spreads contagion during that time."

"Not all illnesses can be transmitted directly from one person to another," Illona pointed out.

Another monk arrived with several novices, bringing enough stools for them all to sit. Illona directed their placement in a rough circle with Fiona slightly to one side. The infirmarian withdrew to the other side of the room, clearly unwilling to leave his charge alone with these women.

Domenic took his place with the others. It felt a little odd to be working in the intimacy of a circle with Grandfather Lew or Sammel and Fiona, whom he hardly knew.

The circle took out their starstones and began focusing their mental energies through the psychoactive crystals. Setting aside his hesitation, Domenic slipped into the familiar trancelike state. Illona's mind touched his. He felt dizzy, as if he had been dancing a wild, spinning *secain* with her. Then he became aware of the steady, rocksureness of Sammel, his grandfather's faceted brilliance. Fiona wound like a silken ribbon through the circle, assuring the well-being of each of its members.

Illona, acting as Keeper, gathered up the *laran* of the others. A sensation of rising, of floating, engulfed Domenic. Awareness of the others faded; he thought only of sending the stream of energy from his own mind through his starstone and into Illona's deft control.

Time lost all meaning as Domenic left his physical body behind. Around him and through him swirled colored mists, glimmering in pastel shades like the light of the Crystal Chamber or a paler version of the Veil at the *rhu fead* at Hali. In the iridescent motes of brightness, he imagined miniature stars. The deeper he went into the trance state, the less he saw himself and the mist as separate. Wonder suffused him, building steadily into transcendent joy.

Break . . . Domenic, you must break now. The mental voice was unfamiliar but distinctly feminine. *Fiona.*

With a reluctance that surprised him, Domenic dropped

out of the circle. Vision returned. He blinked. His eyes burned as if he had been too long in the sun. The others had also roused and were putting away their starstones. Sammel got to his feet, stamping and shaking his arms. Fiona stretched and yawned. Lew looked tired but peaceful.

Frowning, Illona bent over the sick man. His face seemed less haggard, but his breath still wheezed through his lungs. The infirmarian came over and, with a new trace of deference, asked Illona if she had been able to help the patient.

"He fares a little better, I think," she said, "but I do not know how long that improvement will last. This is no ordinary lung-fever. There is some virulence in his blood that I have never encountered before."

"I am not surprised." Sadly, the monk shook his head. "This fever has resisted all our remedies. Anything you can do for him will be appreciated."

Illona rose slowly. "I will search our medical archives, and with your permission, either I or Fiona, who is our most skilled healer, will return later today to tend him."

When the infirmarian hesitated, she said, "This cannot be easy for you, to be set apart so long from women and then to admit not one but two of us. However, as long as the patient remains stable, I can send Sammel or Domenic instead."

Relief flickered behind the old monk's eyes. "That would be better, at least for a time, *vai leronis*. As you have rightly surmised, we are set in our ways and accept change but slowly."

With that, the Tower party took their leave.

22

Domenic returned to the monastery later that same day to check on Garin. He went alone because Sammel was clearly exhausted, although the older man had made no complaint. Fiona mentioned that Sammel had already worked all night in Silvana's circle. "He thinks he can keep going without rest, as if he were one of those *Terranan* machines," she whispered.

Domenic was happy to be of use. He was not especially tired, for a meal had restored him. More than that, he now found Illona's nearness disturbing. She had slept much of the afternoon, but he could feel her presence, as if he had taken the iridescent mist, the stuff of stars, into his soul. He needed to think, to concentrate on something else, to gain some small clarity of thought. He did not want to examine the possibility that he was in love with her. Truly in love, utterly and without reservation, from the very core of his being, as he had never been with Alanna.

The improvement in Garin's condition that resulted from the work of the circle that morning had almost completely disappeared. No faint color touched the sick man's cheeks, although he roused as Domenic settled himself on the bedside stool. A pottery pitcher of honeyed cider, still warm, had been left by the bedside. Domenic lifted Garin's head and held a cup to his lips.

Sighing, Garin licked his lips and rested back on the thin

pillow. The sweet drink seemed to give him a little strength, for he was able to answer Domenic's questions.

As Garin talked, a picture formed in Domenic's mind. This man and his family were exactly the kind of people who had been left rudderless by the failure of the Comyn leadership, those to whom Domenic—and every other lord in Thendara—owed a particular loyalty. Honest and hardworking, they were the heart of Darkover, as much as the *laran* magic of the Towers or the sword strength of the Comyn.

If we had been there to help, they might not have been forced on to the road . . . they might have made it through the winter . . .

He told himself there was nothing he himself could have done to prevent their tragedy. But he was no ordinary man; he was heir to Hastur and the Regency of the Comyn.

Garin fell into a restless slumber, unresponsive when Domenic touched his forehead. Domenic swore softly. The man's body was like a furnace.

He took out his starstone and tried to concentrate on the psychoactive gem. Like every other Tower novice, he had first been taught monitoring, using his amplified *laran* to sense life energies. He could even apply it to himself, enough to keep his *laran* channels clear.

Entering Garin's psychic body was like walking into the heart of a volcano, engulfed by fire. The man's strength was being drained at an astonishing rate as his flesh, muscle and sinew, nerve and organ, consumed itself. He had been a strong, active man, but his resources were almost exhausted, and when that happened, his life would go out like a guttering torch.

As he had been taught, Domenic narrowed his focus, descending through the level of organs and tissues to individual cells and the fluids that bathed them. He sensed a subtle wrongness, a taste he had never encountered in a healthy body. It could not be any of the more common contagious ailments or even those restricted to the Hellers, or surely the monastery infirmarian would have recognized it. Nei-

ther Illona nor her circle were strangers to the various illnesses. Domenic himself had more scientific training than
most Darkovans, for Marguerida had made sure all her
children could pass the University entrance exams.

Could this be some new disease? Something left over
from the time of the World Wreckers? Their agents had not
hesitated to use soil-destroying organisms in their quest to
bring Darkover as a supplicant into the Federation. Why
not a human disease as well, like the one that had killed
Grandmother Javanne? How could it have lain dormant
for so long?

The questions resonated through Domenic's mind as he
dropped out of the trance state into ordinary consciousness. Garin had sunk into a restless slumber. Domenic felt
the heat from the sick man's body on his face. There was
nothing more to be done here. He informed the monk in
attendance that the patient had deteriorated and then
went in search of his grandfather.

He expected to find Lew resting, but the old man was
working in the garden, wearing a broad-brimmed straw hat
and humming as he plied his hoe between rows of toma-
toes, marrow squashes, and salad greens. Bees buzzed
through the companion-planted strawflowers. The smells
of honey, pollen, and moist earth tinged the air.

Lew looked up as Domenic approached, and Domenic
thought he had never seen his grandfather so content. The
lines of suffering that marked his face had eased, and a new
brightness lit his eyes.

They sat on the bench to talk. Domenic poured out his
concerns about Garin's fever being a delayed-onset Terran
weapon.

"No, I don't think so, not after so long a time." Lew
wiped his brow with a scrap of cloth.

Domenic's worry eased, for his grandfather was no
stranger to off-world technology. He must have seen the
Federation at its worst when he served as Darkovan
Senator.

"As I understand it," Lew went on, "this poor fellow and

his family have been on the road, and last winter had been harsh on all his folk. Perhaps his strength held out only long enough to get his people to safety in Nevarsin."

"I fear he is approaching a crisis point," Domenic said.

"Then you should not linger here, but take word to Illona and the others at the Tower. If anyone can bring him safely through, they will."

Domenic said nothing, for the thought was in his mind that Garin would likely die. This was not an isolated case, he remembered. The woman and child who had come to Nevarsin with Garin had died also. How many more would follow?

Domenic found Fiona still awake and told her of Garin's deteriorating condition. "I will go to him immediately," the young monitor said. "You must eat now and rest, or you risk endangering your own health. *Laran* work, particularly when you are not accustomed to it, is exhausting."

Bone-deep weariness swept through Domenic. He knew she was right, but he had grown up with parents who demanded much of themselves, who would not rest while there was urgent work to be done.

"First, I must speak with Illona," he insisted.

"Be brief, then. I do not want another patient on my hands, particularly one who brought his misfortune upon himself from an overinflated sense of responsibility!"

Fiona directed Domenic to the archives, a small room high in the tower. Bookshelves and cabinets fitted with slots for scrolls lined every available wall. A small desk occupied the center, and here Illona sat, paging through a book. Age discolored the parchment pages. Dust motes glimmered in the light pouring through the windows.

Illona was so absorbed in her reading that she did not notice Domenic's presence at first. She wore a loose smock, faded and patched, and had tied her hair back under an equally worn scarf. A few unruly tendrils had escaped, tumbling like copper lace over her shoulders.

She glanced up, her color deepening, and he saw in her eyes a simple acceptance of the state between them. There could be few secrets between telepaths, certainly not something as intense as his feelings for her.

Illona closed the book, went to Domenic, and took his hands in hers. Catalyzed through the physical touch, the heady sweetness of her *laran* rushed through him. The edges of his vision turned iridescent. His breath caught in his throat. He wanted the moment to go on forever, that edge of exquisite agony.

You are my dearest childhood friend, she said mentally, and his heart plummeted.

No, she went on, *I am not about to tell you that we are only* friends. *The boy who changed my life forever has grown into a man, a man with the most amazing gifts*—and here, he felt the trained discipline of her Keeper's mind and knew her assessment was no mere flattery—*a man I have come to love in a very different way.*

For a long moment, he could not trust that he had understood her.

"Nico," she said, her voice softly resonant. "What happened between us on the mountain meant as much to me as it did to you. We were created for one another, I think, and no matter where we go, our hearts will always be calling, each to each, drawing us back again."

He drew her close, and her arms went around him as if they had always belonged there. He dropped his *laran* barriers; his mind was open to hers as hers was to him.

Without warning, Domenic's heart pounded like a caged bird against his ribs. His head whirled with a renewed surge of weakness. The next instant, he felt Illona's strong hands upon him, guiding him to a chair. It was still warm from her own body. A mental touch like a rippling melody played across the back of his mind. Cool energy surged through him.

"Domenic, my dear, I am sorry I did not realize you were in such a state! You are drained from your *laran* work."

She knelt before him, still grasping his arms, her eyes

liquid with concern. Her breath on his face was like honey. He drank it in, drew strength from her closeness. She lent him her own energy through their linked minds. It would not last long, but it was enough so that he could follow her downstairs with reasonable steadiness.

A short time later, Domenic watched Illona bustle about the kitchen, a tidy, scrupulously clean room with an old-fashioned brick oven for baking, a huge stone sink, and bins for storing spices, nuts, and flour. A small cauldron of some kind of soup, fragrant with herbs and green onions, hung just above the banked embers.

Quietly competent, Illona prepared a plate of fruit-studded spiral buns, sticky candy, and sugared nuts. She set the meal in front of him, along with a mug of *jaco* from the kettle on the hearth, and sat facing him across the battered work table. The smell of the food turned his stomach, but he forced himself to eat. After the first few bites, he finished the rest ravenously, yielding to his body's craving for fuel.

In between mouthfuls and gulps of *jaco,* Domenic told Illona about Garin and his own fears of some Terran-born disease, a weapon gone astray.

"I have heard of such things," Illona said with an expression of disgust. "I think Lew is right. Surely too much time has gone by for one of the World Wreckers plagues to now come to life. On the other hand, there is a possibility—and it is only a remote one, with very little evidence to support it—that this may be the recurrence of an indigenous Dark-ovan disease."

"Then why did the monastery infirmarian not recognize it?" Domenic asked.

"Because none of us have seen trailmen's fever for a generation."

"Trailmen's fever?" Domenic searched his memory. Some time after the destruction of Caer Donn, Regis Hastur had led an expedition into trailmen territory to discover a cure. It was one of the first cooperative ventures between Comyn and *Terranan*. "Wasn't that eradicated over forty years ago?"

"That's what the records say," Illona said. "The fever was, and I suppose still is, endemic among the trailmen, but in that species, it's very mild. It used to spread to human populations living near their territory every forty-eight years or so. People superstitiously attributed it to the conjunction of the four moons. According to my research, it starts with a few cases in the mountains, the next month a hundred or so, more widely spread. Then—and this seems to be the defining characteristic—exactly three months later, there are thousands of cases."

Her eyes darkened, as if a cloud had passed in front of the sun. She drew in a breath. "And three months after *that* . . ."

"But we don't have any evidence that Garin's illness is indeed trailmen's fever and not something else."

Illona shook her head. "No, I'm probably conjuring dragons with smoke and mirrors, the way we used to do in the Travelers' shows. Besides, this isn't trailmen's territory. Their home forests lie some distance toward the Kadarin, although no one's reported seeing them in years."

"Too often, our fears drive us to imagine the worst," he said.

She smiled, and the sun shone once more behind her eyes. "Yes, that must be it. We will send word to Neskaya, and if there are no more cases anywhere in the Hellers, that will be the end of my theory. Now, if you are finished stuffing yourself, I will see if Fiona needs my help."

She got to her feet, and so did Domenic. His muscles no longer quivered on the edge of exhaustion, but he would soon have to surrender to sleep.

"Will you come to my bed tonight?" she asked.

Longing flooded him, sudden heat pulsing through his groin. He imagined the silken strength of her body, her skin bare against his, her cries of pleasure. His heart thundered in his ears.

"I have forgotten my manners," she said, blushing a little. "Should I have waited for *you* to ask *me*?"

He sobered. Tower manners and morals were far different from those of the Comyn court. He could make love with her and take away the memory, folded into his heart like a secret treasure. She would never demand anything more.

"Is it safe?" he asked, thinking of Alanna.

"I know my limits," she answered seriously. "We no longer live in the days when Keepers were kept virgin for the Sight. Sometimes the work itself enforces celibacy, but I would not suggest taking you to bed if I could not safeguard both of us. I risk neither harm nor an unplanned pregnancy."

Alanna would never know. To her, it would be as if the night had never happened.

But not to him. Gazing at Illona, with his heart in his eyes, seeing her shrouded in the iridescent glory of their joined *laran,* he knew that once they had consummated their love, he could never walk away from her. Heart and body and mind, he would be hers forever.

The light in her eyes shifted, and he knew she understood. Perfectly, wordlessly, with that same simplicity of acceptance.

You nourish my soul, he thought.

As you do mine. We have already given ourselves to one another, as much as this sad world will permit. Do not sorrow, dearest heart, for my love will be yours always.

She closed the distance between them, brushed his lips with a butterfly kiss, and was gone.

Domenic stood in the kitchen while his pulse slowed and the echoes of her presence died. Within the spiraled chambers of his mind, she was moving toward him.

She would always be moving toward him, her eyes glowing as if lit from within, lips parted in eagerness and delight.

Always, his heart would be rising, reaching for her.

Always.

— ◆ —

Domenic rolled over in his bed, unable to sleep. His body craved rest, but all the fleas on Durraman's donkey seemed to have taken up residence in his skull. His thoughts leaped from one worry to another.

Illona . . . Alanna . . . that poor man, Garin . . . Grandfather Lew falling ill from the fever . . . returning to Thendara . . . what Francisco Ridenow might be up to next . . . Alanna's visions of a dead city . . .

He untangled himself from the covers, stretched out, and tried to quiet his mind by remembering the golden moments earlier in the day. His taut muscles softened. Longing, bittersweet, hovered at the edge of his senses.

Illona . . .

"Yes, beloved. I am here."

Domenic jerked upright as the door swung noiselessly open. He had not deliberately called out to her, and yet she stood on the threshold, bathed in a globe of pale blue light from her upraised hand. Her feet were bare, and she wore only a loose, gauzy shift.

"I didn't—" he began.

"Shhh." She extinguished the light and closed the door behind her. "We have no need for words."

In the near darkness, she shimmered with her own inner light, or so it seemed, for he looked upon her with *laran* as well as eyes. If she touched him, if she so much as breathed upon him, his resistance would shatter.

He tried to summon up all the reasons why he should send her away, all the demands of promises and duty. They withered in the stark light of truth.

He needed her . . . as he needed breath or sleep or the rising of the sun.

She moved toward him. He felt the heat of her body on his face, the whisper of her breath before her lips met his. He felt himself growing hard.

He closed his eyes, drawing her to him, and wrapped

them both in the same blanket. She was shivering, but so was he, and neither of them from cold.

They lay holding each other for what seemed like a long time, speaking with kisses, breathing in each other's nearness. He touched her cheek and neck. She shifted so that the curved muscles of her thigh pressed against his. Heat shook him, the rising arousal of his own body fueling hers.

Joined in rapport, her sensations flooded into his. He could not tell where her passion ended and his own began. Every touch, every kiss, every shift of arm or leg, wove themselves into a mysterious, intoxicating dance. He ached with ever-mounting yearning, until the tension became unbearable.

He came to a climax the first time with her on top, her hands on his shoulders, her body bent over so that he could feel her breasts and the silken fall of her hair over his heart.

For an instant, he felt himself apart from her. Then she gasped, driving with her pelvis, clenching her inner muscles. Waves of melting sweetness surged up through his belly. He had never felt anything like the pulsing ecstasy that seized him, each wave carrying him higher. She opened to him, as he did to her. He felt as if he were flying and drowning, all at once.

The second time was less urgent, yet delirious, riotous, like a headlong gallop down a steep incline in blinding rain. They had rolled over so that she lay beneath him now. His muscles flexed and released, as powerful as those of a racing horse. Surrounding him, holding him, Illona turned hard and melting, all at once. She wrapped him in her long, gloriously curved legs and lifted her hips to meet each thrust. Her desire surged through him, reached beyond them both. Then, suddenly, every place they touched ignited, incandescent as fire, as lightning, as molten silver.

As for the third time, his mind was joined so deeply to hers, they seemed to be one person caught up in the same delirious abandon. He felt her hovering, himself hovering, on the very edge of orgasm. The slightest movement would catapult them into release. Something held them there, gazing into each other's eyes, sharing one breath, one heartbeat. One of them—he could not tell who—gasped and closed his eyes, her eyes, and as one, they surrendered, tumbling down a cascade of ecstasy.

Afterward, they lay in a tangle of blankets. She rested her head on his shoulder, one thigh stretched across his. He sighed, wishing the moment could go on forever.

"Preciosa," he said at last, "I wish more than anything I were free to marry you."

She shifted on his chest. "Why drag politics into it?"

"But—I thought—you feel the way I do, I know you do—you would want to be with me, as I want to be with you."

"Of course, I do! I should very much like to make love with you again." Her laughter was like a mountain stream. "However, I have no desire to marry you or anyone else. I am a *leronis,* not some uneducated country woman who must depend upon a man for her living."

"I would never insult you by suggesting you become my *barragana,"* Domenic replied, stung. "I would offer you all the honor due to my lawful wife."

Illona propped herself up on one elbow. "Domenic, be reasonable. You will be the next Regent of the Comyn; you cannot possibly take a freemate or marry someone who is, to put it bluntly, an unacknowledged bastard. As for the old ceremony, marrying *di catenas,* that is out of the question. It would amount to becoming your property."

Pain shot through him. Miserable, unable to see any way out of their quarrel, Domenic said, "It is all beside the point. Oh, gods, I should have told you before! I am betrothed to Alanna Alar. We made the promise in secrecy, before I knew what love was. I had no idea what I was doing, but I cannot break my word to her. Not even . . ."

Not even if it means spending the rest of my life with my heart in one place and my duty in another.

"She cried so hard when I left," he said, remembering

the protective, helpless feeling as he'd tried to dry Alanna's tears.

"Cario mio." Illona touched his face with her fingertips. "Do you think I begrudge you doing what you must? Or wish you to be anything less than you are? How could I be jealous, after what we have shared?"

If those words had been spoken by any other woman, Domenic would not have believed them. Only from Illona.

Let us treasure this moment together, her thought sang through his mind. *And every other moment, until fate and death separate us.*

——— ◆ ———

The next day, Garin sank into a coma, and three days later he died. The monks at St. Valentine's arranged for his burial in the village plot.

Amid the preparations to return to Thendara, Domenic and Illona shared a bed as often as time and her duties allowed. As they got to know each other's needs and rhythms, their lovemaking became even richer. Sometimes Illona would be too drained by her work as under-Keeper for sex to be safe. She needed rest to replenish her psychic energy and keep her *laran* channels clear. Domenic, acutely aware of how little time they had, lay awake, cradling her in his arms, reveling in the warmth of her bare skin against his, inhaling her scent, or propped up on one elbow, watching her in the pastel light of the moons. He tried to memorize every line of her sleeping face, every exhilarating curve of her body, every strand of her hair.

Soon, he would not have even this much of her. Soon, they would be gone from this sanctuary. Alanna would be waiting for him, expecting him to announce their betrothal . . .

Other times, when his body still tingled with the lingering echoes of pleasure, Domenic wondered how he could endure making love with any other woman, or never doing it again. Yet, when he kept his promise to Alanna, as honor dictated he must, when they were man and wife, they might never be able to consummate their marriage. Certainly, when he left her, Alanna was incapable of any sexual feeling. He might not love her as he did Illona, but he cared too much for her to risk her life again.

Perhaps with time and patience, Alanna's sexuality might return naturally. Perhaps she might consent to return to Arilinn, where the temporary safeguards might be removed and normal functioning restored. He told himself these were foolish, impossible notions, that it was useless to torture himself with hope.

And if not . . . then he must find a way to endure it. The monks at St. Valentine's lived in celibacy, so it was possible. Assuming, he reflected bitterly, you could call that being alive.

As for the other problem, the necessity of offspring, one night Domenic hit upon a solution. At the time of the Sharra disaster, Regis had had no heirs, so he had designated one—his sister's son, Mikhail, who had indeed gone on to be Warden of Hastur and Regent of the Domains. There was no reason why, given such a precedent, Domenic could not do the same. He could wait a suitable time for everyone to conclude that his marriage was not fruitful and to determine the most likely candidate. Not Gareth Elhalyn, who was heir to his own Domain, for all that he was Regis' grandson. Maybe Gareth's younger brother, Derek, or one of the Carcosa Hasturs . . .

Consumed with these thoughts, Domenic rolled away from Illona's sleeping form. All but one of the moons had set, leaving her chamber in near darkness. A terrible silence filled him, as if the night had swallowed up his heart. He felt too empty to weep.

Nico? With a soft rustling of sheets, Illona reached for him. Her fingers, gentle and strong, slid over his bare shoulder, caressed his cheek.

For an instant, he stiffened. Why torment himself with what he could never have again?

We have tonight. We have this moment.

Tenderness swept through him as their minds merged

into rapport. He turned toward her and wrapped her in his arms, holding her tight against his heart. She said nothing, for neither had words for moments such as these. As long as he thought of nothing beyond this present moment, it was enough.

— ✦ —
23
— ✦ —

Jeram had hoped to reach Thendara well before sunset, but the chervine carrying his supplies had gotten a stone wedged in its cloven hoof that morning, slowing his progress. By the time he led the little antlered beast down the slopes and could see the old houses of Thendara ringed by remnants of the Trade City and the abandoned space-port, dusk had crept across the sky.

A rough encampment came into view just off the main road. To Jeram's eyes, the place bore the hallmarks of a crude bivouac rather than a proper traveler's resting place. He guessed there might be four or five dozen men spread out over the site.

Tents and a shed or two clustered around a well of gray, weathered stone. Beyond them, shaggy mountain ponies, chervines, and a swaybacked horse pulled at grass along a picket line. A tall blond man had set up an open-sided shed, its sides draped with blankets, apart from the others. He whistled between his teeth as he used a hand stone to whet a knife.

Jeram approached the camp, one hand holding the lead rope of his chervine, the other extended, palm out and open, to show that he carried no weapon.

One of the men around the fire called out a greeting and gestured for Jeram to join them. His hair was more white than gray, and he wore a fur shirt and boots, mountain style. Neither his accent nor the name of his village sounded familiar, but Jeram was not surprised at the offer of a shared fire. The ancient habits of hospitality and comradeship on the trail under often deadly weather conditions ran deep.

After settling his chervine along the picket line, Jeram brought his rolled-up trail tent and saddlebags to join Ulm, the man who had greeted him, and the others.

Jeram took his seat around one of the fires and accepted a thick-walled pottery cup filled with hot, bitter-smelling liquid. He swallowed, tasting blackroot.

Blackroot. Poor man's jaco . . .

Ulm hunkered around the fire beside his black-haired son, Rannirl, and three or four others, including a grizzled old man in a shearling jacket. A crockery pot holding stew, clearly a communal meal cobbled together from various ingredients, simmered on a bed of cinders. Jeram was reminded once again of the rarity of metals on Darkover. Poor people, such as these travelers, could not afford an iron vessel to boil water in or a tin cup to drink it from.

One of the men handed Jeram a wooden bowl and spoon of carved chervine horn. His stomach growled as he tasted the mixture of boiled grain, potatoes, wild purple onions, and pleasantly pungent herbs. The simple, hearty food nourished his spirit as well as his body.

"That's feeling right better now, eh?" Ulm said as Jeram finished the stew.

"Right better, yes," Jeram replied. "My thanks."

"A good story will set that debt to rights," Ulm said, his eyes twinkling beneath grizzled brows. "By your speech, you come from a far distance."

"A far distance, yes." Jeram noticed that the other men had gathered around, listening. The pale-haired man had strolled over to join them.

For a moment the old habit of secrecy closed around him. In all likelihood, these men had never seen a *Terranan* in the flesh, let along spoken with one. Although the Federation had maintained a presence on Darkover for several generations, most of it had been confined to a few cities or researchers who, while not exactly clandestine, went to a great deal of trouble to avoid attracting undue attention.

To the west, the sun sank with a rush. Darkness, dense and swift, covered the sky like great soft wings. Leaping out in a blaze of sudden brilliance came the crown of stars and the two smaller moons, like colored gemstones.

The time for hiding was over ...

"I've been living in a small village near Nevarsin," Jeram said, "trapping and farming. I was not born there, but far away, on a planet circling a star right about there ..." He pointed upward, to a cluster of glittering pinpoints.

Jeram went on to say that when the Federation departed, he had remained behind. He omitted his part in the Battle of Old North Road and its aftermath. Until he had settled matters with the Comyn Council, he thought it better not to mention it. He had no idea how many laws he had broken or how these men might react. Darkovans had strong notions of honor, and many still held the Comyn in almost superstitious awe.

"Thee has a strange way of speaking, truly." The old sheepherder peered at Jeram and looked as if he'd like to poke the younger man with a stick to make sure he was solid flesh. "I never held with the notion that folk from the stars had horns and tails, like Zandru's demons," he cackled.

"As you can see, I am a man like any other," Jeram said, holding out his hands, "perhaps stranger, but certainly no wiser."

That remark elicited chuckles all around, except from Liam, the blond man. He'd been quiet throughout Jeram's story. Jeram had seen the same stillness, the same concentrated listening, in men in the Terran elite special forces.

"What brings you to Thendara?" Ulm asked.

"Believe me, I would rather have stayed in Rock Glen," Jeram said. "I have business with the Comyn Council that has been too long delayed. I understand the session is to begin within the tenday."

Rannirl let out a whistle. The white-bearded sheepherder shook his head and looked away. On the picket lines, one of the ponies stamped and swished its tail.

"Did I say something offensive?" Jeram said.

"No, lad," Ulm said kindly. "You must truly be from another world. Here, a common man cannot simply walk into the Crystal Chamber. The Comyn do not concern themselves with ordinary people. In my father's day, our own lord often came down among us. He helped us in times of trouble. Now the steward does not know our faces, or we, his. You'll find no favor from that quarter."

"Aye," several men agreed.

"Mine is another sort of problem," Jeram said. "I am not asking for help. Surely, there must be some way to bring a petition before the Council."

"Well . . ." Ulm scratched his head. "The Cortes are for city folk who cannot settle their own arguments."

"Where, then, do you go for justice?" Jeram searched his memory, but the d-corticator programs had said little about the Darkovan government beyond the loosely organized feudal Comyn, their central Council, and a system of local courts. He gathered that most problems were handled locally, through a village headman or the owner of the nearest estate. This made sense, given the difficulty of communication and travel. He wished he'd asked Lew more questions.

"Justice! Justice is for those who can pay for it," Liam said, and several others muttered agreement. "Do you know what the usurper Regent and his cronies say when a man like you or me asks for his rights? They laugh in your face and throw you out!"

"Why, is that how they treated you?" Jeram said warily. The blond man clearly had an axe to grind. The last thing Jeram needed was to be diverted into one man's private crusade.

"I?" the blond man said. "I speak only what everyone here knows!"

A young man, barely past adolescence and dressed more shabbily than the others, said, "Twice now my kinsman and I have tried to take our case to the City Administrative Offices, where we had been told we might petition the Council for a hearing. They told us to *go home,* but they do not understood there's no *home* to go to."

An undertone of agreement ran through the little assembly, resonant with hopeless desperation.

"Jorek speaks true enough," the sheepherder said.

Ulm's gray-laced brows tightened. He lifted the pot of blackroot tea and offered it around. The boy and several others took some. "The world goes as it will, and not as you or I would have it."

"We speak of rights, my friends. Was it *right* that when wolves set upon Ewen's flock last winter—" Liam's gaze flickered to the old sheepherder—"and Lord Ardais, who should have protected him, did nothing? Ardais was doubtlessly too busy whoring to be bothered. So is it *right* that Ewen should have to pay his rents and taxes all the same?"

Ulm looked unhappy. "It's not wise to say such things about the Comyn lords."

"Why not, when they are true?" Rannirl muttered, drawing a sharp look from his father.

"I call no man of us a fool," Liam went on, "but there will be a heat wave in the Hellers before the present Ardais lord—or any of the Regent's pet cronies—honors the promises given by his fathers."

"Let it rest," the old sheepherder interjected. "No good comes from poking a festering sore."

Liam clearly had more to say. "For every one of us with a grievance against the Comyn, there are a hundred—a thousand others—who are still silent. Who will speak for us? Who will shake the Comyn out of their rich palaces and make them see what is going on?"

"Aye, and *do* something about it?" Rannirl said.

Ulm got up to add a few twisted branches to the fire. Cinders shot upward like motes of brilliance against the night.

"What can we do?" Jorek asked, growing agitated. His eyes gleamed in the heightened flames. "Storm the castle gates?"

"Some tried just that, last summer," one of the other men said. "The Guards came out with swords and it looked to be a nasty fight."

"And did they get what they were after?"

The man shook his head. "That part of the story I never heard, only that there was no more trouble."

With that, the little gathering began to disperse. Liam went off with two or three others, the boy Jorek among them, still talking. Jeram remained by the fire with Ulm as the encampment around them fell silent.

From the west, thin clouds stretched across the sweep of stars, dimming their light. The air turned chill and damp.

"What about your story, friend?" Jeram said, holding out his hands to the fire. "It doesn't sound like you found what you came for, either."

"There's little enough to tell. My own tale is much the same as any other man's. You see us, herdsmen and farmers, driven from our homes by famine and fire. Some came here to find work, others for help in restoring their lands. Their fathers were promised protection, and it has taken much hardship to bend their pride enough to ask. A few of them, like old Ewen, still hope that when the Council meets at Midsummer, something might be done."

"And the others, do you think they have given up hope?"

"Some linger for a time. You heard Jorek say there is no home to go back to, and he's not the only one." Sighing, Ulm shook his head and drained the last of his blackroot tea. "My son Ranirrl says if we only keep asking, we will find work. He is just as stubborn and headstrong as I was at his age. There may be hope in this sad world of ours, but not for us."

"So you will give up and go home?"

Ulm paused for a long moment before replying. He looked away, into the night, where even now the stars were fading. Jeram sensed rather than saw the unshed tears. Then, gathering himself, the older man said, "Aye, and scratch out a living from what the fires left. Maybe Rannirl has the right of it. It's no life for a young man, to stay behind when the land itself dies."

The old man's look of hopelessness tore at Jeram, as if he were seeing something strong and fine thrown on a garbage heap. The thought came to him that if he needed an ally, someone to watch his back, it would be someone like Ulm.

But was Ulm's battle one that he wanted to fight? He had come here to face the Comyn Council and any unresolved charges against him. Not to rally powerless men into seizing their rights, as Liam seemed bent on doing.

Jeram lifted his head. Around him, men sat around the campfires that dotted the site, attending to the tasks of informal living. These were proud, independent people who asked only what was owed them.

Justice, denied, festers . . .

If there were some way he could help these people, he would.

— ◆ —

The next morning, Jeram rose early. A fine misty rain had fallen during the night. Droplets clung to the tents and wooden sheds. The gray stones of the well glistened. Even the patches of grass looked brighter, washed new. Only a few filmy clouds remained. The smells of damp charcoal, crushed grass, and horse dung tinged the air.

Jeram determined to be first in line at the Administrative office. A petition seemed his best hope of obtaining a hearing with the Council. Failing that, he supposed he could he could search out Lew's daughter, but from what Ulm and the others said, it wouldn't be easy to speak privately with her. His business was with the Council itself, so with the Council he would start.

Walking toward the picket line to tend to his chervine, Jeram smelled freshly brewed *jaco*. Real *jaco*, not black-root. His mouth watered. *Jaco* wasn't coffee, but it had a satisfying aroma and a pleasant, bitter-edged taste. Liam waved at him from the shelter of the shed. Jeram accepted a mug of the steaming drink and hunkered down to savor it.

"You're up early," Liam said conversationally. "Off to try for a hearing?"

Jeram nodded, cradling the mug between his hands. Warmth spread through his fingers. The mug was skillfully made, the walls of uniform thickness, the orange glaze as fine as any he'd seen off-world. Handmade pottery fetched good prices on Vainwal or Sandoz Three, but there was no hope of ever selling it there.

"I wish you luck," Liam said.

"The same to you, with whatever you've come here for." Jeram sipped his *jaco* and sighed in appreciation. *Jaco* lacked the rich fullness of coffee, but was a lot more satisfying than blackroot.

"I think we are alike," Liam peered at Jeram over the rim of his own mug. His blue eyes glinted, measuring. "We each have something hidden, some untold piece of our story."

Jeram snorted. "What is this, a game? *I'll tell you mine if you tell me yours*?"

Liam did not seem to take offense, but calmly sipped his *jaco*. After a long moment, he said, "Do you think one man of arms would not recognize another? You are no ordinary Terran, no trader or seeker of adventure. You are a man who has fought. And lost . . . And run."

Out of old habit, Jeram's muscles tightened. He had had enough of secret games and seemingly innocent questions that were really probing for something else. "If I am, what business is it of yours?"

Liam shrugged and reached for the pot to refill Jeram's mug. "Only this. That there is only one reason I can imagine for a *Terranan* to remain hidden when the Federation left. You fought in the Battle of Old North Road, didn't you? Now you weary of living as an outlaw? Or perhaps you have come to petition the Council to contact your superiors off-planet so that you can go home?"

Jeram shook his head. "Nothing like that. You still have not given me a reason to trust you, or why you should concern yourself with my affairs. All right, it's your turn to come clean. You said you had something to hide, as well. What's your story? Were you one of the defending soldiers?"

Did I kill your comrades? Are you out for vengeance?

"Trust for trust, then. Truth for truth," Liam said. "I did not take part in that ambush on either side. I have no particular quarrel with the soldiers that did. Some would say that wiping out the old Council—or certain members of it—would have done us all a favor and rid the Domains of a tyrant."

Jeram blinked in surprise. Whose side was the man on, anyway?

"Do you think one man of arms would not recognize another?" Liam had asked. Jeram could well believe it, from the way Liam handled his knife. Liam did not behave like a deserter but a man with a mission. He certainly carried a grudge against the current Regent and had found a receptive audience here.

"My lord is not without influence, and he is sympathetic to cases such as yours," Liam said.

"Your lord? And who might that be?"

"I served *Dom* Francisco Ridenow," Liam said. "And still do, in a number of ways. He no longer holds Serrais, as is his right, or speaks for his Domain. But that is all old history. Today my lord has allies on the Council. Allies with the power to accomplish things. So you see, neither of us is entirely friendless. It may well be, if you are who I think you are, that we can help one another."

Jeram thought for a moment. What did he have to lose in speaking the truth? He had, after all, promised himself that the time of hiding was over.

"You were right," he said, nodding. "I was part of the Terran attack force. I've been living in hiding ever since, and I'm tired of it. It's time to face up to the consequences of what I did so I can make a fresh start."

"A worthy quest." Liam rubbed the golden stubble on his chin. He drained the last of his *jaco* and wiped his mug dry with a handful of grass. "Why did you wait all these years to come forward? Why did you not leave with the others of your kind?"

"That part is difficult to explain," Jeram said, cleaning and handing over his empty mug. "It wasn't until recently— this last winter, in fact—that I fully remembered the battle. My memories had been—I suppose you call it, suppressed. The *leroni* at Nevarsin Tower helped me recover them."

"Suppressed? How?"

Jeram noticed the instant leap of interest in Liam's eyes, the edge of sharpness to his question. The man was Darkovan and had served a Comyn lord. How could he not know about the Alton Gift?

"I cannot say," Jeram said warily. "My people know nothing of such things."

"No matter." Liam shrugged. "I am going into the city on business of my own. Let us walk together, and I will show you where the City Administrative building lies. Otherwise, you may be half the morning searching for it."

Liam's manner was so relaxed and friendly, and he had dropped the question of forced rapport so easily, that Jeram welcomed his companionship. Together, they headed into Thendara.

24

The pen fell from Marguerida's fingers, spattering ink over the concerto she had been trying to compose for the past half hour. The morning had been overcast, threatening rain, and watery gray light cast a gloom over the normally cheery office. Even the bright colors of tapestry and carpet seemed washed out, lifeless.

Without warning, pain shot through her temples. She closed her eyes, fighting the sudden nausea.

What now? Another precognitive warning?

Relax . . . she told herself. *Breathe* . . .

After a few seconds, the throbbing lessened, although her stomach still felt queasy.

The door of her office slammed open. Alanna strode in, tracking mud across Marguerida's favorite carpet. Damp stained the hem of her gown, ruining the rich emerald velvet. Her hair was in disarray, and a high color suffused her cheeks. Clearly, she'd been outdoors, probably playing hoops and streamers with her friends, and was furious at being called away.

"You wished to see me," Alanna announced. "Here I am!"

Marguerida suppressed a frown. Ever since Domenic had left on his tour of the Towers, the girl had been increasingly irritable, back to her old tantrums.

In an effort to maintain control of the conversation, Marguerida said, "Sit down."

Alanna did so, without any softening of her expression.

"In the last tenday, I have had a dozen complaints about your behavior. Temper tantrums are all very well for babies, but you are a young woman now. You simply cannot scream and throw things when you do not get your way. Especially not at servants. You were very lucky the pitcher hit Tomas on the forehead and did not damage his eye. Alanna, are you listening to me?"

The girl muttered under her breath, her expression sullen.

"What did you say?"

"I said," Alanna snarled, "that I am sick and tired of people telling me what to do!"

"Then behave like a responsible adult! You are old enough to control yourself. If you cannot act properly, with courtesy toward those who are trying to help you, then I—"

"Then what?" Alanna broke in. "You'll lock me in my room, the way you did when I was little?" She scrambled to her feet. "Or send me back to Arilinn? I won't go! I won't! I'll make you regret—"

"I WILL NOT BE THREATENED." With the headache tearing at her concentration, Marguerida unconsciously reinforced her words with the Commanding Voice.

Immediately, she broke off. What was wrong with her, to lose control at such a small provocation? Alanna was a child! Wilful and self-centered perhaps, difficult definitely, but not a real threat to her. Confrontation would only escalate the conflict. Why could they not discuss things rationally, the way Marguerida had been able to do with so many people who had once been enemies and were now her friends?

Alanna recoiled from the psychic contact as if she had been physically struck. Her hands curled into fists and her voice trembled. "Go ahead! Use your *laran* on me—you with your shadow matrix and all the power in the world except the power to make me happy! I am your prisoner, and I hate you!"

"Don't be melodramatic, Alanna. You are no one's prisoner, and you know it. Besides, where would you go?" Instantly, Marguerida regretted her words, for it was needlessly cruel to remind Alanna that her own mother had given her up.

"I would go away with Domenic, of course! We—he *understands* me."

Marguerida blinked in surprise. Clearly, Alanna missed her son, but Marguerida had no idea the girl had wanted to go along on the expedition. Alanna had never been physically adventurous, always preferring the comforts of the city to the challenges of travel through rough countryside.

Alanna was going to say something more before she stopped herself. Marguerida sensed the younger woman's effort to control herself, to gather up the shreds of her dignity.

Ignoring the headache as best she could, Marguerida said, "I know you miss him, child. I miss him very much, too." She gave a deep sigh, and glanced at her left hand in its insulated glove, wishing that her shadow matrix could help.

Alanna stood straighter, lifting her chin. "I am sorry I was so temperamental. I have not been sleeping well. Ever since last summer and the attack on the Castle, I have been troubled with . . ." she hesitated minutely, ". . . bad dreams. It was ill-mannered of me to behave so disrespectfully to someone who has been—who will be—a mother to me. I know you have never meant me any harm . . ."

Marguerida's dizziness returned. A psychic storm cloud pressed on the horizon of her mind. The sense of oncoming danger was too nebulous for her to tell if it centered around Alanna, or something else entirely. Was Francisco Ridenow up to something? Or—her stomach clenched and the room turned icy—had something else happened to Mikhail?

"What is it, Auntie Marguerida? Are you ill?" Alanna sounded genuinely concerned.

"Nothing of the sort," Marguerida managed to answer. "I am just a little tired, that is all."

"You had the oddest expression on your face. Please, let me call one of the servants for you. You should lie down now. Come, I will help you to your chamber." Alanna came around the side of the desk, holding out her hand.

Marguerida shook her head, feeling unreasonably irritated. The last thing she wanted was to be fussed over by the young woman who, only a few minutes ago, had behaved so rudely. Allowing Alanna to take care of her would not resolve the friction between them.

For years, I have wished her to be considerate and helpful, and now that she is, I cannot accept it from her.

"I will be quite all right," she said, doing her best not to sound unkind. "I do not need help, only a little quiet to prepare for my work today."

Alanna paused, clearly understanding that she was dismissed. "I will not trouble you any longer, *Domna* Marguerida. Please do not hesitate to call me if you change your mind."

Marguerida waited until the latch clicked shut. Alanna was dealt with for the moment. In a tenday, Domenic would return for the opening of the Council season. Alanna always behaved better in his presence. Already, a number of Comyn had arrived in Thendara, including Marguerida's brother-in-law, Gabriel, and that odious Francisco.

Francisco! He seemed to have a finger in every pie and a network of spies, or worse. Although he himself never attended the Cortes or the Council office in the City Administrative Building, he always seemed to know about any trouble, particularly when it reflected badly on Mikhail's Regency.

And then there was the episode three days ago . . . Only Mikhail, Donal, and she herself knew about the assassination attempt—and the dead man. Disguised as a Castle Guard, the fellow had lain in wait for Mikhail on a night when Mikhail was working late and the corridors were deserted. If Donal had not insisted on remaining at Mikhail's side . . .

No, don't think about that!

The assassin had died in the scuffle before he could be questioned. Nothing on his person linked him with Francisco, but Marguerida had no doubt the Ridenow lord was behind the attack. However, a hunch was not evidence, not even among the Comyn.

To clear her head, Marguerida sent for a pot of her diminishing supply of Thetan tea, for the coffee she loved was long since gone, and something to eat, pastries, cheese, nuts—she didn't care. The tea arrived and she sipped it, letting the comforting warmth spread through her. Her headache eased but did not entirely disappear.

Finally, she could delay no longer. Darkovans did not keep to the strict time schedules of the Federation, but there were only so many hours in a day, even if each contained 28 hours instead of the Terran Standard 24. Some responsibilities could not be postponed with the approach of another Comyn Council season. It was time to get going.

——— ✦ ———

As Marguerida stepped out into the streets beyond Comyn Castle, she shivered despite her thick woolen jacket, a deep inky blue stitched around the high collar and cuffs with snowflakes in lighter shades, and the rather irregular scarf Yllana had knitted for her last birthday. Although she was Darkover-born, she had lived most of her young life on much warmer planets. Even a fine spring day sometimes felt like winter.

Marguerida walked briskly, relishing the sounds and smells of the living city. People passed her, some well-dressed, others in faded, patched cloaks. Pedestrians mingled with riders, carts, and even a brightly painted wagon that surely must belong to a troupe of performing Travelers.

She thought of wandering down to Threadneedle Street to see her old friends, the MacDoevid family, or to the Escalia flower market, but the days when she could indulge such whims were as long gone as lazy afternoons swimming in the crystalline waters of Thetis.

Today, she had committed herself for a shift at the City Administrative building, which also housed a courtroom for commoner business, a subsidiary station for the City Guards, and various offices. She was not looking forward to sorting out those few cases the Council should hear and making sure the others got attended to. Unfortunately, the work turned out to be exasperating and tedious. She believed in doing her fair share; the system was her idea, and, although far from perfect, it was still better than having the Comyn Council inundated with trivial business or, worse yet, turning everyone away unheard.

Things had been quiet since the riot last year, but with the thawing of winter, each day brought new refugees to the city gates. Where they were all coming from, or how they would all be fed and housed, she couldn't imagine. Likely, today's roster of complaints related to these wanderers. Her head ached just thinking about the logistics of sanitation and food distribution for them all, and by the time she neared the Administrative building, her headache had returned.

Dating from the first days of Terran contact, the building struck Marguerida as the worst of both worlds. It was squat and square, a block of unadorned fawn-colored stone, unimaginative and, unfortunately, extremely durable. In all likelihood, her great-grandchildren would have to endure looking at it, too.

A small crowd had gathered on the street outside, mostly men in tattered fur shirts and mountain-style boots, a sprinkling of city dwellers, and the sort of patchwork beggars who had appeared recently. Marguerida pushed her way through them. One or two glared at her, but most made way, pointing at her red hair, bobbing their heads respectfully.

"What's going on?" she asked the Guard at the door, a second-year cadet. She couldn't remember his name, but she thought she had seen him at the Midwinter Festival ball.

He bowed, recognizing her. "Just the usual, *vai domna*. Riffraff and rabble with nothing better to do."

"What do they want?"

He shrugged. "Work, mostly, but there's none here for them. They should have stayed at home."

"*Domna*, can you help me?" one of the men shuffled forward. He looked to be well past his prime, whitened stubble covering his weathered cheeks. "I don't ask for charity, just an honest day's work. I can mend harness, muck out stalls, tend horses. Please—my wife's not well— we come here from Rainsford in the Kilghard Hills."

"I'm sorry," Marguerida said, unexpectedly moved.

"Get back!" The Guard stepped between them, lifting his staff. The man hurried away before Marguerida could say more.

She went inside, her thoughts churning. Surely, something ought to be done for such people. Thendara, like any city, had its share of sorrows, but poverty and homelessness, such as existed on Vainwal or Terra or Sandoz Three, were unknown. Darkovans had always taken care of their own. Something had broken down in the social network.

Or maybe, she reflected, it was a combination of attrition, reducing the ranks of the Comyn; the diversions of one crisis after another, culminating in the death of Regis Hastur; the withdrawal of the Federation's trade and technology; and the too-slow evolution of new social structures to fill the gaps.

She passed through the narrow entry hall into the reception room outside the main office. A half dozen men, a few beggars but also some clearly well-to-do city folk, sat on the long bench, waiting to be seen.

The door to the inner office opened and a man strode out. He hurried away down the hallway, shadowed so that she could not see his face. By his clothing, he was indistinguishable from the men outside, with his worn, travel-stained jacket and boots, and long dusty hair tied back with a loop of leather.

Marguerida was not as skilled as Mikhail or Danilo in the nuances of Darkovan gestures and body language, but she thought this man did not hold himself like a peasant. In

fact, he looked more like a trained swordsman than a poor
mountain farmer.

And yet . . . She frowned as she continued on her way.
She had seen Darkovan sword masters. There was something different in this man's bearing. She could not see him
reaching for a blade, but for some other weapon . . . And,
for the briefest moment, she felt the quiver of *laran*.

"*Domna* Marguerida!" Bowing, the clerk scrambled to
his feet.

She smiled gently as he shuffled from one foot to another and stammered out a response to her greeting. He
was Danilo's protegé, from a poor but intensely proud old
family. Instead of the humiliation of charity, he earned
every *reis* of his small stipend.

"*Dom* Gabriel is still within," the boy said nervously.
"Or so I believe."

So, the man she had just seen leaving must have been
Gabriel's last case of the morning. By the look of him, the
petitioner had not received the verdict he had hoped for.

She pushed the door to the office open. Gabriel looked
up from the desk, where he was finishing an entry in the
log book. His mouth looked tense. Deep creases marked
the skin between his brows. He looked up, met her gaze,
and grimaced.

"I'm glad you're here," he said. "I've never met with a
pack of more insolent rascals in my life. There's no satisfying them!"

"Oh?" Marguerida said lightly, sitting on the edge of the
desk. "Like the one who just left? He didn't look happy, either."

"Of course not! He, and twenty more like him, think
they can come here and fill up the Council's calendar, just
like that rabble last summer! If Mikhail weren't my
brother, I'd thrash him soundly for ever suggesting such a
thing!"

If anyone did the thrashing, she thought, it would be
Mikhail.

"Gabriel, if this work is so distasteful, you need not force yourself to do it. Surely, it was not necessary to leave Armida early for it."

"If I don't do my part, who will?" Gabriel demanded, scowling at her. "What kind of example will I be setting for the young folk? What if everyone decided to act just as he pleases, where would we be then, eh?"

"Perhaps you are right," Marguerida murmured, looking for a way to change the topic. The conversation showed every sign of escalating into an argument.

"So," she said, "what did that man want? Anything interesting?"

"Ha!" Gabriel gave a sharp bark of laughter. "That one just now—if you can believe it—wanted to *apologize*!"

"Really? Apologize for what?"

"Who knows? Who cares? To win a wager? So he could tell his sons he had a private audience with the Council?" Gabriel got to his feet. His spine popped in three places as he stretched. "I sent him packing, of course. Maybe word will get around that we consider only serious matters."

"I wonder . . ." Distracted, Marguerida peered down the hallway in the direction of the disappointed petitioner. She had not gotten more than a brief glimpse of him, and only the haziest *laran* impression, enough to create the disturbing notion that she had met him before.

She darted to the front door and looked up and down the street. It was no use. He was gone, and with him, that faint, fleeting trace. She was probably imagining it all. Some instinct, however, prompted her to ask a Guard to follow the petitioner and see what could be learned about him.

"I'd like to have a word with that man, if you find him."

"I'll do my best, *vai domna.*"

Inside, Gabriel had already put on his cloak. Marguerida settled behind the desk, picked up the pen, wrote an introductory note in her slow, careful hand, and asked the clerk to send in the next petitioner.

———— ✦ ————

The great Red Sun bleared as it dipped toward the western horizon. Shadows of deep mauve and indigo folded Thendara into gloom. Even at this hour, people still thronged the streets, women muffled to their eyebrows in furs or woolen shawls, men in cloaks, uniformed Guards, street vendors, and delivery men.

A thin icy rain began to fall, and the crowd thinned rapidly. Hurrying with the others, Jeram followed Liam to a walled compound. Liam pulled a rope hanging beside the wooden gate. Within the patchstone walls, a bell sounded, sonorous. Jeram glanced over his shoulder at the Guards across the street, even though they showed no interest in him.

Jeram had found Liam waiting for him outside the Administrative building. Liam had given a short, sympathetic nod when he saw Jeram's face and fallen into step with him.

"If you will tell my lord your story, you will find a far better reception," Liam had said.

Before Jeram could reply, Liam's fingers had closed around his arm, impelling him forward. "Quickly now. You're being followed."

A Guard left the steps of the Administrative building and hurried in their direction. Jeram quickened his pace, following Liam through the thickest swirl of traffic. Liam seemed to know where he was going, cutting through a series of alleys with a sureness that suggested he'd evaded pursuit many times.

They had gone to ground in a cheap tavern, one where Jeram would be surprised if any Guard got a straight answer. The owner, who clearly knew Liam, showed them to a private room upstairs.

"You'll be safe enough for a few hours," Liam had said. "I've got a few arrangements to make. I'll take you to *Dom* Francisco once it's dark."

Now Jeram heard footsteps, heeled boots most likely, behind the wall. The gate cracked open. A man peered out, his torch hissing in the rain. Liam spoke a few words in a low, urgent voice, and they were ushered inside, through a garden, and into the house beyond.

"Is this [...]"

"No, on[...]"

upon," Liam [...]

The man w[...] into a small, be[...] set in wall scon[...] blazed brightly in [...] the house of a Dar[...] richness of texture [...] toned carpets underf[...] sumptuously carved, a[...]

Jeram had little time [...] man he had come to see [...] [...]air, lean and saturnine, dress[...] [...]ke green velvet, cut away to reveal [...] [...]ike flashes of gold. Red glinted in his dark [...] aura of power hung about him, power and hunge[...] He was by far the most dangerous-feeling man Jeram had yet encountered on Darkover.

Liam bowed. "*Vai dom,* this is the man I told you about."

"I did not think any of the *Terranan* had stayed behind," *Dom* Francisco said, using the word without a hint of insult.

"Should it surprise you that I have come to love this world and want to make my home here?" Jeram said cautiously.

"Some might question why a man would leave the Federation, with all its culture and diversity, to deliberately imprison himself on such a backward world." The Ridenow lord's eyes flickered. "But I am not such a man. Come, sit down, dry yourself by the fire. It is not a good night to be abroad."

A moment later a servant in green and gold livery brought in a folding table, placed on it a tray of food and drink, then departed. Liam took up a position just inside the door while Francisco poured out hot spiced wine for himself and Jeram. The drink was warm on Jeram's tongue, smooth all the way down.

tale," Francisco said,
ave understood correctly, I

e else to turn," Jeram said. "There
e any way to get a hearing before the
ut inside connections. I should warn you that
e Guards followed me from the City Administra-
ffices. I don't know what he wanted."

"Wisely, you did not linger to find out. Yes, Liam told me that part, too. I can appreciate how frustrating this must be to you. As a Terran, you are accustomed to having certain rights and privileges. Your *democracy,* I believe. We Darkovans have a different way of doing things. Yet in the end, justice prevails." Francisco poured more wine for Jeram. "If you would, let me hear your story from your own mouth. You were stationed with the Terran forces at Aldaran..."

Jeram hesitated, but only for a moment. Francisco already knew that he was Terran military and, undoubtedly, his part in the Battle of Old North Road. Francisco seemed like a reasonable man, willing to help him, and deserved to hear the full story.

Francisco listened gravely, without interruption. When Jeram finished, he said, "I want to be sure I have understood you correctly. You yourself witnessed Mikhail Lanart-Hastur and Marguerida Alton-Hastur use *laran* as a weapon against ordinary soldiers?"

"Yes," Jeram said, "that was what I could not remember."

"But now those memories have been restored? There is no doubt in your mind of what happened? You could not possibly be confused from a blow to the head or the aftermath of a defeat?"

"I am as certain of it as I am of my own name," Jeram said.

Francisco sat back in his immense chair, looking thoughtful. "And afterward, you say, *Domna* Marguerida and her father used the Alton Gift of forced rapport in order to erase the memory of that use of *laran* from all the surviving Terran soldiers? You are sure of this part, as well? If it comes to public testimony, is there anyone who can corroborate your story?"

"The Keeper who restored my memory knows the truth," Jeram said. He did not add that Silvana would in all likelihood refuse to leave Nevarsin Tower.

Jeram paused, not entirely comfortable with the direction the conversation was taking. "My own actions, not theirs, are the issue here. I don't intend to bring charges against anyone else, but to clear up any that remain against me personally."

Francisco frowned and made a dismissive gesture. "Whatever you have done, you are a witness to two crimes committed by members of the Comyn. Using *laran* as a weapon is a direct violation of the Compact. Everyone in the funeral train saw what happened. Since the Regent and his wife have not been charged, I can only assume that the Council was so abjectly grateful for their lives, that they have abandoned their ethical responsibilities. But the second, the suppression of your memories . . ."

Jeram shrugged. He had thought Lew overly fastidious on that point, before he came to understand Lew's horror of involuntary mental contact.

"You are not Darkovan," Francisco said, "but surely in the time you studied at Nevarsin, you must have become aware that the invasion of one mind by another is considered a grave offense."

"Lew and I have already discussed the matter at length. I have fully forgiven him. In the end, he did me no lasting harm."

When Francisco shook his head, Jeram went on, "I did not come to Thendara to press charges against Lew or anyone else. The poor man has suffered enough!"

"I have no intention of calling *Dom* Lewis to account," Francisco said. "He is respected and honored throughout the Domains. No one questions his service to Darkover or the terrible sacrifices he made. But *Domna* Marguerida . . ."

Francisco picked up his goblet and stared into its depths. "If I know any true thing about power," he said slowly, "it is that unless people are held accountable, they will repeat whatever brings them success. The first time is always the hardest, whether it is killing a man face-to-face or blasting his mind with *laran.* Marguerida has already used her Gift to invade the minds of the defeated Terran force. Given another *good cause,* she will do it again. Who then will be responsible? The perpetrator herself, or those who could have stopped her and chose not to?"

Jeram shifted in his chair, growing more disquieted by the direction of the discussion with every passing moment. The fire, which had seemed so cozy at first, was now too hot. The richness of the wall hangings and carpets, the soporific, honey-sweet smoke of the wax candles, now turned nauseating. He realized he was sweating.

"I came here for only one reason only, to clear up my own status," he said. "I'm tired of hiding, and if the Council holds me criminally liable for the ambush, I want to face those charges and be done with it."

Francisco's eyes glittered in the mingled light of candle and fire. "I do not believe the Council has any right to sit in judgment of you. Indeed, they are indebted to you, or will be . . . once they hear what you have to say."

"Do I understand you rightly," Jeram said, "that you will get me an audience with the Council *if* I agree to tell them about how my memories were tampered with?"

"Come now," Francisco protested good humoredly, "you make it sound like extortion. We are friends, are we not? And friends help one another."

"I don't see why you should care. The offense was not against you."

Francisco's smile did not touch his eyes. "Some crimes injure us all."

The room grew still except for the crackle of the fire and the clink as Francisco set down his goblet.

"I said before," Jeram said tightly, breaking the silence, "that's not why I'm here. As far as I'm concerned, the Battle of Old North Road is over, history. The only thing I want cleared is my own conscience. You say I'm a victim of a crime? I say it's forgiven."

Francisco chuckled, a dry humorless sound. "I have heard an old saying of your people, 'All that is necessary for the triumph of evil is for enough good men to do nothing.' "

Jeram cringed inwardly and braced himself for another round of persuasion. *Just sit there and look reasonable,* he told himself. *Make friendly noises and then get out of there as soon as possible!*

"At the risk of becoming tedious, let me explain further," Francisco said. "Mikhail and Marguerida, together and separately, have violated our most fundamental ethical laws regarding the use of *laran.* If they are not stopped, the situation can only degenerate into tyranny. We fought that battle during our Ages of Chaos, when the king with the mightiest *laranzu'in* defined justice according to his own will. My ancestor, Varzil the Good, the greatest of us all, brought an end to that era of despotism through the Compact."

Francisco got up, gesturing as he paced. "Once more, Darkover stands on the brink of dark times. We need a leader, someone with both the vision and the moral authority to forge a new alliance."

"You mean yourself?" Jeram prickled at Francisco's unabashed egotism, but at the same time, the Ridenow lord exuded an almost hypnotic charisma.

"I will not abuse your ears with protestations of false modesty." Pausing before the fireplace, Francisco turned back, so that his form was silhouetted against the flames and his features cast into shadow. "I've known for a long time that I was destined to lead my people."

Jeram sat back in his chair, aware that Liam was listening carefully, with that focused attention. The blond man stood easily, weight balanced on both feet. His body blocked the door.

"—but I lacked the trappings of legitimacy. We are a culture bound by tradition, by honor codes, by symbols. Some years ago, in an act of unbridled greed, Mikhail seized the ring of Varzil Ridenow, a token of moral and political authority. You may not know how the Domains have deteriorated in the last few years. His shadow touches everyone, and with each passing season, fewer dare to stand against him. But with that ring, I could step into my ancestor's shoes. I could lead Darkover back to its greatest age!"

Seating himself once more, Francisco leaned forward. "Until now, the usurper has blinded the Council against all reason. They cannot see what he and his sorceress wife have been doing. She has bewitched them all, bent them to her will, even as she once tried to enslave me."

Francisco's passionate words filled the room. His eyes glowed with dark fire. Jeram found himself drawn in by the man's single-minded zeal, his ardor, his certainty.

"Now, at last, I have the key to open their eyes! *You* are my key! *You* will stand beside me in the Crystal Chamber. They cannot ignore your testimony. Don't you see, you have been sent to me so that I may fulfill my destiny!"

With an effort, Jeram pulled free of the magnetic lure of Francisco's words. He shook his head. "I'm sorry, you'll have to fight your own battles. I don't have anything against you, but all I want is to clear my name and go home to Rock Glen. I don't want to hurt Lew or his family."

I've done enough harm for one lifetime.

"Surely you must see the importance of my cause! I am not talking about petty politics but the future of all the Domains! You are Darkovan by choice—what happens concerns you, too!"

It was too late to back down now. "No, it's not my fight."

"Do you think yourself immune? I tell you, if this evil is not stopped now, chaos will rampage from Dalereuth to the Hellers, as it did millennia ago!"

"I know Lew Alton," Jeram said stubbornly. "I cannot believe that anyone he trusts the way he trusts his daughter could be so vile. I think we've said all we have to say to one another."

Jeram got to his feet and glanced at Liam, still on guard

in front of the door. He drew a deep breath and his pulse sped up, his muscles preparing for action. Now, he would find out just what lengths Francisco would go to to hold him here.

For a moment Francisco looked as if he were going to continue the argument. Then his face relaxed and he raised both hands in a gesture of surrender. "I see that I cannot persuade you. At least, I have done my utmost. Clearly, you are a man who answers to his own conscience, as do I. Surely, we can respect each other even when we differ. I would not have us part with any lingering animosity from our little discussion tonight. Liam, bring us more wine. The special reserve, if you please."

"I believe that you are sincere, *Dom* Francisco," Jeram said, a little surprised at how easily Francisco had given in. Perhaps Jeram had misjudged him. Regretfully, he added, "I am sorry I cannot help you."

A moment later, Liam slipped back into the room with a decanter of garnet-bright wine.

"Come, let us drink once more, as friends," said Francisco.

Since it would have been ungracious to refuse, Jeram nodded. Francisco filled his goblet. The wine, unspiced, was just below room temperature, richly complex, mingling the tastes of fruit, sunshine, and wild mountain spring water. Jeram had no idea that Darkover could produce such a sophisticated vintage.

Sipping their wine, they talked for a little while longer. Francisco offered Jeram housing for the night, since the rain was still coming down hard. Jeram refused, having spent enough time under Francisco's roof.

When Jeram rose to leave, his legs felt strangely unsteady beneath him. The room had come unhinged from its moorings. He could no longer follow what Francisco was saying.

Jeram's stomach twisted and dizziness shivered over him, disturbingly reminiscent of his threshold sickness. He tried to stand. The floor seemed to heave up under him.

Distantly, he felt his knees buckle and his body fold up like a child's paper fan.

The last thing he remembered was Liam standing beside him, a galaxy away, and Francisco's voice . . . something about *kireseth* fractions . . . acting only on those with *laran* . . .

"He'll speak the truth, all right . . ." Francisco's voice echoed weirdly. ". . . when and where *I* command . . . Marguerida's days of glory are over, and she will drag Mikhail down with her . . ."

BOOK III

25

"Look! There's Thendara at last!" Illona, who had ridden a little ahead of the others, stood up in her stirrups for a better view. Her mount, one of the sturdy, shaggy-maned mountain horses from Nevarsin, shook its head, sending the bridle rings jingling in the crisp air. "I can see Comyn Castle and the Terran Headquarters!"

They had taken advantage of the lengthening days to press on, climbing the pass, and now looked down the long slopes to the valley where the old city sat like a faded jewel. Spires and towers of pale stone, set with the translucent blue panels so loved by Darkovans, glimmered in the sun. Over the centuries since the spaceport was first built, the Federation edifices had lost their hard lines and pristine whiteness, softening in the accumulation of seasons. At the same time, a sprinkling of newer Darkovan mansions had been modeled on the stark architecture of the Terran Zone, so that the differences between the two cultures blurred. Even so, the ancient stone Castle remained defiantly untouched by the passage of time.

While they were on the road, Illona's exuberance, as if she were on some wondrous adventure, had infected Domenic. They had made love with the fevered, fragile urgency of a candle burning to its very end. Every glance, every touch, every moment together became infinitely precious, because it might be their last.

He regretted, too, the end of the special joy of traveling through mountains, ragged hills, and sloping pastures, where the ever-changing textures of rock and soil, water and sky, sang through his *laran*.

Now, as they neared the end of their journey together, Domenic dreaded their arrival. Illona would leave him to take her place with the other Keepers for the historic first meeting of their Council, and he . . . he would return to his own life, the politics of the Comyn, and the Regency.

And Alanna.

Domenic's heart plummeted. Never again would he be free to laugh simply because Illona did, or to look at her with his heart in his eyes. Aldones only knew how he was going to hide his true feelings from his mother. He couldn't very well go through his days with a telepathic damper strapped to his belt. He would simply have to rely upon the politeness of a telepathic society and his own meticulously honorable behavior.

Alanna would guess. Oh, gods, what could he tell her? That he had given his heart to another woman? Yet how could he lie? How could he hurt her in that way?

She was his promised bride. They had been friends since she had first arrived at Castle. He had loved her as a playfellow, a cousin, and yes, for a time, as a desirable young woman.

Was there any hope, any way through this tangle? Would Alanna agree to return to Arilinn in the hope of someday being able to enjoy normal sexual intimacy? No, that was only half the problem. Would *he* ever be able to think of her in that way, after what he had shared with Illona?

He could not dishonor his pledge to Alanna, and he did care for her. He would not willingly cause her pain.

It was said that in the ages before memory, group marriages were not uncommon among the Comyn, and in the openness of shared love, jealousy was rare. Even today, many men of his class kept *barraganas*, uncensured as long as they were discreet. *Nedestro* children were often legitimated. Domenic had even heard of friendships between wives and mistresses, but Alanna, he knew, would never consent. She was too insecure, too tempestuous, to tolerate a rival. And his mother—he could not imagine her accepting such a thing.

Domenic's horse now drew even with Illona's. She turned to him, her expression grave. Behind her eyes, he felt her own anguish. Her dignity and courage touched him deeply. They had no choice; they must go on, apart.

"We always knew this time would come, *cario mio,*" she said with a trace of sadness. "Do not mar the memory of what we had with regret."

"Since you ask it," he answered, forcing a smile, "I will try."

They let their horses rest, breathing noisily, as Grandfather Lew and the rest of their escort caught up with them. Thus ended their last possibility of intimate conversation. Their journey was almost over, with the walls and towers of Thendara within sight.

Lew drew his horse to a halt beside them. Since they had first set out from Nevarsin, his spirits had seemed freer, his mood lighter, than Domenic could remember.

Looking toward Thendara, Domenic said, "I can never decide whether it is hideous or beautiful, this mixture of worlds."

"Whatever it is," Lew said, "we must make our peace with it. Darkover can never return to what it once was. For good or ill, the Federation has left its mark on us."

Can never return . . . Domenic repeated silently. *I am not the same person who set out on this very road. I have not yet found my true place in the world, but I am nonetheless moving irrevocably toward it. There is no looking back.*

Lew proceeded down the incline, letting his horse pick its own pace. Domenic and Illona took their places in the middle of the convoy. This deep into Hastur lands, they no longer traveled in a tightly defended formation. Twice along the road from Nevarsin, however, they had been attacked by desperate, lawless men, too ragged and ill-armed to be rightly termed *bandits.*

"What's this?" The captain signaled a halt and pointed below.

Outside the nearest gates, on either side of the road, an irregular encampment sprawled around an old, broken-down well. Domenic made out tents, rude sheds, and a cluster of livestock. The place looked for all the world as if a disorderly, ragtag army had set up outside the city.

Domenic shivered. *We will have to pass through it.*

They have made a city unto themselves here, Illona sent the thought to him. *When winter comes, as it must, what will they do?*

"We'd better see what's going on." Lew nodded to the captain. "Prepare yourselves in the event of trouble."

"We will go cautiously, *vai dom.*" The captain motioned for his men to take up defensive positions. Swords ready, they proceeded downhill. Domenic's mare tucked her hindquarters for balance, stepping carefully along the steep trail.

Illona dropped the hood of her traveling cloak over her shoulders, so that her flame-bright hair was readily visible. She looked very much a Keeper, so much the better. In some parts of the Domains, Domenic had seen, *leroni* were still treated with superstitious awe.

They had not gone very far through the outskirts of the encampment when they attracted attention. Men in farmers' smocks or mountain furs emerged from their tents to stare.

As they went on, Domenic felt increasingly nervous. More men, and some hard-faced women too, gathered around the sides of the road. None bore any visible weapons, but many carried stout walking staves, and a few had axes, pitchforks, or other implements. So far, no one had made any threatening move, yet the mood was unmistakably strained, growing ever more so with each passing moment.

A few men pointed to Illona's red hair and murmured, *"Leronis!"*

Their horses responded to the rising tension, jigging and

dancing sideways. Domenic's hands sweated on the reins. Even Lew's normally sweet-tempered gelding tossed its head, ready to lash out. Only Illona sat easily in her saddle, in perfect control, as her mountain pony trudged along.

A man, young and black-haired, stepped onto the road, blocking their path. He carried a long stick, its tip fire-hardened into a point. A handful of others moved into position behind him. From every side, more people drew in on them.

The captain nudged his prancing mount forward. "Good people, what are you doing here, gathered on the road? What is going on?"

"It's just as Liam told us!" someone muttered. "The Comyn know nothing! They don't care!"

"Comyn!" One of the men barked out the word as if it were a curse. "I say, down with the lot of them!"

"Watch your tongue, man!" the captain said, lifting his sword.

"Get back, you fool!" said another in the crowd. "They've got a *leronis* with them! She'll blast you into cinders as you stand!"

Domenic grasped the hilt of his sword, cold and heavy. He had never used it in earnest, to kill. In the back of his mind, he wondered if he could. These were his own people, men he had sworn to serve. There had to be a better way out of the confrontation than bloodshed!

A man spat on the road. Domenic's horse, at the limit of her temper, reared and lashed out, but her hooves met only empty air. The nearest men scrambled back.

It was a respite only, Domenic knew. The air tasted of unspent lightning. He hauled on the reins, wrestling the mare back under control. She sidestepped and lashed her tail in protest.

"HOLD!"

A voice, raucous as the cry of a great-winged *kyorebni*, cracked the air. The sky reverberated with it. Every nerve in Domenic's body shrilled in response. His horse stood like a carven statue except for the heaving of her ribs. The crowd paused, suddenly irresolute.

A single rider moved to the fore, the horse haloed in blue-white *laran*-generated fire. For an instant, Domenic did not recognize his grandfather, sitting so tall and strong, as if the hand of Aldones, Lord of Light, were upon him. His riding cloak whipped back from his shoulders.

Noises flooded Domenic's hearing—the clatter of shod hooves, Illona's bitten-off cry, a muted outcry from the crowd.

"It's Lord Alton himself!"

"No, I heard he was dead—"

"Lord Alton!"

They drew back, some of them bowing or touching their foreheads.

"Enough," Lew said in his normal hoarse voice. "Captain, have your men lower their swords. These people are not our enemies. You there! If you have a grievance against the Comyn, let me know what it is, and I will do what I can to help you."

The black-haired man rose from where he had fallen to his knees. "I've heard of you, Lord Alton, that you stood against Sharra in my father's time. Everyone says you are a man of honor, that you never break your word."

A shudder went through Lew's body. His horse moved restively beneath him. "What aid do you ask of us? What has driven you from your homes to the gates of Thendara?"

A sigh passed over the crowd. Like the breaking wave of a storm, their stories tumbled out. Grimly, Domenic listened. Despite all the work of the Council during the last year, the plight of these country people had not improved. One sorrow built upon another—flood or drought or fire, crops and herds sickening. Most of it seemed no worse than the normal cycle of bounty and famine, with all the troubles of scratching a life out of harsh land. They had come to Thendara seeking work, loans to buy new seed and livestock, or for relief from taxes or any of the hundred legal difficulties that arose from misfortune.

Domenic exchanged glances with his grandfather. The burst of *laran* energy had almost faded, leaving Lew's face pale. His scars stood out like traces of lightning across his skin.

"An office has been set up in the Administrative Building," Domenic said. "You can bring your petitions there, so that they may be directed to the proper authorities, even the Council itself."

"Your pardon, young lord, but the last man of us who tried that has gone and disappeared," one man said.

"And those before him were turned away!" someone else added.

"Surely, not all," Domenic said, surprised. "Any worthy case must be heard—"

"That's what Jeram believed," the man retorted, "and now, for all we know, he sits rotting in a prison cell."

"If he's not dead already!" one of the women added, shaking her fist.

"If there's no justice for Jeram, what hope is there for the rest of us?" another voice demanded.

"Wait!" Illona cried. The simmering crowd fell back, muttering and averting their eyes. A few made warding signs against ill luck. "Jeram—do you mean Jeram of Nevarsin?"

The black-haired youth nodded. "That's where he said he was from, or nearabouts."

Domenic said to Lew, "Could this be the same Jeram I met?"

"I fear it is," Lew said. "The story fits." He pointed to the youth. "Good man, tell me what happened to our friend."

"*Vai dom,* he went into Thendara to petition for a hearing at the Comyn Council and has not returned."

"That does not mean anything untoward occurred," Domenic said. "Could he not simply have remained within the city, the better to conduct his business?"

"Begging your pardon, young lord, but if that were true, Jeram would have come back for his tent and chervine. No, he's met with foul play for sure. He was seen leaving

the Administrative office, with a Guardsman following
him." The young man's expression turned grim. "My own
father went to search for him and was turned away."

The others muttered in agreement. A few voices called
out, "Free Jeram!" but the fight had gone out of the crowd.

Lew nudged his horse forward and bent down from his
saddle to speak with the young black-haired leader. He
gave his word that he would look into the matter. Amid expression of gratitude and suspicion, the way opened for
them, and they clattered down the last stretch to the entrance to the city.

——— ✦ ———

Domenic did not draw an easy breath until they were
within sight of the Castle. Although Lew made no complaint, ever since he had faced the crowd at the tent city, his
face had gone ashen. Shivering, he clung to the pommel of
his saddle with his good hand. Illona glanced at him, looking worried.

The walls of the city closed around them; the streets
were filled with people, wagons, laden pack animals.
Domenic had forgotten how noisy Thendara was, how dirty
and smelly, how narrow the spaces, cutting off the horizon.
He could hardly sense the bedrock beneath the encrusta-
tion of wood and stone.

The captain did a superb job parting the traffic to speed
their way through the city. In the Castle courtyard, grooms
rushed to take their horses. Servants began unloading their
baggage. Marguerida burst through the main doors, skirts
flying as she raced toward them. She wore a gown of plain,
undyed wool, the sort of comfortable clothing she liked to
wear for writing music.

"Oh my dears, you are here at last!" She swept Domenic
into her arms. "It's so good to have you back again! How
you have been missed!"

Illona, who had drawn herself up, her expression almost
inhumanly composed, inclined her head and said, "It is a
pleasure to see you again, *Domna* Marguerida."

"Goodness, you've grown up," Marguerida said. "You're under-Keeper at Nevarsin now, I understand."

"Mother, what's been going on?" Domenic said. "We just passed through an encampment of very angry men outside the city gates."

Marguerida's mouth tightened. "The shanty town has ballooned over the last tenday. More people come all the time, and we haven't the facilities for them inside the city. So far, there's been no violence, but someone keeps stirring them up—"

"Your pardon, *Domna*," Illona cut in, looking at Lew with an expression of concern. "This is not the time to discuss such matters,"

"What am I thinking, to keep you all out here?" Marguerida slipped one hand through her father's elbow and held out the other to Domenic. Her golden eyes swept across her father's drawn face. "You look exhausted. Once you're settled and rested, we can talk."

"I must attend to *Dom* Lewis first," Illona said. "Where may I monitor him?"

Lew's face hardened. "It will pass. I have ridden through worse pain."

"Pain?" Marguerida looked aghast. "Father, are you hurt? Ill? Why did you not say so at once?"

At the same instant, Illona drew herself up, and her voice rang with authority. "*Dom* Lewis, we warned you that these episodes of chest pain might herald an even more serious condition."

"Enough!" Lew silenced them all. Domenic remembered the stories of Lew's own father, the formidable Kennard Alton. "It is nothing, I tell you, but if it will stop this chatter, then I will submit to Illona's examination and be done with it. We have enough cause for concern as it is."

———— ◆ ————

Domenic's room in the Alton family quarters closed around him like the walls of a prison. The bed with its carved headboard, the chest of inlaid blackwood and

matching dresser, even the chair in which, as a boy, he had
sat daydreaming for so many hours, were all as he had left
them. Yet he felt as if he had returned to someone else's
room, to someone else's life.

One of the Alton body-servants took his cloak and
helped remove his riding boots. Once he had bathed,
shaved, and dressed in clean indoor clothing, his mood
lifted slightly.

On his small writing desk, he found a stack of papers his
mother had left for him. Sighing, he picked up the top
sheet. It was, not surprisingly, an agenda for the first Council session.

He looked up at the sound of footsteps and voices in the
corridor outside. The door swung open and Alanna entered, carrying a tray of covered dishes. Her hair, braided
and coiled elegantly on her neck, gleamed like polished
copper. She set down the tray and rushed to him.

Once, Domenic had welcomed Alanna's embraces as the
most thrilling thing that had ever happened to him. Now
he could not force a response. Her intensity dismayed him,
like a storm sweeping away everything in its path. For a
terrible moment, he froze. What could he say to her, when
he knew now that what they had shared was not love but
infatuation?

Illona, beloved . . . The very thought of her sent a pang of
inexpressible longing through him. No, he must put those
memories behind him. He must think only of Alanna, here
before him.

To push Alanna away would have been unthinkably
cruel. Gently, he took her hands and gazed into her eyes.
She was so beautiful, it was not difficult to summon a smile
of genuine pleasure.

"Oh, how thoughtless of me!" she exclaimed, misunder-
standing his awkwardness, his silence. "Please, have something to eat. Castle gossip has it that you were attacked
outside the city gates. Here I am, thinking only of how glad
I am to see you and nothing of what you must have gone
through! I am self-centered, I know, for *Domna* Mar-

guerida is always telling me so. Now that you are home, I will try to behave more thoughtfully. I am always better when you are here."

Alanna lowered herself to the footstool beside Domenic's chair and watched him eat. As usual, the dishes reflected his mother's taste: a delicate cream soup, fowl simmered in herbs and wine, a terrine of wild mushrooms, and a basket of exquisite little heart-shaped buns stuffed with nut paste. Everything smelled delicious and tasted even better. On the trail and at Nevarsin, he'd become accustomed to plainer fare.

"Please forgive me if I seem less warm in my greeting than you deserve." Between bites, Domenic searched for the right words. "I have been on the road for some time, and, as you have heard, our arrival was eventful. But tell me, why has nothing been done to help those people? What did Mother mean, *Someone keeps stirring them up*?"

Alanna pouted, a pretty gesture. "I am never told anything of importance! *Domna* Marguerida does not even let me sit in on her meetings. Whenever I ask for anything useful to do, she tells me to go practice my sewing! I tell you, it is sometimes all I can do not to throw it in her face that soon I will be your wife, and I have every right to know these things! How can I be a proper help to you if I never hear what is going on?"

"I am glad you managed to say nothing about our engagement," Domenic said, "for we must keep it secret for a little while longer."

"I will try to please you in this, as in all things, my future husband," Alanna said, looking up at him from below lowered lashes. "*Domna* Marguerida thinks that if she tells me nothing, I will remain ignorant. But I see things . . ." her voice changed suddenly, turning thick and dark. "I *know* things."

"Your visions?" he asked, genuinely concerned. "You have had more of them?"

"No, no, only dreams . . ."

Alanna buried her face in her hands and burst into tears.

Domenic put his arms around her and pulled her to him. Sobs racked her slender body. Murmuring, he stroked her hair and back. For a moment she only wept harder, but then a shudder went through her and she quieted.

"I must look a fright." Sniffing, she straightened up. "What must you think of me? A silly girl, weeping at nothing."

"I do not call your dreams *nothing*," Domenic said. "Are you feeling well enough to tell me about them? Perhaps it will help to talk."

"There is one dream that frightens me more than the rest. I look out into the city as it is now, filled with sunshine and festival flowers. But a shadow falls over my mind when I remember the vision of people lying dead everywhere. It will not go away! Night is falling, and I cannot hold it back."

Alanna leaned against him, her eyes open and dry. "Hold me," she whimpered. "Keep me safe."

He pressed his lips to her forehead. "As long as it is in my power, no harm shall come to you."

They both startled as a gentle tap sounded on the door. At Domenic's invitation, Illona stepped into the room. She had changed into the long, loosely belted robe of a Tower worker. Her demeanor was composed, grave. She gave no sign of surprise at finding Domenic and Alanna in this intimate posture.

"I am sorry to invade your privacy, *Dom* Domenic, *Damisela* Alanna," Illona said, "but your grandfather is not merely fatigued from the long journey. He has been taken ill."

Domenic stiffened. He was old enough to remember how, when Regis Hastur had been stricken with a stroke, the alarm blasted from his mother's mind—"*Something has happened to Regis!*"

Had something just as terrible happened to Lew? Not even the immense power of Mikhail's ring had been able to save Regis from his fatal stroke.

"He has suffered a heart attack," Illona said.

Alanna gasped, covering her mouth with her hands. "Oh! Is he—will he—"

"I cannot say. I have done everything that I, as one *leronis* working alone, can do. The Castle healers, who have experience with such ailments, have given him their medicines and ordered him to rest."

Domenic stood up, meeting Illona's gaze. Her eyes, so deep and expressive, seemed like pools of forest-green light. It took all his self-control not to go to her.

"How could this happen? He looked so strong and well on the way back."

"In some ways, your grandfather is older than his years," Illona explained. "In the past, he has suffered not only physical injury but also deep psychic trauma."

"As had Great-Uncle Regis," Alanna murmured. "Everyone said he should have lived much longer."

Illona looked at Alanna, clearly not expecting such insight. "We do not know for certain that such harm shortens a man's life. It may have affected *Dom* Lewis's heart in ways we are powerless to heal. He had an episode of chest pain at Nevarsin at a time when he was under great stress. As far as we could determine, he had made a complete recovery. Perhaps facing those men outside the city, using his *laran* under stress . . ."

Illona closed her eyes, her face tightening. *It is all my fault. If only I had noticed earlier. If only—*

"We cannot live our lives on *if only*," Domenic cut off her anguished thought. *If there is a fault, it is mine as well.*

"He is stable enough for the moment," Illona said, quickly drawing herself together. "I understand that Istvana of Neskaya will be arriving in the next few days, and then we shall know more. Meanwhile, he has asked to see you. I think it would ease his mind."

"Of course," he said. "Alanna, I will return as soon as I can—"

"May I not come, too?"

Illona shook her head minutely and Domenic felt the sweetness of her mental touch. *It is too soon to know how serious your grandfather's condition is,* she told him, *but there are things that must be said—privately.*

You will be there? Domenic asked.

Illona inclined her head, her eyes lowered. *As long as I am needed. As long as you need me.*

Only a heartbeat had passed during their wordless exchange. Alanna stood between them, her chest heaving, her glance flickering from one to the other.

Domenic raised Alanna's hand to his lips. "I must hurry, my sweet. It is difficult to wait, but we are not our own masters in circumstances like this."

Alanna opened her mouth, clearly preparing to protest. Her breath caught and her chin came up. "I—" she began in a strange, choked voice, "I will await your news of *Dom* Lewis. Please do not delay on my account."

At the door, something made Domenic pause and look back at Alanna. Her cheeks had gone pale, her eyes huge and glassy, like those of a stricken deer. She held herself with a desperate, fragile dignity that he had never seen in her before. A word would shatter her.

Summoning a strained smile, he turned away.

26

Arriving at Lew's quarters, Domenic and Illona pushed past a gaggle of body-servants and one of the Castle healers, a gaunt, unsmiling woman of middle years wearing an enormous pocketed apron over her dress. The curtains of Lew's bedchamber had been partly drawn, saturating the air with diffuse light. The panels of pale blue stone set at intervals in the dark-gray walls gleamed faintly.

Propped on pillows on the enormous four-poster bed, Lew lay so still that for a terrifying instant, Domenic feared they had come too late. Then the chest beneath the *linex* nightshirt slowly rose and fell. Lew's head had fallen slightly to one side, his lips parted. The deeply incised scars of his suffering stood out against his withered flesh. Domenic could see the shape of the skull beneath the skin, the frailness of the single hand lying upon the covers. In that moment, his heart understood what his mind had only envisioned.

The old man might die, this bulwark of strength he had known all his life.

Men do die, Illona, behind Domenic, brushed his mind softly with hers. *We all must, in our time. Only death and next winter's snows are certain . . .*

Domenic knelt beside the bed and ran his fingertips over his grandfather's hand. The skin was thin but surprisingly soft, like weathered paper. The contact brought with it a rush of psychic impressions—the laboring heart, the layers of old wounds, the intense faceted brilliance of Lew's *laran*. This man, Domenic remembered, possessed the Alton Gift in full, had trained at Arilinn, the most prestigious of Darkover's Towers, had stood against the immensely powerful Sharra matrix.

Grandfather, don't die! Stay with us, we who love you!

The cry sprang unbidden from the depths of Domenic's heart. Love swept through him, love and pity that the man before him had known so much pain in his long life, and so little peace.

Ah, but I have found peace.

It took Domenic a moment to realize that his grandfather had spoken to him, mind to mind. He blinked away sudden tears to see Lew's eyes open and shining. Bony fingers tightened around his own.

"I do not fear death," Lew said, his usually hoarse voice now softened, "for I have laid my demons to rest. I have done all I could to set right my own sins and have been forgiven. There is but one thing left. Domenic, if I do not—if I cannot—" he paused for breath.

Illona rushed to his side. "Hush, now. You will need all your strength to recover."

I may not have another chance.

"Very well, but if I see you exerting yourself overly, I will intervene." With a nod to Domenic, Illona withdrew to the far side of the room, shielding her mind so that they could speak telepathically in private.

"What is so important?" Domenic whispered.

Jeram . . . you must find him, help him. He may be in terrible danger.

I don't understand. From whom?

Lew's mind opened to Domenic's, and in the swirl of memory and thought, sight and *laran*, the story unfolded. For a moment, Domenic found himself on Old North Road once again. In his mind, he saw the men in dark brown and green rushing the funeral cortege, the mad scramble as the Guards wheeled in defense, and then the flare as the first blaster fired, and, finally, the shimmering brighter-than-bright sphere created by his parents from their joined *laran*.

What . . . ? Domenic looked on the faces of the fallen men, and recognized his grandfather's student from Nevarsin.

Jeram came to Thendara to ask the Council for amnesty, Lew said. *But he never got that far. You heard the story, how he went to the Administrative Building and then disappeared. I do not believe this was random chance. I fear he has fallen into the hands of those who would use his story for their own purposes. I still have a responsibility to him . . .*

Lew fell back on his pillow. Illona, on the other side of the room, looked up sharply.

"Find him," Lew whispered. "Promise me . . ."

"That is enough for now," Illona interrupted. She hurried to the bedside. Her starstone flashed, blue-white, and she laid one hand upon Lew's chest.

At that moment, the latch clicked open. Marguerida burst into the room and rushed to the bedside. She had thrown an old, tattered shawl over her shoulders. Her fair cheeks were flushed. Domenic had never seen her so distraught.

"Oh, Father! I came as soon as I heard. This can't be what my Gift was warning me about! You must fight, do you hear me? Fight! Don't you leave me, like Dio did!"

The healer, stern-faced, followed closely on Marguerida's heels. "*Domna*! Compose yourself!" she barked. "You will do him harm if you carry on this way! To say nothing of turning yourself into a second patient, thereby diverting my attention from where it is needed most. Now, will you behave in a more suitable manner, or must I exclude you from these premises?"

Marguerida straightened herself and smoothed back the tendrils of hair that had escaped from their clasp. "There must be something I can do!"

Illona said, "The healer and I can manage very well."

"Mother, I think Illona has the right of it," Domenic

said, taking Marguerida's ungloved hand and drawing her toward the door. "We will only distract these good women from their work. In the meantime, there is much to do to prepare for the Council session, and when Grandfather is able to join us, he will need all your strength."

Marguerida looked uncertain, but relented under Domenic's gentle persuasion. She allowed him to escort her from the room, after the healer promised to send word at the slightest change in Lew's condition.

——— ✦ ———

In the next tenday, Lew's condition stabilized and improved. Istvana Ridenow and Liriel Lanart, who was a highly skilled matrix technician, had arrived in Thendara early. With Illona, they formed a healing circle. Domenic, watching his grandfather gain daily in strength, thought that few men in the history of Darkover had been tended by such a circle.

Illona had sensed rightly that Lew's body had been affected by what his mind had suffered. The confrontation at the city gates and the use of his *laran* to quell the angry mob had pushed him past his limits. Rest and the medicines prepared by the Castle healers gradually eased the burden on his heart. He responded vigorously to the outpouring of healing energy from the assembled *leroni*.

Istvana observed, after a particularly encouraging treatment, "It is as if he has truly put the past behind him. He has chosen, with his whole spirit, to live."

The Castle filled quickly as more Comyn arrived for the season. Lew continued to improve so well that Istvana and Liriel made plans to meet with Alanna to see what could be done about the safeguards placed in her mind. It would be a delicate task, as Liriel had not been privy to the intervention, and Loren MacAndrews herself had remained at Arilinn, sending Liriel as her representative. Although Liriel was a technician rather than an under-Keeper, her experience, tact, and calm temperament made her an excellent choice. When Alanna heard about the plan, however, she flatly refused to have anything to do with them. Not even Domenic could persuade her. When he tried, she became distraught, the way she did when anyone suggested she return to Arilinn. She even accused Domenic of trying to get rid of her. Rather than risk her making herself ill from hysterics, he dropped the subject.

As the days passed, Domenic searched the city for any clue to what had happened to Lew's friend, Jeram. Danilo knew nothing of the matter, although he offered to have his agents keep watch and make discreet inquiries. Uncle Gabriel remembered his brief interview with Jeram, but nothing more. The Guardsman whom Marguerida had asked to follow Jeram recalled losing track of him only a short distance from the City Administrative offices. No one Domenic talked to had seen Jeram since then. It was as if the city, like some ravenous beast, had swallowed him up.

Men do not simply vanish, not even in Thendara, Domenic told himself stubbornly, and he kept asking questions until his normal Council season obligations forced him to leave off.

The usual festivities that began the season were somewhat subdued compared to previous years, for Marguerida was distracted by her father's convalescence. In her place, Gisela Aldaran and Miralys Elhalyn organized a reception ball. Marguerida's other friend, Katherine Aldaran, was delayed due to an outbreak of a mysterious fever in Caer Donn, still being rebuilt after the Sharra firestorm. In the midst of this, news came that the senior Gabriel had passed away. The younger Gabriel and Rafael took over arrangements for a quiet private funeral, as their father had wished. After his body was taken to Thendara, the family laid him to rest near Javanne's unmarked grave.

Marguerida did not attend the opening festivities, but Domenic did, and he danced several times with Alanna, as well as with Danaria Vallonde and one of the Leynier cousins, a plump, raven-haired girl named Kyria. Gareth Elhalyn was in attendance, along with his brother Derek, both of them drinking lightly and behaving themselves

very well. In contrast, Kennard-Dyan Ardais got so drunk
that Rory and Niall had to carry him back to his quarters.
It was, Domenic thought, hardly an auspicious beginning to
the season.

When the Comyn Council gathered for its first session,
Danilo took his usual seat in the Ardais enclosure, along
with Kennard-Dyan, looking much the worse for his earlier bout of drinking. Two of Kennard-Dyan's *nedestro*
sons, having reached their majority, shared the box.

Men and women filed into the Crystal Chamber. Liriel
Lanart, Istvana Ridenow, and Moira DiAsturien, a pretty,
sweet-tempered woman who had trained at Neskaya but
now was Keeper at the tiny Tower of Corandolis, sat with
their own families. At Danilo's suggestion, Mikhail had
arranged for the other *leroni* to use the empty space in the
Aillard enclosure, and a special banner, a white Tower
against a field of starstone blue, hung beside the Aillard
gray and crimson. Illona took her place there, talking with
Linnea Storn and Laurinda MacBard of Dalereuth Tower.
Laurinda was a pale, homely, heavy-boned woman with a
stern demeanor and a high, nasal voice that Danilo found
abrasive, but her *laran*, what he sensed of it before the telepathic dampers were set, was clear and bright, like sunlight
on a droplet of pure water. Obviously, Danilo reflected,
laran did not necessarily confer a pleasing manner.

Marguerida and Mikhail entered after most of the others had taken their places, followed by Domenic and Rory.
Donal Alar walked just behind and to Mikhail's right side,
as a proper paxman. Alanna accompanied them, attending
Marguerida. In the Alton enclosure, the younger Gabriel
sat as Head of the Domain. Lew's chair remained vacant.
Hermes and Katherine Aldaran had just arrived the night
before, joining the others of their Domain. They had
brought Yllana, as well.

The opening ceremonies proceeded with the usual pomp
and grandeur of the formal roll call. One Domain after an-

other answered the summons, but there was no mention of Gareth ascending to the throne.

Mikhail introduced the members of the new Keepers Council, and Laurinda, as their elected spokeswoman, addressed the assembly briefly. Except in matters affecting both Tower and Council, she said, they would meet separately, reporting any major decisions to the Council.

Marilla Lindir-Aillard asked what sort of questions they were likely to take up. The years had worn heavily on her, and not even her rich gown of gray and scarlet, the colors of her Domain, could hide the frailness of her body or distract from the deep creases around her eyes and mouth.

"Getting to know one another better, for one thing," Laurinda responded. "We often speak to each other over the relays, but we have time for little else besides the messages at hand. All of us feel that the Towers are too isolated and our people stretched too far. Each season, fewer young people come to us for training. Once, it was customary for all Comyn sons and daughters to spend a season or two in a Tower, but now even those with talent stay away or leave after only a short time. The life of a *leronis* is not for everyone."

After Laurinda had finished speaking, Danilo rose at Mikhail's prearranged invitation. "The Towers are not the only place our strength has grown thin. We ourselves have diminished in numbers, so that with each generation, more power is concentrated in fewer hands. Look around this very chamber. Count the empty places."

He paused to sweep the walled-off enclosures with his gaze. Aillard had no heir, nor did Ardais.

"I propose that, for the sake of both the Towers and the Domains, we expand membership in the Comyn," Danilo said. "I ask that all *nedestro* offspring, and even those with lesser blood, be named legitimate, with full right to participate in Tower and Council."

A stunned silence answered him. "What are you saying, that we admit any sort of riffraff among us?" Gabriel was the first to speak, followed by a dozen others, equally outraged.

"*Vai domyn!* Kinsmen! Calm yourselves!" Mikhail said.

"It is not an unreasonable suggestion," Dani Hastur said, once the uproar had quieted. "Once, even within the time of our fathers, a man could not be sealed to the Comyn unless he possessed *laran*. Have you not heard tales of how Kennard Alton almost killed *Dom* Lewis doing just that? Yet how many of us have only the slightest talent and no training to use it? How can we sit here and deny others with far stronger *laran*?"

"It's a preposterous idea!" Lorrill Vallonde said. "We have never—" He broke off as Istvana Ridenow gestured her desire to speak. *Dom* Lorrill, like many other conservatives, held Keepers in great reverence.

"*Dom* Danilo's proposal has merit," Istvana said. "We can easily combine our searches. We all know how much havoc an untrained telepath can create. If every *nedestro* son or daughter is to be examined for *laran,* it must be done under the supervision of the Towers. We can screen and recruit our own candidates at the same time."

"Where would they sit, these talented nobodies?" Marilla said pettishly. "If we admit them to the Council, for whom would they speak?"

"Let us not take on unnecessary difficulties," Linnea said, rising. "There will be time enough to sort out all these details. For now, let us consider the basic principle involved." With her auburn hair touched with only the slightest hint of silver and her graceful air of authority, she commanded the Council's full attention.

"There are precedents for the collateral inheritance of Domain-right," Linnea pointed out. "Regis himself named the son of his sister as his heir, when he had none of his own. Kennard Alton's marriage to Elaine Montray was never accepted by this Council, and yet his son Lewis was named his Heir and Warden of Alton."

When she finished, a commotion broke out again. Everyone tried to talk at once, and the Crystal Chamber rang with raised voices. Again, Mikhail called for order. This time he recognized Kennard-Dyan.

"It is true that too many of us have not fulfilled our obligations to marry and produce sons and daughters to carry on after us," Kennard-Dyan began. It was only by the most extraordinary circumstances that he himself stood here, for his own father had been a notorious lover of men.

"I admit to you all that I have failed in my duty to the future of my Domain." He paused, drawing a deep breath, and Danilo caught the pallor of his cheeks. "I am now prepared to do what is in my power to rectify my shortcomings."

Throughout the chamber, feminine voices whispered. If the most famous bachelor in the Seven Domains was at last prepared to take a wife, there would be no end of matchmaking and gossip.

"Therefore," Kennard-Dyan went on, "I proclaim all of my *nedestro* children legitimate and will present them here as circumstances permit. Any who are worthy by virtue of their *laran* may sit beside me in Council to strengthen Ardais and all the Domains."

He gestured to the two young men behind him, and they stepped forward. Both had the lean, darkly handsome features of the Ardais, but none of the arrogance that had characterized old Lord Dyan.

This could not be easy, Danilo thought, even if Kennard-Dyan were not hung over. The night of the reception, when Kennard-Dyan had gotten so drunk, Danilo had followed him to the Ardais quarters and sat with him through the small hours of the morning.

"I know what they all want of me," Kennard-Dyan had sobbed, lugubrious in his intoxication. "To tie me down, to chain me to some broodmare who's only after my title and the sons I'll give her. Who cares nothing for . . . nothing for . . ."

Regis, too, had once stormed against the ever-increasing pressure to take a wife. To be cared for, truly and without regard for rank or consequence, was that not what Regis and Kennard-Dyan and he himself wanted? Was that not the very thing denied to them by a world desperate for heirs of the blood?

Poor Domenic, he will be next . . .

Kennard-Dyan had found a way out of that trap, for the moment anyway. *"Vai domyn,"* he said with a short but impeccably formal bow, "I present to you my eldest son, Geremy Esteban. It is my will that the Council accept him as Heir to Ardais. And I also present my second son, Valentine."

"We will be pleased to undertake the *laran* examination of both of these young men," Laurinda said.

"I have another child I would acknowledge," Kennard-Dyan went on, "one whose qualifications are beyond question." He gestured toward the half-empty enclosure of Aillard. "Illona Rider, I hereby declare that you are my true daughter, and I offer you a place in the Domain of Ardais."

Everyone turned to stare at Illona. Only the slight movement of her hands, fingers digging into palms, betrayed any emotion. All her young life had been spent poor and rootless, an orphan taken in by the Travelers, performing in one town after another, perhaps going cold and hungry, all because this powerful lord had given no thought to the consequences of a pleasant dalliance. Only a chance meeting with Domenic had given her a chance for anything better.

"Vai dom," she said, "I am fully aware of the honor you do me. Ardais is a noble lineage, and if it is the will of the Council, I will proudly bear the name of your daughter. However, I have come here as under-Keeper of Nevarsin Tower, the place I have earned for myself, and that is the only title I desire."

Good for you! Danilo thought. If the Council was strengthened by women of such integrity, it boded well for Darkover.

Mikhail was speaking again, a gracious acknowledgment of Kennard-Dyan's actions and a formal welcome to Illona as a member of the Keepers Council. Rufus DiAsturien talked forcefully about the lack of heirs to Aillard. The line of Aillard was all but extinct; Marilla held the position only because there was no daughter in direct descent, and her only child was Kennard-Dyan, who ruled Ardais.

As he listened to the discussion, something niggled at Danilo's memory, some footnote to a history text, regarding the name of *Aillard*. Two generations ago, Cleindori Aillard had single-handedly broken the old cloistered tradition that insisted on Keepers retaining their virginity. Her son, Jeff Kerwin, had become a Keeper in his own right. But there had been a woman Aillard cousin as well . . .

"Now that young Domenic has come of age as heir to the Regency and his Domain," *Dom* Rufus said, "he must make plans to marry. I speak on behalf of the entire Council in affirming that we must ensure the proper succession of Hastur."

A wave of renewed excitement swept through the female contingent of the Council at the renewed prospect of a Comyn wedding. Already, they were planning the balls and parties, the receptions, the gifts to be exchanged, the new gowns to be ordered and songs to be composed, the decorations, the guest lists. Danilo wished Domenic a strong constitution and steady nerves.

The guardians of tradition would not rest until they had witnessed the copper *catenas* locked forever upon the wrists of Domenic and his bride. Perhaps Domenic himself had already decided to reveal his choice. Alanna leaned forward, coming more into the pearly light. She was beautiful, Gifted, and of impeccable lineage. At the moment, she was also exultant, glowing with anticipation.

Mikhail had listened with solemn attention to what Rufus said. He turned to Domenic, they exchanged a few words, and then Domenic stepped forward, speaking to the assembly.

"I will in all seriousness consider the matter," Domenic said, raising his voice so that everyone could hear him clearly. "I agree that the future of Hastur must be secured. I thank you for your thoughtful discussion, but I have no intention to marry at this time."

Alanna gave a little cry, quickly smothered, and Mikhail continued with the session. Francisco briefly addressed the Council, requesting permission to add an item to the agenda for the following day. Danilo caught the minute tensing of Mikhail's shoulders as permission was granted.

The session was soon concluded, and within the hour, news of the astonishing developments would spread throughout the higher echelons of Thendaran society. As Danilo lingered to speak to Kennard-Dyan, he could not miss the scrupulous politeness with which Domenic escorted his mother and Alanna from the Chamber, or the way Domenic glanced over his shoulder in the direction of the beautiful young under-Keeper from Nevarsin.

27

The heart has its own reasons, Regis had once told Domenic, *and reason is not among them.*

Why else, Domenic wondered, would he be standing at the doors of Comyn Tower when he should be in his own bed? He had tried to sleep, reiterating the thousand arguments why he should *not* come, until he could recite them backwards. His feet, answering their own desires, had led him here.

Madness, Domenic told himself again, even as his hand lifted the latch. Freshly oiled, it opened silently.

The door swung open. A single *laran*-charged globe filled the space with blue-tinted light. Beyond lay a little entrance hall with a small arched doorway to one side. Stairs led upward into darkness and the common room. Perhaps the Keepers had gathered there, talking or communing mentally. Illona might be among them. Or they might have retired at this late hour. He could not search every sleeping chamber.

Domenic's foot was already upon the bottom stair. The lantern trembled in his grasp. How would he explain his presence to someone like Laurinda MacBard? It was folly to have come.

Wrapped in a shawl so white it glimmered in the shadows, Illona appeared in the arched doorway. Her voice echoed in the stairwell. "Domenic? Is something wrong?"

"I must speak with you." *Please, do not turn me away. I need you now, more than ever.*

"We'll wake the others if we talk out here," Illona whispered. "This place magnifies every sound." She took his free hand and drew him through the doorway, into a corridor and then a small, tidy kitchen. In the center was a simple table, flanked by stools. "Everyone else is in bed like sensible people. I snuck downstairs for something to eat."

"Yes, I remember you did that at Neskaya."

"Old habits, I suppose. I spent too much of my childhood hungry." Smiling, she lifted a cloth from a half-loaf of bread, sliced off two pieces, spread them with butter from a little pot, and handed one to Domenic. "Just like old times. Now, what brings you here in the middle of the night?"

He reached for their deep mental bond and sensed only an impenetrable barrier. *Will you not speak to me as we once did, will you not come into my mind, as you are in my heart?*

"Domenic, you said—we *agreed*—"

"Please."

Leaning across the table, she studied him. Her eyes reflected the light of the lantern. He could read nothing in them, only his own desperate hope. Without speaking, she got up, walked around the table, and sat down beside him. She picked up his hand and held it against her cheek. Her skin felt like sun-warmed velvet.

You are not alone, dearest one. You will never be alone, as long as I have thought and breath.

Domenic turned his head so that his lips pressed against the palm of her hand. Tenderness rose up in him, consumed him, flooded out into the kiss he placed there. Illona trembled in response. Reluctantly, he lowered her hand. They might have only a short time together.

I cannot see my way through this darkness, he thought, and then realized that Alanna had said almost the same thing.

He laid his face against Illona's shoulder, and she

stroked his hair. "I do not know how, but we will find a way," she murmured.

A faint rustle of cloth and softly indrawn breath jerked Domenic upright. Together, he and Illona turned in the direction of the sound, toward the doorway.

Alanna stood there, her face twisted with unreadable emotion.

Domenic scrambled to his feet, knocking over his stool. Wood clattered against the bare stone floor. His worst nightmare—to have the two women in his life confront each other—had come true. He wished the earth would swallow him up. He tried to speak, but the words froze in his throat.

With a sob, Alanna whirled and fled.

Domenic took a step after her, but Illona said, "Let her go. She will not believe anything you say now. What she suspects is, after all, the truth."

Reluctantly, he nodded agreement. "I will go to her in the morning, when the heat of the moment has passed. I intend to keep my promise to her, if she will still have me."

"Yes, I think you must. Now she knows what she has only suspected before. When she has had time to think, she will realize that soon I will be gone, but the two of you will remain. Perhaps she will be satisfied with what you can give her, your honor if not your heart."

Domenic turned to look at her with amazement. Only a few years ago, it seemed, Illona had been a scrawny, uneducated Traveler girl. Where had she acquired such detachment?

"It is not so hard, so long as it is not my own soul I must examine," Illona said with a faint smile. "I am not so wise as all that. Most of the time, I am only passing on what those who are older and far more experienced have told me. You forget, *cario mio,* that I had already seen a good deal of the coarser side of life when we met, and life in a Tower demands honesty and self-examination. It is rather intoxicating, once you get used to it, revealing both the worst and the best of human nature."

She stood up and settled her white shawl around her shoulders. "Do not lose hope or let your fears cloud your vision. Many things can happen, things we cannot even imagine. In this strange and wonderful world of ours, where a Comyn lord can offer a penniless orphan a place at Ardais, where men fly to the stars and *chieri* come down from their forests, who is to say that five years from now, all our present sorrows will not seem like yesteryear's snows?"

———— ◆ ————

There was a saying among the folk of the Armida hills that the old sleep so little in order to make up for all the hours they spent napping as babies.

Unable to fall asleep, Lew got out of bed and sat in his favorite chair by the fireplace, staring into the embers. He hoped the gently flickering glow would make him drowsy, but he remained wide awake. His body did not want to stay in bed; his muscles ached for activity. He thought about Jeram, out there in the city—hurt, lost, in hiding? Dead? And Domenic, still searching when he could, unable to rest.

Lew heard a creaking noise, like old hinges protesting, and then the grating of stone over stone. The tapestry on the far wall, the one depicting Lady Bruna Leynier, bulged outward. From behind it came a distinctly feminine shriek. The tapestry rod rocked off its mounting hooks, and then the whole mass of canvas-backed wool cascaded off the wall, trapping the intruder in its heavy folds. Behind it lay a dark, cobweb-laden tunnel, undoubtedly one of the secret passages rumored to run throughout Comyn Castle. Any ancient place used for clandestine purposes over the centuries must have some means for getting from one corner to another without notice.

Lew watched the figure struggle free from the thick, heavy fabric. He doubted whether even the most inept assassin would present herself in this way. After a short burst of pushing and yanking, the tapestry fell away into a great heap at the feet of a red-faced, dusty, and extremely agitated young woman.

As she stepped into the stronger light, Lew recognized Alanna Alar, Marguerida's fosterling. He had always thought her pretty but unsubstantial, although he had never exchanged more than a few polite words with her. Her hair was disheveled, laced with cobwebs, and several grimy streaks marked her face.

"Oh, this is terrible!" she cried. "How could I have made such a mistake? You are Lew Alton!"

"I am indeed, and it has been a long time since a young woman burst into my chambers," he said, trying not to show his amusement. "Indeed, I cannot recall when one has ever done so before in such an unconventional manner."

"I didn't mean—" she stammered. "Blessed Cassilda, what a mess I've made!" With a visible effort, she drew herself up. "I am sorry to intrude upon your privacy, *vai dom.* I had no intention of emerging in *anyone's* bedchamber, let alone yours."

Lew wondered if her true destination had been the bedchamber of a much younger man. "Now that you are here," he said aloud, "you might as well come in, and see if you can find a way to close that doorway."

The girl turned back to the opening, retrieved a bundled-up cloak and an unlit lantern that smoked as if it had just been extinguished, set them down inside the room, and ran her hands over the wall where the tapestry had hung. It took her only a few moments of pushing and twisting the irregular stones before the door swung closed. Only the faint line of dirt where the tapestry had hung suggested the wall was anything beyond an ordinary wall.

"Would you care for a little late supper?" Lew asked. "There is still some soup, as well as bread and dried fruit, on the table. You must keep your strength up."

"Oh! Actually, I *am* hungry." After helping herself, the girl sat down on the stool opposite Lew. She ate quickly, with a natural neatness.

"Would you like to pack up the leftovers to take with you?" Lew asked. "In my experience, one should always have a generous supply of food for the road."

"If I had known I was going to run away, I would have planned better," she said, giving him a rueful smile. "I apologize for bursting into your rooms like this. Things just—I didn't know what else to do."

"Would you like to tell me about it?"

Alanna shook her head. "It's no use. I suppose I've know for some time now, ever since I first saw them together in my mind. I think I must be going mad, for some of my visions have come true, but they cannot *all* be real. I had thought, for all the time he was gone, *As soon as he comes back, it will be all right. He will love me, and I will never again have to face these things by myself.* And now I cannot even have that. He loves *her*, and I am alone!"

What was the girl talking about? *He* might well be Domenic, for Marguerida had mentioned her concern about a possible attachment between them, and the interloper could only be Illona. No one with a scrap of *laran* could mistake the depth of the attachment between Illona and Domenic, or the incandescent passion whenever their eyes met.

Delicately, gently, Lew reached out with his *laran*, listening, rather than making a direct attempt at rapport. Alanna's thoughts were only partly shielded, a jumble of confusion and immense natural talent. Pictures burst across the back of his mind, streams of energy, flashing scenes of people, dark towers, fire in the night, a city of corpses. Then the fractured images swept away, dry leaves in a bitter-edged wind.

Fear . . . a wild impetuous temper . . . confusion . . . aching loneliness . . .

Someone, Lew thought darkly, *has been tampering with her* laran.

"Will you tell me about these visions?" he asked. "I know something of *laran* matters."

"How can I? You're his *grandfather*."

"Domenic's, you mean."

Alanna flinched. "I suppose that banshee's out of the egg now. Curse this tongue of mine! I couldn't keep a secret if my life depended on it!"

Lew gestured for Alanna to bring her stool and sit beside him. "Rest assured, child, that when the time comes, you will surprise yourself with your own abilities. There is no dishonor in falling in love with Domenic. After all, the two of you have known one another since you came here as a little girl."

"Yes, he was my one constant friend for all those years," she said. "Everyone else thought I was too much trouble to bother with. Domenic was the one person who took me seriously."

For an instant, Alanna's voice choked, but she lifted her chin and went on. "It was like a gift from Evanda herself when he said he loved me, but you know, Grandfather Lew—I may call you that, yes?—I was never sure if I imagined the whole thing. I loved him so much, I was sure I could make him love me back. I used to dream that he'd carry me away from Thendara to some wonderful place—Armida, but without Auntie Marguerida hovering about. Oh, I suppose that's a terrible thing to say to her own father!"

"I take no offense," he told her. "In fact, it is only natural that every young person must find his—or her—own place in the world. We cannot always dwell in the shadows of those who have gone before us, no matter how much we loved and respected them. Nor is it some moral failing on your part to feel pain when the one you love has chosen another."

"Yes, and I want to claw her eyes out!" she cried. "Curse them both! No, I don't mean that! I would never wish him any harm. I've always thought it hideous when the heroine of the story says, 'If I can't have him, no one else will'."

"Yes, even though it costs us everything, we want those we love to be happy."

Alanna nodded, blinking back tears. "I'm afraid that if I

let him go, there will be nothing left for me. No one will ever love me again."

Lew sat quietly, remembering his despair when his beloved Marjorie died in an attempt to control the Sharra matrix. He had never before loved anyone with that exhilarating, soul-deep bond. For a time, he could not imagine living without her. But he *had* lived, and he had healed. He had loved again. Dio had been a very different wife but every bit as dear to him. Now, he looked into his heart and saw a treasure chest of cherished friends, family, lovers. No one of them could ever replace another. All had enriched him immeasurably.

"There are many who love you," he told the quivering girl before him. "Your family and Marguerida, who has tried to be a loving foster-mother—"

Alanna refused to be consoled. "Then why did they send me away? Why does Auntie Marguerida always push me aside, or act as if I have no feelings? Oh, I should not have said that! She—Oh! Perhaps she treats me as if I am a spoiled, selfish, willful child because . . . because that is what I am."

"But that is not *all* you are," Lew persisted gently. "It is said that our past is our fate, but I hope that is not true. I believe you have it within you to become more than what you have been. Stronger, truer. Braver."

A stillness crept over Alanna as he spoke. "If I make Domenic keep his promise and marry me, that will make both of us miserable. But I don't know how I can go on without him."

Lew picked up her hand and stroked it gently. With a sob, she laid her head on his knee. He stroked her hair, brushing away the cobwebs and flakes of rock dust.

"I thought the same thing when I lost my first wife," he murmured. "She was so brave and so beautiful, and I had never known such love. Have you heard the stories of how she perished in the Sharra circle, saving us all? So I know something of grief."

A little sigh passed through Alanna's body, and her muscles softened.

"I think we never forget those we love," Lew said. "They become part of us forever. In time, the pain subsides. The burden becomes lighter. The memory becomes a well-spring of compassion and strength. And sometimes we are given the privilege of passing that wisdom to someone else, so that they know they are not alone."

Alanna's fingers tightened around his own. After a long moment, she straightened up. The childish, petulant quality disappeared from her features. She looked less forlorn, more resolute, as if drawing upon some inner strength she had never before touched.

"I have been a silly, flighty thing," she confessed, "always getting my way by throwing fits of temper and making those around me miserable. But if *you* will help me, as my own grandfather might have, I will try to do what is right."

"I am your friend, and I ask nothing in return." Lew thought of his many conversations with Father Conn. What would the old monk have said? "If you would act with honor, then let it be for its own sake, not to buy any favors from me."

Her eyes gleamed in the reflected firelight. "No, but it would mean a great deal to know that you are watching over me."

Bare is brotherless back, ran the old proverb. No one, not even the highest Hastur lord or the lowliest ragpicker, ought to face the unfolding crises of life alone.

"Then I shall do what I can for you," he said. "I will not take care of you, but I will help you to learn to take care of yourself. Meanwhile, we had best both get some rest. There is an important Council session tomorrow, and I will need a strong young arm to lean on."

Cheerfully, Alanna returned to her own quarters for a few hours of sleep before dawn. Lew could not be sure how long her helpful mood might last; she might abandon all her resolutions at the first trial. Then again, he thought with an inward smile, she might surprise them all.

— ✦ —

Lew woke to a gentle tapping at his door. He had fallen asleep in the same comfortable chair beside the now-cold hearth. Alanna pushed the door open with one hand and slipped through, carrying an enormous covered tray. She wore a fresh gown, a flattering deep forest green edged with snowflake lace around the high neck and cuffs. Her clean hair was neatly braided and coiled on her neck.

"The kitchen was short on help this morning," she said. "Half the cook's helpers were out sick, either they themselves or their families. I ordered everything I thought you might like."

By the time Lew returned from washing his face and changing his shirt, Alanna had finished stirring the fire to new life and setting out the meal. The customary pitcher of *jaco* sat steaming on the little table beside bowls of brown eggs, boiled in the shell and still hot, stewed apples, a basket of nut-crusted pastries, and pots of berry jam, honey, and butter.

"Good provender for a hard day's work," he said approvingly.

"Yes, and you will need all your strength." Smiling, Alanna stirred a spoonful of honey into a mug of *jaco* and handed it to him.

"And you, *chiya*? You must eat as well."

"I had a little bread and soft cheese down in the kitchen while they were making up your tray," she said. "But if it would please you, I will eat more." She bit into one of the pastries.

While they were eating, Marguerida arrived. She was already dressed for Council in dove-gray silk bordered by wide bands of embroidery in shades of blue. She had done up her air in a graceful swirl with strings of tiny Thetan shells instead of the usual coil low on the neck so common among Comynara. Her expression darkened slightly at Alanna's presence, but she said nothing beyond bidding the girl good morning.

"Have you been up all night, Father? I had hoped we could sit and talk."

Alanna bowed with a fragile, self-conscious dignity and

excused herself. When they were alone, Marguerida seated herself in the second chair, opposite Lew.

"Father, do you seriously mean to attend Council today? Illona said you were thinking of it and that neither she nor the healers had any objections, but I didn't believe her. What can they be thinking of, to permit it?"

"I believe," Lew said dryly, "they understand I would do myself more harm by staying here and fretting. After yesterday's astonishing events, how can I miss today?"

"Your presence will not solve anything if you make yourself ill again."

"I am quite recovered, I assure you. Shall I dance a *secain* to prove it to you?"

With a laugh, Marguerida sat back in her chair. "Just listen to me, fussing over you like an old mother hen! I'm sorry I'm so short of temper." She rubbed her temples. "It's this headache."

"Another precognition?"

She shrugged. "Who can say, with so much going on? Every time I think we've passed the crisis, I get another one. I can't stop worrying about what Francisco may do. His scheme to marry his daughter to Domenic came to nothing. Katherine left her and Terése safely back at Aldaran and says she's much happier there, not that Nico was all that interested. Francisco will try something else, I just know it! I don't think Mikhail should have allowed him to make a presentation."

"Don't you trust your husband's judgment?" Lew asked.

She gave him a horrified look. "Of course I do! But he's so bighearted, he sees good in everyone. I've never known anyone less likely to hold a grudge. At the same time . . . isn't there a Darkovan version of *Trust in God but tie up your camel*?"

Lew could not restrain himself from chuckling. "I'm sure the Dry Towners have something like that, only involving Nebran the Toad God and a herd of smelly, foul-tempered *oudrakhi* that no sensible person would want to have anything to do with in the first place."

When Marguerida laughed, some of the tension in her muscles eased. "You see how I've needed you, Father, if only to help me see the lighter side of things."

"Let's go in, then," he said as he rose to his feet. "I do want to have a serious talk with you, but now is not the time."

"We will have plenty of opportunity later," she replied, getting up and kissing his cheek.

Very shortly, they were to discover how wrong she was.

28

After Marguerida departed to prepare for the Council meeting, Lew's body-servant helped him into his formal court attire. The elaborate cloak, trimmed with fur and silver-thread embroidery, never hung properly over his empty sleeve. He would have been just as happy wearing comfortable, ordinary clothing, but as Lord Alton, he felt an obligation to present a certain dignity and grandeur.

Alanna, unusually silent, accompanied him through the maze of corridors, down the stairs and across the courtyard to the entrance to the part of the Castle housing the Crystal Chamber.

Although the Chamber was only half filled, the telepathic dampers had already been set. After greeting Gabriel, Lew settled himself in the Alton enclosure and placed Alanna behind him. She had no official right to appear with him, but Gabriel nodded pleasantly to her and made no objection. Marguerida had gone to speak with Istvana in the Keepers section, and Mikhail already occupied the central position under the blue and silver fir tree of the Hasturs. Domenic was there, his face taut and pale, and Rory as well, looking his usual jaunty self. From across the Chamber, under the banner of Ardais, Danilo nodded to Lew.

Mikhail waited until the Head of each Domain had arrived and Marguerida had taken her seat beside him. Then he called the meeting to order. He began the agenda, calling for old business. To everyone's surprise, Danilo answered.

"Kinsmen, *vai domyn* and *vai leroni*, I would return to a subject we have discussed since our first meeting, that is, the need for an heir to Aillard. Since we have agreed to consider *nedestro* lineage, I believe I have found a candidate to fill that position. He fully understands that he cannot hold the Domain in his own right, but only as Regent for his daughter, when he has one. He will, of course, be subject to the approval of Lady Marilla and this Council."

Beside Lew, Gabriel muttered, "What is Danilo Syrtis up to? The Aillards died out years ago."

"I know no more of the matter than you do," Lew answered in a hushed voice. Then he added, keeping his tone neutral, "Let us hear what he has to say before we pass judgment. It won't be the first time a Domain has passed to a collateral branch." It was only because both Lew and Marguerida had forfeited their rights to the Alton Domain that Gabriel now ruled Armida and sat here in Council.

Marilla Lindir-Aillard got to her feet. This morning, she looked older than her years, her sharp features tired and flushed. "I cannot imagine who you mean, *Dom* Danilo. None now live with full Aillard blood, and every member of the Lindirs and other related families is known to me. Do you perhaps mean some distant Eldrin cousin?"

"No, I speak of one who can trace his lineage from Lady Cassilde Aillard through her son, Auster. As you may remember, he was called Ridenow in order to protect him from the backlash aimed at Cassilde's sister, the Keeper Cleindori Aillard."

"Cleindori . . ." The whispered name spread through the Chamber. "The Golden Bell" was still revered for having challenged the old ways and freed the Towers from the crippling burdens laid on earlier Keepers.

"And so," Danilo picked up his story, "the bloodline was hidden. But Auster in his turn fathered a *nedestra* daughter, and it is her son I would present to you."

"Has he *laran*?" Lorrill Vallonde asked.

"Even if he has none himself," Dani Hastur said, "he may be a perfectly suitable Regent and may pass the talent to his daughters. What sort of man is he, Uncle Danilo? Would he give us wise counsel?"

"I do not think any of us could give better, although he is yet young," Danilo answered. "He has demonstrated his *laran* to my satisfaction."

Lew noticed that none of the Aldarans made any comment. It was not so long ago that the enclosure below the double-headed eagle stood empty, curtained from sight. Aldaran had never taken part in the persecution of Cleindori. Indeed, they had long regarded many of the restrictions imposed by the Towers as obstructive and unnecessary. Sometimes, Lew thought as he rubbed the stump of his right arm, they had been wrong. Beltran Aldaran had sought to harness the power of Sharra for his own purposes, with only disaster as the result. The current family, however, were sound, prudent men. Hermes, who had succeeded Lew as Darkovan Senator, had proven himself an asset to any undertaking.

The discussion continued, ranging in tone from curiosity to veiled suspicion.

"Enough of this bickering!" Marilla snapped with more than a touch of irritation. She pressed one hand to her forehead. "One more word from any of you and my head will explode!"

"Mother, are you well?" Kennard-Dyan asked, from his seat in the Ardais area.

"I'm perfectly capable of making decisions for Aillard while it is in my keeping," she retorted. "Let's have no more useless chatter. I myself will admit this person as my guest. Bring him in, and he will sit here beside me."

Danilo signaled to the Guardsmen to each side of the front doors, and a few moments later, a slight, red-haired young man entered. He wore ordinary clothing, a jacket and long pants of brown wool, well-made and very clean but worn and several years out of style. It was probably, Lew thought, the best the poor fellow could afford.

"Who is he?" Alanna asked Lew.

"I have no idea. Someone Danilo found in one of his searches?"

Danilo had finished introducing the newcomer, Darius-Mikhail Zabal, who in his turn made a few impeccably polite comments, bowed to Mikhail, the assembled Comyn, and *Domna* Marilla, all in proper order. He answered their questions about his parentage and upbringing clearly and articulately. There was no doubt, Lew thought, that he was an intelligent young man, far better-spoken than many who sat here through no virtue of their own but only their birth. The fact that he had been earning his living as a licensed matrix mechanic seemed promising to some and shameful to others. Marilla, who could be as snobbish as any Comynara, nevertheless smiled as she welcomed him.

"*Vai domyn*, worthy members of this Council," Mikhail said, an amused smile playing across his features, "it seems our numbers have grown beyond anyone's expectation. Aldaran is once more united with the Domains. Today we are honored not only by the presence of a company of Keepers in our midst but also by three new Ardais and now a new member of Aillard, who I hope will produce many Gifted daughters to ensure the continued prosperity of his Domain."

The assembly responded with a round of applause. Mikhail's words had touched on all their hopes for a renewed and flourishing Council.

"*Dom* Francisco Ridenow, whom we welcomed back among us last year, now wishes to address us," Mikhail said, once the applause subsided.

Francisco stepped out into the center of the Chamber. In contrast to the elaborate finery of the rest of the Council, he wore a close-fitting jacket so dark it looked black, and matching hose tucked into soft boots, the kind of clothing a man might easily dance—or fight—in. A fire burned in him, igniting his every movement.

Lew's head throbbed with a sense of imminence. Even with the telepathic dampers in place, he sensed Francisco's pride, his arrogance, his barely suppressed triumph . . .

"Lords and kinsmen, *vai* Comyn and Comynara!" Francisco's voice, powerful and resonant, rang out. "I have no desire to spoil the festive mood of this morning, but a matter of utmost gravity has come to my attention, something that cannot be denied or delayed."

The audience shifted restively. Someone—Lorrill Vallonde, Lew thought—asked, "What is he talking about?" and his neighbor hissed for him to be quiet. Rory leaned forward to whisper something to his mother, who shook her head and then turned back to glare at Francisco.

In growing horror, Lew listened as Francisco related how a commoner, a Terran expatriate, claimed to have suffered an abuse of *laran* at the hands of a member of the Comyn, a member of this very Council. The Chamber fell deathly silent.

Jeram . . . it had to be Jeram! No wonder Domenic had been unable to find him, if he had fallen into Francisco's clutches.

Laurinda MacBard surged to her feet. Her features bore the disciplined calm of a Keeper, but her posture revealed her feelings of outrage. "Who among us stands accused of such a terrible act? Where is this *Terranan*, that we may hear his testimony from his own mouth?"

Francisco turned to face the Dalereuth Keeper. His tautly controlled movement drew every eye. Across the Chamber, Marguerida clasped her hands so tightly that Lew could almost hear her joints crack. He could not sense her thoughts through the telepathic dampers, but her eyes shone like molten gold. Clearly, she was wondering what Francisco was up to, bracing herself for some nasty trick.

At a nod from Francisco, the Guardsmen opened one of the double doors. Jeram entered, his hands bound behind his back, flanked on either side by armed men in Ridenow colors. A lanky, pale-haired man in Ridenow livery followed close behind them.

Jeram had changed almost beyond recognition from the man Lew had known at Nevarsin. With his skin gray and dull, his hair hanging in tangles down his back, he swayed on his feet, held upright only by his captors.

Blinking hard, Jeram glanced about the Chamber. His pupils were so widely dilated that his eyes looked black, but his expression was one of bitter determination. His gaze shifted from Francisco to Lew and, finally, to Marguerida. She looked back at him with genuine sympathy but no hint of recognition. Domenic's face tightened, and across the room, in the Aillard section, Illona's chin came up.

Laurinda, with an impatient gesture, broke the shocked silence. She pointed at Jeram, and her high, nasal voice rang out. "Fellow, you have accused one of us of a serious crime. We would hear your name and your story, so that we may determine the truth of it."

Struggling to keep his balance, Jeram shook his head. It took a long moment for the Council to understand that he was refusing to answer. Clearly, he was fighting the drug, whatever it was, probably one of the *kireseth* fractions that lowered inhibitions and impaired will.

Moving in a slow, circular path like a hunting cat, Francisco crossed the floor to where Jeram stood. He spoke in a soft, hypnotic voice. "You don't want to talk? We must convince you. Let's start with something easy. Tell us your name and how you came to be here."

Something in Francisco's tone broke through Jeram's resistance. "Jeremiah Reed." The name burst in staccato syllables from his chapped and swollen lips. "Terran Special Forces, serial number—"

"That's all right, there's no need to be so formal. We're all friends here." Francisco paused, his pacing superb. "Tell us more about yourself. How did you come to Darkover? What did you do here?"

Jeram's chin lifted. Trembling and visibly sweating, he repeated. "Jeremiah Reed, Terran Special Forces . . ."

"Enough!" Francisco's suave control slipped, but only for a moment. "Let's begin again—"

Increasingly desperate for his friend, Lew stood up. "*Vai*

domyn, this man is clearly here against his will. I do not know what *Dom* Francisco intends by this spectacle. This is a Council Chamber, not a theater. Let him take his charges before the Cortes, not here."

"The Cortes have no jurisdiction over the Comyn," Laurinda shot back. "This matter of *laran* ethics directly concerns the Towers."

Mikhail raised his voice. "*Dom* Francisco requested and was granted the opportunity to address the Council. I am sorry to overrule you, *Dom* Lewis, but he has the right, as do any of us, to bring whatever concerns he deems appropriate."

"You would permit this—this blatant torture—to continue?" Lew demanded.

"*Dom* Lewis, you exceed your authority," Laurinda broke in. "The questioning of this witness will go forward at *my* request. *I* will determine how long and in what manner it is to proceed. I need not remind you that this man stands here in full view of us all. No physical or mental force can be applied without our knowledge. Given the seriousness of the charge of *laran* abuse, we will proceed vigorously."

You fool! Can't you see that Francisco is using you? Too furious to speak, Lew sat down again. Francisco had found the right incentive to ensure the Keeper's thorough investigation.

"Thank you," Francisco said with a slight inclination of his head. He turned back to Jeram. "We already know why you were on Darkover. We just want to hear what you did here, in your own words. You were deployed as part of the Terran military force, first to Aldaran and then to Old North Road, isn't that right?"

Whispers flew around the Chamber. Was this man one of *them,* the assassins who had tried to wipe out the Council in one single, cowardly attack? Lew felt any remaining sympathy for Jeram evaporate. Even those who might have been offended by Laurinda's heavy-handed authority or Francisco's manipulations now had a personal reason for wanting to hear Jeram's testimony.

"You were part of the ambush party on Old North Road, weren't you?" Francisco said, circling around Jeram.

Around the Chamber, conversation hushed. Men and women leaned forward to hear, their faces intent, some of them angry. Domenic looked stunned, blaming himself for not having found Jeram sooner.

Francisco moved closer. His voice was silky, almost seductive. "That's why you came to Thendara, isn't it? To tell your story before the Council? Here you are, and they are listening. Now's your chance. Go on, tell them."

At his signal, the two guards released Jeram. Jeram stumbled and caught his balance. Francisco took his shoulders and turned him in a slow circle to face every part of the audience. "Tell them."

"This has nothing to do with the charge—" Domenic protested.

"No, let him speak," Rufus DiAsturien said. "We have a right to know."

For a long moment, Jeram struggled visibly to speak. His face flushed with effort; he swallowed convulsively. "It is true," he began, his voice ragged. "I came here—to confess. To turn myself in. I tried—you were there— blasters against swords—I am sorry—following orders not an excuse . . ."

"Tell them what happened next. Tell them!" Francisco's fingers dug into Jeram's shoulders. Jeram winced but kept on, one dogged phrase after another. It must have taken enormous willpower to resist the drug this much, to say what he willed and not what Francisco ordered him to.

"This is a travesty," Danilo said, rising to his feet. "Can't you see the man is unfit to testify to anything? He's too sick—or drugged—to know what he's saying!"

"Do you dare question my honor?" Francisco retorted.

"Sit down, Danilo," Mikhail said. Lew heard the reluctance in his voice, the stubborn adherence to protocol and tradition. "We must let him continue."

Gasping, trembling, Jeram hung his head. He seemed at the end of his power to resist. Step by step, Francisco

forced him to admit how he had been unable to remember
how the battle ended until the Keeper of Nevarsin Tower
had broken the compulsion spell of forgetting set upon
him. With each revelation, shock rippled through the assembly.

"It was then you realized that *laran*—specifically the
Alton Gift—had been used on you, against your knowledge or consent," Francisco said. "Isn't that true? *Isn't it?*"

Chest heaving, Jeram shook his head. Even though the
telepathic dampers suppressed any psychic contact, the entire Chamber seemed to vibrate with his struggle. The veins
of his forehead stood out in stark relief. Droplets of sweat
dampened the tangle of his hair.

Jeram glanced at Lew, and Lew read the desperate plea
in his friend's eyes.

Throughout the Chamber, a storm was gathering. Lew
sensed it in the air, in the awful expectant *listening,* in the
surge of adrenaline through his own veins. Lives had been
broken in this Chamber before, by heedless words, by deliberate malice.

The pale-haired man seized Jeram's right arm and
twisted it behind him, close to dislocating the shoulder
joint. Jeram's face went white. Francisco bent over him,
"Isn't it?"

Jeram glared at Francisco and shook his head. Between
clenched teeth, he muttered, *"Go to hell,"* in Terran Standard. *"I'll see you there before I go along with any more of
your filthy lies!"*

"You will tell us the truth," Francisco hissed. "One way
or another, you will tell us . . ."

Behind Lew, Alanna cried out, "Oh, this is terrible! Why
doesn't someone stop it?"

Her voice broke the looming sense of inevitability. Lew
could think of only one way to stop Francisco's questions,
and that was his own confession. He had not intended to
make the matter public, but the interrogation had taken on
a life of its own, threatening to sweep away all in its path.

So be it!

No longer caring about the consequences, Lew rose to his feet. "This has gone far enough—"

"Help! Oh, help!"

Lew broke off at the sound of a lady's shriek.

"Look to *Domna* Marilla!"

Kennard-Dyan leaped over the railing of the Ardais enclosure and rushed across the room. One hand raised to her brow, Marilla swayed in her seat. Her waiting-woman let out another shrill wail. Kennard-Dyan reached them just in time to catch Marilla as she toppled over.

"Help, someone help me! My mother is ill!"

Mikhail's voice thundered through the Chamber, calling for order. "Clear the floor! Get that prisoner out of here!"

Francisco's men began to drag Jeram away. Jeram struggled as best he could, but they held him fast. He could barely stand, let alone mount an effective resistance. Marguerida grabbed Mikhail's arm and spoke to him.

"Not you," Mikhail called out to Jeram's captors. "Captain Cisco, you take custody of him!"

Cisco Ridenow gestured to the two Guardsmen at the main doors. The blond man released his hold on Jeram so suddenly that Jeram staggered into the arms of the Guards. Meanwhile, Darius-Mikhail, who had been sitting beside Marilla, took out his starstone, wrapped in a wallet of silk-lined leather and carried in a fold in his belt, and bent over her. He could do nothing in the *laran*-blanketing field.

"Turn off the dampers!" Istvana ordered, as she hurried to the Aillard enclosure. Illona gave a short nod and set about turning off the devices.

The Chamber churned with chaotic emotions. Jeram's anguish struck Lew like a physical blow. Francisco radiated hatred and desperation. Kennard-Dyan's guilt and worry for his mother roiled with Marguerida's burgeoning fury and a dozen other powerful reactions from the room.

Searing white lightning burst from Alanna's mind. A vision swept through Lew's mind. He saw Jeram lying in a pool of blood . . . then it was another man, although Lew could not tell who, a man with flaxen hair . . .

"Help me," Alanna whispered. She clutched the bench to keep herself from falling. A wet, gray sheen covered her skin.

Lew placed the palm of his hand against her cheek. She was cold, going into shock.

It's all right. I'm here with you. Do not give in to your fears, child.

Her eyes widened as his mind touched hers, catalyzed through the physical contact.

Do not feed your fears, Lew sent his thought to her mind. *Let them go, release them. They cannot harm you unless you give yourself to them.*

I . . . Her answer was slow and awkward, untrained. *I am so frightened. I cannot face these visions alone!*

You are not alone, dear child. Once you have mastered your laran, *you need never be alone.*

Into their linked minds, Lew poured his most peaceful memories . . .

. . . the soaring joy of being one with the circle at Arilinn . . . walking through the streets of Caer Donn on a frosty morning, Marjorie's hand in his . . . sitting in the darkened chapel at St. Valentine's as the last sublime chords of a hymn faded away . . .

Alanna's visions lost their vividness and flickered into nothingness. Under Lew's calming images, the psychic storm in her mind died down. Color returned to her cheeks, and her eyes grew steady and clear. Lew had never seen her so free of inner strife, so tranquil.

Lew turned his attention back to the unfolding drama. Half the assembly was on its feet by now. Everyone seemed to be talking at once. Kennard-Dyan and Istvana were in a heated discussion about whether to take Marilla to her own quarters or to the Tower. Francisco loudly protested Mikhail's orders, insisting that the witness was under his protection, not the Guards'.

Kennard-Dyan picked up his mother as if she weighed no more than a child. He followed Illona and Darius-Mikhail from the chamber. Istvana remained behind. The clamor began to diminish as Mikhail loudly announced the adjournment of the session for the day.

Cisco approached Francisco, who had remained in the center of the floor. "Come, Father, I'll see you back to your chambers."

Francisco shrugged off his son's advance. Instead, he strode to the Hastur enclosure, assumed a belligerent stance, and confronted Mikhail.

"Mikhail Lanart, pretender and tyrant!" Francisco omitted Mikhail's rightful surname of *Hastur* as a deliberate insult. "The floor is still mine, and I am not yet finished!"

29

"**C**alm yourself, *Dom* Francisco," Mikhail said, raising both hands in a conciliatory gesture. "There has been enough uproar for one meeting. We will adjourn until the day after tomorrow. You will have your chance then to finish what you have to say."

"By that time," Francisco shot back, his face reddening, "you will have brought my witness over to your side, if you have not silenced him forever. You will not cheat me of my victory, not this time, or bury the evidence of your wife's crimes!"

We should never have let him return, Lew thought with a sickening jolt. *Marguerida was right.*

"I am not your enemy," Mikhail said.

"And I am no criminal!" Marguerida exclaimed. "If you have anything to say to me, do it in plain language. Put forth your evidence for everyone to hear!"

"The events of this morning have overwrought us all," Mikhail said soothingly. "There is no point in continuing to hurl insults at one another—"

"Then you leave me no choice," Francisco broke in. "Here, in the midst of an assembly of our peers, I declare a formal blood feud. I charge you, Mikhail-Regis Lanart-Hastur, with theft and dishonor, and I stand ready to prove the truth with my body!"

A collective gasp filled the room. Cisco stared at his father, plainly appalled by this turn of events. Donal took a step forward, one hand going to his sword. Mikhail restrained his paxman with a glance.

"You forget yourself, *Dom* Francisco," Mikhail said, rising to his feet, "and you bring shame upon your house by these rash words. Retract them now, with full forgiveness and no stain on your honor, or suffer the consequence!"

"The only consequence I see is the end of your worthless life!" Francisco retorted. "Will you stand forth like a man, or must I hunt you down?"

Marguerida stood up, taking her place at her husband's side. The air around her shimmered with intensity. "This has gone far enough. The Council is neutral territory, and we will not have it degenerate into a bar-room or a dueling arena. If you cannot behave in a civilized fashion, *Dom* Francisco, you will have to leave. Guards, escort him from the chamber."

At her words, the Guardsmen at the doors glanced at one another, confusion written on their faces. They were accustomed to taking orders from the Regent himself, not from his off-world wife. Moreover, ancient tradition demanded that a challenge, once issued, must be properly answered.

Francisco spat on the floor at Marguerida's feet. She turned scarlet. Rory's hand moved to the hilt of his sword, but Domenic touched his brother's shoulder and shook his head, restraining him.

Dani Hastur stepped forward, looking more like his father than Lew would have believed possible. As Regent of Elhalyn, which once claimed kingship over all the Domains, Dani was next in line after Mikhail to lead the Council. Like his father, Regis, he had never wanted power. At this moment, however, he carried himself with such authority that the clamor fell away.

"Vai domna," Dani said to Marguerida with impeccable politeness, "that is not possible. This man is Comyn, with full Domain-right that none may deny. He has declared a

blood feud before this assembly. No one has given challenge in this manner since before our grandfathers' time, but, nonetheless, it is the law."

"Then it is time the law was changed!" Marguerida insisted. "We cannot allow such a barbaric custom to continue! This is why we have courts and a Council to resolve our differences nonviolently! Or would you," she raked the assembly with her fierce glare, "have us return to the Ages of Chaos, when might alone determined right?"

What had they come to, Lew wondered, when a man as decent as Mikhail must risk his life at the hands of a traitor, all for the sake of tradition?

"I am sorry," Dani said, gently but firmly, to Marguerida. "You must be silent and let matters proceed. If you cannot control yourself, the Guards will escort you from the Chamber."

"By what right do you—" Marguerida cried.

"*Sit down,* child!" Istvana's voice, with all the authority of a Keeper, sliced through the air. "Sit down, before you make matters worse!"

Breathing hard, her face flushed, Marguerida lowered herself to her seat. Domenic reached out and took her hand. She shot him a look of gratitude.

"What are the nature of your charges?" Dani asked Francisco. "Can they not be satisfied in some peaceful way?"

"I will not be bought off with pretty Hastur speeches, not while my enemy continues to enjoy the fruits of his crimes." Francisco's voice coarsened to a cloud-leopard's snarl. "Nor will I listen to the lies of the *Terranan* woman he has taken to wife, for she has conspired with him, to the dishonor of myself, my son, and my Domain."

"Filthy nine-fathered *bre'suin*!" Rory cried. "How dare you!"

"Father, I beg you, please! Make no such claims in my name!" Cisco interrupted, horrified. "If you're doing this for the honor of Ridenow, I hereby disavow all interest in your quarrel!"

Francisco ignored the outburst. "Mikhail Lanart has unlawfully seized a valuable heirloom belonging to the Ridenow clan—the ring of my ancestor, Varzil the Good. I demand that he either return the treasure or answer the challenge!"

Dani turned to Mikhail. "How will you answer?"

Mikhail was silent for a moment. His choices were few, Lew thought, for the psychoactive crystal in Varzil's ring had keyed into his own starstone, and to separate them would surely cause him serious psychic injury, if not death. He could accept the challenge and fight it out on Francisco's terms, or he could find a reason to refuse. The only legal bases for a refusal were gross disability or difference in rank, which were clearly not the case, or because his death would leave his Domain without an Heir. With two healthy sons and a daughter, Mikhail could hardly claim that hardship.

Marguerida had grasped Mikhail's arm, pleading silently with him. Lew's heart ached for her. He understood how she felt. Once, he too would have done anything to save the life of the one he loved.

Mikhail was no fool; he knew what Francisco had done. If he gave way to the pleas of his wife before the assembled Council, then he would lose all credibility, crippling his ability to govern effectively. Either way, Francisco would have won.

"I accept."

The rush of exultation from Francisco's mind was almost blinding.

NO! Marguerida's telepathic denial roared through Lew's thoughts. Even though it was not directed at him, her psychic blast sent him reeling. It resounded through the mind of every *laran*-Gifted person in the room.

Father, please—help me! Stop them!

Slowly, the effort clawing at his heart, Lew shook his

head. He cursed himself for not having interrupted the proceedings when Francisco first brought Jeram in. But would anything he said have made a difference? Francisco wanted this fight, lusted for it with all his demented obsession. He would not stop until one of them was dead.

While Istvana reset the telepathic dampers so that there could be no unfair use of *laran*, Mikhail and Francisco prepared themselves. Like most of the adult men in the room, they both carried swords. The blades, Lew noticed, were well-balanced weapons, not ornamental toys.

Marguerida was right. The entire situation was unconscionable. The Terrans had good cause to call Darkover barbaric. Two Comyn lords, educated and literate men who had had contact with worlds beyond their own, intended to settle their differences by whacking one another with lengths of sharpened steel.

And what is the alternative? whispered through Lew's mind. *The unbridled force of* laran? *The Alton Gift?*

Maybe it was better to settle differences with swords, rather than blasters or bombs or mental weapons capable of leveling an entire city, even as Caer Donn had burned in the fires of Sharra.

Mikhail stepped into the central area and stood, weapon raised, facing his opponent. The rainbow light glinted on his flaxen hair. He moved with the assurance of a man who has kept up his sword practice. In the Hastur enclosure, Domenic and Rory settled down to watch.

The two men circled one another, feinting. Lew watched them with the experience of his early years as a Guards officer. Mikhail was the better swordsman, Lew thought, but he would not try to kill Francisco, at least not right away. That hesitation would leave him vulnerable.

Francisco stepped in, hard on the offense, blade slashing. Mikhail parried, clearly surprised by the ferocity of the attack. He recovered, disengaged, circled. Again came that quick, almost feline onslaught. Again, the delayed defense.

They drew apart. Francisco stepped to the side, knees bent, shoulders loose. Lew caught the subtle movement as a dagger slipped from his sleeve into his left hand.

Silence filled the Crystal Chamber, broken only by the whisper of boot leather on stone, the harsh breathing of the combatants, and Alanna's muted sobbing.

Mikhail shifted to the offensive, battering away at his opponent. The air shuddered with the power of his strokes. Francisco seemed to crumple under Mikhail's greater weight and power, only to spiral free each time. Mikhail followed up, faster and more aggressively pressing his advantage. He pushed Francisco until they were almost against the railing of the Aldaran section.

Katherine Aldaran let out a little shriek; she had lived on Darkover only a few years and still found swords barbaric and terrifying. Drawing her back, Hermes folded her protectively in his arms.

With a crash and the snapping of wooden rails, Mikhail bore down on Francisco, trapping his opponent's sword. Breast to breast, Mikhail had the advantage of weight and greater muscular strength.

Suddenly, Francisco gave way, collapsing beneath Mikhail. Across the room, Marguerida cried out. Lithe as a catman, the Ridenow lord rolled free and to his feet. Mikhail pivoted to face him.

Francisco sidled in, moving sword and dagger in a circular pattern. Lew's gut clenched as he recognized the distinctive fighting style of the Dry Towns. The men of that land were said to smear their blades with poison. The Ridenow Domain lay on their borders.

Would Francisco dare—would he stoop to poison? Or was he already too lost in madness, too consumed by ambition and revenge, to care about honor?

End it quickly, Lew thought, although Mikhail could not hear him through the telepathic dampers.

By this time, Mikhail dripped blood from half a dozen small cuts. Francisco was wounded too. He placed barely any weight on one leg; the supple black leather over that thigh gleamed, slick and red.

The two fighters closed again, blades clashing, slipping over one another, bodies colliding. They went down, rolling, a tangle of arms and legs. One sword—Lew thought it was Francisco's—clattered free, sliding across the floor. Suddenly, the two men stopped struggling.

Adrenaline surging through his veins, Lew leaped to his feet, slammed open the railing door, and raced across the room.

Mikhail was sprawled on top, his ribs heaving in great tremulous breaths. Lew grabbed Mikhail's shoulder with his one hand and rolled him free.

Francisco lay on his back, eyes open to the prismed ceiling. The rainbow light washed his face, heightening his expression of surprise. Lew touched him and felt a dim flicker, a fading spark . . . and then stillness.

The hilt of Francisco's own dagger protruded from just beneath the arch of his ribs. From the angle, it had gone straight through his diaphragm and into his heart.

Marguerida raced across the room and threw herself down beside her husband. "Mikhail! Speak to me, love!"

Mikhail remained as Lew had placed him, on his back, one arm over his chest. Blood poured from the slash that ran from one hip bone diagonally upward. It drenched the front of Marguerida's gown as she gathered him into her arms. Domenic was only a step behind her, his face ashen, followed by a dazed-looking Rory.

"Oh, no!" Marguerida sobbed. "No!"

"Cut the dampers!" someone shouted.

A moment later, the room roiled with emotion—*pain, shock, terror.*

In a single, decisive movement, Marguerida stripped off the glove from her left hand, revealing the shadow matrix on her palm.

Father . . . She reached out to Lew telepathically. He dropped into rapport with her, as if their minds clasped hands. Her moment of panic receded, held at bay by the need for swift action. After the Battle of Old North Road, she had used her shadow matrix to heal Hermes Aldaran's injuries. Now Mikhail needed her . . .

Lew closed his eyes and steadied his daughter's mind, adding his strength to hers. Power flowed from their joined *laran*. The shadow matrix vibrated with energy. Mentally, Lew followed Marguerida as she plunged deep into her husband's wound. She sensed each severed blood vessel, each layer of torn, damaged tissue. Beneath these images, she touched the rhythms of heartbeat and respiration, the unique cell-deep texture of his life force.

Cario, *I am here!*

During the fraction of an instant when Marguerida paused, caught in the joy that always arose in her when in intimate contact with her beloved, Lew sensed a subtle wrongness in the blood pouring from Mikhail's wound. Acrid . . . subtly malignant. He had never tasted anything like it before.

Lew felt his daughter's sharp mental focus waver. In some way he could not understand, the physical wrongness was affecting her *laran*.

Marja!

Lew gathered himself to dissolve their mental bond, to somehow free her from the miasma that even now worked its way through her mind toward her body.

BREAK!

The mental command, like the ringing of an enormous bell, shattered the rapport. Lew's eyes flew open. Marguerida swayed on her knees. Her eyes showed as gleaming crescents between half-closed, vibrating lids. Her face had gone so pale that her lips had turned white. Covered in blood, the shadow matrix flashed crimson, as if it drank in the gore.

Istvana Ridenow hurried over. Her naked starstone flared into blue-white brilliance. Laurinda, her face furrowed with concern, followed a step behind.

"The wound is poisoned," Istvana said in a voice that

rang with a Keeper's authority. "If you close the wound, you will seal the poison inside Mikhail's body and make things worse."

"No . . ." Shuddering, Marguerida opened her eyes.

A look passed between Istvana and Laurinda. Laurinda nodded, a brief inclination of her head. "I am no healer," Laurinda said, with quiet modesty. "I leave the matter in your hands, Istvana, and will lend you whatever aid I can."

"Thank you, *vai leronis.* Lew, you must take Marja away," Istvana said. "Marguerida, *chiya preciosa,* there is no time to lose. Let us have the care of him. We will save him for you if we can."

So had the Keeper Callina spoken to Lew as she held the broken form of his wife in her arms after the Sharra disaster. And Marjorie had died . . .

Numbly, Lew pulled Marguerida to her feet. She resisted only a little. Tremors shook her body. Any moment now, she would faint. He could not manage her weight with only one arm.

Marja dearest, come with me. You can do nothing here.

I should have stopped it! I should have killed Francisco myself—

She didn't know what she was saying, but he could not find it in his heart to say so.

Come away, he repeated silently. *Istvana will tend to him, and call you if—when it is time to help. You must rest and be strong.*

For a long moment she searched his eyes, as if he were a stranger and not her father. He might hold her and touch her mind with his *laran,* and yet some part of her, perhaps the essence of who Marguerida Alton-Hastur was, had gone where he could not follow. Such was the unbridgeable gulf between parent and adult child.

The moment passed. Behind them, people milled about the Chamber. Cisco shouted orders for the disposition of his father's body. Domenic recovered enough to go look after Alanna.

Marguerida allowed Lew to take her through the hallway and up the stairs to the Alton quarters. All the while, Lew thought that no man could survive a poisoned wound like that, not without Terran medicine. But the Terrans, for good or ill, had left Darkover and taken the dream of a union of the two worlds with them.

30

Marguerida paused on the threshold of a chamber high in the old Comyn Tower. In all the years she had lived in Thendara, she had never explored more than a few dusty rooms on the lowest floors, for the Tower had been abandoned for lack of a working circle decades ago. When it became apparent that the newly formed Keepers Council would need psychically insulated quarters, she had supervised the cleaning and refurbishing of the kitchen, living quarters, and a matrix laboratory or two. She had never intended to create a hospital as well.

Istvana had insisted on bringing both Mikhail and Marilla here for *laran* healing, by far the most effective treatment available for either of them. It was only by the most extraordinary good fortune that there were so many skilled *leroni* present.

Mikhail's room was light and airy at this season, although in winter it would probably be miserably damp and cold. Pressing her lips together, Marguerida told herself Mikhail would not be here for long.

He will recover, he must . . . She swallowed, and her knees threatened to buckle under her, but she steadied herself. She could not afford weakness, not now.

Mikhail's younger sister, Liriel of Arilinn Tower, looked up from where she sat at his bedside. Marguerida felt the

pulse of healing *laran* and caught a flash of blue light from
the other woman's starstone.

Liriel got to her feet, moving with surprising grace for
such a large woman, and took Marguerida into her arms. It
was an unusually close contact for a telepath, but Liriel
had always been comfortable with physical affection, and
the two women had loved each other from their first meeting. For a heartbeat, Marguerida leaned into the warm, soft
strength of her sister-in-law.

"How is he?" Marguerida asked, pulling away. She dared
not say more or her fragile control would shatter. Mikhail
needed her to be strong, now more than ever, as did her
children. She would *not* give way to tears or hysterics.

"It is as we feared." Liriel drew Marguerida aside. "My
brother's wounds are most definitely poisoned. We have
not yet identified the precise agent, for the Dry Towners
use many plant derivatives. That is undoubtedly where
Francisco obtained the poison."

"What about the laboratory equipment in the Terran
Headquarters?" Marguerida said. "Could we use it to ana-
lyze the poison and find an antidote?"

"We do not have the knowledge to operate such equipment, assuming it is still operational," Liriel said, tucking a
stray strand of her thick red hair back into place. Faint lines
of fatigue marked her round face, and her eyes were shadowed with anxiety. In a voice edged with frustration, she
added, "Do you?"

Marguerida hesitated. Her training as a University
Scholar had been in musicology, not chemistry or medicine. She had never entered that part of the Terran base except as a patient. Yet she was not ignorant of research
procedures; she could use a computer as well as any Federation citizen. Surely, manuals and written instructions must
be stored in the records.

"Give me a sample of the poison," she said, lifting her
chin, "and I will figure it out."

Liriel shook her head. "I'm sorry if I misled you. It's not

so simple a matter as identifying the agent and creating an antidote. The poison has bonded to the marrow of his bones."

Marguerida's heart stuttered.

"Ironically, the depth of Mikhail's wounds worked in his favor," Liriel went on. "for he bled heavily, as you know, and that washed much of the poison out of his body before it could act. At the same time, he has a lost a lot of blood."

"Can nothing be done?"

Liriel regarded her with an uncompromising, level gaze. "Mikhail's condition is grave, we cannot deny it, but there is still hope. Istvana and I have already made good progress in tracing the course of the poison and stimulating his own body to produce new blood. That will take time, and meanwhile we have lowered his bodily functions, very much the way the monks at St. Valentine's do while in deep meditation. Do not despair, *breda*. My brother is a strong, healthy man, with a great will to live, and that must work in his favor."

"I—I would like to sit with him."

Liriel gave Marguerida's arm a squeeze. Her worried expression lightened into a warm smile. "I think that would be an excellent idea. Even if he does not respond overtly, I am sure he will feel your presence, the bond between you is so strong."

Her eyes stinging, Marguerida nodded. She heard the click of the door latch as Liriel departed and then took the empty seat beside Mikhail's bed.

His wounds had been bandaged, his hair combed. She touched the stubble along his jaw, smoothed the strands of frosted gold. One hand rested on top of the sheet, where the ring of Varzil Ridenow sparkled. Mikhail usually wore a glove on that hand, even as Marguerida did to cover her imprinted matrix. She remembered how he once used the ring for healing.

If only he could use it to heal himself . . . Her heart ached as if it, too, had been torn apart. A pulse throbbed in her temples. She slipped off her glove and took her husband's hand between her own.

"Mikhail, *precioso* . . ."

Closing her eyes, she reached for the special link they had shared from the first awakening of their love.

Dearest heart, I am here . . .

Dimly, she felt a flicker of response, Mikhail's distinctive mental touch. The next instant, it faded. Again she reached out, but this time she sensed nothing. His life forces were perilously low. His *laran* nodes glowed dully, like dying embers.

Where have you gone, beloved? I know you can hear me. I know that somewhere, you are trying to get back to me. You must not give up, not after everything we've been through together!

Her thoughts flew to their journey back through Darkover's past, to their strange meeting with the legendary Varzil the Good, who had given Mikhail his ring, to their battle in the Overworld against the malevolent spirit of Ashara, who had overshadowed Marguerida as a child. Marguerida remembered thinking that as long as they were together, they could weather any crisis.

Try as she might, she could not reach his mind, as she had so many times before. He lived, his chest rose and fell, and the essential spark still burned within him, but the man she loved, heart and soul and mind, was slipping away. Shadows rose up to engulf him, darkening with each passing moment.

Marja? The voice was familiar, compelling. It dragged her back toward the light. She did not want to answer. Instead, she longed to sink into the darkness where Mikhail waited for her.

"Marguerida, wake up. It is time to go."

She lifted her head and blinked in the brightness of the afternoon. Her father stood beside her, his single hand on her shoulder. Behind him, Liriel and Istvana waited, their faces expectant.

"We must let the healers continue their treatment," Lew said, gently lifting her to her feet. "Let me take you back to your chambers, where you can rest."

No! she thought wildly. *I cannot leave him! What if he were to wake, and I was not here?*

"My dear, we will summon you immediately," Istvana said. "Listen to your father's wisdom. Let your family comfort you."

And leave us to do our work.

With an effort, Marguerida admitted that the other woman was right. There was nothing more she could do. She must leave Mikhail in the hands of those who could help him.

"Is there any news of *Domna* Marilla?" she asked without thinking, not because she really wanted to know, but because as chatelaine of Comyn Castle, she was responsible for everyone in it.

"Illona is tending to her," Istvana said, "along with Lady Linnea and Darius-Mikhail Zabal. You see, there are enough of us to do all that is necessary."

Numbly, Marguerida allowed herself to be led away. She hardly saw the corridors and stairways until they arrived at her familiar quarters. Domenic was deep in conversation with Rory and Yllana in the family parlor. The room, usually bright and cheerful, looked subdued. Gloom hovered in the corners. The flowers in the center of the table had wilted, their petals browning around the edges.

All three looked up, anxious for news about their father. Gathering herself, Marguerida gave them a brief version of her conversation with Liriel. She tried to sound optimistic: Mikhail was receiving the very best care that matrix technology could provide; Istvana and the others would keep searching until they had found a cure; they had every reason to hope.

Rory and Yllana accepted her reassurances, but not

Domenic. She could not read his reaction; he'd gone back into secretive mode. He had always been a strange child, with a maturity beyond his years.

"I will take this news to Alanna, as well," Domenic said.

"Yes, that would be a kindness," Marguerida replied, distracted. "And I suppose we should send word to Rafael and Gabriel."

It was, Marguerida thought, just as well that Alanna was keeping to herself these days. At least she would not have to deal with the girl's tantrums on top of everything else.

With a quick nod, Domenic ushered his siblings out, leaving Marguerida and Lew their privacy. In a daze, Marguerida searched for something to do, some task to take her mind off the fear and pain. She picked a flower from the vase and began pulling off the dead petals.

"Come here, my Marja." When Lew put his arm around her, something inside Marguerida gave way. She had been holding herself together for so long now, fighting off her fears. Sobs racked her body. She buried her face against his shoulder.

What will I do without him? she cried out silently. *I love him so much! He is my heart, my very life!*

Take heart, daughter, Lew said gently, speaking to her mind with his. *Liriel has said there is hope. She is a* leronis, *learned in these matters, and she too loves Mikhail.*

If only I had stopped them from fighting! Marguerida's mood shifted like quicksilver from torment into fury. Her eyes flashed, as if ignited by golden fires.

I should have killed Francisco myself!

She could have done it, too. Under the right conditions, fueled by unbridled anger, the Alton Gift could be lethal. She possessed the Gift in full measure. She'd used it in self-defense before against bandits, against Terrans. If only she had intervened while she still had a chance, Mikhail might not be lying there, wounded, poisoned, dying—

Lew's voice, now grimly serious, brought Marguerida's thoughts back to the present. "*Chiya,* you are distraught or you would not think such a thing."

"Don't patronize me!" Marguerida leaped to her feet. "Or prattle to me about scruples! If it had been Dio, and you could have saved her, would you have hesitated, even for an instant?"

"It's not as simple as that," he said. "Using *laran* against Dio's cancer is not the same as using it to strike down a man—and a Comyn, at that. The first oath we swear in the Towers is *never to enter another mind save to heal or help*—"

"That is nonsense, and you know it, Father!" She should not be picking a fight with him, of all people, not so soon after his heart attack, but she could not help herself. What had gotten into him?

Words spilled from her mouth. "We have a responsibility, yes, an *obligation* to use our talents for the greater good! Do you think men like Francisco would obey such rules?"

"It is not a matter of standing by while tyrants and assassins commit unspeakable crimes, unopposed." Lew shook his head. "Those same weapons you would use for good carry with them an even greater potential for harm. The foundation of our society, the Compact, was designed to prevent such abuses."

"Oh, spare me the lecture!" Marguerida strode to the cabinet at the far side of the room, poured herself a goblet of *ravnet* and drained it. "Why is this even an issue? You yourself used the Alton Gift for the greater good. We both did, after the battle of Old North Road. How could we have done any else?"

"Gods, daughter!" he cried, as if she'd struck him. "Do you think I'm *proud* of what I did for Darkover?"

Realizing she was on the verge of losing her temper entirely, Marguerida turned away and took a deep breath. The muscles of her neck and shoulders ached. Mikhail would have rubbed them into delicious relaxation.

"At any rate," she said tightly, "that is all history now. We cannot change what happened, then or now. The best we can do is forget the whole matter."

"We cannot just go on as if the issue of *laran* abuse had never been raised," he said, in that infuriating, persistent tone. "Sooner or later, whether we like it or not, the charges must be answered."

"Abuse? You call saving Darkover *abuse*?" Marguerida strode over to the window, her arms crossed protectively over her chest. "I expected to hear language like that from Francisco. He was just looking for something to use against me. But I always thought *you* were on my side."

"Come here, child." Lew held out his hand. "I *am* on your side, as you put it. What I want you to understand, more than anything else, is that I will always love you. That does not mean I approve of everything you do, only that my devotion to you does not depend upon your actions."

Tears sprang to Marguerida's eyes as Lew spoke. "We worked *together* after the Battle of Old North Road to erase the memory from the Terran soldiers," she said, trying hard not to give in to frustration. "We *agreed* it was too dangerous for the Federation to find out about how powerful *laran* is. Didn't you do the same thing, years ago, to make certain Senators 'forget' about Project Telepath? If I'm guilty of 'improper use' of the Alton Gift, trying to protect Darkover, then you are, too!"

"Yes, I am," Lew said quietly. "I of all people, who knew what it was like to have my mind and will taken over by another, should have known better."

Marguerida's anger melted. From one instant to the next, her heart filled with pity for the old man before her, for all the pain and guilt he had suffered and, for all she knew, would carry to his grave.

She held out her ungloved right hand. His strong fingers closed around hers. She remembered how freely, how generously he had linked his *laran* to hers when she tried to stop Mikhail's bleeding. Love welled up in her, sweeping away the last shreds of the argument.

"Let us not quarrel," she said. "Surely there are enough

battles for us to fight without creating one between us. On this, let us agree to disagree. I will need all your support while Mikhail pulls through this crisis."

"You shall always have it."

31

With no small feeling of regret, Domenic accompanied his brother and sister to the entrance to the Alton suite and closed the door. Rory returned to the Guards and the solace of Niall and useful work, and Donal escorted Yllana back to the Aldaran town house. Marguerida and Grandfather Lew were still talking in the family parlor. Alanna had wafted in, looking for Lew; she had taken the news of Mikhail's condition with surprising calm and then departed again.

After the bright and familiar comfort of the parlor, the old main hall of the Alton quarters seemed shrouded in gloom. No fire brightened the ancient hearth, but a faint radiance came from the light-emitting panels scattered on the walls. The stones themselves had been shaped by *laran* so long ago that they had gone silent, as if dreaming.

For the moment, Domenic thought, no one would come looking for him. He had a few precious moments, surrounded by these sleeping stones, to gather his thoughts. Marguerida's distress affected him more than he could put into words. Since he could remember, she had been the anchor of his world, resourceful and steady.

Domenic forced himself to consider what would happen if his father died. Rationally, he knew it was a possibility, although under the care of Istvana's healing circle, Mikhail's condition was stable. There was nothing he could do to help.

The Council was another matter. They would not meet again today, but the recess must be brief. Too many matters required action, and the old balance of power was disintegrating. With Marilla ill and Darius-Mikhail an inexperienced substitute for Aillard, with the addition of the Keepers Council and the indomitable Laurinda MacBard ... the changes made Domenic's head spin. At this critical time, the Council needed a leader to bring them all together. And now they had lost Mikhail.

Dani Hastur might officiate for a time, but he had maintained a steadfast refusal of power over the years. He could never be more than a custodian, holding things steady and making few if any changes. The Council needed someone who could inspire and direct, not just continue things as before.

I have no choice, Domenic thought, and then realized that he had been training for this time, in one way or another, since he was born.

The door swung open and Donal Alar entered. He had changed from court garb into his ordinary clothing, cut for easy movement along the lines of a Guards uniform but with the blue and silver fir tree badge of the Hasturs on one shoulder. Shadows darkened the skin around his eyes. He inclined his head in greeting.

"Your sister is safe at the house of Hermes Aldaran," Donal hesitated, his competent, square hands loose at his sides. "Is there—might I be of service in any other way?"

"Please, sit down." Domenic gestured to the chair nearest his own. Donal did so.

"This is a difficult business, so please bear with me," Domenic said. "I don't know how long it will be before my father can resume his Council duties—" *He will recover, he must* ... "—but events cannot wait for him. I would like you to act as my paxman during this period. Temporarily, of course, with no permanent commitment. I would not expect you to—to—"

"Yes, of course. I have always served my lord's family." In the glow of the luminescent stones, Donal looked puzzled. "What do you wish me to do?"

"To begin with, advise me. I know what I want to do, but not how to go about it. I must call the Council into session—not today, of course, but soon. Tomorrow if possible."

Donal shrugged. "That's easy enough. I have arranged such meetings for *Dom* Mikhail many times. But why—you aren't thinking of taking your father's place as Regent?"

"This is a poor beginning if *you* have so little faith in me," Domenic said.

"No! I didn't mean—" Donal stammered, covering his lapse. "Everyone knows that you will follow him some day. You are his heir—I just did not anticipate it so soon."

Nor in the middle of a crisis. "Neither did I." Domenic nodded grimly. "I will, as my mother says, have my work cut out for me. I must seize the initiative. For that, I need your help."

The dull sheen lifted from Donal's eyes. He suggested that Domenic speak privately with as many influential members as possible before the Council met next.

"Thank you," Domenic said, "that's excellent. See how many of these private meetings you can set up. I should talk with Dani Hastur, my uncles Gabriel and Rafael, Hermes or Robert Aldaran—" Domenic ticked off the names on his fingers as Donal nodded agreement with each one— "the new Aillard heir, and Kennard-Dyan Ardais, if he's willing. Cisco Ridenow, I suppose. My mother and grandfather and Danilo Syrtis, those I can see on my own."

"Very good, *vai dom.*" Donal stood and bowed before taking his leave. They had no time to lose.

——— ◆ ———

Oh gods! Standing outside the door to the family parlor, Domenic was seized by a moment of panic. *How am I going to tell Mother?*

He'd delayed telling her about his promise to Alanna and had only made the situation worse. He might have consulted her before making this decision . . . but he had not, and the sooner he brought her in on it, the better. Bracing his shoulders, he tapped on the door and, at her invitation, went in.

Marguerida was sitting next to Grandfather Lew on the divan, his one arm around her shoulders her face flushed. Clearly, she had been weeping.

"Nico." She got up and enveloped him in a hug. Her cheek felt hot and damp against his. "I'm sorry. I have not given much thought to your feelings, I have been so preoccupied with my own. How can I help you?"

"I need to talk, and it's good that you are here as well, Grandfather. It's about business, not personal matters." Domenic pulled up one of the chairs and took a deep breath. "With Father disabled, someone must take his place on the Council."

"Yes, I suppose you are right," Marguerida said, her face tightening. "I had thought to remain at Mikhail's side, but I must not allow personal feelings to interfere with my responsibilities."

"Marja, you cannot possibly assume the post of Regent," Lew protested. "It's politically impossible."

"What would you have me do? Sit back while everything Mikhail and I worked so hard for falls apart?" Marguerida cried. Behind her words Domenic heard the desperate need to do something active, to wrest some measure of control from the whirlwind of changes around her.

"*Someone* must take up the reins of power," Domenic repeated, "but it should be me. Not Rory, not Grandfather. Not Dani Hastur. Not you, Mother. *Me.*"

He paused for emphasis, his heart beating a wild dance

in his ears. "I am the one Father trained for this work, just as Great-Uncle Regis trained him."

"Nico, are you sure you can do this? We expected that some day you would take Mikhail's place, but not for a long time yet." Marguerida glanced at Lew, searching for agreement.

"History speaks of times when great leaders arose," Lew said, "often before anyone thought they were ready . . . sometimes before they themselves felt they were. Domenic is neither arrogant nor prideful. If he is moved to step forward, might it not be because he, like others before him, feels . . . summoned?"

"Please, do not make me out to be some kind of hero chosen by the gods," Domenic said, raking his hair back from his forehead. "I'm terrified enough as it is. I only know this is something I *must* do."

Lew regarded him steadily, with a sense of undemanding acceptance, flaws as well as strengths. "That is exactly what I meant."

"The Council may not see it that way," Marguerida said. "We have friends, but also enemies, who will see you as an untried boy, unfit to shoulder so much responsibility during a crisis."

"If they will not have me, let them say so and choose who they will!" Domenic said. "But after what has just happened, we cannot go even a single day without firm leadership."

"Of course. I will support you in any way I can." Marguerida gave a brief, brave attempt at a smile. "Forgive me, Nico, but it is always a shock for a mother to discover that her son is grown and longer needs her."

Domenic's heart ached for her. She needed a challenge to absorb her restless energy and keen mind. Sitting by Mikhail's bedside or composing chamber music would never be enough.

"Mother, I still need you. I rely on your good counsel and yours, too, Grandfather. I cannot do this alone. Don't desert me now!"

"I shall not," she replied.

Lew added, "And neither will I."

In all the sessions of the Comyn Council that Domenic had previously attended, he had never taken his father's seat in the Hastur enclosure, nor did he now. The huge, carved chair must remain vacant until he was confirmed. Until then, he sat on a nearby bench, while Marguerida occupied her usual place. Grandfather Lew sat under the Alton banner, with Alanna by his side.

Today, the multicolored light in the Crystal Chamber seemed muted, as if the prisms set in the ceiling and the very walls were numb from shock after the recent tragedy. Istvana and Casilde Aldaran-Lanart, the Tramontana Keeper, moved about the Chamber, setting the telepathic dampers. The familiar hum of *laran* gave way to the even less comfortable numbness of the interference fields. Domenic's temples throbbed. For the hundredth time, he wondered if he could go through with his plan.

The murmur of conversation died down as the Guardsman at the door announced, "Danilo Felix-Rafael Hastur, Warden of Elhalyn!"

Domenic rose with the others as Dani passed through the massive doors and walked at a stately pace to his place beneath the Elhalyn banner. Miralys was already seated there, along with Gareth and her sister, the *leronis* Valenta Elhalyn. Gareth looked somber and composed. Watching him, Domenic reflected that sooner or later the issue of an Elhalyn who was competent to occupy the throne—and hence bring the Regency to an end—would come up. Gareth had shown no sign of such ambition, not since that disgraceful incident four years ago. Domenic hoped that Gareth, under his father's steady guidance, would not use Mikhail's absence to try again.

"Kinsmen, Comynari," Dani said, his voice ringing

through the hush, "I bid you welcome in Council. As you know, this session has been convened at the request of Domenic Alton-Hastur, son and Heir of the Regent."

Heads turned in Domenic's direction, some hopeful for good news about Mikhail, others apprehensive, all of them expectant.

Taking a breath, Domenic stepped forward. "I am Domenic Gabriel-Lewis Alton-Hastur, the legitimate son of Mikhail Lanart-Hastur, Warden of Hastur and Regent of the Comyn. As my father is temporarily unable to perform his usual duties, I claim the right and responsibility of serving in his place until he has recovered."

The assembly murmured in surprise, punctuated here and there by expressions of approval or dismay or simple surprise. Dani gave Domenic an encouraging nod and asked, "Does anyone challenge the rightful wardenship of Domenic Alton-Hastur?"

In a moment of self-doubt, Domenic almost wished someone would stand forth and insist that he was not old enough, not experienced enough, not ready for such a position.

He set the thought aside. He *was* ready. During the past year some part of him, some germ of strength, had roused and stretched forth. Whether it was a love of power or of justice, or the simple exercise of his heritage, he could no longer deny it existed. He imagined Grandmother Javanne, Great-Uncle Regis, and so many others who had gone before, looking down on him, waiting to see what he would do.

The thought came to him that his unique *laran* gave him a vision not just of the Domains, the cities and castles and Towers, but of Darkover itself. The very bedrock of the mountains sang to him, the melody of the rivers danced through his dreams, and the slow molten planetary rhythms hummed below his breath. If there was a way to bring together the disparate elements of Comyn and commoner, Dry Towns lord and Hellers mountain folk, even the nonhuman trailmen and *chieri,* it would take a vision as big and deep as Darkover itself. Where he would find the words to turn that vision into reality, he did not know. He could only pray to whatever god was listening that the words would come.

The audience shifted, the rustle of rich fabrics blending with whispered comments. Rufus DiAsturien got to his feet, and the muttering fell away into a respectful hush, for his family traced their nobility back to the farthest reaches of Darkovan history.

"With all due deference to young Lord Domenic's rank and character, I do object. I do not call his right into question, only his age. In ages past, when the world was simpler, a boy of his years could assume such a responsibility. But these are difficult, complex times. Any man who holds a Domain, let alone the Regency of the entire Comyn, must have solid understanding and judgment. In time, I hope Domenic will acquire the necessary experience, but he does not yet have it. He is too young and untried to hold such a post."

"Regis Hastur was not much older when old Danvan died," Lew answered in his hoarse voice. "Would you have accused *him* of being unready, as well?"

"We all know that Domenic is your grandson, *Dom* Lewis," Rufus protested. "Your judgment is biased—"

"I knew Regis," Lew cut him off. *As you did not.* "And I know Domenic."

After an awkward pause, Dani asked who else among them supported the challenge.

Kennard-Dyan got to his feet, looking unhappy but resolved. "Ardais challenges also. Domenic indeed is the rightful Heir to Hastur, but he is too young to serve as Regent."

"Yet the Comyn cannot continue without either King or Regent," Gabriel spoke up. "We are not at the point of adopting some degenerate *Terranan* democracy."

"Someday an Elhalyn may once again sit upon the throne," Dani said in a steely voice, "but this is not that time. With both *Dom* Mikhail and *Domna* Marilla unable to speak for their Domains, this Council would be best served by the continuation of the Regency. We must give Mikhail's Heir serious consideration."

Marguerida had been sitting so still, Domenic had not even heard her breathing. Now she stood up. "I am Marguerida Alton-Hastur. You all know me. I have advised my husband for many years. I now offer myself in the same capacity to my son, as guide and councillor. Will this satisfy your objections?"

An older lord, one of the traditionally conservative MacArans, answered. His voice rumbled like that of some huge, awakened beast. "That would be equally unacceptable, to grant a woman such power. *Domna* Marguerida is clearly still a stranger among us, or she would know this."

Scattered about the chamber, heads shook and voices murmured in agreement. Marguerida showed no outward reaction, but Domenic felt her quiver in outrage. In all her years on Darkover, she had steadfastly refused to accept a lesser role because of her sex.

"We of the Comyn have never submitted to the rule of a woman," Rufus insisted, "weak-willed and unreliable as they are. And we never will!"

"Weak-willed? Unreliable?" In the Keepers' area of the Aillard box, crimson draperies swirled as Laurinda stepped to the railing. "How dare you say such a thing!"

Rufus paled, but Robert Aldaran broke in with, "The Council, not the Towers, rules the Domains!"

"Quiet! All of you!" Dani's voice soared above the uproar. "*Domna* Marguerida is not proposing to act as Regent herself but only to offer her son the benefit of her experience."

With each passing exchange, Domenic felt increasingly uneasy. The last thing Darkover needed was a Council torn apart, paralyzed with internal dissension. He raised his hands and shouted, "Kinsmen, nobles, Comynari!"

"Silence, let him speak!" Lew shouted.

"Since before the dawn of time," Domenic said, once the commotion died down, "this Council has operated by virtue of our allegiance to a common cause. Even when blood feuds ran rampant among us, within these halls we met in truce to decide what was best for all."

He paused, then repeated, "*All* of us. Not one Domain over another, not Tower against city, Lowlander against mountain folk. I am not ignorant of history. I know that many times since the founding of the Seven Domains, one or another has sought to use the Council for advantage. I would like to believe—I *hope*—that whenever our common welfare is at stake, we are able to set aside such narrow-minded concerns."

Around the Chamber, heads nodded. In their somber expressions, Domenic sensed the echoes of shock. The taint of blood and poison from the duel still lingered in the air.

"If we turn on one another now," Domenic said, "what hope is there for any of us?"

As he spoke, Domenic rested his fingertips on the railing, the wood worn smooth by generations of kinsmen. Knowing he was taking an irrevocable step, he opened the gate and walked into the center of the floor. He was acutely aware that he now stood in the same place where his father had fought and almost died.

No, he would not think of that now. The need for unity was only part of what drove him. Something else was brewing inside him, in the dark at the back of his mind, in the wordless music of his *laran*, pushing its way into day.

"My friends, Comyn and kinsmen, we cannot return to the old days, nor should we wish to. Each age leaves its mark. Each generation receives the world in one condition, changes it for good or ill, and passes it on. Our fathers strove to keep Darkover from being absorbed and exploited by the *Terranan*. Now that the Federation is gone, we need a new purpose, a new vision of our world . . . this vast, harsh, beautiful, wild planet of ours."

He spoke of the wonders of the world, those he had seen, those he had only heard about, but, most of all, those he had felt in the innermost part of his mind.

With each phrase, the vision became clearer and stronger. Domenic opened his arms. For the moment, he had captured his audience. Words rose to his mouth, and he let them go, like the Kadarin in flood, like a Dry Town sandstorm, like a Hellers avalanche.

In his mind, the Council, the city, the Domains themselves, diminished, ephemeral and infinitesimally small.

We are men, after all, not mountains.

The old proverb rose to his mind, *Only men laugh, only men weep, only men dance.*

In that moment, it seemed that the assembled Council—and the hills beyond Thendara's walls, and the soaring mountains beyond them, from the swelling ocean beyond Temora to the Wall Around the World—laughed. And wept. And danced.

The moment stretched into silence. Then someone coughed. Dani Hastur shifted from one foot to the other. Marguerida stood, her face rapt, her golden eyes alight.

Domenic returned to himself. "This is my vision. If you will not have it, if I myself present a source of discord and rift in this Council, then I will withdraw my claim."

It was the last thing they expected. The entire chamber shuddered with a shared, quickly indrawn breath.

"Lad," Dani said, "that will not be necessary. Not a man in a thousand would have spoken as you did." The pale, fractured light of the ceiling prisms glinted off his eyes. "Does anyone still question the fitness of Domenic Alton-Hastur to become Acting Warden of Hastur and Regent of the Comyn?"

For a long moment, no one spoke. No one moved.

"If I—" Marguerida began, her voice hovering on the edge of emotion, "if I myself am an obstacle, I withdraw my proposal, as well."

"If I may be so bold to present an alternative suggestion." The calm, quiet voice of Danilo Syrtis filled the Chamber. "It would be as badly done to reject *Domna* Marguerida's experience and wisdom as for a fighting man to cut off his own left arm. How often in battle does the shield and not the sword save a man's life? I say, let the *vai domna* continue to counsel *Dom* Domenic, but let him select other advisors as well, subject to the approval of this Council."

"Aye, that will serve," said the elderly Leynier lord, "so long as they are steady men and true."

When it was clear there were no remaining objections, Dani asked Domenic whom he would choose.

"I would indeed consult my mother," Domenic answered, "for she has studied much, seen even more, and traveled in the company of great men. One of those great men is my grandfather, *Dom* Lewis-Kennard Alton. I would also seek the wisdom of the *leroni* of the Towers, a representative of their own choosing, for it is in their matrix sciences that we Comyn have found our deepest strength. And for his understanding of the affairs of Thendara and its people, I would ask *Dom* Danilo-Felix Syrtis-Ardais."

Deliberately, he used Danilo's full name, with the additional Domain-right granted to him so many years ago by the old Lord Dyan Ardais. In this way, he reminded the Council of Danilo's long years of service, not only as paxman to Regis Hastur but also as Warden of Ardais, with all the responsibilities that entailed. No one could possibly challenge him on the basis of inexperience or lack of knowledge of the affairs of the Comyn. No one dared to suggest that Domenic had selected Danilo not on the basis of his merit but as a reward for his support.

After a long moment, Dani said, "These are sound choices, *Dom* Domenic. I speak for the Council when I say none here can have any objection."

Dani formally asked each of the candidates present whether he or she was willing to perform the duties of advisor to the provisional Regent. Then, with an almost tangible sense of relief, the telepathic dampers were released and the session adjourned.

Domenic watched the crowd disperse, filing out through either the main doors or the private entrances for each Domain section, and wondered what he had gotten himself into.

32

After the Council session, Domenic spent several hours in earnest conversation with one member or another. Donal stayed at his side, smoothing out awkward moments, lending an added touch of normality. Some, like Danilo and the Aldarans, seemed pleased with him as Acting Regent; others were carefully neutral, and even those who had opposed him seemed disposed to give him a chance to prove himself. Domenic understood, without the need for overt explanation, that neither Cisco Ridenow nor Darius-Mikhail Zabal could be seen to take sides. At least, Jeram was now in Cisco's scrupulously neutral hands.

When, at last, Domenic and Donal returned to the family suite, they found Marguerida alone. She had been arranging a bouquet of starflowers and rosalys in an elegant blue-glazed vase, a gift from Marilla's pottery. Domenic asked where Grandfather Lew was.

"I finally convinced him to rest," she replied with a slightly distracted smile. "I suspect he didn't trust this morning's business to go right unless he was there. He says work is the best medicine, and I suppose he's right. I think I would go mad without something constructive to do."

"This part, at least, is over." Domenic's nerves still quivered with tension. He stretched his shoulders, trying to relax.

"Are you hungry?" Marguerida's usual practical nature reasserted itself. "Dinner should arrive any minute now. Donal, you'll stay and eat with us, won't you?"

"If it pleases you, *Domna,*" Donal replied with a short bow.

Servants brought in trays of food and placed them upon the table. To Domenic, the young girls looked like scullery maids. They curtsyed, blushing, and hurried away without setting the table properly. The food was simply prepared but still hot, and among them, Marguerida, Domenic, and Donal laid out the dishes and served themselves.

A few minutes later, Illona came in, flushed and out of breath, as if she had just run the length of the Castle. Her step, usually so fluid and strong, faltered.

"What is it?" Marguerida asked, her soup spoon clattering against the bowl. "Is there—is there some change in Mikhail's condition?"

"No, as far as I know, he is neither better nor worse," Illona panted. "I have come about an entirely different matter. I am sorry to invade your private family meal, but as Acting Regent, Domenic, you should know at once. I dared not entrust this news to a messenger."

"Here, sit down. You look unwell." Domenic put one arm around her, for she was visibly trembling. "Let me get you something to drink—*jaco*? Some of this good soup, then? Or—Mother, do we have any wine?"

From behind a glass door on the sideboard, Marguerida brought out a bottle. "Here it is. *Ravnet,* a rather good vintage."

Illona allowed herself to be seated at the table but refused any refreshment. "I am quite well, thank you. It is the news I bear and not any personal malady that affects me."

"Then tell us at once," Domenic said.

"Is it *Domna* Marilla?" Marguerida asked, setting the unopened bottle down. "Is she gravely ill?"

Illona drew a breath, and a degree of composure returned to her. "I fear that she is. It is worse than any of us imagined. She has trailmen's fever."

"Surely that is not possible." Marguerida blinked in surprise. "There has not been a case since before I came to Darkover. It was wiped out like Terran smallpox or greenplague on Thetis."

Illona shook her head. "No, it was contained at that time but not eliminated. The host for the virus is the trailmen themselves, you see, and although we believe their numbers have been greatly reduced in recent years as a result of forest fires started by the World Wreckers, they are not yet extinct. I found records in the archives at Nevarsin Tower of the Allison Expedition, the one that Regis Hastur led."

"That was well before the World Wreckers' time, wasn't it?" Marguerida said.

"Yes," Illona said. "As a result, a vaccine was developed, and mass immunization halted the worst of the outbreak."

Donal asked what made her think it was the same disease.

"I have seen it before." Illona's voice turned hard and clear. "In Nevarsin, I monitored a patient who subsequently died from this very same fever. I have just come from a *laran* examination of *Domna* Marilla. The vibrational signatures of their infections are are identical."

Lord of Light! Domenic swore silently.

Illona turned to Domenic. "You remember our discussion. At the time, I suspected that Garin's illness was a recurrence of a Darkovan disease, not some toxin left from the World Wreckers. In the end, I could not be sure. Not until now." She explained to Marguerida, "The defining characteristic of trailmen's fever is not its symptoms but its timing."

"Timing?" asked Marguerida.

"It comes in waves," Illona explained, "each one worse than the one before."

Domenic's belly clenched. "If you are correct, Illona, where are we in the cycle?"

Her gaze met his, the delicate skin around her eyes as dark as if it had been bruised. "This is almost exactly three

months after Garin's case. I think we are in the second
stage, with many cases scattered throughout the city and in
the encampment outside. Perhaps, the same is happening
in other cities as well."

"Mother of Oceans!" Marguerida closed her eyes. *First
Mikhail and now this . . .*

"The refugees must have brought the fever to Thendara." Donal's voice roughened in anger.

"It does no good to blame them," Domenic said. "We
must act quickly to prevent panic. I did not expect to begin
my duties as Acting Regent with such a crisis. I may have
to suspend all regular Council business until we have the
situation under control. I will confer with Cisco about
quarantine measures and safeguarding food and water
supplies. Mother, I will need your help now more than
ever."

Marguerida gave her shoulders a little shake. Her golden
eyes regained their focus. "I will enlist Istvana and the
Keepers Council in organizing healing circles. It's fortunate we have so many *leroni* in the city now. We'll need
clinics throughout the city to care for the sick."

"Don't forget the city's licensed matrix mechanics,"
Domenic added, "and the Terran-trained healers of the
Bridge Society."

"Do not place too much hope in those measures," Illona
warned. "In the past, our best efforts—including *laran*—
saved only a few of those infected. And that is not all we
must face. In another three months, when the third stage
strikes, it will be far, far worse."

Domenic caught the images in her mind. *Thendara deserted, corpses gray and bloated in the streets because there
were too few left to bury them—Alanna's vision? Fires
raged unchecked through the Hellers, farmsteads empty,
fields untended . . . famine and more death. And then, in another forty-eight years or so, the whole cycle would repeat
itself.*

"We stopped it once with Terran medical technology,"
Donal said. "Now that we need them most, they are gone."

Marguerida looked thoughtful. "Yes, the Federation is gone . . . but not their library and medical facilities. I must organize a research team at once. I'll need people who can operate computers and read Terran Standard . . ."

Domenic felt a surge of admiration for his mother, that she could so quickly set aside her own sorrows for the greater good.

She would fall into a nest of banshees, he thought, *and manage them all into becoming herbivores . . . and liking it.* Perhaps there was hope, after all.

——— ✦ ———

Within the hour, Domenic found himself standing before a hastily reassembled Council. Donal had done an extraordinary job contacting everyone, sending pages running all over the Castle and to private residences throughout the city. Not every member could be found at such short notice. Darius-Mikhail remained at Marilla's bedside. Half the Keepers were already meeting with Marguerida. Laurinda, who insisted she had little talent for healing, attended.

Domenic kept his opening brief and direct. "I did not call this meeting lightly, so I will get to the point. When you confirmed me as Acting Regent earlier this morning, none of us could have guessed that we would be facing an even greater crisis than my father's incapacity."

The entire Chamber held its breath, listening. From one instant to the next, he had captured their attention. Using plain terms, Domenic told them of Marilla's diagnosis.

Fear jolted through the room. "Plague!" someone yelled. A dozen people leaped to their feet and started to leave.

"Sit down!" Domenic shouted. The chamber's acoustics caught and amplified his voice. "Remain where you are! Do you think you can save yourselves by rushing about like a herd of headless barnfowl?"

Surprised, perhaps shocked by the ringing command in his voice, they paused. A few sank back into their seats.

"Do none of you remember your history?" he thundered. "This is *trailmen's fever!* If one of us has been exposed, we *all* have. If you scatter to your homes, you will only bring the plague with you. Do you want that?"

"But what are we to do?" one of the women—Domenic thought it was Lorrill Vallonde's daughter—cried.

"Stay here, where we are working on a cure. Carry *that* back to your lands and families!" Domenic had no idea if he could keep such a brazen promise.

Whether you believe me or not, you will not spread panic and chaos, which would only make the situation worse! The people in Alanna's dire vision could have died by one another's hands as well as from the plague.

Domenic poured all the authority he possessed into his next orders. "No one is to leave the city. Order will prevail. The Comyn will not descend into savagery. We will search for a cure, and we will care for those who become ill."

"Cure?" Robert Aldaran said, his face torn between terror and blatant skepticism. "There *is* no cure!"

"The Terrans—" someone said.

"The Terrans found a vaccine, not a cure!" Robert retorted. "Now they're gone, and we don't even have that! You fools! We're all going to die, don't you know that? I for one would rather end my days in my own mountains, with my own people!"

Cisco Ridenow, who had been standing with his Guardsmen just inside the double doors, looked pointedly at Domenic, awaiting the signal to close in and enforce order. If that became necessary, Domenic thought, he would already have lost control. He needed these people as cooperative, committed allies, not prisoners. He had to give them reason to hope, to believe that working together offered their only chance of survival.

"Listen to me!" Domenic said. "The Federation is gone, that is true, but not their knowledge. Their Base still stands, and in the Medical Center is a library of everything they learned about the fever. Even as we speak, a team of experts is searching those records. At the same time, the Keepers Council will be using their *laran* to develop an effective treatment. Even if you mistrust the technology of the *Terranan,* do you also doubt the Keepers of not one but five Towers? Do you think a mere disease can stand against our matrix science?"

For a long moment, no one answered. Domenic sensed fear give way to tentative hope, or at least acceptance. He had them . . . almost.

Shaking his head, Rufus DiAsturien stood forward. "*Vai dom,* you mean well. None of us doubts that. But if a cure were possible, would not the *vai leroni* of those past times have found it?"

"These are not past times." Domenic shook his head. "Before, each Tower worked in isolation. Now we can share our strength and knowledge."

Across the room, under the white tower banner, Laurinda MacBard raised her head. Her homely features brightened as if lit by an inner fire. She was the only member of the Keepers Council present. All the rest were either tending Mikhail and Marilla or in conference with Marguerida.

"Young Lord Domenic speaks the truth," she said. "We of the Towers have kept to ourselves for far too long, each answering only to the conscience of our own Keeper. We have spoken to one another over the relays, but we have always guarded our secrets, hoarding our discoveries. Now, for the first time in memory, we have the opportunity—and the duty—to work together."

Pausing, she fixed Robert with a fierce glare. He gulped and sat down. "Here in Thendara, we have representatives— Keepers and under-Keepers—from *five different Towers.* Who is to say what we can accomplish when we put our united minds to it?"

Domenic let a long moment pass for Laurinda's words to sink it. "Not only that, we can combine the wisdom and strength of the Towers with the medical science of the Terrans. This too has never happened before, and I believe we will prevail! Who is with me?"

Rufus, who was still on his feet, bowed slowly and for-

mally to Domenic. It took Domenic a long moment to realize that the old man acted for them all. That they had
agreed to his command. That he had won this round.

For the moment, he had the cooperation of the Council.
For how long? he wondered as the meeting adjourned. If
the search of the Terran records and the efforts of the
Keepers could not contain the fever, it would no longer
matter who ruled over a dying city.

33

Domenic craned his neck to look up at the tall, rectangular buildings that formed the Terran Federation Base, thinking how different the place looked from when he had visited it as a child. Once it was a beehive of activity, with men and women in outlandish, immodest clothing hurrying about their business, spaceport police in black leather, Renunciate travel guides and translators, workmen and suppliers. The Base had been a city unto itself, steel towers and stark white walls, austere and yet beautiful with its own exotic customs.

Most of the Trade City was gone now, absorbed into the living city of Thendara, but these towers remained, locked and deserted. Few Darkovans had ventured inside the perimeter fence once it became evident that there was no easy access for looting, and even fewer made their way through the vicinity today, for the growing epidemic kept many indoors.

"Strange, isn't it?" Domenic said to Donal, who now went everywhere in the city with him. "This place belongs on another planet, and yet it's been here since the time of our grandfathers."

"As you say, *Dom* Domenic," Donal replied, "but not even the *Terranan* could teach Durraman's donkey to sing."

"Or to make anything like this truly Darkovan?" Domenic

permitted himself a chuckle. "I suppose you're right, but I can't imagine Thendara without it."

Now our fate may ride on what lies within.

"There you are! Have you been waiting long?" Marguerida hurried up to the gate and kissed Domenic's cheek. From the practical way she'd pinned up her hair and the utilitarian comfort of her clothing, a tunic of soft wool loosely belted over a simple underdress, she was eager to get to work.

She'd brought assistants: two grim-faced Renunciates, healers who had participated in the Bridge Society exchanges, and Katherine Aldaran, who had married Hermes Aldaran while he was the Darkovan Senator to the Federation. Katherine looked nervous and a bit strained. That was not surprising, for she had reason to be concerned about Terése and Sibelle, back at Castle Aldaran, and the outbreak of fever in Caer Donn.

Domenic was sorry not to see his Uncle Rafe Scott, who was climbing in the Hellers at this season, since Rafe's knowledge of the Base would have been very useful.

Domenic nodded to his mother's other companion, who returned the greeting with an easy smile. It had been some years since Domenic had seen Ethan MacDoevid. Ethan was about ten years his senior, with dark hair and open, generous features. He came from a crafter family of cloth-makers and had known Marguerida since her first tenday on Darkover. As a boy, Ethan had been caught up in the spaceman craze, wild to learn everything about the Federation.

"My cousin Geremy's searching for others who were employed on the Base," Ethan said. "There may be dozens of other families in the city who once had *Terranan* ties— traders, scholars, the like. No one ever thought to keep track of them once the Base was closed."

Marguerida slipped off the thin leather glove from her left hand to reveal the glimmering outlines of a faceted stone, imprinted into her flesh. As she touched the locked door, the shadow matrix flashed blue-white. Domenic winced at the raw *laran* power, harsh like salt over abraded skin. Then something mechanical shifted within, and the door swung open.

With Donal at his heels, Domenic entered a vast, cavernous chamber, lightless and deathly still. A moment later, a row of yellow-tinted lights appeared above his head.

Safety lights, he thought, *running on backup batteries.* The Federation intended to return some day, but it didn't make sense to waste energy on heat and light for a place that no one used.

Domenic smiled at himself as his eyes adjusted to the partial light of the lobby, bemused that he even knew about such things as *backup batteries.* Marguerida had been adamant that all her children receive a minimum education by Terran Federation standards.

"You can never tell, one of you might want to study off-world. I won't have you growing up as illiterate savages," she'd said on more than one occasion. Somewhat to her disappointment, none of them had developed the slightest interest in going to University. Who could have guessed that he would use that training right here in Thendara?

Ethan went to one of the consoles facing the entrance and tapped in a pattern on a screen. Domenic sensed rather than heard some vast machinery start up in the depths of the building, perhaps the underground power plant that had been installed when the Base was first built.

A few moments later, Domenic felt the whisper of air on his cheek. The safety lights gave way to brighter illumination. With the return of ventilation came an acrid smell. Domenic coughed, his eyes watering, and even the Renunciates could not disguise their repugnance.

"The air should freshen as the scrubbers kick in," Ethan said with infuriating cheerfulness. "That delightful stench is out-gassing from the synthetics. When I worked here, I eventually got used to it."

"Yes," Marguerida said, "we humans can adapt to almost anything. Come on, the Medical Center is this way."

The sound of their boots echoed in the long, bleak corridor. They kept together, reluctant to become separated in this strange, lifeless place. As they continued, lights sprang on.

Marguerida quickly located the records facility within the Medical Center and led them to a nearby conference room. Within minutes, she had organized everyone into teams. She and Katherine would search the computer for information on the Allison Expedition and the resultant vaccine. The two Renunciates were to make a more general study of the virology of the infectious agent. Ethan, who was more familiar with the physical layout of the place, went off in search of paper records.

"For a society that was supposed to run entirely on computers, we always had a stack of forms, logbooks, requisition slips, you name it." Katherine's mouth twitched into a wry half-smile as she settled at one of the computer stations. Tucking back a strand of glossy, ebony-dark hair, she switched on the screen.

"In triplicate!" Marguerida said, and they both laughed.

Domenic exchanged a puzzled glance with Donal, unable to understand what was so funny, and then left to continue his own work.

———— ✦ ————

Domenic returned to the Terran Base late in the same afternoon, with Donal as his silent shadow. He had been able to reassure the members of the Council about the efforts of the research team, but the situation in the city was rapidly worsening. The number of new cases of fever increased hourly. Danilo and Darius-Mikhail had been setting up clinic shelters, drawing from the city's matrix mechanics, herbal healers, anyone with nursing experience.

Domenic had already ordered the distribution of supplies of water, food, blankets, and medicines from the Castle. In addition, he realized they needed a central location for planning and coordination. Donal had suggested using the Grand Hall, and he set about making arrangements.

As he entered the conference room in the Terran Medical Center, Marguerida looked up from the table covered with diagrams, file folders, and piles of discolored flimsies. From the lines between her brows and the faint tremor of *laran* in the air, she had been battling one of her headaches.

She extended her hand to Domenic with a wan smile. "Bless you for interrupting us! We've worked far too long without a break."

"I now know a hundred places *not* to look." Dispiritedly, Ethan tossed another folder on the pile. "I've combed through personnel files and supplies requisitions. I can tell you how many pounds of flimsy substrate and detergent were needed every tenday or everything about agricultural beetles of the Valeron Plains. But nothing on human diseases or the Allison expedition."

"What about the rest of you?" Domenic asked. "Did you have any better luck?"

The two Renunciates shook their heads. From her computer station, Katherine sighed. She had found references to the expedition, but very few details and none of them medical.

"How could the Terrans lose the records of such an important scientific expedition?" Domenic said.

"Look," Katherine said. "I'll show you."

Domenic looked over her shoulder as she slowly tapped in, *MEDICAL PERSONNEL.*

Name? The computer inquired.

ALLISON, JAY, M.D.

The computer hesitated, as if mulling over her request. Then a man's portrait appeared in the upper right of the screen, lean and composed, with a pleasant mouth and shadowed eyes.

Surgeon, Terran Federation Medical Service. Consultant, Department of Alien Anthropology; specialist in Darkovan parasitology . . .

Leaning over Katherine's shoulder, Domenic skimmed the details of Allison's schooling, his internship and residencies, his publications.

. . . participant in Allison Expedition, Project Telepath . . .

Katherine touched the key that froze the narrative and highlighted, *ALLISON EXPEDITION.*

Mountaineering expedition to trailmen territory, organized by Dr. Randall Forth and Lord Regis Hastur; personnel included . . .

"No, that won't help. I've read that same summary a hundred times." Marguerida reached over and tapped in, *TRAILMEN. DISEASES OF.*

Again there was a pause. A box, bordered in red and black, appeared in the center of the screen.

Security authorization? it read.

"What in Zandru's Seven Frozen Hells does *that* mean?" Domenic stared in disbelief. Why require a security clearance on nonhuman diseases?

"Who organized this database, anyway?" Exasperation edged Katherine's voice. "And why didn't they include a decent search function?"

"Some pea-brained bureaucrat, anxious to keep his librarian nephew in permanent employment, no doubt," Marguerida answered, sighing. "It probably never occurred to them that someone not already familiar with the system would have to find something, particularly as obscure as a native trek to uncharted territory relating to a disease thought to be extinct."

"I suppose it was too much to hope for results in a single day," Domenic said, masking his disappointment.

"Research can be like that." Marguerida stretched, arching her back. "We'll come back tomorrow with reinforcements."

"Good idea," Katherine said. "I've got tight muscles all over."

"We should leave the power on standby," Ethan said as they retraced their steps. "The plant should be good for a couple of centuries, but I wouldn't want to count on it."

"There's no point in wasting energy," Marguerida said. "A hundred years from now, or two, or three, our descendants may need this very same library. That is, assuming the Federation hasn't returned to reclaim the Base before that."

They came out into the street. Dusk was falling, a swift velvet shadow through the light drizzle. Orange and yellow lights dotted the old city. In the distance, the sound muffled by walls and wooden gates, a dog barked.

"Do you think they will ever return?" Katherine asked, tilting her head back to peer through the darkening clouds.

Marguerida grimaced. "That depends, I suppose, upon how thoroughly they blow one another up. I can't imagine them abandoning Darkover forever. Even if we have nothing else they want, our position in the galactic arm makes us invaluable as a transit point. No, I very much fear that whoever comes out on top will come back and take what they need, regardless of whether it is to our benefit or even our liking."

She paused and turned back to the lock, resetting it with the matrix imprinted on her left hand in much the same manner as she had released it.

They made their way back to Comyn Castle. Far fewer people than usual were abroad at this hour. The nearly deserted cobblestoned streets of the old Trade City seemed darker and narrower than ever. Even the air bore a close, dank edge. Many of the taverns were shut up, but a few braziers burned outside closed shops, and men in tattered clothing hunched beside them, drinking. They looked up with glazed, smoke-reddened eyes. When they saw Donal's sword, they shambled away.

From time to time, Marguerida rubbed her temples.

"Mother, are you all right?" Domenic asked. "Shall I send Donal for a sedan chair for you?"

"I am well enough, and I don't mind a little rain," Marguerida answered, although her strained voice belied her words. "This is no ordinary headache, to pass with rest and quiet. It is a sort of warning, and it will plague me until whatever it portends has come to pass."

"Can you see what will happen?"

She shook her head. "No, only an infuriatingly vague sense of foreboding. I would like to tell that part of my mind that I already know bad things are about to happen, and could it please leave me alone to deal with them, but I doubt it would do any good."

As they neared the Castle, the streets broadened, and the air grew fresher. Night-blooming flowers grew in planters along the way. Marguerida sighed and slipped her hand through Domenic's elbow. "Still, it is reassuring to know I do not face it alone."

34

Once at the Castle, Katherine returned to her own quarters, but Domenic, Donal, and Marguerida went on to the Grand Hall, where only a few days ago they had feasted and danced. Gone was the elaborate holiday buffet. The festive decorations had been removed, including the mirrors, so the hall seemed smaller and darker. The Castle servants had transformed it into a working headquarters. Tables had been set up, some as work spaces, others holding simple, nourishing food. A cluster of Guardsmen, cloaked for patrol, were helping themselves from a steaming soup tureen. Others stood, talking and sipping mugs of *jaco*.

Domenic took a bowl of thick bean stew, nut bread smeared with cheese, and a goblet of watered wine. He and Donal sat down at a table where Danilo and Darius-Mikhail were poring over charts and lists. A moment later, fortified with *jaco* and a plate of honey-nut pastries, Marguerida joined them.

"The craft guilds are reluctant to open their halls to outsiders. They say it's enough to care for their own," Darius-Mikhail said, finishing up a point he had made to Danilo. "The clinic shelters will soon be overtaxed."

Domenic took a sip of soup. It was too bland for his taste, but it was hot and filling. After Darius-Mikhail had explained the problem, Domenic authorized Danilo to speak with the guild masters, since the older man had special contacts there. "I'd rather their cooperation be voluntary."

"It will take some persuasion, but I will try," Danilo answered. "To ease the burden on the shelters, we are encouraging those who are better off and can afford servants, or who have families still able to care for them, to stay at home."

Darius-Mikhail reminded them that not everyone had that option. "Those newly arrived in the city seem to be disproportionately stricken. Unfortunately, they have far fewer resources. Some have no shelter or clean water and no money to buy food."

"The poorer areas of the city are not much better," Danilo agreed. "Sometimes an entire family falls sick, and their neighbors are either overwhelmed with their own needs or too frightened to help."

Domenic asked for the latest estimate of casualties.

"We have only guesses, because we have no way of knowing for certain how many are tended at home." Consulting his notes, Darius-Mikhail gave alarmingly high calculations.

Donal looked grim. "And it's only beginning."

A group of servants had carried out fresh covered dishes and set them on the food tables. The lady supervising them approached the table, and Domenic recognized Alanna. She wore a white head scarf and an apron several sizes too big for her over a faded green gown. Quietly, she slipped on to a bench opposite Domenic. Darius-Mikhail stared at her, color suffusing his cheeks and throat, and then hastily lowered his gaze.

For an instant, Domenic glimpsed the image in Alanna's mind, the vision of Thendara streets silent and gray, bodies lying everywhere.

"What is the mortality rate?" Marguerida, having finished the last of her pastries, asked. "How many of those affected will die?"

"It is too soon to be sure." Darius-Mikhail shook his

head. "Many continue to go about their business in the early stages."

"Spreading the disease still further," Donal said.

"Such fears serve no one," Domenic pointed out. "They only divert us from our true goals: tending those who need us most and discovering how to stop this dreadful epidemic."

"*Domna,* have you had success finding the Terran medical records?" Danilo turned to Marguerida, who shook her head. "Alas, I myself have little to offer. I was at Ardais during the time of the Allison expedition. Regis told me about it afterward, but not in any scientific detail. We thought we had eliminated trailmen's fever forever."

Domenic frowned as he struggled to recall the biology Marguerida had insisted he study years ago. Immunity from some vaccines wore off with time, but others lasted a lifetime. Which type applied to trailmen's fever? Danilo had been vaccinated, as had many others still alive. They would be middle-aged or older. Would immunization decades earlier give them even partial protection?

When he voiced his question, Marguerida immediately understood its importance. "If older people who have received the vaccine don't get sick, then we can use the old formula. When we find it, that is."

"But if they are as vulnerable as younger folk," Domenic said, following the thought along its logical progression, "it could either be because the immunity wears off or the disease has changed. How would we know the difference?"

"That's a very good question," Danilo said.

"I don't have lists of specific individuals," Darius-Mikhail said, "but I will ask those in charge of the shelters if any have fallen sick who were previously . . . *vaccinated.*" He stumbled a little over the unfamiliar word.

"What of those among us who are already sick?" Domenic said. "*Domna* Marilla, for example. Was she immunized?"

Just at that moment, Illona entered the hall. She accepted a laden plate and a steaming mug from one of the serving maids and stood looking down at what she held as if she no longer recognized it as food and drink. Then, as if sensing his gaze upon her, she lifted her eyes to meet Domenic's.

He wanted to go to her, to fold her in his arms, to surround her with his love, to pour his strength into her. But he could do none of these things, not in public, not with Alanna and his mother sitting here, watching him. The weight of his position as Acting Regent pressed down on him like a mantle of stone. He was no longer a private person. With the fragile cohesion of the Council dependent upon him, with the healers and organizers looking to his leadership, he dared not falter, no matter how pressing his personal desires.

Illona came toward them. The men started to rise, but she gestured for them to remain as they were. She took the nearest seat, beside Alanna, and set the mug and plate on the table.

"I bear sad news," she said. "This very hour, Marilla Lindir-Aillard has passed from our midst."

Domenic sat back, stunned. "So quickly? The fever is that virulent?"

"It is a dreadful disease, and she was not strong," Illona said, "not like that poor man at Nevarsin. She slipped into a coma at midday and never awakened. Kennard-Dyan stayed with her until the end. *Domna* Linnea . . ." she inhaled, visibly gathering the shreds of her strength, ". . . ordered me to rest."

"And so you should, child," Marguerida said. "You must replenish your energies so that you do not also fall ill."

Illona picked up a slice of pastry studded with nuts and dried fruit and set it down again.

Alanna touched her gently on the back of the wrist, telepath-style. "I cannot eat such rich food when I am tired, either. May I bring you a custard or a baked apple instead?"

Domenic felt a sudden lump in his throat as Illona nodded and said in a thin, strained voice that she would like that very much. Alanna sprang up and hurried away toward the kitchen. Darius-Mikhail followed her with his eyes. She returned in only a few minutes with a simple egg custard garnished with cream and berries.

Illona took a spoonful and swallowed it. "It's very good. Thank you."

Alanna lowered her eyes and did not reply. Domenic had no notion of what such kindness to her rival had cost her. Whatever her feelings, she had behaved with dignity.

While Illona ate, Darius-Mikhail finished showing the others a map of the city, with locations of improvised hospitals marked.

He has not yet realized what the death of Lady Marilla means, Domenic thought with an odd, dispassionate clarity. *Now he will be Warden of Aillard, with everything that entails.*

"We must make provision for disposing of the dead," Donal said. "*Domna* Marilla must be buried at Hali."

"But—" Darius-Mikhail broke in.

"Even now, at such a time," Donal glared at him. "Would you deny her the honor of her caste because it is inconvenient? She was Comynara, a noble lady, and the head of her Domain."

Before Darius-Mikhail could reply, Domenic directed the conversation back on a more practical course. "Danilo, Marilla was about your age. Do you know if she had been vaccinated?"

"Yes, she was, for I remember Regis talking about all the Lindir-Aillards receiving the serum. *Domna* Callina was alive then and was the formal head of the Domain."

"So we cannot count on any immunity." Marguerida began to say something else, but she paused as her father came into the hall. His scarred face looked more battered than ever, but he moved with firm purpose, very much the still-vigorous man who had ridden from Nevarsin.

"Father, what is it? What has happened? Is it Mikhail? Please sit down."

Lew shook his head. "There is no time to lose. The reports of the epidemic grow more alarming with each passing hour."

For a moment Domenic feared his grandfather would insist on joining one of the healing circles, as he had at Nevarsin, but Lew went on, "Domenic, we must use every resource at our command. You must send word to Cisco Ridenow to release Jeram and ask for his help."

"Jeram, your friend from Nevarsin?" Domenic said, surprised. "If you believe he has something to offer, I will certainly ask him. If nothing else, as a Terran, he must know computers."

"Would he agree to help us?" A shadow passed over Danilo's still-handsome features. "He has little reason to love the Comyn, given what he has endured at our hands."

"Let us put that question to Jeram himself," Lew said.

"After all," Marguerida added tartly, "we are not all like Francisco."

"We should discuss this with him in a private location," Domenic said. He would eventually need an office, not his father's but some other place.

"Perhaps my chambers?" Lew said, as if sensing his thought.

Domenic asked Donal to have Jeram brought there. "Mother, will you come with us?"

He caught the edge of her quickly masked emotion. This Terran, Jeram, might not have willingly collaborated with Francisco, but he reminded her all too painfully of the scheme that led to her husband's current critical condition

"I have too much work of my own." Shaking her head Marguerida stood up. "First, I must go and see Kennard-Dyan. He will be devastated."

"Just so you do not overtire yourself," Lew said. "You must follow the good advice you gave to Illona."

Promising, Marguerida bent to kiss the old man's cheek before leaving the hall.

"I will join you, if I may," Illona said, "for I tended this man at Nevarsin."

As they got to their feet, Alanna said, with a pleading glance at Domenic, "May I not come, too?"

It would be cruel to exclude her when Illona could come and go wherever she willed, as a *leronis*. Alanna had tried so hard to behave well, to be of use.

As she is to be my wife, she should not be shut out or kept ignorant. Domenic nodded and held out his arm for her. From the corner of his vision, he saw Darius-Mikhail's quickly masked expression of disappointment. It was a pity Alanna was utterly oblivious to him.

Ah, well, Domenic thought. *As Father always said, the world goes as it wills and not as we would have it. Especially in affairs of the heart.*

—— ✦ ——

Donal escorted Jeram into Lew's quarters a few minutes after the rest had arrived and were settling around the small table before the fire. Domenic settled himself in one of the chairs beside his grandfather, noticing that the old tapestry of Lady Bruna Leynier tilted at an odd angle. Domenic wondered if the housekeepers had been careless or if Lew had been trying to rehang it one-handed.

Domenic was pleased to see the change in the *Terranan*. Over the last several days, Jeram had lost his pallor. Moving with assurance, he crossed the room and bowed to Lew.

"My friend," Lew said, holding out his single hand. "Excuse me for not embracing you as comrades should, but I claim an old man's privilege. It is good to see you looking well once more."

Jeram touched Lew's hand for a brief, telepath-style greeting. "You lend us all grace, *Dom* Lewis," he said in fluent, heavily accented *casta*. "And you, *Domna* Illona."

"I am glad to see you, too," she said.

"*Dom* Domenic," Jeram said, bowing again.

"This is my cousin, Alanna Alar," Domenic said.

Another bow, this time accompanied by a smile of genuine warmth. "*Damisela.*"

"I remember you from the Council meeting," Alanna said. "*Dom* Francisco was absolutely horrid to you."

"Let us not speak ill of the dead," Jeram replied, "but I thank you for your concern."

"Please, sit down," Domenic said. "I do not know if news has reached you about the illness in the city."

"I have heard a little," Jeram said in a guarded tone, "enough to realize people have reason to be frightened."

Illona explained to Jeram that in earlier times, what was a harmless childhood illness among the trailmen sometimes passed to humans, building in cycles to a devastating epidemic.

"My grandfather thinks you can help us," Domenic said.

Jeram glanced sharply at Lew. Lew said, "I said nothing. It is your story and your choice entirely."

"Trailmen's fever used to decimate our population until the Terran Medical Corps helped us develop a vaccine a generation ago," Domenic explained. "Now it has returned, and my mother and her friends have spent all day trying to find those records. Without any success, I might add."

Jeram's eyes glittered in the light of the fire. He seemed to hesitate. Domenic wondered if Danilo had not been right, that the Comyn had already made an enemy of this man. Then Jeram said something utterly unexpected: "Those records would be heavily encrypted, invisible unless you know the codes and where to look."

"Encrypted?" Domenic thought of the SECURITY CLEARANCE warning that prevented access to information on the Allison Expedition's findings.

"This trailmen's fever of yours is a perfect biological weapon. You'd have to seed only a few target areas, not necessarily densely populated. In seven months, either your enemy would be dying, or all his resources would be committed to nursing the sick."

"*Biological weapon*?" Domenic repeated, stunned. The Terran Federation had thought to use this dreadful infection as a tool of warfare? He was so horrified that for the moment, he could not speak.

Lew nodded darkly. "The Federation wanted to preserve the knowledge and keep it secret. The potential to make such things is itself a powerful threat."

"But to *deliberately* expose thousands of innocent people, with no way of defending themselves . . ." Donal muttered. "What kind of monsters are they?"

"It is no worse than what we ourselves did during the Ages of Chaos," Illona said. "Clingfire, lungrot, and bonewater dust killed or maimed uncounted ordinary folk. The only difference is that we created them with *laran* instead of science. In the end, we became so ruthless that we faced a choice between the Compact and utter destruction. I fear the *Terranan* have not yet reached that point."

"So they hid the medical records of trailmen's fever, including its prevention and treatment, in order to keep the knowledge for themselves," Domenic said, still deeply disgusted.

"They did," Jeram said. *"But I know how to find it."*

They all stared at him.

"Before I came here with the Special Forces unit, I was an expert in biological warfare, and that includes treatment and prevention as well. I know those encryption systems. If you're willing to trust me, I can dig out everything we know about trailmen's fever. By the time I'm done, we'll have this bug nailed down to its genetic sequence. If there's even a hint of how to cure it, we'll have that as well."

From the expression on Lew's battered features, he had known about Jeram's special expertise. For some reason, he had left it up to Jeram to step forward. The offer had been genuine, of that Domenic was certain.

"We would be most grateful for any help you can give us," Domenic said to Jeram.

"There is, however, a price for my assistance," Jeram said.

Domenic's belly clenched. Jeram had been Francisco's prisoner, had been drugged and then tortured. He had been the unwilling victim of *laran* assault and had every reason to extract compensation, even revenge. Yet when Domenic glanced at his grandfather, he sensed the bond between Lew and Jeram, love and trust and something more.

"Just this," Jeram said. "Only that whatever I find—a treatment, a vaccine, I hope—be made available without charge and to *everyone,* regardless of economic or social status, no special privileges for the Comyn or anyone else."

"We have limited resources," Donal protested, "and cannot send *laran*-trained healers to every person. For some, warm blankets and food will have to do. Certainly every life is worth saving, but how many might die needlessly from a rash action?"

Alanna flashed him a look, near defiance. "If it were our own people, if only Comyn got this wretched fever, we would find a way to save them all. Wouldn't we? And if we could not, if we are so feckless and—and *unresourceful,* then I think we are not fit to rule."

Lew reached out and patted her hand. "Well spoken, child."

Illona had been listening, hands lightly clasped in her lap. "Alanna is right. I must go out among them—"

No, you must not risk yourself! She had not yet fully recovered from her fruitless attempt to save Marilla's life.

"I *will* go out among them," Illona repeated, her voice now carrying the icy authority of a Keeper, "even as I tended the man Garin in Nevarsin. Equal treatment for all is an honorable price, one that we all should be eager to pay."

"Thank you, *vai leronis,*" Jeram said. "I promised myself that if there were some way to help those people, I would. I had no idea it might come in such a form."

35

Marguerida leaned forward, her elbows braced on the conference room table, and rested her face in her hands. She had never felt comfortable in the Terran Headquarters complex, and now the air scoured her lungs and left her eyes red and itching. The ventilation system might remove the worst of the chemical stench, but it could not restore the natural sweetness of Darkovan air. Her head had gone beyond aching, her eyes refused to focus properly, and yet she searched on. What else could she do, with the pressure of foreboding pounding through her temples?

One more time . . . she thought wearily.

"*Domna* Marguerida?" came a man's voice from the direction of the door.

Startled, she swiveled her chair around. It was that man, Jeram or Jeremiah Reed, whatever his name was, the one Francisco had paraded before the Council to support his charges. Silently, she swore to find whoever let Jeram in and flay him alive.

"What are you doing here?" she said.

Jeram stepped into the room, carrying an insulated bottle. "I brought you some coffee."

Coffee! She could almost taste it, bitter and invigorating. The last of her own stores had been used up a year ago, and there would be no more. Darkover's climate would not support the cultivation of coffee beans, only the ubiquitous *jaco.*

"Where did you get it?" Her hand reached for the bottle with a will of its own. She snatched it back.

He set the bottle down on the work surface. "Never mind where I got it. I'm here to help."

Help? What could he possibly do except get in the way? If Francisco were still alive, she would suspect this offer was some nefarious scheme of his. No, not even Francisco at his most devious would think to bribe her with coffee!

Jeram drew up a second chair beside Marguerida's. For the first time, she realized what an interesting face he had. It was not a simple face, but it was a strangely attractive one, with guarded eyes, strong bones, and a small triangular scar over one cheek. Under other circumstances, she would have wanted him as a friend.

"I am here with the knowledge and permission of the Acting Regent of the Comyn and your own father," he said, looking at her with a disconcerting directness. "People are dying out there—in the city, in the encampment. People I care about, and I assume you do, too. This thing is bigger than either of us. Separately, I do not believe we have a chance to stop it."

Marguerida thought of Marilla, pale and utterly still when they laid her out. The two women had not been close, but she had known Marilla since her first year on Darkover. When Marguerida had fallen ill from threshold sickness on the trail, Marilla had offered her hospitality. There, in Marilla's house, Marguerida had first set eyes upon Mikhail. With Marilla's passing, she lost not only a fellow Comynara but yet another tie to the man she loved.

"I do not see what you can do," she said. "Katherine and I are both knowledgeable about computers. We've combed the files and found nothing of any use."

"You could look from now until doomsday, and still you won't find it," Jeram said. "You are looking in the wrong place."

"Good heavens!" Marguerida's chin jerked upward. "Is

there another, independent database? How can that be? You're supposed to be able to access everything from Medical."

"I don't think you'll find information on trailmen's fever, the vaccine, or even the expedition that brought back the immune serum, not in any unsecured system." Jeram's voice took on a new, steely edge.

He got to his feet and held out one hand to her. "Come with me, and I'll show you where we will find it."

Refusing his help, she got up. "And where is that?"

"Military HQ. To be specific, the Bioweapons Archives."

—— ◆ ——

"There," Jeram said, pointing to screen. "That's the virus the Allison team isolated."

Marguerida peered at the fuzzy electron-microscopic images and shivered. She was still in awe at the skill with which Jeram had maneuvered through the security systems of the military computers. It had not occurred to her that this system might be entirely independent of the civilian databases; she had had no idea it even existed.

"So that's what it looks like," she murmured. "A twist of fluffy yarn. What now?"

"See those codes?" he pointed to the side bar, where triplets of letters filled the space. "That's the genetic sequencing. And here," he tapped in a few instructions, and a different code appeared, "is the analysis of the protein coat. That determines, among other things, how the virus is transmitted, whether it can survive outside a host cell, and the severity of the illness it causes."

He shook his head. "This is one nasty bug. Normally, it's mild, like the common cold, but tinker with the receptors here and here—" he pointed to the diagram, "and, wham! it goes virulent."

Marguerida stared at Jeram. In a surprisingly short time, he had located the records of the expedition and the manufacture of the vaccine, as well as the exhaustive analyses of the virus.

"What next?" she asked.

He raked his hair back from his forehead in a gesture that reminded her of Domenic when he was thinking hard. "The beauty of this organism is that we don't need to vaccinate the entire population. The immune serum developed by the Allison team caused the fever virus to revert to its benign form. That will be our goal, too. The hard part will be making enough of it before we enter the terminal phase of its cycle."

At least, we've made a start, Marguerida thought. *We have something to work with.*

"What equipment will you need?" Marguerida asked.

"I can sequence the proteins from here, but to synthesize the serum in quantity, we'll need a lab and some pretty sophisticated equipment. This place isn't set up for anything that complex. I hope the facilities in Biochemistry are. I have to tell you, though, that my lab skills are seriously out of date. Is there anybody here with protein sequencing experience?"

"You mean, anybody still on Darkover? I don't think there ever was. I know a few dozen people who can read Terran Standard and operate a computer. I doubt any of them has so much as held a test tube."

He picked up the opened bottle of coffee, looked into its empty interior, and sniffed. "Then I'll have to come up with more of the good stuff."

Marguerida's curiosity finally got the better of her. "Where *did* you find it?"

Jeram's grin turned rakish, making him look years younger. "You've never been in Special Forces, have you? The first thing we do in a new port is to find a local source of coffee. Sometimes it's less than legal, but my conscience is clear in this case. This coffee came from a fellow with the Pan-Darkovan League. He made a small fortune selling it to us. Once the Federation left, so did his customers. He'll be thrilled to get the rest of his stock off his hands."

"Not as thrilled as *I'll* be to help drink it!"

— ✦ —

Lew Alton rode out from Comyn Castle and through the gates of Thendara shortly after dawn the next day. Illona, looking pale but strong in the manner of Keepers, went with him. At Domenic's insistence, a pair of Guardsmen accompanied them. They carried packs of food, skins of clean water, and rolls of blankets as well as swords. The night had been mild, with only a light drizzle. Raindrops dotted every blade of grass along the road. The air was moist and rich, the sun warm as it burned off the damp.

Already, men and beasts and carts filled with summer's bounty—crates of fresh greens and root vegetables, bushels of summer-pears and early apples, sacks of nuts and flour—had begun entering the city.

Beyond the gates, Lew nudged his horse off the main road and between the clusters of tents, past picketed chervines and cooking fires. The shanty encampment was larger and more orderly than he remembered. Crudely constructed sheds clustered around a rough dirt road leading to a pavilion cobbled together from smaller tents and blankets.

"It's Lord Alton and the *vai leronis*!" A cry went up.

A handful of men came out to meet them. Lew recognized the black-haired youth who had challenged them on their return to Thendara.

"We are here," Lew said, "to do what we can for those who are already ill. Kindly lead us to them."

The youth's face hardened. He stepped forward in an aggressive stance. "Liar and tyrant! Do you come to view our misery for your amusement? Or are you here to collect taxes for the air we breathe?"

One of the other men grabbed the young man's shoulder. "Don't be a fool, Rannirl! Talk like that will get your right hand chopped off! Besides, your father's beyond any medicine we have. His only hope is *laran* healing, and for that we need the good will of the *leronis*."

Face suddenly pale, Rannirl dropped to one knee. "I beg you, do not punish my father, who is old and sick, for the foolishness of his son. If there is anything—if only you can save him, then I will—I have nothing to give—"

Lew swung down from his mount during the boy's speech. He moved stiffly, for his joints did not bend easily this early in the morning. With a touch, he silenced the torrent of words and lifted Rannirl to his feet.

"Whatever talents I have were not granted to me for my own glorification but for the benefit of others. So let us hear no more of this, but bring us speedily to him."

The central pavilion had been set up as a hospital, with improvised pallets of straw and rough-spun sacking. Inside, three or four dozen beds were crammed together around narrow aisles, all of them occupied. Scattered coughs came from the men who lay there. Several Renunciates moved among them, pausing to speak with a patient here and there.

Illona followed Rannirl down the aisles. Lew ordered the Guards to bring in the blankets, waterskins, and hampers of food. One of the Renunciates supervised their distribution.

A short time later, Illona finished her examination and rejoined the two men. Her starstone hung unwrapped on its chain between her breasts. Blue fire sparkled within its crystalline depths as she tucked it under the neckline of her gray Tower robe. "Your father is indeed ill, but he is still strong. I have done what I can for him for the moment."

Lew refrained from mentioning that *laran* healing had not saved Marilla or that poor man at Nevarsin.

"Your father's name is Ulm," Illona said to Rannirl. "Was he the one who went in search of our friend, Jeram of Nevarsin?"

She had an exceptional memory for names, Lew thought. Whether this was due to her natural quick wit, early years performing memorized plays with the travel-

ers, or her training as a Keeper, he did not know. The
more he saw of her, the greater his appreciation for
Domenic's attachment to her. The two lovers had behaved with perfect propriety since returning to Thendara, but they could not disguise the depth of their
longing for one another. Lew's heart ached for them. He
hoped matters would work out, that Alanna herself
would come to see that her own best hope for happiness
lay elsewhere.

Rannirl looked surprised at Illona's question. "The very
same, to his cost if he contracted the fever in the city."

"It makes no more sense to blame city folk for carrying
the disease than to blame those from the country," Lew
said.

"It should ease your mind, as well as his, to know that by
the order of the Acting Regent, Jeram is well and free
among us," Illona said. "Even now, he is using his Terran
science to help find a cure."

"Truly?" Rannirl breathed. "Magic from the stars?"

Illona bit her lip and simply nodded, for to common people, *laran* was magic as well.

—— ✦ ——

When Lew returned to the city, Illona stayed behind to
work with the patients. In the Castle, Alanna was waiting in
her usual place beside Lew's fireplace. After settling him
with a hot drink, she plied him with one question after another about conditions in the shanty camp.

"Why, then," she said when he had finished relating the
events of the morning, "I must go down to those poor people, like Illona. I have no skill with a starstone, but surely,
there is need for a willing nurse."

"Alanna, think carefully. There is no need for you to go,
and the work will be difficult, the conditions stark." Lew
wondered whether he was right to oppose her wish. The girl
had spoken from an earnest desire to do good. She would
benefit from both hard work and a sense of usefulness.

She faced him, a fierce light in her eyes. "How can I sit here, in ease and idleness, when I might be of use? Why should Illona have meaningful work and not me? Am I to pass my life like a plaything, some doll, fit only for displaying fine dresses?" She held up her hands, spreading her soft, perfectly manicured fingers. "Was I not given two good hands, like everyone else? Why should I not be allowed to use them?"

"Calm yourself, child." Lew could not resist smiling. "You have convinced me!"

"And," she said, with a last triumphant lift of her chin, "in the company of the Renunciate healers, no one can question whether it is proper for me to be there! Not even Auntie Marguerida could object!"

———— ◆ ————

The plague had changed everything. Domenic felt the shift in the ambient texture of *laran* throughout Comyn Castle, in the very air he breathed. He had been too young when Regis Hastur died to appreciate how irrevocably his world had shifted. Now he was older, a participant as well as witness. Now he knew the difference.

He arrived early for a meeting of his advisory council in the Grand Hall that now functioned as the coordination center. A cold meal had been laid out on the tables along one side, nut-bread, cheese, and sliced roasted meat, with platters of buttery pastries and baskets of tawny Lowland peaches. Guardsmen, matrix mechanics, Renunciate healers, and crafters sat side by side, eating a quick meal and exchanging news.

Whether we find a way to stop this thing or limp on, our ranks decimated and our society in disarray, things will never be the same.

Marguerida walked through the arched doorway leading to the interior of the Castle, closely followed by Lew and Danilo. To Domenic, she appeared on the ragged edge of exhaustion. Shadows surrounded her golden eyes, and her lids were puffy from lack of sleep. Her skin had lost its glow, and her body seemed fragile rather than slender.

Domenic found himself irrationally angry with her. How dare she go without sleep or food, as she so obviously had, when so much depended upon her?

Marguerida flinched, clearly having caught his flash of emotion. She set her lips into a thin, defiant line, but Lew said to Domenic, "Let it be, *chiyu,* and do not add your own worry to her troubles."

"None of us has the right to render ourselves unfit," Domenic said. "We belong not only to ourselves but to the people we are trying to save. If, through pride or simple carelessness, we push ourselves to collapse, how can we help them?"

"Say no more on my behalf, Father," Marguerida said. "Nico, you are right to chide me. Work can become an obsession, like anything else. I must remind myself that our problems will not be solved in a single sleepless night."

Before Domenic could say anything more, the last two members of his informal council, Donal and Danilo, arrived. When they had all supplied themselves with *jaco* and settled in their places around the table, Domenic asked each of them to report any progress.

"Well, you want to know how we are getting on in the laboratory," Marguerida said, "and the answer is, not nearly well enough. Jeram's analyzed the viral DNA from the current fever and compared it to records of the old one." She rubbed the fingers of one hand over her temple. "As we suspected, they're not identical. We are definitely dealing with a new strain."

"So those who received the vaccine years ago have no immunity." Danilo's shoulders tensed, as if bracing for battle. He relaxed them forcibly, but his dark eyes lost none of their grim expression.

"That's right," she said. "And the worst of it is, we can't use the antibodies in their blood, either. Jeram says there's something in the enzyme receptor sites on the protein coat, or something like that, that make this one particularly tricky. So far, nothing he has tried has worked in a test tube. It could be months—years, even—before he hits on the right one."

"By then, there may not be anyone left to save," Donal muttered.

"Try to be a bit *less* hopeful, will you?" Marguerida said with unwanted sarcasm.

"I'm only saying what we're all thinking—" Donal gulped and lowered his gaze. "Forgive me, *vai domna.* I had no right to speak to you in such a manner."

"And I was unkind and impatient for my part," she answered, more gently.

"We're all tired and frightened," Domenic said. *Or if we are not, we soon will be.* "Let us not quarrel among ourselves. We have enemies enough."

"Yes," Marguerida said with a tiny sigh, "several trillions of them."

Donal inclined his head in agreement.

"Our best hope is to find someone who has survived this current strain," Marguerida said, briskly returning to the topic, "and use the antibodies in his blood to create a new immune serum."

Domenic shivered inside. Donal had reason to be pessimistic, even though it was tactless to speak those fears aloud. The figures from the Medical Center had put the mortality rate at an extremely high percentage when the disease reached its final cycle. The numbers of the dead kept climbing as more of the sick succumbed.

Marguerida wrapped her arms across her chest. Even without mental contact, Domenic knew what she was thinking, the heart-wrenching despair of watching those she loved slip away into darkness and being able to do nothing. In his mind, he saw her sitting at her husband's bedside, Mikhail's limp hand between hers, unshed tears glimmering in her eyes.

All the powers I have, my skills, my training, the shadow matrix, and still I cannot save him . . .

Another, darker, image rose up behind Domenic's eyes, and it seemed that he walked alone through Thendara's streets. Dusk had fallen, pooling like molten charcoal against the deserted buildings. Bodies the color of clay lay tumbled in doorways.

Alanna's vision . . . oh, gods, let it not come to that!

BOOK IV

36

The funeral for Marilla Lindir-Aillard took place a few days later, when she was laid to rest in an unmarked grave beside the Lake of Hali. Domenic attended in his capacity as Acting Regent of the Comyn and Hastur, along with Kennard-Dyan and his two sons. Illona insisted on coming, too.

"Although I never knew her, she was my grandmother and deserving of my respect," Illona said, forestalling Domenic's objections. "There are no Federation soldiers lying in ambush this time."

Marguerida and Lew had stayed behind in Thendara, continuing their search for a cure for the fever and dealing with the increasing numbers of its victims. Although she made no complaint, Domenic sensed that his mother would have liked to attend. The fever, and the fear it generated, shredded the very fabric of their society. Rituals like this funeral helped to bring them together.

The traditional ceremony was brief, with each person sharing aloud a memory of the dead woman. Marilla had not been an easy person, or openly loving, and yet each mourner drew out something positive about her. Perhaps, Domenic thought, she was more beloved in remembrance than in life. It was a sad thing to think about anyone.

Now whatever had tormented Marilla in life was over.

She would lie in the earth, and the seasons would pass, snow and rain and flowers, each in its proper time.

For a moment, all the sorrows of the world settled over Domenic's shoulders. His *laran* senses picked up a faint groaning, as if the planet itself echoed his sentiments. The sky shimmered, layer upon layer of veiling clouds, and the grasses bowed down in the fitful breeze.

How many more unmarked graves would there be in the days to come?

•   —— ◆ ——

After Marilla's funeral, Danilo rode out to the encampment outside the Thendara gates. The site was much larger than he expected, having swelled as the plague claimed more victims. His saddlebags held packets of herbal remedies, willow bark tea to reduce fevers, golden-flower to aid sleep, and firenze blossom poultices to soothe bed sores. He could have sent someone else, but he wanted to see for himself how the rotation of matrix healers that he and Darius-Mikhail organized had worked out.

Within the patchwork pavilion, men huddled under blankets in neat rows. Other men, and women too, crouched beside the pallets, sponging foreheads or spooning out cups of broth.

At the far end Alanna knelt by a makeshift bed. She wore an old gray gown and had covered her bright hair with a plain head scarf. So intent was she on her work that she did not see Danilo as he slipped past the door flap. Closing her eyes, she pulled the blanket over the face of her patient. She sat back, her hands loose across her lap, looking too exhausted to weep.

Varinna, from the city matrix mechanics, came forward to greet Danilo. She too looked tired, but infused with a new pride and purpose. The edge of defensiveness had left her features. She and her colleagues had, at long last, been recognized as skilled and valued professionals by the assembled Keepers.

Varinna accepted the packets of herbs with a smile.

"These are always welcome! Menella!" she called to a woman tending the sick, a Renunciate by her breeches and neatly cropped hair.

"Our thanks, *Dom* Danilo," the Renunciate, a plain-faced woman of middle years, said. "Our supply of willow bark is almost gone. We have been trying to control the worst fevers, for some believe it is the heat and not the disease itself that kills. Often the body burns itself out before it can recover."

"We have lost several who I think might have lived if their strength had not been depleted," Varinna added.

Danilo knew little of healing, but what Menella said made sense. "Jeram had word that a friend of his had fallen ill and asked me to check on him—Ulm, I think he is called. Which one is he?"

Varinna's smile brightened even more. "Come, see for yourself."

Outside the tent, a crude awning had been cobbled together of tattered bits of cloth, enough to keep off the midday sun. An old man sat on an improvised camp chair in the dappled shade, a blanket tucked around his legs. As they drew near, Danilo noticed the pallor beneath the grizzled beard, the hollowed cheeks. The old man turned his head at their approach, eyes bright beneath shaggy gray brows, and lifted one hand in greeting.

This man was sick . . . and is now recovering!

"He is our first success," Varinna said with a hint of triumph in her voice, "although I cannot claim sole credit. I suspect he was simply too stubborn to let a deadly plague get the better of him."

"Watch who you're calling *stubborn,* for 'tis much like the ember complaining of the fire's heat," Ulm replied. His voice was thin with an undertone like granite. Danilo liked him immediately. "And who have you brought to torment me today?"

"I am Danilo Syrtis, and I am more glad than I can say to see you well."

Ulm's eyes narrowed as if he were considering whether

the man before him, slight of build and dressed simply, might indeed be a Comyn lord. The moment of doubt passed. The old man pawed at the lap robe and struggled to rise.

Varinna insisted that Ulm remain seated. "You stay put, do you hear? None of this popping up and down! I won't have you relapse on me, you recalcitrant old chervine. Nursing you once was enough, but twice would be an insult."

As he settled back in his chair, Ulm peered up at Danilo. A wink twitched the corner of one eye. "I'd best mind her, m'lord. She'd got a tongue as sharp as a banshee's beak."

"Mind your own wagging tongue," Varinna responded, clearly enjoying the repartee. She tucked the blanket back into place and went inside the tent, leaving the two men to continue their conversation.

Danilo dragged over a square-cut log and set it on one end for an improvised stool. "Your friend Jeram will be pleased to hear of your recovery."

"Aye, he's been so concerned about his old friends, he has not set foot in this camp. Not that I complain, for what could he do here? Best that he keep to his own business— but he has not taken with the fever? Or fallen afoul of the Council?"

"Jeram is well, I assure you," Danilo said. "He is even now in the laboratories at the Terran Base, searching for a cure."

And you, my friend, may well be the key.

"Cure?" Ulm fell silent for a moment. "Now, then, that would be a thing indeed, even greater than flying through the stars."

"Jeram seeks your help in this," Danilo said.

"Mine? What can an old man like me do, who never sets foot off my mountain except to buy a bit of salt or a few ribbons for my wife? Is it with nuts and firewood, or wild chervines perhaps, that you aim to defeat this thing?"

"No, no," Danilo said, smiling in spite of himself. "Jeram can explain it himself. In this matter, my own understanding is as poor as that of the chervines you spoke of. Are you well enough to ride, or shall I send for a litter?"

Ulm said the only way he would be carried while lying down was after he was dead, and as for a horse, none would suit him better than his own pony. Varinna objected strenuously to Ulm going anywhere but back to his own bed. It took all of Danilo's diplomatic tact to convince her of the urgency. In the end, Ulm declared that useful work was the best medicine, and Varinna relented. Even so, she insisted that Ulm rest while his son saddled his pony.

Before they left, Danilo went back inside the pavilion to speak with Alanna. She had gone on to tending another patient. She held a basin of herb-infused water and a damp cloth on her lap.

"*Chiya,*" he said gently, "there was nothing more anyone could have done for that patient. Do not blame yourself."

She looked up from sponging the forehead of a sick woman, all the fire in her green eyes quenched. The woman burst out coughing, bringing up gobbets of blood-flecked sputum. Alanna waited until the fit had passed and then gently wiped the woman's lips and face.

"How long has it been since you slept?" Danilo asked. Alanna shrugged. "You return to the Castle at night for a hot meal and your own bed, do you not?"

Alanna shook her head. "I make up a pallet in the corner. Do not scowl at me. I must be near if one of the patients needs me."

"Child, you must rest, or you will become ill yourself."

She shot him a fierce look. "*Now* is when these people need my help, and I will not sit idly by while they suffer."

"Alanna—"

"No, I will hear no more!" she cried, with a passion that surprised him. In her words, Danilo heard something more than stubbornness or pride. Desperation, certainly. *Despair?*

"Stay then," he said, knowing that nothing he said would change her mind, "and may the gods watch over you."

———— ✦ ————

Danilo expected that even the short journey from the shanty camp would tire the old man, but for most of it, Ulm seemed as comfortable on his shaggy mountain pony as sitting in a chair. The placid beast, a blue roan with a lopsided star on its forehead, stepped along with almost no need for rein or spur. The two seemed to understand one another perfectly.

Ulm chuckled at Danilo's concern and said that being up and doing was as good medicine as any. Danilo agreed, but he noticed that Ulm clung a little more tightly to the pommel of his saddle as they passed the city gates.

The Terran Base was strange and forbidding even to a man in good health, so Danilo persuaded Ulm to visit his own chambers in the Castle while someone went to fetch Jeram. A short time later, warmed by a small summer fire and plied with hot soup and even more spiced cider, Ulm nodded off.

Watching the old man sleep, Danilo remembered spending many hours in the very same chair. He had felt old and useless, corroded from within by unremitting grief.

Ulm is right. The best medicine is knowing you are needed, that it matters whether you live or die.

Danilo roused from his meditation at a tapping at the door. As Jeram entered, Danilo raised a finger to his lips and pointed at Ulm, now snoring gently.

Frowning, Jeram hissed, "I didn't mean for you to drag him from his sick bed!"

"He's only tired out from the ride," Danilo whispered back. "There was no time to be lost, and he refused a litter."

"What's that?" Ulm straightened up with a start and looked about. "Jeram! It's a sight to see you! I was only resting my eyes."

Jeram crossed to the old man and took his hand. "It is good to see you, my friend."

"Aye, laddie, though you're no vision of beauty yourself."

Jeram grinned. Purplish shadows rimmed his eyes, and he was in obvious need of a shave.

Danilo said firmly, "I did not bring this man here for a social call but because he has *recovered.*"

For a long moment, Jeram stared at Ulm. Realization dawned. Jeram's eyes widened. He whispered something in Terran Standard, a prayer of thanks perhaps.

"Is this true, Ulm?" Jeram said. "You are well again?"

"Aye to that as well, although a bit wobbly in the legs. It takes more than a spot of fever to put me in my grave."

From the heavy wooden sideboard, Danilo brought Jeram a mug of cider, still warm and aromatic. "I said only that you needed him. I thought it better that you explain why."

"Some nonsense about finding a cure," Ulm said. "The Lady from Nevarsin tended me, and what more could any man ask? The gods willed that I live, and so I have."

"Perhaps it was the will of the gods," Jeram said carefully, "but how they went about accomplishing this miracle is something we men may do as well. I will try to explain."

Jeram took the chair Danilo indicated. The leather upholstery creaked comfortably under his weight. He took a sip of the cider, grimaced, and set the mug down on the low table. "We talk about *fighting* the fever, as if it were an army we could defeat. In a way, it is. A tiny one, with many thousands of soldiers, and the battlefield is your own blood."

Ulm glanced down at his chest with a skeptical expression, but uttered no protest.

"To defeat this army," Jeram went on, "your body creates its own soldiers. Sometimes the defenders are too few and too late. In your case, however, they were strong and clever. They won. Should the enemy attempt another invasion, they would be instantly ready."

Now Ulm nodded in understanding. " 'Tis said that any man who lives through the trailmen's fever cannot fall sick from it again. And there are other illnesses—patchfoot in chervines—that are the same way."

"Yes, a case of the fever confers lifelong immunity. Now, you know I am *Terranan* and have training in their science.

What I mean to do, with your permission, is to create enough of these soldiers to protect other patients. A mercenary army, if you like, that we can send anywhere."

Ulm's expression was so incredulous that Danilo thought if the speaker had been anyone but Jeram, the old man would have laughed in his face. Danilo suggested that if Ulm had rested enough, they might all go to the laboratory, where Ulm might see for himself. The old man agreed, and they left the Castle for the Terran Base.

The Medical Center churned with activity. Worktables filled Jeram's laboratory, slabs of flat black set on frameworks of gleaming metal and covered with racks of the most flawless glassware Danilo had ever seen. Tubing connected various beakers and flasks, transparent corkscrews and vats. Some contained colorless liquids, others held what appeared to be weak broth, but Danilo doubted that was what it really was. A team of men, and some women, too—Renunciates and Marguerida's friend, Katherine—moved about the laboratory, operating small devices, measuring liquids with graduated tubes, mixing powders.

"Zandru's frozen backside," Ulm muttered. "Who would have thought such a place existed?"

One of the workers broke off what he was doing and hurried toward them. "Jeram! Praise Aldones, you're back. The protease sequencer is down to sixty percent efficiency, and as near as I can make out, the reagent's contaminated. It'll take two days to synthesize another batch—"

"It's all right, Ethan," Jeram said, patting the young man on the shoulder, "I'll look at it in a minute. Come this way, Ulm, and you, too, *Dom* Danilo." He led them to a quieter corner of the room. The wall-mounted shelving held various strange devices of metal, plastic and glass. A table-high freestanding cabinet doubled as storage and workspace. "Your body, Ulm, has done in a few days what it would take weeks—tendays, I mean—with all this equipment."

Ulm looked blank, so Danilo asked, if that were true, why did so many die?

"Because this is a particularly virulent agent," Jeram

said. "It acts so fast and generates such a high fever that most people don't have time to produce enough antibodies."

"So they die first?" Danilo said.

Jeram placed a chair beside the cabinet and gestured for Ulm to sit. "If we could keep the patients alive long enough, more might recover. That's one of the approaches we've been trying, medicines that slow down the rate of viral replication. Now," he looked at Ulm, "we can use your antibodies as a template—a set of instructions—so we can give sick people the same level of immune response they would eventually develop. If we do it right, they will then pass on an attenuated, harmless form of the virus."

Ulm looked confused and frightened. His gaze flickered over the room, its strange equipment, the bustle of incomprehensible activity. Danilo, who had years of encounters with off-worlders, did not understand half the things Jeram said. How could Ulm comprehend what was asked of him? How could he give consent?

"This will only take a minute." Jeram told Ulm to sit while he rummaged in the shelves and brought out a flat box covered with panels of dark glass. He set the box on the cabinet and touched the panels along its side. An array of colored lights winked across its top surface.

Danilo knew something of Terran medicine. Giving a sample of blood was neither dangerous nor painful. With his *laran,* he sensed the old man's bewilderment shift toward terror.

Gently, Danilo took Ulm by the arm. "Let me go first. Jeram, you will take some of my blood and explain to Ulm what you are doing."

"*Vai dom!*" Ulm, stunned, blurted out. "You must not bleed for me!"

Danilo hushed him with a gesture, then sat quietly as Jeram rolled up his sleeve and went about taking the sample. He was not afraid of shedding his own blood; he would have given it all, and his very life, to defend Regis.

The procedure was accomplished in a few minutes, and

then Ulm took Danilo's place. The whitened eyebrows lifted slightly at the touch of the automated tourniquet, but otherwise Ulm gave no sign of any distress.

"Is that all there is to it?" Ulm asked, rolling down his sleeve.

"To your part, yes," Jeram said. "Our work will be fractionating and analyzing the sample you've given us. Once we've programmed the sequencers, the computers will do the rest. Ulm, I can't tell you how grateful I am—we all are. If this works, you will have saved thousands of lives all over Darkover."

"Well, I don't know about that," Ulm said, looking uncomfortable.

"Speaking for the Comyn Council as well as myself, we stand in your debt," Danilo said. "Will you accept the hospitality of the Castle?"

Ulm shook his head. "No, what would I do in such a place? Besides, Rannirl will fret if I'm not back soon. My place is in the camp, and then home before snow closes the passes."

"You came to Thendara for help," Danilo said, "and you will not return empty-handed. Let us at least show our gratitude."

For a moment, Ulm's expression took on the aspect of a hawk newly freed from its hood. "Never came asking for gratitude. Only justice. Only what's due."

Danilo had handled birds of prey as a boy, and he recognized the flash of pride. Any further offers would only shame this proud old man. "Then let me ride with you back to your people at the camp," he said gravely, "while you explain to me exactly what the matter is, that you came to Thendara for your rights."

37

Jeram had been full of optimism at first, for the immune serum he extracted from Ulm's blood performed perfectly in both test tube and computer simulations. When he tried to synthesize it, however, he met with dismal failure. Something in the sample, some incorrigible trace of biochemical chaos, defied replication.

He ran the protein assembly program four times and came up with four different and equally useless results. Each seemed to make sense, but when he tested them, the proteins were physiologically inert. He didn't think the molecular assemblers were at fault, so the problem must lie in the information he fed into them.

In the laboratory, Jeram stared at the computer screen, his eyes watering with the strain of a second night on double-strength coffee instead of sleep, and restrained himself from putting his fist through it. At least then he would be doing something, instead of retrying the same futile tests.

Jeram cleared the screen and leaned back. The chair creaked under his weight. In an instant, he became aware that he was not alone in the laboratory. He turned his head, his neck joints popping.

Marguerida stood at the door, wrapped in a thick shawl, earthy green wool knitted in interlocking cable stitches. "When was the last time you slept?"

"*Domna,* don't badger me. I need a miracle, not a mother."

"Point taken." She gave a self-deprecating smile and brought up a second chair. "Now, tell me what's going on."

"It's what's *not* going on." He tapped the last coding algorithm on to the screen and explained the problem.

Marguerida nodded, her eyes thoughtful. She might not have advanced scientific training, Jeram reminded himself, but she was University-educated and literate, an intelligent woman who had been exposed to a variety of cultures and had successfully adapted to them. Sometimes he forgot she was not Darkovan.

"I am and I'm not," she said absently, responding to his unvoiced thought. "I was born here and spent my first five years in Thendara, most of that time in the John Reade Orphanage. After Sharra was destroyed, Father took me away. I grew up on Thetis."

"A very different world from this one." Jeram had heard of the balmy climate and warm, shallow seas of that planet.

"Returning to Darkover in my twenties was a strange experience. I had almost no memories of this place, and yet it felt like home. I knew things I couldn't possibly have learned. It wasn't until I fully recovered my *laran* that everything began to make sense. It was like remembering who I truly was. I don't know what I would have done without Istvana and my other teachers at Neskaya. Gone mad, I suppose."

Jeram looked away, thinking how similar their stories were. Not where they were born, but the suppressed memories and newly awakened psychic abilities, the way their pasts had shadowed them. The teachers who had saved their sanity.

"I wonder . . ." she said. "How much do you know about *laran* monitoring?"

Jeram replied that it had been done to him at Nevarsin Tower. Puzzled, he asked, "Why?"

"I learned a little, first at Arilinn and then at Neskaya. It's the most basic level of Tower training. I never had the desire to go further, but anyone who works as a monitor must be able to not only sense but also actively adjust the physiological processes of those in their care—breathing, for example, or heart rate. Even hormonal levels."

Jeram shook his head, confused. He knew she had a point, but he was too tired to follow her logic.

"How different can this antibody be from the other natural substances of a human body?" she said. "If a trained circle, working under the direction of a Keeper, can separate out atoms of copper from crude ore, then it stands to reason they might also be able to complete your analysis."

"I don't know, it's pretty tricky stuff. If the computers can't handle it . . ."

Another part of Jeram's mind insisted he was thinking like a head-blind Terran, trying the same thing over again in the insane hope of getting a different result. Maybe it was time to start thinking like a Darkovan.

Marguerida pressed on, her voice gaining in certainty. Her golden eyes glowed faintly, as if some inner fire had sprung to life. "Maybe your computers can't replicate the Darkovan antibodies because there's more to them than a simple chain of molecules. Maybe there's another dimension, the *laran* that's bred into us."

"Certainly, your psychic abilities go beyond anything in the Federation," Jeram admitted. "I have some *laran* myself . . ."

Enough to blow me out of the water when you blanked out my memories.

Marguerida flinched visibly at his thought.

"*Laran* is just a human trait, developed through natural selection and isolation," Jeram said. "The computers should compensate for the genetic drift."

"That's where you're wrong," Marguerida said. "There's no question that Darkover was colonized by a Lost Ship. Some time after Darkover's beginning, if the stories are true, human women bore children fathered by *chieri*"—seeing Jeram's look of confusion, she explained—"a nonhuman sapient race, strongly telepathic, hermaphroditic, and extremely long-lived. They may be extinct now, but at least one was still alive during the time of Regis Hastur. Linnea or Danilo may know more of what happened to him—her, I'm not sure. Legend says that our *laran* originated with them. You can see traces of their heritage in the Comyn— not only our *laran,* but the six fingers many of us have, as well as pale eyes and slender build."

"That still doesn't explain why I can't replicate the immunoglobulins from Ulm's blood," Jeram said doggedly. "First of all, the donor is not Comyn, and second, as I told you, the computer protocols already include the necessary adjustments."

"That is, if the changes are purely physical," Marguerida said. She paused, rubbing her fingertips across her temples and muttering under her breath about *this damned headache.* "What if there's a *laran* field around the protein molecule, a psychic vibration, something that can't be measured by ordinary instruments? Something that could be perceived and manipulated by a trained telepathic mind? I know how fantastical it sounds, but in the twenty-odd years I've been on this planet, I have seen more things than are dreamt of in *anyone's* philosophy."

It was as outlandish an idea as Jeram had ever heard, and he had half a mind to tell Marguerida so. But what better idea did he have to offer?

It was time, he repeated to himself, to think like a Darkovan.

The decision of whether to perform the experiment in the Terran Base or in the newly refurbished Comyn Tower, as well as all the subsequent arrangements, took far longer than Jeram expected. He understood that ordinarily the Keeper simply decided things, and her word was law. This circle, however, consisted of Istvana Ridenow, Linnea Storn—the elegant beauty who, Jeram gathered, had once been consort to Regis Hastur—Moira DiAsturien, and Laurinda MacBard, with Illona acting as their monitor.

Each one of them was accustomed to having her own way, and while they were exquisitely courteous to one another, their discussions amounted to exercises in diplomatic pigheadedness.

At last, the Keepers agreed that, despite the advantages of working in the Terran Medical Center, with supplies at hand and where their results could be easily verified by computer analysis, they preferred a setting that could be safely shielded. The Terran Base provided only flimsy protection against the fear and anger pervading the city. Comyn Tower, on the other hand, had been designed to insulate the minds of those who worked within.

Despite Jeram's reluctance to relocate, Marguerida accepted the decision as an accomplished fact. She recruited Ethan and his friends to transport the blood samples, reagents, and various portable instruments that Jeram determined were the bare minimum.

Comyn Tower, as he understood it, had been abandoned for some time. Another Tower, referred to in strained whispers as *Ashara's,* had functioned in one capacity or another until fairly recently. He asked Marguerida why it was not still in use, and she pretended not to hear.

Housekeepers had clearly been at work in Comyn Tower, for the entry hall and stairwells had been dusted, and intricately woven rugs laid on the stone floors. The room they were to use was three-quarters of the way up the physical tower itself, a space Marguerida called a *matrix laboratory,* although Jeram could not imagine doing experiments here.

The room had a surprisingly light, airy atmosphere. Panels of translucent blue stone alternated with the smooth, fine-grained granite of the walls. A sideboard bore an array of pastries, candies, honey-glazed nuts, and beverages. With a good deal of bustle, the equipment from the Medical Center was arranged on a round table, and benches and cushions were brought in for everyone.

After Ethan and his friends left, a hush fell over the room. Laurinda MacBard took the centripolar place. Ever since their first meeting, Jeram had found her intimidating, although she treated him with scrupulous politeness. The other Keepers assembled around the table, with Illona sitting on a bench set to one side. Marguerida led Jeram to a seat along the opposite wall.

"I'll need to tell them—" he began.

"They will know. Illona says she has linked to you before. She will be monitoring, but she'll also be facilitating the rapport with you."

Marguerida left, and the work began. The women in the circle set their starstones on the table around the vial containing a sample of Ulm's blood. The sparkling blue-white stones caught and intensified the light. Then, as Jeram watched, they began to glow. Slowly, the light grew into a ring and then spread through the room. It bathed the faces of the Keepers in a pale, eerie radiance. Jeram closed his eyes against the brightness . . .

. . . and felt a faint touch, like silk brushing the inside of his skull. Although he could not have told how, he recognized the mental presence of Illona and, through her, Laurinda.

For a long moment, he hovered, suspended in a sea of misty blue-white, surrounded by cool, pulsating globes of the same light. Gradually, the colors shifted, so that he traveled between swirling disks of red, in a sea of golden liquid. The disks faded to mere ghosts, residual energy imprints of the red blood cells. Vision shifted, as if he were approaching a planetary system from space. He passed between spheres of color and energy, some as huge as gas giants, others tiny asteroid belts. These were not celestial objects but particles of infinitesimal size.

A sound like a vast ocean filled his hearing. He shrank further and now perceived that the golden sea was not entirely liquid. Shapes emerged from the faint currents, complex threads and globules, the tiny nodes of electrolytes, nutrients, and waste.

Show us, whispered a distant voice, so subtle it did not disturb the slow, floating dance of the molecules. *Which one?*

How could he tell? The long, immensely complex chains loomed ever larger. There were dozens of them, all different. With an effort, he summoned an image, the pattern on the computer screen. Some parts of the molecule resembled any other immunoglobulin, but the specific sites *here* and *here* . . . He forced himself to concentrate, to bring the configuration into focus.

Ah, yes! responded the voice, and then trailed away.

Nausea rose up, and his throat stung with acid. He blinked, his eyes focusing reluctantly.

Illona leaned over him, one hand on his arm, and urged him to close his eyes. Sick and disoriented, Jeram obeyed. He felt a cool touch on his brow, and his unease vanished.

When he opened his eyes again, Illona was smiling at him. The women of the circle had risen, some stretching, others helping themselves to the food and drink that had been laid out on the sideboard. They had, Illona explained, been working for over an hour, and that was a long time for anyone who was not accustomed to it. At her advice, he ate some fruit, sweet and intense like sun-dried apricots. It helped to steady his nerves.

With a nod, as one acknowledging an equal, Laurinda handed him a small vial of serum.

As soon as Jeram felt steady enough, he took the sample back to the Medical Center laboratory. Excitement thrilled up his spine, sweeping away the last remnants of fatigue, as he watched the indicators change.

Positive . . . positive . . .

Marguerida joined him a short time later, just as the computer simulation confirmed the test tube results. "Well?"

He grinned. "Break out the champagne. We still need the final litmus test, a live subject, but yes, I think we've got a biologically active serum here."

In the end, Jeram decided to test the serum on three people in the city clinic-shelters, each in a different stage of the fever. The most ill, a young woman, had been unconscious for the last day, her body radiating heat like an oven.

The next morning, the fevers of all three patients had broken. Over the following days, even the woman who had been critically ill was able to sit up and take some food.

Jeram sent word to Domenic and then returned to Comyn Tower to ask Laurinda to reconvene the circle. She received him in the kitchen, of all places. When he entered, she was kneading bread on a floury work table, rhythmically folding and pushing the elastic dough. With her hair tied back under a gaily striped kerchief, her sleeves rolled up to the elbows, and her forehead glistening with sweat, she looked like a peasant wife, not the Keeper of Dalereuth Tower.

"Oh, it's you," she said. "Sit down, but don't talk to me until I've got this settled."

Laurinda smoothed the dough into a huge earthenware bowl, scraped the table surface clean, rinsed her hands, and sat down facing him. "There. I feel almost human again. I take it from your expression and the jubilation you're practically shouting mentally, you have good news."

"The serum worked better than we hoped!" he told her. "How soon can we have more?"

"That depends," she said heavily, wiping her face with her kerchief, "on how much you need."

An icy trickle shot down Jeram's spine. "We need enough to treat everyone who's sick. I thought that was understood." He gave her Darius-Mikhail's current figures. "We'll also need to begin a prophylactic program, beginning with health care workers. Of course," he went on, trying to sound encouraging, "distribution will take time. We won't need it all at once."

Laurinda shook her head. "Your heart is good, but you do not understand what you are asking. A circle of Keepers, the most powerful minds on Darkover, took an entire session to produce what we gave you."

"Which was enough for a dozen patients," Jeram said.

"That is all we can do at any one time. *Laran* work is exhausting on both physical and psychic levels. It will take us days to regain enough strength to do the work." Her expression gentled. "We will make more serum for you, do not fear."

"Just not at once, or any greater quantity?"

Laurinda's gaze flickered, and in that brief instant, Jeram caught her own frustration. No wonder she'd been punching the bread dough.

We've come so close! There must be another way, something else we can do!

"You are all Keepers," Jeram said desperately. "Could you not each head up a circle, so that we have four—or five, if Illona can do the work—groups working on it? What about asking the other Towers to help?"

"Even if that were possible, the work would take far longer, so there would be no advantage in dividing our forces," Laurinda said. "As it is, there are not enough circle workers in Thendara, perhaps in all the Domains, to do what you ask. Once, perhaps, but now we are few and scattered."

Jeram gulped, remembering how appalled Lew and then Silvana had been by his desire to rid himself of his own *laran.*

"What are we to do then?" he cried. "Let people die, when we know how to save them?"

"I am more sorry than I can say," Laurinda said, "but we can help no one if we burn ourselves out."

Jeram had once caught the edge of a blaster beam. Sick and shaken, he had been confined to a rejuvenation tank while skin and nerve and muscle healed. Now he felt as if he had been shot full in the belly. Numbly, he walked from Comyn Tower, across the courtyard, through the Castle gates and toward the city beyond. Someone called out to him, but he had not the will or voice to respond.

Until now, he had thought the worst thing would be to accomplish nothing, to watch the people he loved and the planet he called home die, helpless to save them. But this was far, far worse.

Some will live, and some will die. Who will decide?

The Council? Would the Comyn seize the tiny supply of serum for themselves? No, he could not believe that. He knew Lew and Domenic and Danilo—yes, and Marguerida—too well to believe they would act in such a selfish way.

Me? Will I be the one to deal out life or death?

He walked along the streets, through swirls of activity. Even the fear of the plague could not keep everyone inside. Life must be lived, and Darkover's summer was all too brief. In a market square, half the stalls stood empty, but others were laden with food and leather goods, finely worked knives, harnesses, beaded scarves, and ribbons. A musician sang while another strummed a guitar and a little girl danced. Down an alley, two ragged boys played with hoops and sticks. Through it all, Jeram moved like a ghost.

His feet carried him to the entrance of the Terran Base. *I'm the one with the training. It's up to me to find another way. There must be something else . . .*

In the laboratory, his crew rushed to meet him. They looked edgy and exhausted, worn thin with worry and relentless work. Their faces fell when they saw his expression.

"What's the matter?" Ethan asked.

"What more can go wrong?" said someone else.

"At the maximum rate the Keepers' circle can produce the serum, it will be only a trickle," Jeram said. "We'll make more, of course, but it will be too little, too late."

Ethan looked away, chewing on his lower lip. "My cousin, Geremy, is sick. We won't have the serum in time for him, will we?"

"I don't know—" Jeram bit off the words. There were a few more doses left from the batch the circle had made. They'd used three from the dozen the Keepers had made. That left nine doses. He could eke the serum out to ten if he dared to dilute it. If he took one dose for Ethan's cousin, would it be stealing? Who would die then, who might have lived?

How will we decide?

— ✦ —

"Jeram, I'd like to speak with you."

Lost in his own tortured thoughts, Jeram had not seen Marguerida enter the laboratory. A quality like steel energized her. Ethan and the others stepped back to let her pass. She moved briskly between the tables of equipment.

"I have an idea, a way around the production problem," she said, "but we'll have to clear the lab. I can't take any chances."

Her plan sounded mysterious and somewhat sinister to Jeram, but that could be his own bone-deep weariness speaking. Marguerida's last idea, he reminded himself, had been a good one. Within short order, she tactfully but firmly ejected everyone but the two of them. She managed to give the rest of the team important tasks elsewhere, so there were no grumbles.

"I'll need a work space with absolute privacy," she said briskly, "a sample—either the original serum or the one the circle made—and the protein substrate solution. As much of it as you've got."

Surely she'd gone mad, Jeram thought. The team had indeed prepared quantities of the amino acid building blocks ready to be turned into serum. The circle of Keepers had worked with a soupy mixture, the ingredients dissolved in a sterile solution. Jeram loaded the storage vat on a cart, wheeled it into the laboratory, and assembled the rest of the supplies Marguerida asked for, including a small sample of Ulm's immune serum. At her direction, he placed a chair between the vat and the work table.

After making sure everything was within easy reach, Marguerida nodded in satisfaction. "You'd better go, too."

Suspicion curdled inside Jeram. She had strong *laran*, but as far as he knew, no single person could act as a circle. Wasn't it dangerous to work without a monitor? He asked what she proposed to do.

"You're going to have to trust me on this. And no, I've never done it before, but I don't want to risk anything hap-

pening to you." She fixed him with her tiger-bright gaze.
"Now *go.*"

Jeram walked to the door and stepped through, but he
did not close it completely. He left a crack open and
paused just outside, where she would not be able to see
him. The only sound from the laboratory interior was her
breathing, quick and light.

He leaned toward the crack, peering through. Marguerida bent over the vat, as if trying to penetrate its secrets or, by force of will, to transform it into the life-saving
serum.

A tracery of lightning crackled on the inside of Jeram's
skull. Marguerida was using her *laran.*

She was planning something dangerous, or she would
not be doing it secretly. Any properly trained monitor
would certainly halt the operation right now.

Did she know what she was doing? Did she realize the
risk?

Jeram put one hand on the door and then drew back. His
own life had been a series of risks, everything from fleeing
into the Hellers when the last Federation ship departed, to
deciding to trust Silvana and Illona and then Lew, to making his confession to the Council.

The plague had eliminated safe, tested options. Marguerida, with her husband, had saved the Council once, at
the Battle of Old North Road. If there was even a remote
chance she could succeed now, he had no right to interfere.
The risk was hers to take.

Slowly, without taking her eyes off the vat, Marguerida
removed her glove. The skin on the back of her hand
looked ordinary enough, pale from having been covered
for so long. Then she raised her hand and held it over the
vat. Jeram discarded all notion of it being *ordinary.*

Imprinted on her palm, melded to her flesh, something
glowed blue and white like a living starstone. That was impossible—how could the psychoactive crystal be *inside* her
hand? And yet, there it was, and with each passing moment, it pulsed more brightly.

Jeram watched, unable to tear his gaze away and yet filled with an ever-increasing sense of dread. He had seen the work of Marguerida's matrixed hand before, under very different circumstances.

... the Old North Road, the caravan of funeral carriages and men on horseback. Shouts, horses neighing, wheeling. Swords raised ...

... a woman with hair like a flame and golden eyes, lifting her hand ... her hand a starburst of eye-searing brilliance ...

He had thought, in that wild moment before the trees caught fire and men fell screaming to the muddy earth, that she held a miniature sun, a hand-sized nuclear device, far beyond the Federation's technology.

She did not hold the white-hot sphere, she *was* it. Even across the room and behind the metal and duraplas door, Jeram felt her power. Through his own *laran,* he experienced her ability to perceive and manipulate molecules.

Time lost meaning for Jeram, except for the gradual awareness that he was no longer an observer. Unconsciously, his mind slipped into rapport with hers. Although he did not know how, he began sending her mental energy. She took it, spun it together with her own *laran,* and funneled it through the imprint on her palm.

Brightness surged through their linked minds. Amino acids shifted, aligned, bonded. Patterns emerged, mirroring those in his memory. From his work with Laurinda and the others, Jeram recognized the molecules forming in the center of the vat. Working alone, this single woman had created the same amount of immune serum as had an entire circle of Keepers.

A shimmer swept through the dissolved substrate. At first, Jeram sensed it as a ripple in a still pond. Then the waves *shifted.* A reverberation emerged, initially subtle, then building in intensity. At last, it filled the entire container of solution. Here and there, proteins vibrated out of harmony, sharp motes of dissonance. He felt her stretch farther and deeper to eliminate impurities and inactive molecules.

Somehow, beyond all possibility, Marguerida was using the matrix and the immense force of her mind to convert the entire vat to immune serum. Jeram feared she would bleed herself dry, but he dared not interrupt her concentration. All he could do was pour out his own energy through her mind, as best he could.

Eventually, the flow of power faltered. The blue-white radiance on Marguerida's palm dimmed, shifting to lavender, then darkening to blood-red.

Physical awareness returned to Jeram. He was breathing hard and his pulse thundered in his throat. Trembling, he steadied himself against the doorframe. A sound came from within the room, the thud of a falling body.

Heedless of his own exhaustion, Jeram darted into the laboratory. Marguerida lay in a graceless sprawl on the floor. Her skin had turned the color of ashes and she did not seem to be breathing.

38

Domenic stood upon a balcony overlooking the garden courtyard of Comyn Castle and the city beyond. Late afternoon sun slanted across the paving stones, the benches and arbors, the beds of ornamental herbs. The flowers had faded, and the first dry leaves lay in rumpled piles. By tomorrow, the gardeners would have raked them up, only to have even more tumble to the ground. The brief, glorious Darkovan summer was drawing to a close.

He thought how little had been accomplished this season, with the interruption of the trailmen's fever, and yet how much. The alliances born of dire necessity were already evolving. He was beginning to see a way through the current crisis. Only this morning, he had received word that Jeram's serum worked. Now the problem was to make enough for everyone, but Domenic felt hopeful that, too, would be solved. Sooner or later, his father would recover . . .

When Domenic's thoughts turned to the dilemma of his feelings for Illona and Alanna, however, he could see no solution.

Behind him, a door opened. As if summoned by his thoughts, Illona glided into the room. His heart brightened at the sight of her. They had each been so occupied with their respective tasks this last tenday that he had seen her but little. She looked thinner and more intense.

"Domenic, *cario mio,* there is no easy way to say this. I am sorry to be the bearer of bad news once again. Something terrible has happened to your mother."

For a long moment, Domenic could not speak. His heart leaped in his throat. For all his life, Marguerida had been a tower of strength, a steady, constant presence, endlessly resourceful, in turns opinionated and kind, but never ill . . .

Never ill . . .

Somehow, he forced his fear into words. "Has—has she contracted trailmen's fever?"

"No, nothing like that. Please, sit down, and I will explain. You know that Jeram's serum has proven effective?"

"Yes, he told me so, himself." Domenic lowered himself to the stone bench and Illona sat beside him.

Was there some unanticipated difficulty, some questionable side effect? Had Mother, in her typical impetuous manner, tried it on herself?

Illona glanced at him, startled. "No, it seems to be safe. The patients we gave it to are recovering. But the Keepers' circle can make only a small amount of it at a time, and only slowly. You know your mother—"

"She would find some way, not counting the risk to herself. What did she do?"

"*Domna* Marguerida used her *laran*—her shadow matrix, that is—to produce a massive amount of serum. Unmonitored, she did the work of an entire circle a thousand times over. Aldones only knows how she generated that much power. It's possible she reached through the shadow matrix into the Overworld."

The Overworld . . . Domenic shivered.

"One thing is certain," Illona went on. "Her accomplishment was not without cost. Jeram found her, unconscious and not breathing, beside the vat of transformed serum."

"Is she—Did she—"

Illona took his hands in hers. Her touch, added to their *laran* bond, calmed him.

She is alive, that is the important thing, but in a strange state, neither sleeping nor awake nor in an ordinary coma.

These we could deal with. None of us can reach her mind, not even Domna *Istvana.*

"What can I do? Where is she?"

"We took her to Mikhail's chamber, hoping that being near him would bring her ease." From Illona's expression, Domenic understood this had made no visible difference. "As for what you can do, that is why I am here, to bring you to her. Sometimes, love finds a way when skill cannot."

Domenic and Illona hurried down the interior corridor and down a flight of stairs, through the labyrinth of the Castle.

"Does my grandfather know?" Domenic asked, as they crossed the inner courtyard, heading for the Tower.

"He is with her even now."

"And my brother and sister?"

The news would strike both of them hard, but Yllana would be more deeply affected. She had rallied after Mikhail's injuries in part because of Marguerida's steady presence. What would she do now, how would she manage, when Marguerida was stricken? At least, she would have the loving support of Katherine and Hermes.

Domenic was less concerned for his brother. Rory loved both their parents, but he had made a life and home for himself in the City Guards. He had the discipline of his work, and Niall, to sustain him.

"Istvana decided not to send word to them yet," Illona said, clearly uneasy, "just you and *Dom* Lewis. They will have to be told soon, but we are still evaluating your mother's condition. Until we know more about what happened to her and her prospects for recovery, the fewer people who know, the better. We cannot risk premature news generating wild rumors that the serum is tainted."

"We have to tell them!" Domenic stormed. "We can't keep something like this secret, not about their own mother!"

Illona flinched and instantly, Domenic regretted his hot words. The decision was not hers to make. Nor was it Istvana's or Laurinda's, or even Grandfather Lew's.

No, it's mine.

Together, they rushed up the stairs of Comyn Tower. Domenic burst into the chamber where his parents lay, Illona on his heels. He had visited his father a number of times since the duel, although not nearly as often as his mother had. On those occasions, he had been struck with a sense of light and stillness, the faint shimmer of the *laran* field that preserved Mikhail's life. Now the room seemed narrow and dark. The air tasted of unshed tears.

Marguerida lay on a second bed, her upper body propped on pillows and wrapped in her favorite knitted shawl, the one with intertwined cable stitches. Lew and Istvana attended her. The Keeper looked grim but resolved; her uncovered starstone shone like a piece of the sun at her throat.

Domenic bent over his mother. Her cheeks had gone pasty pale. No hint of color brightened her lips. The corners of her mouth were drawn down. Her brows tensed, creating an expression of intense concentration or of great pain. Behind her closed lids, her eyes jerked from side to side. Her breathing was irregular, a few shallow pants followed by a pause and a deep inhalation, as if she were gathering herself for battle.

Mother! I'm here—Domenic, your Nico.

Marguerida's lips parted, as if she would speak, but only a gasp passed them. She opened her eyes, their gold now faded, unseeing, and then closed them again. The fingers of her right hand clenched and straightened. Her left hand, bound with bandages, lay motionless, as if paralyzed.

Mother!

Domenic drew back, dazed. Never in his life had his mother failed to respond when he called. When he was lost in the Overworld, searching for Alanna, she had known. With her mind, she had found him.

In his memory, a maelstrom of blue-white energy buffeted him, uprooted him, swallowed him up. He had seen no way through the storm. The blasts of chaotic *laran* had shredded away his very sense of self. Hope had faded with every passing moment. He remembered thinking what a fool he'd been, that all was lost.

Then he had heard his mother's mental voice, clear and resonant as a summoning trumpet. *"Come back!"* she had called. *"Come back to me!"*

There was no place on Darkover or beyond, he had thought, *that she could not reach, nothing she would not do, to save the ones she loved.*

How could he do any less for her?

Something roused at the back of Domenic's mind, a pressure, a gathering of raw power, a melding of desperation and deep, instinct-driven impulse.

MOTHER, WHERE ARE YOU? ANSWER ME!

"Domenic, stop!" Grandfather Lew's voice broke through Domenic's mental summons.

The room snapped back into focus. Domenic tasted shock and adrenaline in the air. Istvana clutched her starstone and wavered on her seat, her face ashen. Gently, Illona took Domenic's hands and guided him from the bedside to a chair. Tears glimmered on her cheeks.

Lew said, his voice even more hoarse and distorted than usual, "You cannot reach her that way. None of us can. We've all tried."

"I don't understand," Domenic said. "She's just . . . gone."

Where can we look for help? We can't just give up! Domenic cried.

We will not abandon her, Illona thought.

The door opened. Linnea Storn entered and silently joined them. Her hair, soft auburn curls shot with silver, was dressed in a simple style, and she wore the unadorned gray robe of a Tower *leronis.* Domenic did not know her well; as consort to Regis Hastur, she had always been kind, if distant, to him. Before she left Thendara for Arilinn Tower, he had not known that she was once a Keeper.

Domenic turned back to Istvana. "Exactly what is the matter with my mother?"

Istvana gathered herself. "You know that she used her shadow matrix to transform the serum?"

"Yes, Illona told me. What difference does that make? I assume that Mother used it as one uses a starstone, to amplify her natural psychic energies."

"That much is true, although Marguerida never needed a starstone because of the embedded matrix. In fact, the shadow matrix is likely responsible for her extreme sensitivity to the matrix screens at Arilinn, which prevented her from working in a circle. It's quite a powerful device, but it is not the same as a natural starstone. We are not sure ... perhaps the matrix provided more raw power than her channels could sustain."

"Do you mean this is some kind of *laran* overload? Like threshold sickness?" Domenic said. "We know how to treat that, don't we?"

Istvana shook her head. "No, *not* like threshold sickness. That much, we can be sure of. We cannot tell, however, whether generating and controlling so much power burned out the *laran* centers of her mind. That would be terrible indeed."

"I don't care if she keeps her *laran* or not!" Domenic exclaimed. "I want my mother back, here among us!"

An awkward pause followed. Illona said gently, "If she has lost her *laran*, and what is wrong with her is psychic, not physical, we may not be able to reach her mind."

During the discussion, Linnea shook her head minutely. "There may be another cause. Istvana disagrees with me, but the possibility must be explored."

"With all respect, we've been through this before," Istvana said. "The matter was laid to rest years ago."

"I know from my own experience that being controlled by *laran* is a thing not easily erased from the mind," Lew said.

At Domenic's bitten-off exclamation, Linnea said, "Marguerida entered this state after she drew unimaginable power through the shadow matrix. I believe the shadow matrix may be more than it seems. For one thing, it did not come to her in the usual way, like an unkeyed starstone. She obtained it in the Overworld, from a Tower erected there by Ashara. It was created and tuned to Ashara's mental vibration long before it ever came to Marguerida."

That much was true. Over the years, Marguerida had drawn upon the immense power of the shadow matrix, but she confessed she had never fully understood its nature.

"For that reason," Linnea went on, "and because Ashara had overshadowed Marguerida from the time she was a small child, the embedded matrix may yet retain the resonance of Ashara's personality."

A tendril of ice crept down Domenic's spine. Since childhood, he had heard tales of that ancient *leronis,* who prolonged her existence by dominating the minds of generations of Keepers. Marguerida had told Domenic a little about that terrible psychic struggle in the Overworld. In her attempt to free herself from the disembodied spirit of the ancient Keeper, she had seized the keystone from the astral Tower of Mirrors, the stone that had preserved the strongest presence of Ashara, the stone that now glimmered in the flesh of Marguerida's left hand.

"Has Ashara come to life again, through my mother?" Domenic asked.

"Not yet, may all the gods be praised," Linnea said. "Marguerida has considerable strength of will. She would never permit that monstrous entity to come back into the world, not if she could prevent it. If I am correct, however, the tainted crystal is even now draining her life force, and we have no way to protect her."

Linnea lifted Marguerida's left hand and unwrapped the bandages. When he saw the matrix embedded in Marguerida's palm, Domenic's courage almost failed him. No longer pale blue-white, the pattern pulsed with the color of freshly spilled blood. It seemed to have taken on a life of its own. He wondered what lurked behind those shifting crimson facets.

Feeling sick, Domenic tore his glance away from the crimson matrix. Whether Linnea was correct or whether the crystalline pattern had turned red for some other reason, one fact remained. Cut off from the animating power of her spirit, Marguerida's body would in time wither and die. The more time passed, the less chance she had of ever returning.

Where had she gone, that none of them could reach her?

How could he call her back, even as she had called to him?

Domenic's strange *laran* roused. A pattern slowly emerged, like mountains rising through mist. Before, the planet had called to the deepest core of his consciousness. He had heard it as song, as wordless melody, as deep groaning, as the shifting harmonies of a single entity.

Now his innermost perceptions intensified. He sensed not only the physical manifestations of rock and magma, river and cloud, but their psychic forms as well. Interpenetrating the ordinary world, he saw the Overworld, a realm of infinitely elastic thought, of power, of dreams. His mother—and, for all he knew, the spirit of his father— wandered lost in that limitless realm.

How to reach her?

Domenic let the question die away into silence. He would not find the answer in words. Instead, he allowed his psychic focus to expand even more, softening his peripheral senses.

With eerie, doubled sight, he glanced at the other bed, where his father lay, eyes closed, hands folded on his chest. The *laran* field preserving his life shimmered slightly, iridescent shades of blue. The ring on Mikhail's right hand glinted.

The form of the ring did not waver as Domenic shifted his own vision between physical and psychic. Some objects, then, existed in both planes. They were bridges between one world and another, drawing their power from both.

The pulsing, blood-red matrix on Marguerida's palm was another such object. It was linked to her mind, even as the ring was bound to Mikhail's. Was there a way to use the power of the two devices to bridge the gap between worlds?

Domenic had been taught at Neskaya that it was dangerous for anyone but a trained Keeper to handle another person's starstone. The results might be fatal for both individuals. But Mikhail's ring was no ordinary matrix. Mikhail often wore it openly and uninsulated. Moreover, he had joined all its power to his wife's shadow matrix at the Battle of Old North Road.

Domenic's resolve hardened. Some risks must be taken. He could not believe that Marguerida would ever bring harm to Mikhail, even involuntarily. Domenic had never known two people more compatible. Was he willing, though, to stake his mother's life on it?

What if he were wrong?

What choice did he have? She was dying anyway, and Mikhail would not choose life without her.

"I don't know about Ashara or the shadow matrix," Domenic said, searching for the words, "but I do know one thing. If she were lost, cast adrift, cut off from everything and everyone . . . there is one person she would find, no matter what barriers stood between them."

He strode to his father's bedside. His hand passed through the *laran* field with a faint tingling sensation. The ring slipped from Mikhail's finger, as if it understood Domenic's purpose, and gave its consent.

Domenic lifted his mother's left hand, carefully avoiding contact with her shadow matrix. He placed his father's ring against the blood-hued pattern on her palm and closed her fingers around it.

———— ◆ ————

Marguerida had no idea how long she had floated here, in this place of formless mist. Invisible currents swirled around her, unstable composites of wind and sound, voices and air, fragmented memory. How she knew this, she could not tell. She seemed to be shifting in and out of phase with the storm, so that at moments it battered her from the outside, and at others there was no outside, no inside, no *herself.*

"*Marguerida . . .*"

Something curled on the gusts, a thread of sound. A man's voice, calling to her. He cast out her name like a fisherman's net. The wind snatched the name away.

Name . . . she had a name . . .

She felt herself condensing, no longer vapor but something infinitesimally more substantial. The voice, dim and blurred, formed words.

"Marguerida . . . breathe, damn you! Breathe!"

Dimly, she felt fingers pinching her nose, a mouth over hers, forcing air into her lungs, the desperate pressure of a mind reaching for hers.

She knew the pattern and texture of that mind. She had thrust against it with her own. As the tremendous power of the Alton Gift flowed through her, she had felt the man's natural *laran* barriers crumble and give way.

The voice receded into silence. Memory faded. Vision fractured into tiny mirrored bits, spreading on the wind. The sparkling motes sifted downward.

Gradually, she felt herself separating from the color-bleached firmament. Her feet touched a surface, and she found herself, her body, standing upon the unending, featureless plain of the Overworld.

A Tower glowered before her, the stones veined like inflamed living flesh. Ashara's Tower, shining with uncanny mirrored light . . .

No, that was destroyed! she raged silently. *Mikhail and I brought it down.*

Still the Tower stood, mocking her. Beckoning her. The reflected brilliance intensified, avid . . . hungering.

Marguerida's left hand burned. She looked down to see the matrix embedded in her palm, no longer pale starstone-blue but crimson, like blood, like sunset, like a Keeper's robe.

Time, she knew, had no meaning here. Somewhere, two decades ago, a much younger self had battled the mind that had overshadowed her since childhood.

This is where I obtained the matrix. Did it bring me here for some purpose?

Purpose . . .

As she thought this, distance compressed, so that she stood *within* the Tower that was crimson and blue-white, facing the spectral figure of Ashara. Strength surged through her, and she sensed that now, as then, she was not alone.

Ashara glared at her, features distorting, shifting. For a fleeting, sickening moment, Marguerida looked into a mirror.

"You are mine! Mine! You always have been, and you always will be." A voice like granite shattering shocked through Marguerida. *"I will live again through you!"*

Marguerida's instinct urged her to resist, to fight, even as she had so long ago. In that first struggle, just as her own strength had failed her, Mikhail had found her. His determination had flowed into her, pulling her free. What was left of Ashara's spirit had disappeared in the destruction of her astral Tower.

Wrestling her panic under control and her focus to the present moment, Marguerida forced herself to think.

If Ashara exists only in the past, then why am I remembering her now? She's the last thing I want to think about!

Dimly, as if over an unimaginable distance, Marguerida heard her father's voice, *" . . . being controlled by* laran *is a thing not easily erased from the mind."*

Marguerida and Lew had each survived the experience of another psychic presence in their minds, powerful and dominating. In their turn, each of them had used the Alton Gift to impose their will upon another.

. . . Jeram . . . the Battle of Old North Road and its aftermath . . .

I didn't know! I didn't realize . . .

There was no help for it. She could do nothing to change the past. She must face the menace within her own mind.

Ashara cannot harm me now . . . not unless I give her the power to do so.

Drawing herself up, Marguerida faced the image of Ashara. The ancient *leronis* glared back, her eyes burning with ravenous anticipation and triumph. The air shuddered under the accumulated malevolence of centuries. Light melded with heat and crushing psychic energy.

Marguerida's nerve almost failed her. Ashara's will and her lust for domination had not abated during the intervening decades. This time, there would be no Mikhail to stand beside her . . .

With an inhuman shriek of triumph, Ashara leaped forward. Marguerida caught a whiff of the aura streaming from her form, a concatenation of rot and *laran* energy.

You . . . do . . . not . . . exist! Marguerida cried out with all her strength.

The words, spoken so bravely, disintegrated under Ashara's attack. Marguerida knew that her own fear was fueling Ashara's power, and yet she could not stop herself. The old Keeper was almost upon her, but she could not move . . .

No single human agency could defeat the monstrous psychic entity before her. Alone, she had no chance.

But *together* . . .

Mikhail! Beloved, help me!

Pain shot through Marguerida's left hand. Startled, she looked down. Something lay in her palm, sparkling against the blue-white pattern on her palm.

Mikhail's ring!

She had no time to wonder how it had gotten here. Her only thought was that once she and Mikhail had combined their special *laran* instruments, her shadow matrix and the ring of Varzil the Good upon his hand.

Together!

She gripped the ring. It dug into the matrix in her hand. As the two psychoactive devices made contact, a clamor like the sky breaking open deafened her. For an instant, she sensed another presence rushing through her.

The world exploded in a glory of light.

At a deep, cellular level, Marguerida *felt* the violent clashing of energies around her. The node of desiccated consciousness that had been Ashara thrust back. Twisting, evading.

Ashara tried to flee, to hide herself in the adamantine

lattice of the shadow matrix. But the light was too powerful; it flooded the flesh-embedded crystal, bleaching away all traces of crimson rage.

A shriek of inhuman despair shocked through the psychic firmament. Marguerida staggered under the blast. With a swift velvety hush like falcon wings, the clamor fell away.

For a brief moment, Marguerida gazed upon the empty spot where Ashara's Tower of Mirrors had once stood. Nothing, not even the smallest particle of dust, remained.

She's gone . . . she's really gone.

Light died. Distance thinned to void. She was alone in a vast, spinning emptiness.

39

Curling in on herself, Marguerida cradled Mikhail's ring against her heart. Pain beyond words, beyond tears, beyond bearing, filled her.

It is over. I am free ... but I will never see him again.

Never say the thousand things she wanted to share, never laugh at the way the morning sun turned his hair into spun gold. Never lie in his arms, drinking in the light of his eyes, as if their joy would never end.

Never again see her children, or hold her grandchildren. Never see her old friends, or that quick hushed nightfall over Thendara that always made her breath catch in her throat with its beauty. Never put right her regrets.

She thought of Jeram, who had tried to save her, even after what she had done to him after the Battle of Old North Road. What could she say to him if she ever had the chance? Could he understand that she and her father had had no other choice unless they slaughtered the entire defeated Terran force?

Did that make what they had done right? Lew felt it did not, but he spoke from his own tortured guilt.

And I, what do I believe?

Life was rarely so simple as pure right or pure wrong. Every choice carried the possibility of unintended consequences. She had made the best decision she could, perhaps the only right decision, and now there was nothing she could do to change it.

Ah, what did it matter? Here in this timeless place, she had lost all sensation of her physical body. She had not the least notion of which direction it lay in or how to get there. She could have drifted a minute, an hour, a year. Did she still have a body to which to return?

If I could only see Mikhail again . . . just once . . .

Yet . . . for a fleeting moment, as she faced Ashara for the last time, Mikhail *had* been with her.

Marguerida's practical nature reasserted itself. *Just listen to me, wallowing in self-pity!*

Nothing was over yet, not while she still had her wits about her. Mikhail's spirit was somewhere out there in the Overworld. Even if neither of them could return to the physical plane, at least they could be together. Her heart, with its own instinctive wisdom, would guide her now.

Taking the ring in her right hand, she raised it to the level of her eyes. The crystal glinted with inner fire. On the palm of her other hand, the imprinted pattern of the shadow matrix shone faintly, pallid blue-white. With the final vanquishing of Ashara, all other color had drained away.

Mikhail's ring . . . her shadow matrix. The two were linked, just as their hearts and minds were connected, ever since that strange journey to the past, when Varzil the Good himself had given Mikhail the ring and then married them.

Varzil had said the marriage ceremony itself created a bond . . . what was it? Something about the symbolism of the *catenas* bracelets, locked upon the wrists of the man and woman in the old tradition.

Symbolic of what deeper truth?

Locked, joined . . . as their separate *laran* talents had become fused together. Before, they had loved each other sweetly, passionately, with intense mutual delight, but always as two separate people. When they had returned to the present time, however, they shared a constant, abiding connection. They might go about their daily lives, sometimes seeing each other only briefly if things got too hectic, but always she could feel his presence in her mind.

She studied the ring that was the touchstone of her husband's *laran*. The great colorless crystal had been keyed to Mikhail's starstone.

You are part of him. You must know where he is. Take me to him!

There was no change in the flickering brilliance within the crystal or the gray monotone that surrounded her. Again, she reached out, aiming her will and concentration at the ring.

TAKE ME TO HIM!

Silence answered her, silence and utter stillness.

Her fingers closed in a fist around the ring. What good was it if it could not bring her to her beloved? Temper and frustration flared up in her. She wanted to hurl the ring as hard and far as she could.

No, that would not help anything. It wasn't the ring's fault it could not fulfill her wish. The ring might have many powers, but it lacked the will to deliberately thwart her. She imagined its sadness at seeing the two people it had united now parted.

At that, Marguerida smiled. *What a fanciful thought!*

She opened her fist and studied the ring, lying on the unmarked palm of her right hand. "If you can't bring me to him, what *can* you do? Why do I have you?"

As she asked the question, Marguerida's thoughts cleared. Her body became more solid, as did the Overworld. She was on the right track. The overhead light strengthened, and the flat gray terrain firmed up beneath her feet. She felt her arms and legs, torso and head, the supple, articulated strength of her spine, the texture of the flimsy robe that had materialized on her body.

What did she know about the ring? She knew where it had come from. That Varzil had given it freely to Mikhail. That Mikhail had worn it ever since. That Francisco had coveted it.

"Quite a troublemaker, aren't you?" she said to the ring,

but lightly, so it would know she did not blame it for Francisco's treachery.

Mikhail had used it at the Battle of Old North Road, its power joined to that of her shadow matrix. But that was not its first use.

Originally, Mikhail had used the ring for healing.

Healing . . .

A shiver tickled Marguerida's spine, a ghostly hope. Not a sure thing, of course. The ring was not all-powerful. It had not been able to save Regis after his stroke. Yet, if there was any force on Darkover that could restore Mikhail, she held it in her hand.

But he's not here! wailed through her mind.

Think like a Darkovan, she told herself. *Since when has distance made any difference in the Overworld?*

The ring itself lacked the power to find him. But together with its counterpart, the shadow matrix that was part of her own flesh . . .

The ring had appeared in the Overworld in her left hand, in direct contact with the shadow matrix, yet no harm had come to her. Or, she was sure, to Mikhail. Ordinarily, she insulated her matrixed hand from accidental contact with a silk-lined glove or mitten. Now it occurred to her that in the Overworld such precautions might not be necessary. This was, after all, a realm of thought and energy, where only willpower and imagination mattered.

The ring and the matrix existed in the ordinary world as well, but they were essentially devices to channel and amplify *laran.* Carefully, Marguerida replaced the ring over the crystalline imprint on her left palm. A shock, like living electricity, shot up her arm. Her nerves tingled. The feeling was not unpleasant, but it was *strong.* She wondered, but only for an instant, at the vividness of the sensation, here in the Overworld, where she had only an astral body.

Mikhail's ring and her own matrix began to glow, moment by moment ever more strongly. Their combined brilliance stung her eyes. Energy that was neither light nor

heat streamed out in all directions. The gray of the Overworld paled, almost to white.

It was, she thought, as if their love, combined, now filled
the entire world.

One love, combined . . . one love, one heart . . .

Of course!

Joy rose in her. The ring had been unable to bring her to
Mikhail because in this place, neither time nor distance
had any meaning. He was *already* with her. Her own fear
had created the illusion that they were apart.

Marguerida turned her sight inward, trying to see
Mikhail with her heart instead of her eyes. In memory and
longing, he stood before her, his hands clasping hers. She
could almost feel that sure touch . . .

Eyes blue as the clear sky of Thetis smiled at her . . .

Sun glinted on hair the color of new-minted gold . . .

*No, that was Mikhail as he had been when they first met;
he was older now, and silver frosted the gold . . .*

The lines of his face came into sharper focus, a face neither young nor old, but Mikhail as he would always be to
her, the radiant spirit behind those eyes, that smile . . .

She willed the form before her to condense into flesh.

Beloved, be with me now!

Gradually, Mikhail took form before her, at first a shimmer, like heat rising in the shape of a man. He seemed to
be made not of flesh but of glass. His eyes, as colorless as
the rest of him, looked right through her.

As Marguerida watched, a glint of yellow appeared in
Mikhail's flowing hair. His eyes shaded from gray to palest
blue. Like her, he wore a white robe, fluttering as if caught
in a wind. His feet came to rest on the smooth gray plain.
Moments passed as his outline grew sharper. His eyes focused. Yet still he remained insubstantial, transparent.

Lips shaped her name. *Marja!* Preciosa!

Unable to contain herself, Marguerida rushed toward his
outstretched arms. Her body passed through his with only
the faintest suggestion of contact, an almost imperceptible
crackle of electricity. She whirled around, even as he

reached for her again. When her hands touched his, she felt only empty space. They tried several more times, with the same result. Finally, they drew back, gazing at each other across the unbridgeable gap.

For a long time, Marguerida could not speak, caught between frustration and longing. She forced herself to face the truth. She could not hold him, nor he, her. Here in the Overworld, in this manifestation, at least, they were thought, not flesh, insubstantial as ghosts.

Mikhail . . . She could not bear to be so close, and yet to lose all hope of him.

My Marja. His smile dimmed. *Are you dead, too?*

I don't think so. I don't think either of us is, although I have no idea how to bring us back. The last time I saw you—your physical body, that is—you were still alive, poisoned by Francisco's dagger, and in a laran *stasis field.*

Mikhail shook his head, as much a gesture of love as negation. *You should not have come looking for me,* preciosa. *It was too dangerous. But when have you ever listened to sense when someone you love was involved?*

I did something rather foolhardy, but necessary, she admitted ruefully. *I used my shadow matrix to transform enough of Jeram's serum to immunize everyone who needs it against the fever, at least I hope so. But I didn't count on—*

Slow down! he said, laughing. *What fever? By Jeram, do you mean that poor fellow Francisco was using for his phony charges?*

Mikhail could have no way of knowing what happened after the duel . . . and, she thought, the charges of *laran* abuse were true, although not in the way Francisco had intended. If she lived, she would eventually have much to sort out.

Briefly she explained how Thendara had been struck by an epidemic of trailmen's fever and Jeram, the Terran Jeremiah Reed, had used his expertise in infectious disease control to help.

With both of us absent, who is acting as Regent? Mikhail asked. *Who rules the Comyn?*

Marguerida smiled. *Domenic, who else?*

Domenic? Astonishment and delight shone through Mikhail's mental voice.

He's grown up in an amazing fashion, Marguerida replied. *As long as we were pushing him to be responsible—and face it, Mik, we did pressure him with our expectations—he fought us. But when it was his own choice . . . well, he is as resourceful as his father. He held the Council together, kept everyone from panic, and organized the care of the sick. You would have been so proud of him!*

Then we must return immediately, so that I can tell him so. Something in her husband's words tugged at Marguerida's heart. She remembered all the years of her own young life when she yearned for her father's approval.

Marguerida looked down at the ring, still lying in the palm of her hand. Clearly, it was the key to healing Mikhail, but she did not know how to use it.

She held it out to him. *Here, take it. Use its healing power to cleanse the poison from your earthly body.*

When he reached for the ring, his fingers passed through it, even as they did her own hand. They tried placing the ring on the ground and tossing it through the air before admitting the impossibility. The ring belonged in the same dimension as Marguerida. She herself would have to use it.

Mikhail tried to explain to her how it worked. She did her best to follow his directions, but without any result. She might as well have tried to use his starstone. The crystal was, after all, a type of matrix, keyed to Mikhail's mind.

Or was it?

Marguerida peered into the faceted brilliance of the crystal. Through it, she could barely make out the shadow matrix on the palm of her other hand. As she watched, the two patterns began to interweave, each enhancing the other, like harmony and counterpoint in music. She heard their combined melodies in her mind.

One love, combined . . . one love, one heart . . .

One matrix . . .

She could not wield the ring, but she could use the

shadow matrix embedded in her own flesh, keyed to her own *laran*. If she channeled her mental power through her shadow matrix, and then through Varzil's ring . . .

A ball of coruscating fire burned in her memory. She remembered how it had leaped out from their hands, blinding the attackers at the Battle of Old North Road. Then, their Gifts had been used as a weapon.

Now I need a different sort of weapon. Just as the immune serum changed the particles of the trailmen's fever virus, now she envisioned a stream of healing *laran* altering the molecules of poison in Mikhail's body.

Yes, that just might work!

The transformation would take every scrap of *laran* she possessed, right down to the dregs, and she knew by now that her Gifts were considerable. What had Lew said, *"I would have given anything, done anything to save the one I love"*?

Anything to have Mikhail live.

Marguerida reached deep within her mind for her Gift. She found a wellspring of strength, and poured it through the matrix on her hand.

One love, one heart . . .

One matrix . . .

One . . .

She felt the two matrices become attuned to one another. Building on each other's vibrations, they began to glow even more brightly than before. Crystal fire ignited in their depths. Brighter and stronger they burned, until two spheres of brilliance fused into one.

Marguerida tried to picture Mikhail's physical body as she had last seen him. He had been lying under a light blanket in the chamber in Comyn Tower, a protective field of *laran* surrounding him. His face had been pale, his features composed. Even as she attempted to bring the image into focus, it blurred, weak and indistinct, as if viewed through a badly warped lens.

How could she have forgotten the face that was as familiar to her as her own? Had she floated in the Overworld

for so long? Had she lost all connection with the physical
plane?

During that moment of uncertainty, Marguerida's concentration faltered. Patches of darkness appeared in the
searing brilliance of the joined matrices. They pulsed, red
and sluggish, like congested *laran* nodes. The energies fluc-
tuated, peaking irregularly and falling away.

Marguerida struggled to bring the luminous orb under
control, to smooth out the variations. Her efforts were of
no use. The sphere was rapidly becoming unstable. In only
a few moments, she would not be able to contain its power.
She had no idea what would happen then, how much dev-
astation would result. In horror, she realized that once she
had lost control of the matrices, she would also destroy the
only hope of either of them surviving.

She had built up this nexus of power to be used, but she
had nowhere to send it. The power had no mooring, no ties
to the physical plane. She had generated it from her own
mind, and she was adrift in the Overworld, cut off, even as
Domenic had been when she reached him on the night of
the Midsummer Ball riot.

Domenic! She had found him, lost and drifting, in the
Overworld. What if they were still connected? Could he
reach her in the same way?

Nico . . . she called out to him across the void. Mikhail
joined her, his strength flowing effortlessly into hers.

She caught the distant, eager response.

Mother! Father!

Her son's mental voice echoed weirdly through her
thoughts. She could not sustain the contact. She was rapidly losing her ability to concentrate as the shifting energy
of the matrices tore and pulled at her.

Hold on! The words formed in her mind.

Nico, where are you?

Here—I am here, in the light.

Marguerida bent her mental focus again on the joined
matrices. They no longer radiated unblemished white light.
Instead, she looked upon streams of energy, vibrating at

many frequencies. Her rational mind understood this was impossible; she could not perceive such harmonics, so far above and below the visible range. Yet her imagination turned the vibrations into a panoply of rainbow lights, shifting from blue-white brilliance, to the green of tender shoots in spring, the blue of Lake Mariposa on a clear summer's day, the varying crimson shades of blood and lava and the great Bloody Sun itself, the gold of a sunrise high in the Hellers, the dusky slate of basalt, the pale ivory of Temora sands . . .

She seemed to be seeing all the colors of Darkover.

Vision shifted into hearing. A symphonic blending of sound spread through her mind, even as she had imagined it when Domenic spoke before the Council . . .

. . . *the sweet high singing of storm and river, the deep, rumbling groan as massive sheets of crust slowly buckled under unimaginable pressures, the resonant hum of the molten layers beneath* . . .

HOLD ON! Domenic's mental voice now came through, louder and clearer than ever.

Suddenly Marguerida understood what was happening, why she saw those colors and heard that music. Her son's unique *laran* bound him to the planet itself, and he was using his Gift as an anchor in the physical plane, reaching out to her through his mind.

The unending gray of the Overworld faded. She no longer stood upon a chill, featureless plain. Once again, she was floating, but no longer alone. Mikhail was beside her, both of them swept up in a single multicolored sphere. Streams of variegated energy, light and heat, matter and energy, rushed past without touching them.

Suddenly, all sensation of movement ceased. Marguerida blinked as the intense radiance receded. To all sides, gray stone walls emerged, as if from a disappearing mist. Below her, a spot of brightness remained. She found herself floating, looking down on her own body, lying wrapped in a her favorite shawl . . . in the same room, high in Comyn Tower, where Mikhail lay. People clustered around her. She recognized them, even though she was looking down at the top of their heads. Domenic grasped her left hand in both of his. The mote of brightness issued from their joined hands.

Mik? Are you with me? Can you use the power from the ring now?

No, I cannot. His mental presence was very near, as if he were whispering in her ear. *But together we can.*

Marguerida gathered up the power from the Overworld matrices. Anchored by the sure, steady contact with Domenic's *laran* to the physical plane of Darkover, she and Mikhail became conduits for the ring's healing energy. It passed through them like silk, like sunshine, like a thundering waterfall.

Power flowed first through the astral form of Mikhail's body, then settled into his *laran*-carrying nodes and channels. Deftly, Mikhail shifted the vibration of the energy so that it now infused his every tissue, every fluid, every cell.

Marguerida sensed the minute particles of Francisco's poison like bits of caustic darkness. As Istvana had said, the toxin had bonded to Mikhail's bone marrow.

As the healing energy shifted, the composition of the particles altered. They brightened, infinitesimal suns, before fading away. Only healthy marrow tissue remained.

On the bed, Mikhail's body drew in a deep breath. Already he looked less pale.

Marguerida felt a pulse of reassurance from her husband. To return to the physical plane and their own bodies, they had only to follow the lifeline Domenic had created. Yet Mikhail hesitated, restraining her.

While we are still here in the Overworld, he said, *there is one more thing that can be done, if you choose.*

What is that? What could be more important than to return to life together?

Mikhail shifted his focus to Marguerida's left palm, where the shadow matrix still pulsed with power. She had encountered Ashara again, with almost fatal results, because of the device. The ancient Keeper was destroyed, but as long as Marguerida remembered her, there remained the possibility of recreating her.

You can be free of her, Mikhail said, *if you leave it here.*

Marguerida understood instantly what he meant. The shadow matrix had originally been the keystone, the heart of Ashara's Tower of Mirrors. With it, Marguerida could recreate Ashara's Tower . . . or she could build a new Tower, one never tainted by Ashara's lust for domination. The Tower as it ought to have been. She could place the shadow matrix at its heart, build its graceful walls with her imagination . . . and then walk away.

If she had never acquired the shadow matrix, what would have happened at the ambush at Old North Road? Who would have defeated Belfontaine's forces? Would the Comyn have been wiped out with that single bold attack?

Yes, the shadow matrix came with a heavy responsibility, the burden of constant vigilance . . . just like the Alton Gift. And just like the Alton Gift, it should never be used lightly.

What had Lew said about the Alton Gift, that it was a weapon when all else had failed? Could she leave her world and everyone she loved without the added defense of her shadow matrix?

For a long moment, she made no answer. She did not need to. Mikhail understood her.

Then let us go home, he whispered, a kiss for her mind.

A sense of completion filled her. Then, with a rush like wings, like the astonishing, swift Darkovan nightfall, the last mote of brilliance faded.

Some time later—an eon, a heartbeat, she could not tell—Marguerida returned to herself. She felt her body, muscle and bone, her left hand clenched around a ring. She lay on a bed in a room in Comyn Tower, the same room she had looked down upon. Someone put an arm around her, steadying her. Someone else, with a Keeper's cool deft touch, gently opened her fingers and removed the ring.

Sound reached her, people breathing, her father's voice, too low and hoarse to make out his words. Nico, sobbing softly with exhaustion and relief and joy. The rhythm of her own heart. She opened her eyes and sat up as Mikhail came toward her on unsteady feet. Linnea supported him, and the ring gleamed once again on his right hand.

She could not speak, she could only gaze into that face that was as dear to her as breath. Tears and laughter bubbled up in her. Running her hands over his damp cheeks, she gave herself over to the rapturous moment.

40

Even with careful tending, it would be some while before Marguerida and Mikhail were fully recovered. With Domenic's blessing, Donal resumed his duties as Mikhail's paxman. Domenic was able to give Yllana and Rory the simultaneous news of Marguerida's perilous experiment and that both their parents were now awake and recovering. Relief and rejoicing swept away any momentary indignation at being kept ignorant of Marguerida's condition. Yllana took over much of the nursing, under the supervision of Katherine and the Castle healers. Rory was offered leave from his duties to be with his family, but he took only enough to visit frequently. Niall accompanied him whenever his own assignments permitted.

Domenic tore himself away from his parents' bedsides to tour the city. When he visited the treatment centers, he wore a formal cloak of Hastur blue and silver, so that he could be easily recognized, and rode his gray Armida-bred mare. It was important that people see the Acting Regent out on the streets, that they hear his voice.

The shelters originally set up by Darius-Mikhail now served admirably as distribution centers for the serum. The matrix mechanics and *leroni* supervised teams of healers administering the serum. Many who were originally brought there were well enough to return home.

One morning, not long after Marguerida's crisis, Domenic

found Jeram and Danilo in one such place, in the poorest area of the city. The building they were working in had once been a barn, with worn timbers and a dirt floor. A faint tang of hay and horses remained. The late summer day was mild enough so that the wide doors stood open, as did the shutters of the unglassed windows. Only a short time ago every pallet had been occupied. Now about half were empty, and the remaining patients did not seem seriously ill. In fact, several were sitting up, playing a game of knuckle bones.

A table had been set up at the far end of the shelter, and Jeram and Danilo bent over it, making notations in a log book. Smiling, Domenic approached them.

"It's going better than we expected." Lines of fatigue etched Jeram's face. "It's too soon to tell if the serum can actually prevent infection or simply attenuate it. I still have to run the final analyses, but I'm hoping that we've reduced the number of cases below a critical level."

"Critical level?" Domenic said. "I don't understand."

"The phenomenon is called *herd immunity,*" Jeram explained. "That is, once enough individuals in a population are immune, the disease cannot spread past a scattering of new cases, not the pandemic of previous years. Even if we don't achieve that degree of prevention, we still can treat those who contract the fever, and we can develop a new serum in case the virus mutates again."

We've done it! Domenic caught Jeram's exhilaration.

"Darkover owes you more than we can ever repay," Domenic said.

"It was a team effort." Jeram looked uncomfortable about being singled out for such thanks. "You, Ulm, Marguerida, Danilo, Darius-Mikhail, the Keepers, every person who came forward. None of us can claim sole credit. By working together, we found a solution that combined your own healing skills and matrix science with Federation scientific knowledge."

Danilo looked thoughtful. "I think that's been a dream ever since the *Terranan* came to Darkover. Sometimes our two cultures have clashed more than we have cooperated, but we have always been richer together than apart."

"So Great-Uncle Regis always said," Domenic said.

A strange look passed over Danilo's face, and for a moment he was silent. Jeram excused himself to continue about his work, reminding Domenic that the serum must still be distributed and patients tended, lest they succumb to secondary infections.

"Doesn't Jeram ever rest?" Domenic watched the Terran hurry out the doors.

"Not that I've noticed. I've rarely seen a man drive himself so hard, as if his soul depended on his making atonement for past sins. May the Bearer of Burdens grant him peace," Danilo murmured, making a sign of blessing.

Yes, Domenic thought, that felt right, even if phrased in *cristoforo* terms. He remembered the look that had passed between Lew and Jeram during the meeting when Jeram agreed to help them. A look of understanding, forgiveness. Hope. Jeram's knowledge, and what he chose to do with it, could kill untold thousands . . . or save a world.

As Domenic turned to leave, Danilo said, "If you have not already visited the encampment outside the gates, would you please do so? I am concerned about Alanna. She has scarcely left the healing pavilion, even when others offered to take her place. More than that, the last time I spoke with her, she still refused to take the serum."

Domenic had already received his dose. Katherine Aldaran had administered it to everyone in Comyn Castle with a ruthless efficiency that would have done Marguerida credit. The Terran hypospray was quick and not particularly painful. Domenic could not imagine why Alanna had declined it.

Taking his leave, Domenic guided his horse along the streets toward the gates. The shanty camp had shrunk since his last visit. Trampled grasses and scattered ashes marked empty sites around the old gray stone well. A handful of men moved between cookfires and the few remaining sleeping tents or tended their beasts on the single picket line.

The pavilion was a motley of blankets and scraps of tents, some still bright, others so faded and dingy that their original color could not be determined. Domenic stepped inside, his eyes adjusting to the dimness of the interior. The place was almost deserted. Only a few pallets were occupied. On one, a white-bearded man lay curled on his side, snoring loudly. He was fully dressed in shepherd's clothing and did not appear to be ill; in fact, he seemed to be enjoying a comfortable midday nap.

Ulm's black-haired son, Rannirl, stretched out on another pallet, arms raised and crossed behind his head. He sat up as Domenic approached.

"A fair day to you, *Dom* Domenic. I would greet you properly, but—

"No, do not disturb yourself," Domenic said. "Is there no one here to tend you?"

"There is no need." Rannirl shrugged. "I had a touch of the fever, nothing more. *Mestra* Varinna was going to give me the medicine yesterday, but I was already on the mend. I told her to save it for someone who really needs it. Even so, she wanted me to stay in bed for another day. I don't suppose there's an urgent task I can do for you?"

Grinning, Domenic shook his head. Jeram was right; the virulent fever had changed into a benign form that would give the same immunity. The primary danger to those infected with the new strain was, in Rannirl's case, simple boredom. The original fever, however, still carried a grave risk.

"Where is *Damisela* Alanna Alar, who was nursing the sick here? Has she returned to the Castle?" Domenic asked.

"Over there." Rannirl pointed to the farthest corner. "Though she's not stirred since I woke this morning."

Alarmed, Domenic hurried over. It was indeed Alanna, but this was no normal sleep of exhaustion. She had curled into a ball, shivering under layers of blankets. Her eyes were closed, her cheeks flushed. He could hear her breath as coarse rattling in her chest. When he brushed her cheek with his lips, he felt the intense, brittle heat of her body.

What had Alanna been thinking, to take such a risk? Why hadn't she taken the serum, as the other nurses had? His head seethed with questions to drive out the one that terrified him—*What if she should die?*

No, that would not happen. She was not beyond help. Many who had been even more critically ill had recovered.

"Alanna?"

Through chapped lips, she murmured something he could not understand.

"Rannirl, can you help me?" Domenic called. "I must get her to the Castle right away." He lifted Alanna to a sitting position. She had always been small, and her oversized garments disguised how thin she had become.

Looking relieved to be of use, Rannirl helped Domenic settle Alanna in front of him on the gray mare's saddle. The horse snorted, unsure of what to make of this extra burden. She quieted at Domenic's touch and moved out easily. They headed for the city at a brisk pace. Alanna's head lolled against Domenic's chest, swaying with the motion of the horse's stride. As they passed the gates and threaded their way along the noisy streets, she roused.

"Nico, is it winter again? I'm so cold . . ."

"Hush, darling, I will take you home and light a fire to keep you warm. Now lie still. I am here with you. Everything is going to be all right."

With a sigh, she rested her face against him and slipped back into unconsciousness.

Immediately upon their arrival at Comyn Castle, servants carried Alanna inside, and others went in search of a healer. Domenic turned his horse over to a groom and then hurried through the labyrinth of Castle stairways and corridors to the Alton family quarters. While he paced the hallway, Illona and Charissa examined Alanna in her chamber.

Domenic remembered standing here, outside Alanna's

door, the night of Grandmother Javanne's funeral. He'd been half drunk, boiling over with frustration and rebellion. Had it been only a year ago that Alanna had so enchanted him, that the last thing he wanted was to step into his father's place? How little he had known then of duty . . . and of love.

The door opened, and Illona stepped out. Domenic struggled not to fling himself into her arms. Her fleeting smile and the steady light of her eyes were as shelter to a man caught in a Hellers blizzard. Warmth spread through him. His pulse quickened. His heart ached with longing. Then he felt disgusted with himself. What was he doing, when Alanna was so sick?

"We have done what we can," Illona said gently. She gave no sign she was aware of Domenic's emotional turmoil, although she could hardly have mistaken the intensity of his feelings. "Before you go in, there is something you should know."

Dearest, she spoke to him mentally, *I do not think she wants to be helped.*

Aloud, she said, "We have given her willow bark infusion to lower her fever. She knows how ill she is and that if she does not receive treatment, she will most likely die. Yet she adamantly refuses to take the serum and has forbidden us to administer it if she becomes unconscious. Domenic, I know she has a reputation of being willful, but I have never seen anyone so determined. She even called upon my monitor's oath to prevent me from taking any action."

Domenic was too stunned by this news to think clearly. It sounded as if Alanna *wanted* to die.

"We swear never to enter the mind of another except by consent," Illona went on, "and Alanna has extended this to mean we cannot treat her body either if she has refused permission. She is correct in principle, of course. The only way around it is to presume she is mad, and that is clearly not the case."

"Blessed Cassilda! What are we to do?"

"Go to her, *precioso.* She spoke of the strength you give

her. Perhaps that is what she needs to regain the will to live."

Illona brushed her fingertips against the back of Domenic's wrist, a telepath's butterfly-light touch. Unable to contain his emotions, he caught her hand and brought it to his lips. An aching tenderness rose from the core of his being and flowed into the kiss.

"You would send me to Alanna, knowing my only chance of saving her may be the promise I once made to her?"

"Of course." Illona pressed their joined hands to her breast, over her beating heart. "How can your honor in keeping that promise in any way diminish what we have together? If you were capable of turning away from her, now when she needs you most, you would not be the man I love."

"Do you wish nothing for yourself, then?"

She released his hand and turned away with a little sigh. "I already have more than I ever dreamed possible. I have your love and the song that rises in my heart when we are together. I have a place in the world. I will someday be a Keeper, beholden to no man, not even the Regent of Darkover."

As long as I am pledged to Alanna, he lashed out, *you do not have to choose between Tower and marriage. How convenient for you!*

Illona's chin came up and she glared at him. An instant later, her expression softened. "Let us not quarrel. Rather, let us treasure the time we have together, and its memory when it has passed."

For a moment he was too overcome to speak. His heart rose in his throat so that his next words came as a sob. "I will never love anyone the way I love you."

Her lips trembled, and her beautiful jade-green eyes glittered with tears. He remembered the taste of her kisses, the velvet of her breasts, the silken fall of her hair across his bare chest. Some part of him wanted to cry out that he could not live without her and that once he was married to Alanna, he would never know such lovemaking again. The *catenas* locked upon his wrist would separate them forever.

The moment fled, and the under-Keeper once more looked out at him. With a bow, he left her and went in to Alanna.

Alanna was sleeping when he entered her chamber. Katherine had been sitting with her, reading aloud from an off-world book of children's stories.

Domenic was stunned by the change in Alanna. The flush of fever had lifted, leaving her skin, even her lips, as pale as alabaster. Her breathing was shallow, almost tentative, except when a fit of coughing shook her.

"Perhaps I should return another time," Domenic said, moving as if to withdraw.

"No, she will be glad of your presence. She has been asking for you." Katherine bent to smooth the damp, tangled hair back from the girl's forehead. "Alanna, little love, he is here."

Alanna's lids fluttered open, revealing eyes like faded emeralds against the whiteness of her skin.

Katherine excused herself, saying that she would wait in the family parlor should she be needed. Domenic followed her to the door.

"You will convince her to take the serum, won't you?" Katherine said. "The healers say she has very little time left before it will be too late. None of us can understand what the child is about, refusing treatment like this."

Domenic thought of the visions he had shared with Alanna and the torment they brought her. Had she reached the end of her endurance and wanted only dreamless sleep? Or had she chosen death rather than see him with another woman?

If that were true, if Alanna died, then he would be guilty of her murder. It was his selfish indulgence, his lustful infatuation, that had secured her affections. She had never faltered in her devotion, while *he* had moved on to another love.

Was he not entitled to follow his heart? Must he be loyal to a first, mistaken promise? Did it count for nothing that he had at last found the full, deep meaning of love?

Did his personal feelings have any weight when the life or sanity of an innocent was at stake? A young girl, his childhood friend, rejected by her own mother, a girl who had trusted his honor and never wished him ill . . .

"You've got to do something," Katherine went on, outrage simmering behind her words. "No one else will intervene, not even to save her life. This would never happen on a civilized—I mean, a Federation world. We have laws governing such situations."

"But *we* do not," Domenic said.

Katherine gave a sigh of exasperation. "Then maybe it's time you did!"

"I will do what I can," Domenic said.

The door closed behind her. Domenic knelt at the side of the bed and took Alanna's hand in his. Her skin felt cool. That was the temporary effect of the willow bark tea, he knew, and not any true improvement in her fever.

"Do not scold me," Alanna whispered. "It is better this way, truly it is. I feel no pain, except when I cough, only a great weariness."

"Alanna, why are you doing this? We have enough serum for everyone who needs it. You will not be depriving some other patient of treatment."

"I am not afraid of death. It will be like falling asleep, only without dreams. Oh, how I wish to never dream again."

"You don't know what you are saying," Domenic said. "What about all the good things you will never see again—spring in Thendara, the fish-birds in the Lake at Hali, Midwinter Festival Night, wildflowers in the Hellers! Get well, and we will see them together."

When she shook her head, he plunged on. "What about the life we planned together? The promises we exchanged? Our marriage?"

Alanna closed her eyes, and a stillness settled over her

flesh. Then she took a deep, shuddering breath. "Please do not torment me, Nico. I am not blind, nor am I a child to be bought off with pretty lies. You love Illona in a way you could never love me. What reason have I to live, knowing your heart belongs to her?"

Oh Blessed Cassilda, Holy St. Christopher—any god who will listen! I cannot lie to her, but I cannot let her die! Help me! Give me the words!

Slowly, choosing each phrase with care, Domenic began, "We cannot change the way we feel, any more than we can alter our natures as the gods have made us. But what we can do is choose our actions."

"Yes," she murmured in the hesitant pause that followed, "that is true enough. I—I have tried to behave better than I once did."

"Then let us honor the promise we made to one another. I do care for you, Alanna, and I would cut off my right arm before I would let any harm come to you. Please, please believe that. Perhaps," he swallowed, "this is not the grand romantic passion we dreamed of, but if you will give me the chance, I will be a true and faithful husband to you. I will send Illona away—I will never see her again."

She turned her head on her pillow to look him full in the face, her eyes wide. "You would do this for me?"

Domenic's vision shifted, and he saw the world through a wavering mist of pain. His voice formed words that could never be unsaid. Never to be free . . . Never to hold Illona in his arms, to feel the sweet rapturous union of their bodies and minds . . .

To look only upon Alanna, with whom he might never share any intimate touch. Even if she could overcome her conditioning, he could not. Another Darkovan would have been able to accept that he could love two women in very different ways. But his upbringing had been shaped by the offworld attitudes of his mother and her single-minded devotion to his father. After Illona, he did not think he was physically capable of making love to a woman with whom he could not also share his mind and heart on the deepest levels.

As for offspring, he could not bring himself to cast any blame on Alanna if that was not possible. Rory might never father children, but Yllana might marry, and if she didn't, Domenic could designate one of his cousins by his uncles Gabriel or Rafael as heir.

"Take the serum," he begged, "and live. *Di catenas,* bound forever."

A shudder passed through Alanna's body, and slowly she nodded. "Then yes, I will be your wife."

41

While Alanna and the other victims of trailmen's fever recovered, Marguerida regained her strength after her own ordeal. Seeing Mikhail alive and growing daily more fit, holding him each night in her arms, feeling his breath sweet against her skin and gazing into the blue depths of his eyes, these restored her spirit far better than any medicine. The tender care from Yllana and Rory's frequent visits, often with that nice Guardsman friend of his, warmed her heart.

On a bright morning, Marguerida and Mikhail sat in the family parlor, lingering over a last cup of Jeram's aromatic coffee. A fire crackled in the hearth, scented with her favorite balsam. Someone—Marguerida suspected it was Yllana from the haphazard arrangements—had strewn vases of orange and pink flowers throughout the parlor. Marguerida ignored the clashing colors, resting her gaze instead on each dear, familiar object. Each chair, each table and ornament, each carpet that cushioned her tread, even the warm-textured wood paneling and leaded glass windows, hummed contentment and belonging.

Home, she was home.

Her moment of tranquility came to an abrupt halt as Domenic and Rory entered and confronted her with the most unexpected announcements. Each of them, it seemed, had formed a romantic attachment.

She faced her sons, and she did not know whom she was more exasperated with—the two of them, for having kept secrets from her for so long, or herself, for having missed all the clues. From his favorite chair beside the fire, Mikhail grinned at her. Her aggravation melted into joy.

One look at the relief in Rory's eyes was enough to dispel any lingering doubts. Marguerida stood up and held out her arms. Rory returned her hug enthusiastically. Holding him at arm's length, she said, "Oh, my poor, dear boy, how difficult it must have been for you!"

Rory's shoulders tightened in a shrug.

"I suppose everyone but me guessed," she went on, blushing at how many times she had asked about his interest in girls.

"Certainly everyone in my Guards unit knew," Rory said. "Don't worry, I've done nothing to blacken the family name. I keep my professional and love lives quite separate, but I don't lie about who I am."

"No," Marguerida said softly, "I'd never want you to do that." She wondered where her wild, heedless boy had learned such discretion.

She sat down again, her thoughts whirling. It seemed that her dreams of seeing Rory happily settled with a wife were going to turn out very differently from what she'd imagined. She reminded herself that here on Darkover, men formed lifelong commitments, as respectable and honorable as any conventional marriage. Regis Hastur and Danilo Syrtis had stayed together, *bredin* and devoted friends, lord and paxman, from the time they were Rory's age. Regis had even married and fathered children.

"Well," she said, gathering her wits, "what's his name, and when do I get to meet him? Is he also in the Guards?"

Rory hesitated for a moment, looking as nervous and euphoric as any young man in the throes of his first serious love affair. "You've already met Niall. His people come from the Venza Hill country and are related to the Castamirs. I'll invite him to dinner when things settle down after the last Council meeting, if that's all right, so you can get to know him better."

"I'm sure we will all love him as you do." She turned to Domenic, struck by his mixture of sadness and resolve. "And you, Nico?"

Alanna was the last person Marguerida would have chosen for her firstborn. Perhaps that was why, for all her fears, she had failed to see what had grown between them. There had never been any doubt of Domenic's fondness for his foster-sister, but Marguerida had assumed it was no more than a childhood friendship. Alanna was beautiful and talented, and since her recovery from the fever, she had been a model of decorum. But could Alanna truly understand Domenic, with all his complexity? Could she stand by his side, whatever happened?

When Marguerida had seen Domenic with Illona, she could have sworn to the depth and passion of their connection. In fact, they reminded her of herself and Mikhail when they were first in love. Perhaps she had been mistaken in this as she had been in other things. Or perhaps . . . her heart ached to think of Domenic marrying out of a sense of obligation.

Are you sure? she asked, speaking mind to mind.

Domenic glanced away. "Alanna and I have been sworn to one another for a long time. I am sorry I did not tell you earlier. We feared your disapproval. I know that your relationship with Alanna has not always been an easy one. Still, it was wrong to keep it from you, and from you, too, Father."

Mikhail nodded. "That is behind us now. Both you and Alanna are grown. If she is your choice, then we wish you happiness together."

"I am sorry that I made it difficult for you to confide in me," Marguerida said. "I will try to be a good mother-in-law, or as close an approximation as I can manage."

Domenic kissed her on the cheek, murmuring his thanks. As he and Rory took their leave, Marguerida thought about the difference between them. Rory was all high spirits and jubilation, but then, he had always been more open in his emotions. Domenic did not look like a man contemplating a joyous, much desired union. He looked like ... she did not know what. Yet she sensed no uncertainty in him, no reservations. He was completely committed to this course of action.

Marguerida went to stand beside Mikhail and, sighing, laid her arm across his shoulder. He touched her hand, intensifying the light rapport that always linked their minds.

Nico will be well, beloved, Mikhail sent his thought to her.

And happy? she answered. *Will he be happy?*

He has never had an easy time of it, and yet he has found his own way in his own time. A year or two ago he could not have stepped into my place or led the city through a crisis. He has become a leader of men. We must trust that in this marriage, as well, he knows what he is doing.

Marguerida bent over and kissed her husband, trying to convince herself to be satisfied with his faith in their oldest child. "Well, that's settled. Now I must be off. There is an interview I cannot put off any longer."

"You will be careful, won't you, to not overexert yourself?"

She paused by the door. "Only if you do, Mikhail Lanart-Hastur, but you know perfectly well that neither of us is going to take that advice!"

Marguerida had only a few minutes to settle herself in her office when a servant announced Jeram's arrival. She remained at her desk as he came in, then realized she was hiding behind it and forced herself to sit on the divan. They each took some *jaco* from the pitcher on the sideboard. She did not really want any, not after the coffee earlier, but pouring and stirring in honey to her taste gave her something to do with her hands. The small gestures eased the tension of opening the conversation.

"Thank you for coming to see me," she said.

"It's a welcome diversion," he replied with an engaging half-grin. "I've been packing serum to send to key distribution points throughout the Domains and training Renunciate volunteers to administer it. It's tedious but necessary work. I'm glad to see you recovering."

"I didn't ask you here to talk about my health but about quite another matter. About the Battle of Old North Road and what happened afterward." She paused, waiting for his response. "That is, if you're willing to discuss it."

"That issue has not been resolved, has it?" he said. "The Council means to take it up again before they all go their separate ways."

"I don't mean the charges Francisco brought. He is— *was*—a hateful, mean-spirited, vindictive man who didn't care two pins about *laran* ethics. He just wanted to hurt Mikhail through me. No, I mean what happened between you and me. I mean that I used the Alton Gift on you. I imposed my will upon yours."

Jeram met her gaze. His eyes were steady, a deep clear russet. She saw none of the hostility she expected, no bitterness or resentment. "I've talked with your father about this issue on more than one occasion. You don't need to apologize or justify what you did. I'd be the last person to let the Federation get their hands on a weapon like your *laran.*"

Marguerida rubbed her sweating palms on her skirt. How odd it was, she thought, that her hands were wet and her mouth was dry. She cleared her throat.

"Sometimes things are not so simple," she said. "I may have forced you and the others to forget the battle for a good reason, but I still may have . . ." . . . *harmed* you.

Her voice faltered. This was harder than she'd thought. She could still pull back, say it was a mistake, drop the matter, gracefully send him on his way. Had Jeram not said she did not need to apologize?

Her father had tried to warn her. *"I of all people, who knew what it was like to have my mind and will taken over by another, should have known better."*

At the time, she had seen only a tortured man inflicting

unnecessary guilt upon himself. She had seen only the political consequences of their actions, not the effect of using the Alton Gift upon herself and her father personally.

Lew had made his amends, but she could not seek the solace of Nevarsin Monastery. She belonged in the world, not a cloister or a Tower. So she must find her peace in some other way.

She plunged on. "When I was in the Overworld, I met a ghost, no, an entity from my past. When I was little, she overshadowed my mind. I didn't even remember for a long time, but nonetheless, she . . . influenced me. So you see, I know what it means to have someone else controlling my thoughts and memories."

Something broke open inside her. "I am so sorry! I wish there had been some other way!"

Jeram looked directly at her again, his expression calm and sympathetic. "You have not injured me. If anything, you *helped* me by activating my latent *laran*. When it kicked in, I got pretty sick, but that part isn't your fault. As a result, however, I had to face things in myself— what I had done. That would not have happened without you."

"I don't understand," she said.

He leaned forward and took her hands in his. Living among telepaths, she had become unaccustomed to casual touch. But this was not casual.

"You made your choice in order to preserve life," he said, his voice low and intense. "I made mine to destroy it. By the grace of whatever gods exist, I was given a chance to use that training to do good instead. Thank you."

Unable to bear the intensity of the contact any longer, Marguerida drew her hands away. In her heart, she felt Jeram's forgiveness and also his own yearning to be forgiven.

Marguerida did not know what she could say to ease his burden. Surely, what he had done to save Darkover from trailmen's fever must atone for his past. But she was not Jeram any more than she was her father. Each of them must find his or her own resolution. With as much warmth as she could summon, she wished him well.

After Jeram left, she stood at the window, blankly looking out. After the Battle of Old North Road, she had made a deliberate choice, weighing the alternatives. But that was not the only time she had used the Alton Gift. The first time happened not long after her arrival on Darkover, when she did not even know what *laran* was. Taken by surprise, she had sent a young boy to the Overworld. He could have died there.

When those bandits ambushed me on the trail, I used the Gift again. I could have killed them, as well.

Memories flashed by, the small uses of her Gift as well as the bigger ones. She remembered her father's anguished cry, *"Marja, no!"* on the night of the riot at the Castle gates.

I've been lucky so far. I haven't killed or maimed anyone with my Gift. How long can that luck hold? How can I trust myself not to make the wrong choice in a moment of desperation? Father was right. Laran *is too powerful to be used lightly or on impulse.*

Only yesterday, Istvana had spoken with Marguerida on the charges still pending against her. With an expression that would have been apologetic for anyone but a Keeper, Istvana explained that although the Comyn Council might overlook Francisco's accusation of *laran* abuse, the Keepers could not. The Comyn were naturally grateful to Marguerida and Mikhail for saving their lives at the Battle of Old North Road. They also understood the necessity of making sure the Federation never found out how powerful *laran* was. But the Keepers, especially conservatives like Laurinda and Moira diAsturien, took another view. They felt responsible for enforcing the traditional limits on *laran,* and they were accustomed to wielding absolute authority.

So, Marguerida had responded, they might not admit any valid justification for erasing the memories of the Terran soldiers. *And what about my father? Hasn't he suffered enough?*

Istvana, seeing Marguerida's stricken reaction, had attempted to reassure her. "You are not without friends, we who know and love you. My fellow Keepers may be strong-willed and opinionated, but we all want the best for Darkover. Surely, once all sides of the question are presented, we will reach an acceptable resolution."

An acceptable resolution . . .

The only place Marguerida knew where her Gift could be safely used by those standards was a Tower. She'd studied at Arilinn and then Neskaya in her youth and thought she was done with it. More than that, she was no longer a single woman who could afford the luxury of withdrawing from the world; she had a husband, children, responsibilities as chatelaine of Comyn Castle, even a musical career.

Sighing, she returned to her desk and picked up a stack of papers. Indulging in fruitless maundering would get her nowhere. Her natural optimism began to assert itself. In time, a solution would present itself. Until then, there was more than enough work to distract her.

42

The Comyn Council gathered in the Crystal Chamber for its last session of the year. The season had already continued overlong, and the fair weather of summer was quickly giving way to nightly snow and the threat of storms to come. Those who had traveled farthest or who must negotiate mountain passes on their way home were anxious to begin their journeys.

Domenic settled into his place under the Hastur banner of blue and silver, watching as people filed into the Crystal Chamber. The Chamber itself seemed as ageless and untouched as ever, yet many of the faces had changed. Darius-Mikhail Zabal was now Warden of Aillard, sitting beside Laurinda MacBard, presiding head of the Keepers Council. Most of the other Keepers, including Linnea Storn, kept together beneath their new banner. The Ardais enclosure, once almost empty, now held Kennard-Dyan, his Heir, and his second legitimated son, as well as Danilo Syrtis, quiet and solemn.

Mikhail's heavy carved chair remained empty, awaiting his return. Marguerida, her face pale but radiant, sat in her usual chair, while Rory and Ylanna occupied benches behind them.

Grandfather Lew had announced his intention to return permanently to Nevarsin at the conclusion of this final session. Alanna had taken her seat beside him. Once she had

accepted the serum, she had made a rapid recovery, but
Domenic had never seen her so withdrawn, so pensive. She
would not tell him what troubled her. When they were
married, he promised himself, he would coax the truth
from her, although how he might give her ease, he had no
idea.

Illona finished setting the telepathic dampers and took
her place with the other Keepers. The massive double
doors swung open, and the senior Guardsman announced
Mikhail's arrival.

Mikhail entered the Crystal Chamber, moving slowly,
for his muscles had not yet fully recovered their flexibility.
Donal followed a pace behind. The effect, combined with
Mikhail's stately bearing, was dignified rather than stiff.
Watching him, hearing the hush of respect that swept the
Chamber, Domenic's eyes stung.

Surveying the assembly, Mikhail began the formal, time-
honored greeting. "Kinsmen, nobles, Comynari! I bid you
welcome to this, our final gathering for the year. We have
come through a terrible time, a season that has tested us
all, as individuals and as a Council." He did not add that
the years to come would prove whether they had risen to
the challenge or irrevocably damaged the old social order.

"Now, as we prepare to bid one another farewell, we
have cause for rejoicing. It is my very great privilege to
present to you a man who, more than any other, has labored on our behalf during the epidemic of trailmen's
fever. You met him once before, under far less favorable
circumstances. Now I ask you to welcome the *Terranan* Jeremiah Reed, who has chosen to live among us as Jeram of
Nevarsin."

Mikhail nodded to the Guardsmen standing to either
side of the entrance. They opened the doors, and Jeram
walked in. He came alone, without an honor guard, proceeding at a dignified pace down the length of the Chamber, and halted facing Mikhail.

In a single fluid movement, Marguerida got to her feet,
followed an instant later by her father. Across the Chamber,

in the Ardais enclosure, Danilo stood up, followed by Hermes Aldaran. A ripple spread through the assembly, and within the span of a handful of heartbeats, every person had risen.

Jeram stood there, his face impassive but his eyes far brighter than normal. Not even a hint of tension in his jaw betrayed any emotion. Only when the Council had seated themselves again did faint color wash across his face.

"Jeram of Nevarsin," Mikhail said, "as Regent of the Comyn and Warden of Hastur, I bid you welcome to this Council and extend to you our deepest gratitude."

"*Vai dom.*" Jeram bowed to Mikhail, a brief inclination of the head. "My lords, my ladies. It has been my privilege to serve. I never expected to draw upon my Terran skills in this way, but I am profoundly grateful that I was able to use them in such a worthy cause."

Around the Chamber heads nodded in approval. Jeram had answered as graciously as any of them could wish.

Darius-Mikhail, as Warden of Aillard, rose to speak. "On behalf of myself and my Domain, I invite Jeram to sit with me as my guest for this closing session."

As Jeram took the seat offered to him, a ripple of tension passed through the room. His presence served as a reminder of the matter still unresolved, the charges Francisco had made against Marguerida. Jeram might not be the plaintiff, but the words had been spoken, and the accusation still stood.

Domenic braced himself when Laurinda rose to address the Council and was surprised that it concerned quite another matter.

"Thendara has long been in need of a working Tower," she said, somehow managing to modulate her high, nasal voice, "both to facilitate communications by telepathic relay and to participate in the search and training of new candidates. The Keepers Council has therefore decided to reopen Comyn Tower, and *Domna* Linnea Storn has consented to serve as its Keeper. The circle will be small at first, drawn from volunteers from existing Towers, but we hope that with a vigorous recruitment program, it will soon grow to full strength."

Glancing around the Chamber, Domenic thought that even the most imaginative members of the audience could barely encompass such an astonishing announcement. There had not been a new Tower in the Domains within recorded history, or a renewed Tower either, only closures. Once, he knew, there had been many more, but time, attrition, and the slow decay of the Comyn had caused too many to be abandoned.

"And now," Mikhail said, "my son and Heir, Domenic, wishes to announce a more personal reason for celebration."

Domenic stepped forward so that the entire assembly could see him. For an instant, his resolve wavered. The next words, once said, could never be taken back.

The telepathic dampers made mental contact with Illona impossible. If he so much as looked at her, or felt the sweetness of her mind touching his, he would break down. He must find a way to endure their parting, and he would do his best to treat Alanna with respect and kindness, even though they might never share physical intimacy. Honor demanded no less.

He took a breath, carefully avoiding even a casual glance in Illona's direction. "I have asked *Damisela* Alanna Alar to become my wife, and she has consented."

Domenic's voice sounded remote and impassive to his own ears. He had rehearsed the announcement so many times in his own mind that all emotion seemed utterly spent. His heart felt like a lump of stone.

Excitement buzzed through the Crystal Chamber. Domenic imagined them making plans for his wedding and all the attendant festivities. They had not had such an occasion—a Hastur wedding—since Dani had married Miralys Elhalyn.

The murmur died down as Alanna stepped to the front of the Alton enclosure. People nudged their neighbors to stop talking so that they could hear the bride's acceptance speech.

Alanna had rarely looked so beautiful or carried herself so gracefully. She was paler and thinner than before her illness, her skin like milk against the gleaming copper of her hair and the muted green of her gown, her breasts crossed by a tartan in Alar colors.

"*Vai domyn,* kinsmen and kinswomen." Her voice had never been very strong, but the audience had fallen so still that even a whisper could be heard. "I am aware of the great honor offered me by *Dom* Domenic Alton-Hastur and by this distinguished assembly. I will not insult you with protestations of my own unworthiness, but I must respectfully decline."

"Decline? What does she mean, *decline*?" one of the ladies chirped.

"She cannot seriously intend—"

"Hush!"

Domenic stared at her, dumbfounded.

"Such an action on my part," Alanna went on, "requires an explanation, lest anyone think ill of the man who has so honored me with his proposal. Let me be absolutely clear on this point. No fault whatsoever belongs to Domenic. He is . . ." and here her voice faltered, but only for an instant, "he is everything I dreamed of in a husband. But I am not free, I *cannot* enter into a marriage with him or anyone else."

"Did I hear right? Is she *refusing* him?" Voices buzzed throughout the Chamber.

"What is the girl thinking, to turn down such a marriage? Has she lost her senses?"

"She *cannot*? What does that mean?"

Expressions of disbelief and astonishment mingled with those of curiosity. Domenic recovered his wits enough to notice that neither his mother nor Grandfather Lew seemed surprised.

"Darkover has survived the trailmen's fever, thanks to the efforts of Jeram of Nevarsin and *Domna* Marguerida

Alton," Alanna went on. "We Comyn still face many problems. At the beginning of this season, we discussed the need to train those with *laran,* wherever they may be found. I—I am one such person. The events of the past year have convinced me that no matter how hard I try, I can never lead an ordinary life."

The last of the objections fell away into silence tinged with respect and not a little awe. Watching her, Darius-Mikhail looked sad and resigned.

"For the future of the Comyn," Alanna went on, her voice gaining in surety, "for the example I will set to others, and for my own sanity, I must withdraw to a Tower. There I hope not only to master my Gifts but to use them for the benefit of others. Whether I will ever be able to return to normal society, I cannot say. Therefore, it is only right that I release Domenic from his promise, that he may be free to choose another wife."

With those words, Alanna returned to her seat, cutting off further discussion. From the Keepers section, Linnea Storn nodded in solemn approval.

Domenic could not think of what to say. As his mind took in the meaning of Alanna's words, one part of him reeled in exhilaration—*he was free, his honor intact!*

Another part cringed in embarrassment at being publicly refused, and yet another in shame, to have his dearest wish fulfilled. What should he say? What *could* he say?

Fortunately, Dani Hastur, who had taken over the duties as director of the agenda, filled the awkward silence with a series of routine business details needed to conclude the session. When he had finished, he glanced down at the document in his hands.

"There remains the unanswered charge made in this very Chamber, which we must decide whether to address, to dismiss, or to postpone until next season," Dani said. Everyone understood that Mikhail, because of his relationship to Marguerida, could not preside over this last matter.

There was a stir in the Keepers section. Laurinda spoke again. "We of the Keepers Council believe this case falls solely under our jurisdiction. It is a matter of *laran* abuse by one who is—or was—oath-sworn to a Tower. As a novice at Arilinn, Marguerida Alton solemnly took the vow of a monitor, *Never to enter the mind of another without consent, and then only to help or heal.* Therefore, it is we, the Keepers, who must determine her guilt."

Sitting behind Laurinda, Istvana's expression turned grim, and Domenic remembered that she had been his mother's oldest and dearest friend on Darkover, and her mentor as well. How difficult this must be for them both, he thought with a rush of compassion.

"And you, *Domna* Marguerida," Dani said, "do you accept the right of the Keepers Council to pass judgment on you? Will you abide by their decision?"

"I do, and I will," Marguerida replied gravely.

Dani turned to Jeram. "Will you, also, accept the decision of the Keepers Council?"

"I have already withdrawn the charges that were made, most unwillingly, on my account," Jeram said. "In these last tendays, we have faced problems far more important than whether one person acted as she thought best to defend her entire world. Therefore, I ask the Keepers Council to dismiss all charges against Marguerida Alton."

Across the galleries, people exclaimed in surprise.

"The Keepers Council refuses!" Laurinda declared. "The offense was not against you personally, Jeram of Nevarsin, but against the principles of *laran* ethics. The Towers have been entrusted with the guardianship of matrix science. Therefore, this is a matter for our sole judgment."

"The Council has not agreed to this!" Robert Aldaran jumped to his feet. "The Keepers do not dictate to the Council! *Dom* Francisco brought these charges as a member of this body, and we Comyn, not an assemblage of Keepers, must determine the outcome!"

"Do you speak for Aldaran?" Dani said.

Gabriel Lanart-Alton answered, "He speaks for all of us. We Comyn have never been ruled by an assemblage of Keepers."

"Is this not a matter for *both* the Council and the Keepers?" Danilo Syrtis said.

"That's true enough," someone said.

"But what if we cannot agree?" another voice asked.

"No!" Lorill Vallonde cried. "It is ours as a matter of principle!"

A renewed murmur sprang up, subsiding only when Dani shouted for order.

"We Keepers cannot let such a matter pass," Laurinda continued, "no matter what the Council decides. Jeram, you must accept that these matters are beyond your understanding. *Laran* abuse is a very serious issue. Ask *Dom* Lewis Alton what *laran,* acting through the Sharra matrix, did at Caer Donn. That is only a tiny fraction of its potential. It must be handled with utmost care and the highest integrity."

"I know a little about what happened with the Sharra matrix," Jeram said, once Dani motioned permission for him to respond. "I also remember the Battle of Old North Road. This lady and her husband were not the aggressors. They were the victims of an ambush, and I was among those who lay in wait for them, armed with blasters against swords. There are two sides to every story, and I think you should ask Marguerida to tell hers."

Another flurry of exclamations followed, quickly dying away.

"*Domna* Marguerida Alton," Dani said, "you stand accused of using your Gifts in a manner contrary to your oath. What have you to say in your own defense?"

Marguerida got to her feet. Droplets of sweat gleamed on her face in the light of the ceiling prisms. "The charges are true."

Stunned silence answered her. Then Hermes Aldaran, who had been glowering beneath the eagle banner of his Domain, lunged to his feet.

"Marja, you cannot be serious! Tell them the rest of the story!" He turned to the crowd. "*Vai domyn!* You all know that *Domna* Marguerida used her *laran* at the Battle of

Old North Road. So did *Dom* Mikhail. Most of you, like me, were part of Regis Hastur's funeral cortege. *All of us* could have been killed, without Marguerida's Gift and her willingness to use it. Do you propose to punish her for defending us?"

Around the Chamber, heads nodded. Expressions turned somber, even those who had not been present at the battle. They all knew how easily the Council could have been decimated, if not entirely eliminated.

Before the pause became uncomfortably awkward, Hermes went on. "After *Domna* Marguerida helped defeat the Terran soldiers, what other choice did she have? Should she have allowed those men to return to their Federation commanders with the knowledge of what *laran* can do? Should we have turned Darkover into a military asset for the Federation?"

"No, never!"

"Zandru curse them—the likes of Belfontaine!"

A few people shook their heads, muttering. Hermes might have represented Darkover in the Federation, but he was an Aldaran, and the ancient suspicion still ran like a dark undercurrent through the Council.

When Rufus DiAsturien stepped forward to address the Council, however, the muttering subsided. Domenic braced himself, for the old lord had never been friendly to his family.

"As Keepers, then, what else would you have had *Domna* Marguerida do?" *Dom* Rufus demanded. "Murder those men as they lay helpless? Was this not a *compassionate* use of the Alton Gift, to allow them to return home with no greater loss than a few minutes of their memories?"

Domenic thought of Grandmother Javanne, serving her family and Domain, even as his mother had served the Comyn and Darkover. For each of them, there had been a price.

"I move that all charges be dropped!" Hermes said. Across the room, some scattered few raised their voices in agreement, but others grumbled in dissent. The Keepers sat like granite images.

Marguerida closed her eyes. Domenic caught the gleam of silvery runnels on her cheeks. She grasped the railing of the enclosure for support.

"I thank you, but that does not change my decision to accept the judgment of the Keepers Council," Marguerida said. "My father once said to me that he was not proud of what he had done. I must share that sentiment, or risk falling prey to arrogance and pride. *Domna* Laurinda is right; our Gifts must never be used lightly or without precautions. I have entered into the minds of others, without consent, neither to help nor to heal but for my own purposes. I cannot deny it."

Laurinda signaled for a pause in the proceedings while the Keepers conferred together. "*Domna* Marguerida, we understand that you did not intend to misuse your Gift," Laurinda said a few moment later, "and also that life is filled with unexpected events and unpredictable crises. Under other circumstances, you would not be permitted to use your *laran* except under the supervision of a Keeper. We would have confined you to a Tower until we were certain that you had learned restraint and mastered your impulsiveness."

Clearly unable to speak, Marguerida nodded. Mikhail paled, but he held himself motionless. Domenic, thinking of what such an incarceration would mean to them, after all they had been through, felt sick at heart.

"This would not be an easy or lightly made decision," Laurinda said. "We understand that you have no vocation as a *leronis*. The separation from your family would be a terrible hardship. We also recognize that under other conditions you might have lived your entire life without any need to use the Alton Gift, and those very circumstances give rise to our gratitude to you, on the part of the Council, the Domains ... and ourselves." She paused, glancing at Linnea Storn.

Linnea, who had been listening with an expression of calm

interest, now spoke. "Fortunately, with the re-establishment of Comyn Tower, there will now be a working circle close by. One could say, since you are the chatelaine of the Castle, it lies within your own home. You need not go into exile in order to study further. Will you accept this judgement and place yourself under my direction as your Keeper?"

Marguerida lifted her chin. "I will."

Relief surged through Domenic. He had known Lady Linnea his entire life; she was firm but kind, and she loved Marguerida almost as a daughter. Surely there could be no better outcome, unless the Keepers themselves reversed their decision.

"What judgment does the Keepers Council have for me?" Lew Alton's hoarse voice rang out. "My daughter was not alone in using *laran* to tamper with the memories of the Terran soldiers."

Domenic shuddered and saw the same anguish reflected on the faces of the assembly. Was there any man among them who had suffered or sacrificed more than his grandfather? Any man more deserving of peace during the time left to him?

Laurinda bowed her head. "Your own conscience has exacted a far heavier penalty than anything we could impose, Lord Alton. We have no concerns about your future actions. If it is your wish to return to St.-Valentine's-of-the-Snows, to spend your remaining years in peaceful contemplation, you are free to do so with our blessing."

43

After the session closed with the usual ceremonial formalities, Domenic's first thought was to find either his mother or Alanna. He wasn't sure which one had astonished him more. Just when he thought he understood everything and had steeled himself to make the honorable choice between one painful alternative and another, the situation had changed. A completely unforeseen outcome had arisen, and the people he had known all his life had behaved like strangers.

He was not able to leave right away. Half the Council gathered around him to talk about one thing or another. The Aldaran lords, the diAsturiens, his Uncle Gabriel, and even Kennard-Dyan stopped to offer congratulations for a job well done, as if Domenic were personally responsible for both the end of the plague and the dismissal of the charges against Marguerida. Had things gone otherwise, they would doubtless be blaming him now. People needed someone visible to either praise or condemn, and if a king were not available, a regent—even a former acting regent—must suffice.

The last of the court ladies took their leave, clucking like ruffled barnfowl and implying that they hoped to be celebrating his engagement to some other lady in the near future.

Domenic leaned on the railing of the Hastur enclosure,

his head lowered, too drained in spirit to move. The Chamber was almost empty except for the Guardsmen and a few minor family members, who had been seated at the rear of the enclosures and now followed their more distinguished relatives out.

A footfall at the back of the Hastur section caught his attention. The telepathic dampers had been turned off, and he sensed Illona's nearness. His throat filled with a dozen things he longed to say to her, but all he could do was to gaze into her eyes.

"My poor Domenic," she murmured. "You are too severe with yourself. Even Regis Hastur and old Danvan were young and inexperienced once, and I doubt that either could have done better than you have."

Domenic shook his head. "I was lucky, nothing more. Jeram and my mother developed the serum in time, Danilo and Darius-Mikhail had the city and the outer encampments organized so it could be distributed, not to mention addressing the problems that brought those people here. My parents are both recovering." *Alanna released me from my promise.* "Things could have gone far worse."

"But they did not," she insisted. "When next year's troubles come, as they surely must, you will not face them alone. None of us—not Regent, not King, not Keeper— works in isolation. In the Tower, every member of the circle is vital to its success. Here in Thendara, in the Comyn Council, you have drawn together an extraordinary group of people to help you—Danilo, Lew, Jeram, Darius-Mikhail—"

"You."

She stopped, considering. "Well, yes."

"And now that my father has assumed his duties again and the season is over, you are all to go your separate ways. The Keepers have already been too long from their Towers."

He added, *I will miss you more than I have words to say.*

Illona looked away, her lips curving in a gentle smile. "I shall not tease you for being tired and grumpy. Let's leave so the servants can do their work. Your mother has planned a small family supper, and I'm to ensure your safe arrival."

Just as Domenic and Illona stepped through the double doors, a page trotted up with a message from Linnea Storn, asking Illona to come at once.

"Yes, of course." Illona turned to Domenic. "Since Lady Linnea is to be Keeper here, I must show her proper deference and not delay. Promise me you'll eat something and try not to worry."

She looked so beautiful and so severe at the same time, Domenic smiled despite himself. His heart ached at the prospect of a single day without her. He said he would do his best, and then she was gone, hurrying after the page in a swirl of gray skirts.

Domenic was half tempted to leave the Castle and spend the remaining daylight losing himself in the old Terran Trade City, but he had given Illona his word. As he climbed the stairs to the family quarters, he realized that he was too emotionally drained to think clearly. The Council session had left his head spinning. He could not imagine Thendara without Grandfather Lew or Alanna, or with his mother spending a good portion of her time in the newly reopened Comyn Tower. Yllana would depart for Castle Aldaran tomorrow, and Rory had his own life with the City Guards and Niall. Domenic tried to cheer himself up with the thought that Danilo would still be here, as would Darius-Mikhail. Perhaps now would be a good time to select a paxman, someone who would stay with him always and not be leaving on his own affairs.

And that, his own voice whispered through his mind, *is the worst reason of all, to bind a man to your side because you are lonely.*

In his own chambers, his body-servant helped him change from formal court attire into more comfortable clothing, a loose shirt of blue *linex,* lightly embroidered around neckline and cuffs, vest and pants of butter-soft suede, and his oldest pair of house boots. A sword and dagger, each in its sheath and buckled on a belt, lay on the bed.

The very notion that he must go armed in the Castle, in his own family's quarters, nauseated him. It took only a few minutes to splash his face and hands with cold water and cross the short corridor, leaving the sword belt behind.

——— ✦ ———

Domenic found Grandfather Lew waiting for him in the family parlor, along with Yllana and Mikhail. The table had been set with a fine cloth and beeswax candles. Instead of summer's flowers, Marilla's vase held a garland of yellow and orange leaves.

"So here we are," Lew said. "Marja has satisfied both the Council and the Keepers, Jeram has set his conscience to rest, Yllana can hardly wait to leave us again—"

"Grandpapa! What a thing to say!"

"—and Alanna will follow her own path and find her own happiness."

"I will miss you, *chiya*," Mikhail said, patting Yllana's hand.

"Oh, Papa, I have to grow up *sometime*. Terése and Belle are waiting for me! At least," Yllana paused, lacing her fingers through his, "I go with the knowledge that you will be all right."

"Grandfather Lew," Domenic said, taking his seat at the table, "you and I have had so little time since we came back to Thendara. Can you and Illona not delay your return for a little while?"

Lew gave him an odd look. "I must travel while the weather is kind to these old bones."

Marguerida emerged from her office and embraced them each in turn, lingering with her hand on her husband's shoulder. "Goodness, what a day! Can you imagine, so many surprises! How have you been holding up, Father?"

"As well as any man my age," Lew answered, "though I confess I am weary for the peace of St. Valentine's."

"Then it is good that all matters have been laid to rest, so that you may return with a light heart," Marguerida said, taking her seat.

The door swung open, and Alanna walked in, not with her old breathless flurry but with a new poise. "Pardon me," she said, curtsying to Lew and then Marguerida and Mikhail, "am I interrupting a private conversation?"

Marguerida said, "It is one in which I would gladly include you, child. Now that we are all gathered, we can begin."

The meal, served by a pair of servants Domenic had known all his life, began with mushroom soup, fragrant with herbs, followed by savory onion and cheese tarts, crusty nut bread, and fruit compote topped with clotted cream. After the first bite, no one spoke much. Domenic had not realized until that moment how hungry he was.

"I've always been amazed at how much *laran* energy you burn under those telepathic dampers," Marguerida said, just as if he'd spoken aloud. "Pass the bread, Yllanna dear."

"I wondered about that, too." Alanna picked up the basket at her elbow and offered it to Yllana. Yllana, looking puzzled at this act of courtesy, handed it to her mother.

"Is it true for normal—I mean people without *laran*—as well?" Alanna asked.

"I shouldn't think so," Mikhail said.

"Even when we are not speaking mind to mind, we are always in some degree of rapport with one another," Lew explained. "Our *laran* creates a web that binds us together. What touches one affects us all. It is not possible," he said directly to Alanna, "for any sorrow to be truly private."

"That is why we must be especially polite to one another," Alanna said with a trace of diffidence in her voice, as if asking for his approval. "Because we all need something—some place within ourselves—that is ours alone."

"Exactly," Mikhail said, smiling at her in approval.

Marguerida sighed. "Sometimes, I fear, that lesson takes a lifetime to learn."

Lew reached out to brush her wrist with his single hand. "We have all the time we need to do all the things we must. Not one minute more, not one minute less."

Domenic rubbed his temples, which had begun to

throb. "I don't understand any of this. Grandfather Lew is leaving tomorrow and Alanna's going who knows where, Yllana's off to Aldaran again, Mother is to return to a Tower, even if it is in our back yard, and here you sit, talking *philosophy*!"

His words sounded peevish to his own ears, but no one laughed at him. Instead, Marguerida answered seriously.

"I know this will come as a surprise to you, Nico. It certainly did to me. I am feeling—I supposed the correct word is *relieved*—to have this whole matter done with. You see, in some part of my mind, I *knew* it was wrong to use the Alton Gift to control other people. When I was only a small child, I was overshadowed by that horrible old witch, Ashara. It took all my will and strength, not to mention a good deal of rescuing by Mikhail, to finally get her out of my mind. You would think, wouldn't you, that I would be the last person to use my *laran* on anyone else?"

Domenic stared at her, horror-struck. "Are you saying you have been *overshadowing* someone?"

"No, of course not!"

"Don't be silly, Domenic," Alanna said. "Auntie Marguerida would never do anything so vile. She may be bossy, but it's only because she loves us."

Something in Alanna's tone, so like her old impertinence, made Domenic want to laugh. The tension in the air evaporated. Even Yllana, who had endured a great deal of Alanna's bad temper, relaxed.

"No," Marguerida said, more slowly, "what I mean is that I may have been born here, but I was raised off-world. I never received the intensive training in *laran* that I would have here on Darkover. When I was surprised or frightened or sometimes just too tired to think straight, I reacted without thinking. I used the Alton Gift."

She paused, her golden eyes thoughtful. "In ordinary matters, I believe I manage my temper well enough. But the Alton Gift, because of its lethal potential, demands more than ordinary control. I'm looking forward to learning how to trust myself completely with it."

"So, you're not unhappy about having to study with Lady Linnea?" Domenic asked.

"Not at all. She's always been kind to me, and it will be fun learning from her," Marguerida said. "She's like me, a woman who had a career, and a very important one, and then gave it up for husband and family. Now she has returned to the work she was trained for, but in new and exciting ways. She not only helped to create the Keepers Council, she will have a Tower of her own, one that has not functioned for years!"

"I think you will understand one another very well," Mikhail said. "Linnea knows the pressures a woman of the Comyn must face. I suspect you will find in her a friend and ally, as well as a teacher."

Domenic turned to Alanna. She had been listening quietly to most of the conversation, her face reflecting her understanding. Mirrored in her eyes, he saw her own hopes, that she might find the strength to live with her visions, a purpose for her life, a use for her talents.

"Now, I suppose it is my turn," she said, looking up at him with a new straightforwardness. "Domenic, we could never have made each other happy. At least, *I* could not have made *you* happy, and no man alive could have done for me what I needed to do for myself. To grow up."

She glanced at Lew, and again Domenic was struck by her obvious admiration for the old man.

"All my life," she explained, "I have gotten what I wanted by throwing childish tantrums. I behaved especially badly to you, Auntie Marguerida, and to you, my foster-sister, Yllana. No one took me seriously because I did not *deserve* their respect."

Alanna turned back to Domenic. "I could not understand why, when you were so clearly in love with Illona, you were still willing to marry me. The only reason that made sense was that you were too honorable to do otherwise. But as I felt the serum working in me, another thought came to me. You did not want me to die—you *cared* about me."

"Of course I did," he said. "I always have."

"If you cared," she went on, "then there must be something in me worth caring about. Something beyond bad temper and selfish behavior. It was then, I think, that I started paying attention to my other visions, the good ones."

She paused, her eyes shining. "Yes, mixed in among the city of the dead, the explosions in the sky, the fires and floods, I saw things of beauty. I saw myself standing on a balcony overlooking a valley filled with flowering trees, and their perfume rose up to fill me, and I was laughing. I saw myself cradled in a circle of light, made up of people who knew me and loved me. I . . . well, never mind. Nowhere did I see myself with you. So I went to Illona and asked her advice."

"To *Illona?*"

"She, too, was once terrified of being sent to a Tower," Mikhail pointed out.

"Remember when you discovered her among the Travelers?" Marguerida said. "She'd heard nothing but horror stories about 'the witches of the Towers.' And look where she ended up—under-Keeper at Nevarsin, and now at Comyn Tower."

"Here? At Comyn Tower?" In a moment of wild confusion, Domenic wondered if he were still asleep and dreaming this entire conversation.

Illona was to stay in Thendara!

"I believe I said that," Marguerida said. "Didn't she tell you?"

He shook his head. "She was called away . . . to talk to *Domna* Linnea."

Yllana giggled at him. "You goose! Couldn't you guess why?"

When Lew smiled, it seemed to Domenic that the old scars on his face faded into crinkles of delight.

Of course. Now it was all beginning to make sense.

"So where will you go?" Domenic asked Alanna, trying to distract his thoughts from dizzying conclusions.

"To Nevarsin Tower. It's a fair journey, but I believe the

separation from home will be good for me." She gave Lew a shy smile. "I will still have you as my teacher."

"Poor Darius-Mikhail," Marguerida sighed. "How he will miss you."

Alanna lifted her chin. "There is nothing to miss. We have not exchanged more than a dozen sentences. All he can know of me is a pretty face, and when I marry—*if* I marry—I want to be valued for more than that!"

For a long moment, there did not seem to be anything more to say. They all looked at one another with expressions of satisfaction.

The servants returned with a pitcher of Terran coffee. Its distinctive aroma filled the air. Sighing in contentment, Marguerida poured it out for everyone.

At the first sip, a grin stretched Lew's scarred features. "Wherever did you get this, Marja?"

"Jeram has connections it's best not to question too closely," she said.

"Then there's only one thing to do," Domenic said, lifting his own cup, "and that is to tell you all how much I love you and to wish everyone the blessings of the gods, wherever they may go. *Adelandeyo.*"

"Yes, indeed," Marguerida said, laughing. "I'll drink to that."

— ✦ —

EPILOGUE

— ✦ —

The first winter snows fell gently upon Thendara. At first the flakes melted as they touched the ground. By morning, however, white draped the roofs and piled in drifts along the streets. Children darted through the marketplaces where farmers were still bringing in late-harvest sweet gourds and bushels of oats, hazelnuts, and hearty rye.

Snug and warm behind the walls of Comyn Castle, Danilo lingered over breakfast in his sitting room with Linnea. It had become their custom once or twice a tenday after her night's work in the newly constituted circle of Comyn Tower. He had been concerned about her at first to take up such a demanding post at her age.

"Do not trouble yourself for me," Linnea said. "Instead, be happy that I am once again doing the work I was trained for. I did not have to give up marriage or children"—*or love, as we both well know*—"the way Keepers trained in the old tradition were forced to. Look at Illona and how well she balances her own work as under-Keeper and her relationship with Domenic."

Domenic and Illona had been quietly discreet about their relationship, and Illona was so respected that no one would have dared to call her a *barragana*. In fact, the winter court had taken to referring to her as his *leronis*-consort.

"I have never seen him so happy, either," Danilo said.

She laughed. "It seems there is no end to goodness!"

Some good things end.

A pang of loss brushed his heart, sweet and bitter. In the very edge of his vision, he caught the brightness in her eyes as well.

Linnea picked up her thick knitted shawl, a gift from Marguerida. She yawned, covering her mouth with one delicate hand. "I fear there is one way in which I do show my age, and that is I no longer have the stamina for staying awake past my bedtime."

"Rest well, then," he said, getting to his feet. "Come again when you will."

Linnea paused, one hand on the latch of his door. "It is good to speak with an old and dear friend. For all our differences, there is even more we have shared, and those memories now form a tapestry of life between us. We have both loved and been greatly loved in our turn, and for one lifetime, that is enough."

——— ✦ ———

Thendara. Once Jeram had never wanted to see it again, and now it would very likely be his home for the rest of his life.

He reined his sturdy gray mountain pony to a halt at the crest of the pass, letting the beast catch its breath while the wagon bearing Morna and their household goods caught up. He wanted to see her face when she looked down at Thendara's walls and spires. She'd never been to any city larger than Nevarsin and had never seen anything like the Terran Zone. He felt as if he were seeing the world anew through the lens of her delight.

The edifices of metal and glass, now showing the effects of decades of harsh Darkovan winters, faced the beautiful old stone towers of Comyn Castle. Another place, he thought, he once never wanted to see again.

"What do you think?" He turned in his saddle.

Her mouth made an O of surprise. "Who would have

thought there could be so many people in one place? Are we truly to live here?"

At first she had not believed his story, not to mention his adventures since leaving for Nevarsin. In the end, however, she relented. No sane man, she said, could have made up such a tale. She did not care where he had come from or where he proposed to go. Like everyone else in her mountain village, loyalty and adaptability had been bred into her bones. __

Jeram was happier than he could express that she had chosen to come with him. Their relationship had begun with shared comfort, a way to ease their loneliness, or so he had thought. When he had returned to Rock Glen at the close of the Council season, his heart had opened to her. Or perhaps he had discovered that he already loved her for her generous spirit, her honesty, her simple acceptance. He could face his new life in Thendara with confidence because she was at his side.

It began snowing again as they approached the Thendara gates. Only a few traces remained of the old encampment. Ulm and his son had long since returned to their own village with a line of chervines laden with seed stock, some precious metal tools, fine woolen cloth, and leather—riches enough to ensure a good life for years to come.

The Guardsmen at the gates recognized Jeram by name if not by face and admitted him with an almost embarrassing degree of courtesy. They made their way through the maze of cobbled streets to the old Terran Trade Zone, where Jeram had, with Marguerida's help, purchased a walled compound with a comfortable house, kitchen garden, and stabling for a couple of animals.

Morna's expression showed that he had guessed rightly at what would please her. A ball or a banquet at the Castle would be all very well for a treat, but she would derive far more joy from her own plot of herbs and vegetables beside her own house. Two servants, a married couple, greeted them at the front door and began unloading the cart and caring for the ponies. A fire burned merrily in the central room, and the aromas of fresh-baked nut bread and herb-laced stew hung lightly on the air.

Morna flew from one room to the next, exclaiming at the spacious kitchen, the chests filled with bed linens and blankets, the furnishings, the wide bed with its beautifully carved headboard.

"'Tis big enough for a Dry Towns lord and all his wives!" she exclaimed.

"Yes, we must take care not to get lost in it," he laughed. Perhaps life in Thendara, in a home that blended Darkovan and off-world, might not be so bad. With Morna, he need never hide who he had been or pretend to be other than what he was.

"Tomorrow or the next day, when you have rearranged everything to your satisfaction—" he began, sitting on the bed.

"Oh, surely it will take longer than that!" Slipping onto his lap, Morna put her arms around his neck. Her eyes gleamed.

He kissed her tenderly. "We must get you some city clothes. My friend Ethan comes from a tailoring family on Threadneedle Street."

"What would I do with such finery? Am I not well as I am, a simple country woman?"

Jeram shook his head, half in disbelief. What other woman would not jump at the chance for a new gown?

"You are exactly perfect," he told her, smiling, "but do it to please me, as a favor to my friend. Ethan is a proud man—all you Darkovans are—proud and stubborn. It would be a generous gift on your part to allow him to do this for me."

Morna frowned. "Yes, you talked about your work here, but I did not understand it. You will be teaching your *Terranan* ways to this man, Ethan? Why, if they have gone?"

"They will not stay gone forever." Jeram set her aside and walked over to the window. The bedroom was on the second story, and from here, he could look over the wall of their compound toward the old spaceport. It lay empty now, but for how long?

How long before the Federation's vicious civil war reached Darkover? How long before one side or another wanted the strategic advantage of Darkover's position on the galactic arm? Or some bureaucrat discovered a forgotten record about matrix science? How long before some band of refugees or smugglers decided the planet of the Bloody Sun was easy prey?

Jeram had not saved Darkover from trailmen's fever only to lose it to politicians or scavengers. His knowledge and skills ran beyond immunization protocols. He knew war, he knew men, and he knew communications equipment.

Morna stood beside him, soft and sturdy and loving. He put his arm around her, drawing her close.

"Not forever," he repeated, "but we will be ready for them." Starting with Ethan and his friends, perhaps working with the *laran*-trained youngsters Danilo would enlist, he would begin searching the skies, listening . . . and preparing a defense.

Let them come, he repeated to himself. *Darkover will be ready.*

Marion Zimmer Bradley
& Deborah Ross

A Flame in Hali
A Novel of Darkover

On Darkover, it is the era of the Hundred Kingdoms—a time of nearly continuous war and bloody disputes, a time when Towers are conscripted to produce terrifying laran weapons—weapons which kill from afar, poisoning the very land itself for decades to come. In this terrifying time of greed and imperialism, two powerful men have devoted their lives to changing their world and eliminating these terrible weapons. For years King Carolin of Hastur and his close friend, Keeper Varzil Ridenow, have dreamed of a world without war. But another man, Eduin Deslucido, hides in the alleys of Thendara, tormented by a spell so powerful it haunts Eduin's every waking moment—a spell of destruction against Carolin Hastur... and all of his clan.

To Order Call: 1-800-788-6262
www.dawbooks.com

Kristen Britain

GREEN RIDER

As Karigan G'ladheon, on the run from school, makes her way through the deep forest, a galloping horse plunges out of the brush, its rider impaled by two black arrows. With his dying breath, he tells her he is a Green Rider, one of the king's special messengers. Giving her his green coat with its symbolic brooch of office, he makes Karigan swear to deliver the message he was carrying. Pursued by unknown assassins, following a path only the horse seems to know, Karigan finds herself thrust into in a world of danger and complex magic....   0-88677-858-1

FIRST RIDER'S CALL

With evil forces once again at large in the kingdom and with the messenger service depleted and weakened, can Karigan reach through the walls of time to get help from the First Rider, a woman dead for a millennium?   0-7564-0209-3

MERCEDES LACKEY

Reserved for the Cat
The *Elemental Masters* Series

In 1910, in an alternate Paris, Ninette Dupond, a penniless young dancer, recently dismissed from the Paris Opera, thinks she has gone mad when she finds herself in a conversation with a skinny tomcat. However, Ninette is desperate—and hungry—enough to try anything. She follows the cat's advice and travels to Blackpool, England, where she is to impersonate a famous Russian ballerina and dance, not in the opera, but in the finest of Blackpool's music halls. With her natural talent for dancing, and her magic for enthralling an audience, it looks as if Ninette will gain the fame and fortune the cat has promised. But the real Nina Tchereslavsky is not as far away as St. Petersburg...and she's not as human as she appears...

978-0-7564-0362-1

And don't miss the first four books of
The Elemental Masters:

The Serpent's Shadow	0-7564-0061-9
The Gates of Sleep	0-7564-0101-1
Phoenix and Ashes	0-7564-0272-7
The Wizard of London	0-7564-0363-4

To Order Call: 1-800-788-6262
www.dawbooks.com

DAW 23

MERCEDES LACKEY

The Novels of Valdemar

To Order Call: 1-800-788-6262
www.dawbooks.com

DAW 25

The Novels of
Tad Williams

To Order Call: 1-800-788-6262
www.dawbooks.com

DAW 102